Praise

and her novels

"This sizzling hot historica... you panting for more! Monica Burns writes with sensitivity and panache. Don't miss this one!"
—Sabrina Jeffries, *New York Times* bestselling author

"No one sets fire to the page like Monica Burns." —*Ecataromance*

"[Monica Burn's] excellent love scenes and bold romance will have readers clamoring for more." —*Romantic Times*

"A cinematic, compelling, and highly recommended treat!"
—Sylvia Day, national bestselling author

"The love scenes are emotion-filled and wonderfully erotic . . . Enough to make your toes curl." —*TwoLips Reviews*

"Elegant prose, believable dialogue, and a suspenseful plot that will hold you spellbound." —Emma Wildes

"Historical romance with unending passion." —*The Romance Studio*

"Wow. Just wow." —*Fallen Angel Reviews*

"A satisfying read complete with intrigue, mystery, and the kind of potent sensuality that fogs up the mirrors." —**A Romance Review*

"Monica Burns is a new author I must add to my 'required reading' category . . . Everything I look for in a top-notch romance novel."
—*Romance Reader at Heart*

"Blazing passion." —*Romance Junkies*

Berkley Sensation titles by Monica Burns

KISMET

PLEASURE ME

Order of the Sicari Novels

ASSASSIN'S HONOR

ASSASSIN'S HEART

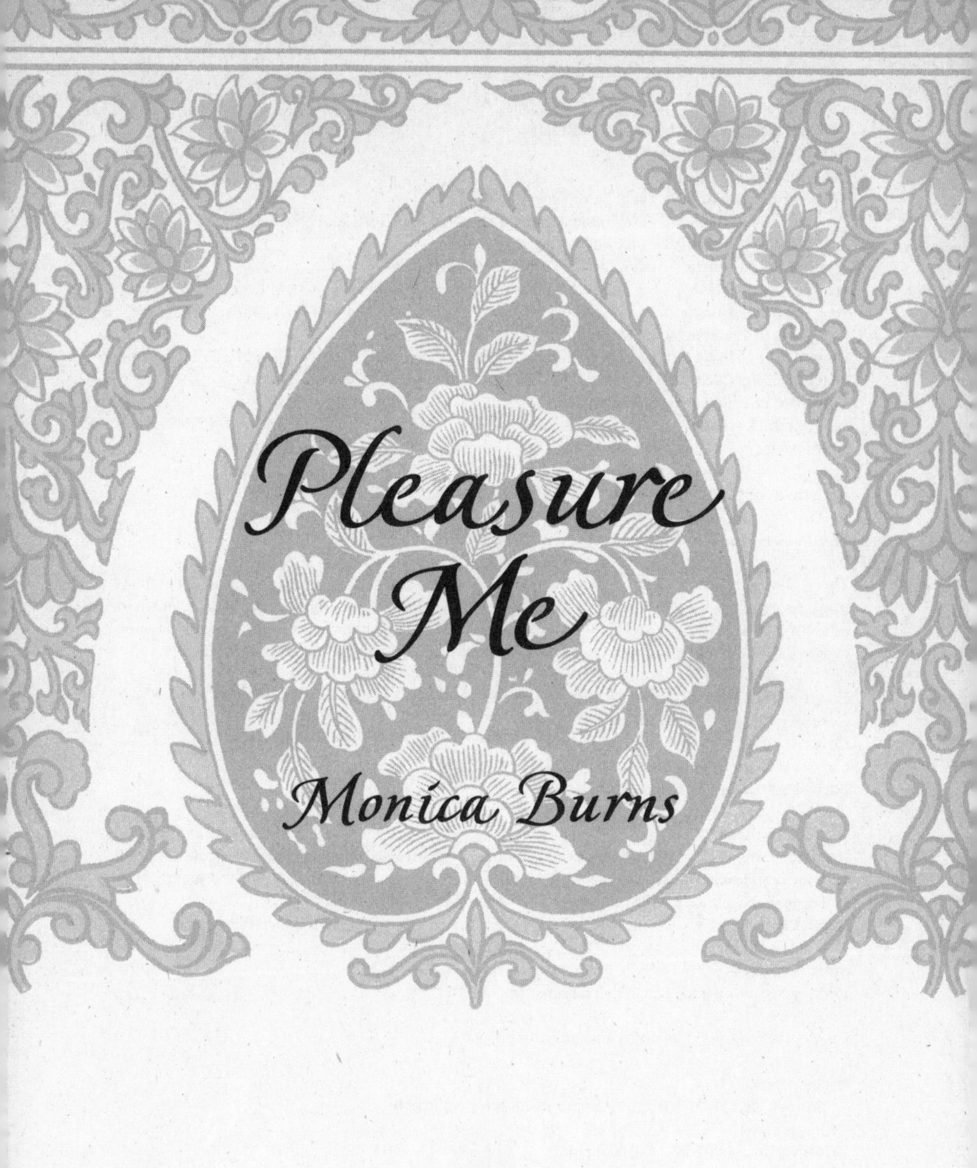

Pleasure Me

Monica Burns

BERKLEY SENSATION, NEW YORK

THE BERKLEY PUBLISHING GROUP
Published by the Penguin Group
Penguin Group (USA) Inc.
375 Hudson Street, New York, New York 10014, USA
Penguin Group (Canada), 90 Eglinton Avenue East, Suite 700, Toronto, Ontario M4P 2Y3, Canada
(a division of Pearson Penguin Canada Inc.)
Penguin Books Ltd., 80 Strand, London WC2R 0RL, England
Penguin Group Ireland, 25 St. Stephen's Green, Dublin 2, Ireland (a division of Penguin Books Ltd.)
Penguin Group (Australia), 250 Camberwell Road, Camberwell, Victoria 3124, Australia
(a division of Pearson Australia Group Pty. Ltd.)
Penguin Books India Pvt. Ltd., 11 Community Centre, Panchsheel Park, New Delhi—110 017, India
Penguin Group (NZ), 67 Apollo Drive, Rosedale, North Shore 0632, New Zealand
(a division of Pearson New Zealand Ltd.)
Penguin Books (South Africa) (Pty.) Ltd., 24 Sturdee Avenue, Rosebank, Johannesburg 2196,
South Africa

Penguin Books Ltd., Registered Offices: 80 Strand, London WC2R 0RL, England

This book is an original publication of The Berkley Publishing Group.

Cover illustration by Jim Griffin.
Cover design by George Long.
Cover hand lettering by Ron Zinn.
Interior text design by Laura K. Corless.

PRINTING HISTORY
Berkley Sensation trade paperback edition / March 2011

Library of Congress Cataloging-in-Publication Data

Burns, Monica.
Pleasure me / Monica Burns.—Berkley Sensation trade pbk. ed.
p. cm.
ISBN 978-0-425-23879-0 (trade pbk.)
1. Courtesans—Fiction. I. Title.
PS3602.U76645P54 2011
813'.6—dc22

2010048803

PRINTED IN THE UNITED STATES OF AMERICA

10 9 8 7 6 5 4 3 2 1

For Marie and Olivia.

The easiest thing about being a parent is how you love.

I love you more than you can possibly imagine.

Acknowledgments

With gratitude to Kati Dancy for her meticulous attention to detail and her demand for excellence. A shout-out to my BFFs Rosie Murphy, Becke Martin, Keri Stevens, Keri Ford, and Renee Vincent for patience in listening to me whine, your commiseration, your jokes, and the HAWT male model pics that keep dropping into my inbox. You all are the best!

London, 1897

"I'm sure you understand, my dear. Miss Fitzgerald and I have formed a tendré for each other that transcends what you and I have had over this past year. I'm amazed she's even countenanced my suit as she's so much younger than me."

Ruth flinched as she stood at the window with her back to Marston. What he really meant was that Ernestina Fitzgerald was younger than *her*. There was just enough complacency in her lover's voice for her to know the bastard was enjoying himself. She'd been through this type of event so many times over the past twenty some years, but this time it was worse. This was the second time in less than two years that a lover was leaving her for a younger woman. And at forty-one years of age she was old—wasn't she? Her hands trembled despite her death grip. Steeling herself, she pasted on a smile and turned around to face him.

"Of course, I understand, Freddie." She deliberately used the nickname and earned a glare from him. She knew how much he despised anyone calling him that. "I'm certain Miss Fitzgerald will suit you well. As I understand it, her talent for skilled conversation equals yours."

Marston sent her a suspicious look, but she knew he would never understand the double entendre. The man wasn't nearly as intelligent as he liked to think. In fact, he was hopelessly inept at conversing intelligently about any subject other than hunting and fishing. Suddenly, she despised herself for even entering into a liaison with him. She knew why she had. She just hadn't wanted to admit it until now. She'd been scared, afraid that time was running out for her. And now it had.

"Naturally, I'll see that your allowance is paid through the end of the month."

"Naturally," she said coolly, not about to let him see she was shaken by the parting. It wasn't as much unexpected as it was humiliating. "And Crawley Hall?"

"I am sorry, Ruth, but that seems a rather extravagant parting gift, don't you think?"

"I prefer to think of it as a promise you made several months ago."

She narrowed her gaze at him. She needed the estate. The orphanage on Aston Street was overflowing, and the more sickly children would benefit from the fresh country air.

"Did I? I don't recall agreeing to any such thing."

"Then perhaps I should have Wycombe refresh your memory, as he was present at the time you agreed to purchase the property for me."

"I'm sure Wycombe will remember it differently," Marston said with more than a hint of smug arrogance. "Besides, you already have property in the country. I see no reason why you would have need of another one. If you're concerned about money, you can always sell the jewelry I've given you."

The sanctimonious pig. The bastard knew why she wanted Crawley Hall. He also knew good and well that the house she owned near Bath was far too small for her needs. There was barely enough room for her, Delores, and Simmons let alone half a dozen orphans. And the jewelry he'd given her would bring her barely enough for half the purchase price of Crawley Hall. His refusal to buy the Hall meant she would need to dig more deeply into her resources. Something she'd hoped to avoid. She'd managed her finances well over the years, but buying Crawley Hall meant utilizing her long-term investments much sooner than she liked. Especially when her future was far from bright when it came to securing a new patron. She sent him a contemptuous smile.

"The jewelry you've given me? Darling Freddie, those trinkets will hardly fetch even a paltry sum. But if you refuse to keep your promise with regard to Crawley Hall, who am I to question your honor." She caught a glimpse of the anger darkening his face as she turned away from him with a small shrug. "Since we've nothing further to say to each other, I think it's time you left."

Seconds later, a rough hand snaked through her hair and jerked her head backward. She never liked to show fear, but Marston pulled painfully on her hair and she cried out not only in surprise, but anguish as well.

"Listen to me, you old hag, if you even suggest that my attentions to you were ever anything but honorable, I'll show you just how *honorable* I can be."

A door opened behind them, and her butler entered the room. Tall and burly enough to make any man cautious of crossing him, Simmons occasionally acted the bodyguard in addition to his many other talents.

"I heard a scream, my lady. Is everything all right?" It wasn't a question. It was the butler's way of telling Marston to release her, which Freddie did with a rough shove.

"Don't forget what I said, Ruth. I'll not have anyone sully my good name."

She remained silent, despite her desire to tell him exactly what she wanted to do to him, starting with castration. Lord, how could she have actually thought the man attractive? Because he was the *only* man who'd been interested enough to enter into a liaison with her. Nauseated by the thought, she swayed slightly on her feet.

As Marston left the parlor, she crossed the floor and gripped the arm of the settee as she slowly sank down into the cushions. Simmons didn't comment. He simply followed her ex-lover out of the room, obviously intent on seeing the man out of the house. The trembling of her hands expanded to wrack her entire body, and she closed her eyes against the pain sweeping through her. First one tear and then another rolled down her cheeks.

She'd always known this day would come, but it was even more horrible than she'd possibly imagined. Age had always been her enemy, and she'd never been able to find a way to defeat it. Bent over, she cupped her face in her hands to cry softly. A warm arm wrapped around her shoulders, and she looked up to see her maid's concerned expression.

"Did he hurt you, my lady?"

"Not really, Dolores." She pulled a handkerchief from a side pocket in her skirt and shook her head as she wiped the tears from her cheeks. "More my pride than anything else."

"I never cared for the man. He never treated you as well as your other beaus."

"I'm well aware of how you felt about Marston." She couldn't help but release a small laugh at the vehement distaste in her maid's voice. "I'm surprised I didn't come around to your way of thinking a long time ago."

"You're stubborn. That's why. Stubborn, right down to the core, you are. Always so certain that man was the best you could do."

"He was the only man who seemed remotely interested at the time as I recall," she said with a self-deprecating laugh. "I can no longer fool myself, Dolores. My age has begun to show."

"Nonsense." The maid snorted with disgust. "You still have the figure of a young girl, and a face as lovely as an angel's."

"Thank you, Dolores. You are a true friend, loyal and blind to the obvious."

She winced at the truth. It wasn't necessary to look in the mirror to know that her looks weren't what they once were. She knew she was still an attractive woman, but her days of garnering accolades for her beauty were long gone.

"*Harrumph.* My eyesight is as good as it was twenty years ago." The maid straightened her shoulders, hands clasped in front of her, and scowled down at her. "There are plenty of men who would be more than happy to enter a room with you on their arm. You're far too hard on yourself."

The woman's chiding lifted her spirits slightly as she contemplated the way Lord Mackelsby had complimented her several nights ago. Marston had even spared enough time to leave Ernestina Fitzgerald's side to come claim her as if she were a piece of property he owned. The analogy had been accurate at the time. Marston paid her bills and as such was entitled to her full attention.

But now he was gone, along with her monthly allowance. She released another sigh. It wasn't the money that troubled her as much as the fact that Marston, like her lover before him, had left her for a younger woman. No matter how much she fought it, the knowledge threw her into a state of despair.

She swallowed back another rush of tears. Crying would do little good, and there were more important matters to consider than her bruised ego. She stood up quickly to pace the floor in front of the fireplace. The children had to come first. Whatever it took, she'd find a way to purchase Crawley Hall or another estate like it.

In addition to the few trinkets Marston had given her, she owned several other pieces of jewelry she could sell, but she knew it wouldn't be enough. She breathed a sigh of resignation. In order to fetch the remainder of the Hall's purchase price, she would have to sell her house outside of Bath. She cringed inwardly at the thought before dismissing her regret. She could just as easily retire to Crawley Hall as anywhere else.

"I think it's time I sell some of my investments."

"What?" Dolores's horrified astonishment made her smile.

"My jewelry should fetch at least half the sale price of Crawley Hall, and selling the country house should make up the balance *and* hopefully pay for the necessary improvements to the Hall. If that's not enough, I can easily rent the town house. There should be sufficient monies from my annual annuities to support me, as long as I'm careful with money." Ruth glanced around the parlor wondering how much the house would rent for. It was in a reasonably fashionable district, which should make it an attractive offering.

"But you bought the house in Bath for your retirement, my lady. And if you rent this house, where will you live?"

"I shall live at Crawley Hall." She saw her longtime companion flinch, and quickly moved forward to grasp the older woman's hands. "And you'll come with me, Dolores. And Simmons, too. You do want to come, Dolores, don't you?"

"Yes, my lady." The maid's expression of fear disappeared. "I just thought perhaps you might not have need of me anymore."

"Don't be ridiculous." She sat down next to the woman and squeezed her hands. "I don't know what I'd do without you. Who else will keep me on the straight and narrow?"

"This is true, my lady. Although I think you've a heart that's far too big for your pocket where those children are concerned."

"They haven't anyone else to look after them, Dolores. I can't simply abandon them as Marston has me."

The words were a vivid reminder of her current state of affairs, and she fought off the wave of self-pity threatening to wash over her. As much as she wanted to give in to the emotion, she refused to do so. She'd always been practical in her outlook, and it was time she accepted the fact that her days as one of the Set's darlings were quickly coming to a close. Marston leaving her for a younger woman would make her an object of pity among the Marlborough Set, something she would abhor. The appearance of Simmons at the parlor doorway interrupted her train of thought.

"Lady Pembroke has arrived, my lady."

As the butler stepped aside, Allegra Camden, the Countess of Pembroke, swept into the salon as Simmons retreated from the room. The smile on her face only enhanced her younger friend's beauty, as Allegra took her outstretched hands in hers then kissed her on the cheek.

"I'm sorry I'm late, but Shaheen and the children took longer than usual with breakfast."

"It's quite all right." Ruth returned her friend's affectionate greeting then turned to her maid. "Dolores, bring us some tea, please."

The older woman bobbed her head and left the room to do as Ruth had asked. With a small gesture, she invited her friend to sit down. Her movements elegant, Allegra sank into a wingback chair as Ruth took a seat on the settee across from her. A frown on her face, her friend eyed her carefully.

"Something's happened. Are you ill?"

The concern in Allegra's voice tightened her throat, and she shook her head. "No. I'm fine."

"You look rather peaked." Allegra leaned forward then suddenly gasped. "You've been crying."

Before Ruth could say a word, her friend sprang to her feet in a soft rustle of expensive silk and joined Ruth on the couch. Taking her hands in hers, Allegra studied her with an expression that said she intended to get to the bottom of whatever was troubling her.

"Tell me." The command didn't surprise her. Allegra had always been as protective of her friends as they of her. She sighed.

"Marston has left me." Saying the words made tears well up in her eyes again. She blinked hard, fighting them back. The man wasn't worth the effort.

"Oh, my dear. I'm so sorry, but I confess I never liked Marston at all. He has never treated you with the respect you deserved."

"I've been a fool." Ruth drew in a deep breath and shook her head.

"You most certainly *have not*. You did what you thought you had to do to survive."

"No, not survival . . . a refusal to admit the truth. I am old, Allegra."

"*Nonsense*. You're only four years older than me, and you *look* younger." Her friend sent her a look of admonishment. She rejected the observation with a shake of her head.

"He left me for Ernestina Fitzgerald. She's at least fifteen years younger than me."

"And the woman is twice as dim-witted as Marston. The two shall make a handsomely dull pair." The disgust in her friend's voice made Ruth choke out a laugh.

"See, you agree with me," Allegra said with great satisfaction. "There are plenty of men who would find themselves enthralled with you. And when you attend the Somerset ball this evening I've no doubt you'll see how quickly men will flock to your side."

"I couldn't possibly go this evening." She stared at Allegra in horror. "Marston will be there. He'll have Ernestina with him, and everyone will know he left me for her."

"Well, they'll notice it more if you're *not* there. You know as well as I do the sharks will close in the moment they smell blood." Allegra eyed her sternly before suddenly flashing a wicked smile in her direction. "Besides, what better time to announce how delighted you are that Marston has finally found someone who equals his intellectual standing in the Set?"

This time Ruth laughed easily. "When you put it like that, it's easy to see I'm crying over the man for no reason at all."

"Precisely," Allegra said firmly.

She forced herself to smile at the woman seated next to her. No, there was no reason to cry over Marston's departure. But her lost youth? She had no doubt there were far more tears still to be shed for that loss. How had it happened? It seemed only yesterday that Allegra had invited her, Bella, and Nora to stay with her while her friend weathered the scandal that had made her the renowned courtesan she'd been before her marriage to the Earl of Pembroke.

How could twenty years pass in the blink of an eye? She didn't *feel* old. Her hopes and desires were still the same, although the ones buried deep inside her seemed doomed to go unanswered. She envied Allegra and the happiness she'd found with the earl. Her gaze drifted up to where her portrait hung over the fireplace. The Viscount Westleah had commissioned it when she was twenty-three. They'd spent almost three years together before they'd parted as friends.

Westleah had bought this house for her then taught her how to manage the generous allowance he'd given her. It was how she'd made several sound investments that would ensure her retirement wouldn't be one of abject poverty as was that of so many other women like her. She had simply hoped to have a little more time before being forced to retire.

The soft rattling of china caught her attention, and she turned her head to see Dolores entering the room with tea. The woman set the tray on the round table in front of the settee, and eyed her carefully for a moment. With a quick shake of her head, Ruth indicated she was fine and reached for the teapot. The maid, somewhat satisfied with Ruth's silent assurance, released a soft grumble then left the salon. Eager to talk of something other than her future, Ruth smiled and offered her friend a cup of tea.

"Motherhood and marriage suit you, my dear. You've found a happiness most can only dream of."

"I *am* happy, Ruth. If you had told me five years ago that I would be living such a wonderful life, I would have laughed at you."

Neither one of them said it out loud, but for a courtesan to find love, let alone marriage, was a rare thing. The soft glow on Allegra's face emphasized how happy her friend was despite the trials she'd endured in the Moroccan desert. Allegra had only shared some of the pain she'd experienced, but she knew her capture at the hands of Pembroke's enemy had taken its toll on her friend.

Every so often, a dark emotion filled Allegra's eyes that said the trauma would never leave her. When Lord Pembroke was present, he seemed to instinctively sense his wife's distress and was immediately at her side. Robert, she would never grow accustomed to his Bedouin name, Shaheen, was devoted to his wife and children. The sound of a teacup clinking loudly against a plate pulled her out of her reverie.

"We're not going to let him get away with this."

"What?" Ruth sent her friend a puzzled look.

"Marston. Tonight, we're going to see to it that everyone thinks Marston a fool for leaving you to take up with that flibbertigibbet Ernestina."

"And exactly *how* do you propose to accomplish that?" she asked in a skeptical tone.

"Do you remember how Mrs. Langtry stood out among the rest of the Set by wearing a simple black dress before Bertie took her under his wing?"

"Lillie Langtry stood out because she was beautiful, not because she wore a simple black dress to catch the eye of the Prince of Wales. I'm reasonably attractive, but far from beautiful."

"Nonsense. You're lovely, *and* you have presence, Ruth. When you enter a room everyone stops to look at you. And that mysterious smile of yours makes men eager to discover all your secrets. Tonight you're going to use that to your advantage."

"And *how*, pray tell, am I going to do that?"

"Dolores is going to modify that hideous monstrosity of a dress Marston insisted you wear to his house party last winter."

"The purple one with the enormous pink flowers?"

"Yes." Allegra's smile broadened. "The dress matches your eyes beautifully, but the flowers are horrendous. When Dolores makes the changes I have in mind, everyone will think Marston a fool for choosing Ernestina Fitzgerald over you."

"Such a transformation seems highly unlikely, but I suppose a miracle is always possible," she said with a skeptical laugh.

"Well, I for one believe in miracles," her friend replied quietly. "And so should you."

She met Allegra's affectionate look with a doubtful smile, but her friend's words were still in her head hours later as she climbed the steps to the Somerset town house. She should have known better than to question Allegra's determination. With Dolores's skillful sewing and Allegra's vision, the two women *had* managed a miracle. The result was a daring dress that emphasized her ample bosom and rounded hips. But most of all, it was devoid of any lace, flounces, ruffles, or bows.

The sleeves, what little was left after Dolores had finished, barely clung to the edge of her shoulders, mere slips of material. The entire dress was one of stark simplicity, but symbolically, it represented her casting Marston off. The flowers, the ruffles, every decoration on the dress that had once weighed down the satin were gone, with the exception of a trail of pink flower petals bordering the hem. It would give her enormous satisfaction to point out that Dolores had refashioned Marston's ostentatious choice into something much lovelier.

Her maid had pulled the original flowers apart to tack the pink trimming along the edge until they appeared to be actually falling off the hem. Before the night was over, they would be crushed and dirty. A silent sign of how unimportant Marston was to her. At her throat was the amethyst necklace she'd worn in the portrait Westleah had commissioned.

Her only other extravagance was a mauve-colored feather fan. As she entered the house, a tremor streaked through her as she caught sight of Marston entering the ballroom with Ernestina on his arm. In a mechanical fashion, she undid the frog loops of her cape, allowing the footman to gently remove it from her shoulders.

As more guests arrived, she stepped out of the way to inspect the sides and back of her gown for any unexpected wrinkles. It was more a need for time to collect herself than concern over her dress. The sudden whisper of sensation trailing across the back of her neck made her hand reach up to touch her skin. Satisfied her hair hadn't unraveled from the knot on top of her head, she turned toward the ballroom. Another frisson skimmed its way over her skin as her gaze met that of a man who casually handed off his overcoat to the household staff without looking away from her.

He was almost a foot taller than her with hair the color of a moonless night. There was something intense and riveting about him. If Allegra thought she had presence, her friend hadn't met this man. He seemed to dwarf everyone and everything in the entryway. He studied her for what seemed an eternity, yet she knew it was only a few seconds before another man she didn't recognize drew his attention away. But the stranger's look was enough to leave her heart racing.

She swallowed hard and gripped her fan tightly. Good lord, she was no longer twenty and attending her first soiree. She flinched at the thought. Suddenly overcome with the need to flee, she forced herself to cross the foyer floor toward the ballroom rather than claim her cape and head back out into the night. The sensation she'd experienced moments ago warmed her neck again, but she refused to turn around to look at the man. She hadn't come here this evening to find a new paramour.

The moment she reached the ballroom doorway, her courage sagged. She didn't see a single friendly face in the room. Dear God, where was Allegra? She wasn't certain she could do this alone. The moment the thought entered her head, she stiffened her back. Her youth might be gone, but not her dignity. She'd hold her head high, and she'd make damn sure no one, not even Marston, would be able to tell how she was feeling inside. As she waited for those in front of her to pass through the receiving line, the tingle at the nape of her neck became a blazing heat.

Lord, it had been years since she'd had this type of a reaction to a man. In the crush of arrivals pushing their way toward the ballroom, the space between them evaporated. He was so close to her that the warmth of his breath singed her shoulder. The sudden image of his hands at her waist, pulling her back into his chest, flashed in her head. The mental picture sent a shudder rippling through her that she was certain everyone around her could see.

Confused by the strength of the sensations assaulting her, she almost stumbled forward in her haste to greet Lord and Lady Somerset. The reception she received was a polite one simply because of her relation to the Marquess of Halethorpe. Her stomach lurched at the thought of her father. She didn't know whether to despise the man or thank him for sending her down the path she'd chosen so many years ago. Either one was painful to contemplate.

She turned away from the Somersets and slowly descended the steps into the ballroom. Despite her attempts to deny it, she wanted to know the stranger's name, and as she made her way down the staircase, she heard him introduced as Lord Stratfield. The moment she reached the ballroom floor, a small group of women to her right caught her attention and her heart sank. *Ernestina.* The last thing she wanted was a scene. Desperate to find a friendly face, she strained her neck to see over top of an older woman with three tall feathers sticking up in her hair.

"Once an old cow is put out to pasture, you would think she'd stay there." Ernestina's comment sliced deep, and Ruth stiffened as she continued forward. She didn't get far.

"Lady Ruth, what a delightful surprise to see you here this evening."

Words failed her as the renewed tingling on the back of her neck ignited a fire that raced across her skin. Dear God, was that the way he always sounded? Like he'd just woken up and was inviting her to sin in ways she'd never dreamed. The wickedly deep, dark note of his voice sucked the air out of her lungs as she slowly turned toward him and extended her hand.

"Good evening, my lord." She fought to keep her voice steady, and a shiver streaked up her arm as he politely kissed the back of her hand.

"Simplicity becomes you, my lady. I've never seen you look so exquisite."

His gaze suddenly shifted to stare at the ruffles, lace appliqués, and bows adorning Ernestina's gown. It was a deliberate snub, and everyone within hearing distance knew it. A part of her almost felt sorry for Marston's new paramour. Still, she experienced a twinge of pleasure to see the other woman's viciousness silenced, but she was leery of the man's motives for coming to her rescue. When her eyes met his again, his gaze revealed nothing, but he smiled as he offered her his arm. Her heart immediately skidded out of control.

It was a smile that would be lethal to a woman's heart if she allowed herself to fall under its spell. She accepted his arm and allowed him to guide her away from Ernestina and her friends. The frisson skimming over every inch of her body made her want to run as far away as she could. This man was far too attractive for his own good, which made him dangerous. Besides, he looked younger than her. A flirtation with him would only serve to make her feel that much older, and she was feeling far too vulnerable tonight.

"While I appreciate your gallantry, my lord, I can assure you I was not in need of rescue." She heard the catch in her voice and forced herself not to look in his direction.

"It was a sincere compliment. The fact that it served to rescue you was secondary." The husky note in his voice made her blood flow sluggishly. Lord, but the man was a mesmerist. She caught sight of Allegra and came to a halt. He turned his head toward her, his eyebrow quirking upward in either amusement or curiosity. She couldn't determine which.

"Then I thank you again. If you'll forgive me, I see a friend I must greet." Something flickered in the depths of his vivid blue eyes, and it made her mouth go dry. Lord Stratfield bowed his head in her direction.

"A pleasure, my lady. I look forward to our next meeting."

There it was again, that husky note of sin in his voice. Her chest tightened in reaction. Blast it, she was acting like a woman half her age. She was too well seasoned to allow herself to be affected so easily. She swallowed hard and gave him a slight nod as she fled his side. And she *was* fleeing. She was crossing the floor entirely too fast, not in her usual restrained manner. Despite reaching the safety of her small circle of friends, her pulse was still racing. Allegra offered her a small hug then stepped back to study her with a look of concern.

"Good heavens, you're shaking."

"It's nothing, simply nerves."

"Are you certain it's not a devilishly handsome stranger that has you in a dither?" The amusement in Allegra's voice sent a wave of heat into her cheeks.

"Of course not." She sniffed with irritation as her friend eyed her with skepticism, but chose not to question her.

"You look stunning. I knew Dolores would make this dress a work of art. And the petals bordering the hem . . . it's a masterpiece at saying the man isn't good enough to kiss the hem of your gown."

"Let me add to my wife's observations, my lady." The Earl of Pembroke offered her a slight bow. "You look enchanting."

"Thank you both."

"Might I add my own compliments as well, my dear? Everyone is talking about how radiant you look tonight." The warm voice of Lord Westleah drifted over her shoulder, and she turned around with a smile of delighted surprise.

"William. How lovely to see you again."

He greeted Allegra and the earl with warmth before turning back to her and leaning down to kiss both her cheeks. It had been months since they'd last seen each other, and to see him here tonight reminded her how long ago it had been since they'd first met. She pushed the thought aside as she stared up at her old lover.

"It's been far too long, Ruth. How have you been?"

"Quite well."

She forced a smile as she saw him narrow his gaze at her. Westleah knew her well, and could easily see through the façade she'd deliberately thrown up for the evening's event. She was grateful when he didn't press her. As Allegra and the earl turned away to greet another couple, Westleah eyed her carefully.

"How do you know Baron Stratfield?" The question caught her by surprise, and she darted a quick look at her champion, engrossed in a conversation with several gentlemen across the room.

"I don't. He overheard a rather nasty comment directed at me when I arrived and rescued me from further insult."

"Doesn't surprise me. He's a decent fellow. Rarely takes offense at anything except the mistreatment of others."

Allegra turned back to them at that moment, and her friend

tipped her head to one side in a questioning manner. "What doesn't surprise you, Westleah?"

"Lord Stratfield. It seems he rescued Ruth from some rather unpleasant gossip when she first came into the room."

"Do you mean the handsome gentleman headed our way?"

Allegra's question made her turn her head toward the last place she'd seen Lord Stratfield. To her astonishment, the man was coming toward them. No, her. He was heading directly toward *her*. Instantly, her palms felt clammy and her heart was pounding a hard rhythm against her chest. What in heaven's name was she going to say to him? The question irritated her. Had she suddenly lost her wits? The art of flirtation was something she'd excelled at for years. Now suddenly one man had her doubting herself. No, it wasn't him. The break with Marston had shaken her confidence. Nothing more.

Not to mention Lord Stratfield had to be at least five years younger than her, although there was something about his mannerisms that made him appear older than his years. She winced inwardly. Her interest in him was bordering on the absurd. The strains of a waltz faded into the background as her body hummed a melody all its own the moment the man joined them.

Westleah dealt with the introductions before excusing himself to speak with another friend, and in seconds Allegra had dragged her husband away to greet other guests. If she hadn't known better, she would have thought the entire thing was staged to leave her alone with Lord Stratfield. The silence stretched between them for a long moment before he cleared his throat.

"Might I have this dance, my lady?" The low sound of his voice skimmed along her senses as she struggled to reply in a quiet, reserved manner. Instead, she simply nodded, then placed her hand in his. A moment later he whirled her out onto the dance floor. The electricity pulsing its way through her was as exhilarating as it was terrifying.

Not even Westleah had affected her this way. Frustrated by her faltering composure, she straightened her spine. For more than twenty years she'd perfected the art of seduction, and she refused to let this man reduce her to a state of confusion, especially when he was younger than her.

"How is it we've never met until this evening, my lord?" She offered him a small well-practiced smile.

"When it comes to events such as this, I've seen far too many of my acquaintances ensnared in the spiderweb of some mother with a marriageable daughter. I prefer my freedom." His straightforward response made her laugh. He smiled with a hint of satisfaction.

"Good, I've made you laugh. It suits you."

As much as she wanted not to, it was impossible to keep the heat from flooding her cheeks. The man was far too charming, and it was irritating to know how susceptible she was to him. She breathed in his clean, woodsy scent, and her heart skipped a beat. Even at the most base levels her body responded to him. When she didn't say anything, he studied her with an intense look that sent a shiver racing down her spine.

"The man's a fool."

There was a dark note of outrage in his voice, and she stumbled. He immediately pulled her closer as she collected her wits.

"I beg your pardon?"

"Marston. The man needs his head examined."

"Oh." Forcing a smile to her lips, she gave him a brief nod. "And I should have *my* head examined for ever having been seen with the man."

He released a soft laugh that drifted across her skin like sinful velvet. His large hand in the middle of her back pressed her into him even tighter. As the heat and scent of him filled her senses, she found it difficult to breathe normally. A primitive rhythm hummed in her blood, and her mouth was so dry not even champagne could wet her tongue enough. She tried desperately to regain control of her senses.

"And I'm certain there are many here tonight who are delighted to know that your heart is no longer occupied," he murmured as the music came to a halt.

Slowly letting her go, he stepped back from her as she sank into a low curtsy. His words eased her bruised feelings for only a split second before she realized he hadn't included himself in the compliment. Why would he ask her to dance if he had no interest in pursuing her acquaintance?

Confused, she frowned. What was it Westleah had said? The man rarely took offense except at the mistreatment of others. Anger slashed through her. Damn him. The bastard had asked her to dance out of pity. She came upright and snapped her fan open to flutter it quickly in front of her then collapsed it again in a sharp movement.

"Thank you for your second rescue attempt this evening, my lord. But in the future, please note that I neither want nor appreciate your interference in my affairs."

Without giving him the opportunity to respond, she swept away from him with her back ramrod straight. The insolence of the man. She was more than capable of looking after her own interests. And she certainly didn't need any man treating her like a lost cause.

The fist connecting with the Right Honorable Lord Stratfield's jaw sent his head flying backward. Garrick could taste the blood in his mouth, and he quickly stepped to one side to avoid another blow from his opponent. Out of the corner of his eye, he saw Worthington's fist heading toward him and quickly ducked before sending his own fist upward into the man's lower jaw. Somewhere in the back of his head, Garrick heard the sound of cheers and jeers from the men forming the circle around him and Worthington.

He blocked the sounds out of his head and landed another hit to the man's jaw with his other fist. The minute he hit the man, he knew Worthington would fall. Garrick danced back a couple of steps and watched the younger man collapse on the grass fresh with early morning dew.

With dueling outlawed, a boxing match was the next best thing for avenging his sister's honor. Grace was more than worthy of marrying the Earl of Bainbridge, even if their mother had abandoned them and their father had committed suicide. Defeating Worthington would also ensure his reputation as a man of principle when it came to protecting his family's honor. A hand slapped him on the back as his friend Charles, the Viscount Shaftsbury, congratulated him.

"Brilliantly done."

Garrick accepted the cloth Charles handed him and wiped the blood from his cut lip. He wouldn't go so far as to say his performance had been brilliant, but he was satisfied with the result. Grace's honor had been redeemed, and he knew Worthington wouldn't have the audacity to make any other comments. He looked at his unconscious opponent, and met the gaze of one of the man's friends. He tossed his head toward Worthington.

"I suggest you ice his jaw or he'll not be able to eat for a week," he said. Lord Millbourne nodded his head with a chuckle.

"I'll see to it. Although if it keeps the boy's mouth closed for a while, it will do him no harm. I feel certain he'll be calling on you to humbly beg your forgiveness in a few days."

"Then I shall make the apology as painless as possible for him."

With a cool nod, he turned away from Worthington's friend and accepted his coat from Charles. Damn, but he was tired. He needed sleep. After being up for almost twenty-four hours, he was dog-tired. And the boxing match had done little to ease his exhaustion or his restlessness. He raked his black hair back off his face and met Charles's amused gaze.

"What?" he asked as he shrugged into his coat with a wince. His young opponent had managed to land a couple of well-placed blows, and he was feeling decidedly uncomfortable.

"You let the boy hit you." At the observation, Garrick arched his eyebrows at his friend.

"He got lucky. I wasn't paying attention."

"That I find difficult to believe, but I'll indulge your delusions and not argue with you."

Garrick snatched his top hat from Charles's hand. His friend's amusement irritated him. It was the second time in less than a day that he'd been caught acting magnanimous to his fellow beings. He preferred to keep his benevolent tendencies hidden from the Marlborough Set. To do otherwise could easily make him appear weak and impotent. He tightened his mouth at the thought.

Last night the Lady Ruth. Now Worthington. Charles was too damned observant. The truth was Worthington's youth and penchant for one too many brandies had gotten in the way of his tongue when he'd insulted Grace. And what was his own excuse for rushing to the Lady Ruth's rescue? He pushed the question aside.

While he couldn't let Worthington's insult go unanswered, he'd had no desire to humiliate the boy. He'd been young once and understood how shame could leave brutal scars. He grimaced. Worthington was only six years younger than his own twenty-nine years. He felt fifty at the moment.

"You should have let Bainbridge handle the matter. She's his fiancée."

"My future brother-in-law would have pulverized the boy."

It was an honest statement. If the Earl of Bainbridge had heard the insult, Worthington would be in the care of several physicians at the moment instead of just his friends. The earl was as good a pugilist as he was, perhaps better. But Grace's betrothed would have made Worthington pay in a far more savage contest.

"True. Bainbridge would be furious no matter how trivial the insult where your sister is concerned. Short of my cousin Robert, I've never seen a man so devoted to a woman."

"It's the only reason I accepted his offer for Grace's hand," he said coolly.

He'd had Bainbridge investigated thoroughly before he'd agreed to let the man marry his sister. No one was going to marry into his family without his believing they were devoted to his siblings. The fact he'd failed Lily in that regard had made him even more vigilant in determining Bainbridge's suitability for Grace. He could only hope Lily and her husband worked out their differences. He wanted his sisters and brother to have the one thing their parents had never had—a happy marriage. As for him—his fate was already sealed.

"With Lily married and Grace soon to be wed to Bainbridge, that leaves you free to find a wife."

Charles's cheerful tone made Garrick clench his teeth until his jaw ached. Taking a wife was something he'd never do. Nor did he bother to explain the less than happy state of Lily's marriage. He had no desire to let his sister's marriage become fodder for the gossip mill.

"You're forgetting Vincent," he said in a tight voice.

"Surely the boy is capable of finding a wife." Charles narrowed his eyes at him. "I thought he was courting the Clayton girl."

"He is, but I've some concerns about her suitability." He looked away from his friend's surprised expression and headed toward his carriage.

"Care to join me for lunch later?" Charles asked as he fell into step beside him. Garrick shook his head in an apologetic fashion.

"I've plans to visit a piece of property I'm thinking of purchasing."

"Another estate. What the devil are you planning to do with another piece of property?"

"It's an investment."

"Yes, but must you buy up the whole of England? Pretty soon, we'll be calling the country Stratfield. And I can just imagine how Her Majesty would react to that."

His friend's comment tugged a small smile to Garrick's mouth. He could see where others might view his numerous holdings as extreme, but they were more than simple investments. They were necessary. As he opened the door of his carriage, he arched his eyebrow at Charles.

"Property that pays for itself is always a good investment."

"And a sound means of providing for your children when you get around to marrying."

His fingers gripped the edge of the carriage door until they ached from the pressure. The only heir he would ever have would be Vincent. When he didn't answer his friend, Charles quirked an eyebrow at him.

"For a man who's just avenged his sister's honor, you're looking rather dismal."

"I'm tired and my jaw aches."

"Perhaps your mysterious *mistress*, Mary, could minister to your . . . aches."

The words made him grimace. The none too subtle implication was meant to amuse him, but did just the opposite. It was depressing to acknowledge that the only thing he did when he visited his mistress was sleep. Alone. But for Charles to call her mysterious . . . he frowned.

"Exactly what do you mean by mysterious?"

"Nothing, except that after more than what, two years without ever having seen the woman, people are beginning to do more than speculate—"

"Speculate?" His terse response made Charles suddenly look uncomfortable.

"Well there's always been talk . . . people have always wondered if the woman even exists . . . or if she's actually a . . ."

Garrick's body went rigid at the unspoken implication. He quickly forced himself to make his expression unreadable to cover up the sense of stunned dismay he was feeling. Christ Jesus, he'd been a fool to think he could convince the Set he adored his mistress too much to take her out in public. There had always been gossip about why he never showed Mary off.

Some rumors he'd overheard, while at other times, friends and family had delicately shared the fact that he was the topic of curiosity. But this was the first time it had been suggested the Set was viewing him in less than a manly light. His stomach lurched at the sound of his uncle's mocking laugh echoing in the back of his head. He could have at the very least taken Mary to one of the finer establishments catering to men and their mistresses. No. He could never have subjected her to that. Not after what Tremaine had done to her, but he could have done something different. Furious with himself for his lack of foresight, he sent his friend an icy look.

"I can assure you that Mary is quite real. The two of us simply prefer not to socialize in public. It would be extremely uncomfortable for her. She wasn't brought up to handle the savagery that is the Marlborough Set."

That was entirely true. Mary's parents had owned a farm on one of his properties. He'd seen that her education would allow her to mingle with those in the upper classes, but she'd openly expressed her objection to the idea.

In fact, she seemed far more content with her book learning than she did anything else. Not even clothes seemed to interest her all that much, although lately she'd taken a heightened interest in them. He'd taken her to Paris for new clothes twice in the last eight months alone.

"I believe you, but perhaps showing her off from a distance might not be a bad thing either. I know how you loathe gossip. Perhaps a carriage ride in the park?"

"I have no intention of appeasing the Set's curiosity."

"Fine. But be prepared for *some* people to do more than speculate. I understand Wycombe made a bet with Marston the other day at the Club that he would prove this Mary of yours didn't exist."

"Bloody hell." This time he couldn't hide his shock.

"You've a great many friends who will stand by you, Garrick, but we both know Wycombe will do whatever he can to discredit you."

His head jerked in a sharp nod. Older by several years, the Earl of Wycombe had been one of his tormentors at first Eton and then Cambridge. The man had made him the brunt of malicious pranks for more than three years until Garrick had learned how to box. He'd beaten the man in a match that was now legendary in the halls of Cambridge.

Wycombe had arrived unconscious in the university's infirmary, while Garrick had walked away without even a scratch. The man had even missed his graduation ceremony as a result. While Wycombe had never crossed him since, the earl hated him beyond measure for that humiliating defeat. If Wycombe thought he could bring humiliation upon his head, the man wouldn't hesitate. Even if it meant lying.

He climbed into the carriage, his body aching more from the

battering his friend's news had given him than his match with young Worthington. As Garrick closed the door behind him, Charles looked at him through the window with a sympathetic expression on his face.

"I understand your desire for privacy, Garrick, but you cannot ignore this. I think a weekly carriage ride might go a long way toward satisfying the avid interest the subject has raised. Perhaps even an introduction to the Prince himself will prevent Wycombe from making any mischief."

"The last thing I intend to do is present Mary to His Royal Highness. The man would terrify her simply by virtue of his position. I won't subject her to that."

"At least introduce her to several of your friends—"

"No. I'll not sacrifice her simply to protect my own skin. I appreciate your warning, Charles, but I have no intention of putting Mary on display."

"Devil take it, Garrick. Wycombe will be merciless where you *or* your Mary is concerned."

"The Earl of Wycombe be damned," he snapped. "I took care of him once, I'll do it again." With the silver head of his cane, he tapped the carriage ceiling to instruct the driver to leave. Charles eyed him with worry and grimaced, but didn't argue with him. He gave his friend a sharp nod good-bye as the carriage pulled away.

It was a bumpy ride across the grassy expanse at the farthest edge of Hyde Park. But then he'd chosen the isolated spot not for its access, but its seclusion. The quiet grove, in the early morning hours, had seemed the most logical place for his match with Worthington, but the rough ride was doing little for the headache he'd suddenly developed.

Damn it to hell. He should have anticipated his refusal to bring Mary out into the limelight would pique people's curiosity. He'd kept her hidden away to protect her, while insulating himself from anyone learning the real reason he kept a mistress that no one ever saw. He groaned and rested his head on the leather squabs behind him.

Now what was he supposed to do? Perhaps Charles was right. Maybe a weekly ride through Hyde Park would lay to rest some of the speculation. He knew it wouldn't allay all the gossip, but Charles was correct. He couldn't abide rumors or innuendo. Nor could he allow Wycombe to poke around in his personal affairs.

The thought brought the Lady Ruth to mind. Last night he'd meddled in her affairs and had earned her wrath. He rubbed his sore jaw in contemplation and immediately grimaced with pain. No doubt, she would enjoy knowing he was feeling suitably chastened where she was concerned. It hadn't been his intent to interfere, but he'd not been able to help himself.

In the Somerset foyer, he'd watched the way she'd gathered herself as if preparing to face a horde of barbarians. She'd been a beautiful warrior princess ready to do battle with an enemy whose weapons were words. Word of Marston's break with her had reached the Marlborough Club long before evening. It had taken great courage to enter that ballroom alone. And the moment he'd heard that insult flung at her, he'd been unable to do anything but charge to her rescue.

He hadn't helped matters any when he'd asked her to dance. His motives had been not quite as suspect as she'd believed. While his first rescue had been rooted in sympathy, dancing with her had been a spontaneous action. It had also been a mistake. Not because he'd angered her, but because holding her in his arms had been far too pleasurable.

The carriage rocked to a halt, and he grunted with annoyance. What else could go wrong with his life at the moment? He got out of the vehicle and wearily climbed the steps of the small house he'd provided Mary with. He'd been so busy thinking about the Lady Ruth, he still had no solution as to how to handle Wycombe's intent to malign him. He sighed. Sleep would help clear his head, and he'd be able to come up with a plan of action later today.

He didn't even have to pull his key from his pocket, as Carstairs opened the front door when he was only two steps from the top of the stoop's stairs. He handed the butler his top hat and cane then headed toward the staircase. Carstairs cleared his throat.

"Forgive me, my lord, but Miss Mary would like a moment of your time."

"Now?"

He pulled out his pocket watch to see the time. It was only six forty-five. She was an early riser like him, but never quite this early. He frowned. What could be so urgent—had Wycombe been so crass as to visit her unannounced? The staff had explicit instructions not to let anyone cross the threshold unless he or Mary said otherwise. Sleep would have to wait.

"Where is she?" he asked as he met the butler's stoic gaze.

"In the parlor, my lord."

With a nod, he headed toward the salon where Mary spent a great deal of her time studying with the tutor he'd hired for her. As he entered the room, she was waiting for him. She jumped to her feet at his entrance, a look of trepidation on her face. Her blonde hair was piled fashionably on top of her head, and her blue day dress complemented her peaches and cream complexion. While he knew other men would find her exquisite, he'd never found himself aroused while in her company. It was one of the reasons he'd offered to provide for her with the understanding that their relationship would be strictly platonic.

"Good morning, Mary. You're up unusually early."

"I wanted to talk to you." She seemed nervous. He frowned, but forced himself to smile at her.

"What about? Is the new cook not working out to your liking?"

"Oh no, Mrs. Boardwine is wonderful." She hesitated then rushed onward. "Actually, I needed to tell you that I'm getting married."

If she'd pulled a gun and shot him, he couldn't have been more stunned. What the devil was happening to his life? First, the Set trying to root out information about his mistress, and now Mary was telling him that she was leaving him for another man. No, she was getting married.

"Who is he?" It was impossible to keep the sharp note of anger from his voice, but he was too upset to care.

"Jeremy . . . Mr. Routh."

The tutor. Christ Jesus, he'd been cuckolded by the goddamn tutor. His mistress no less. No, that wasn't possible. One couldn't be cuckold if one hadn't consummated the relationship. And he and Mary had never been together in that way. The fact was he'd *never* been with a woman. At the ripe old age of twenty-nine, he'd yet to discover whether a woman could find him desirable. He cringed inwardly.

Did it matter? Did he really care what anyone thought? He didn't need to explain himself to anyone. The harsh voice in his head sounded as clearly as if his uncle were standing in the same room with him. *You're half a man, boy. No woman will have you, let alone want you. You'll never understand what it's like to be a real man.*

"I see." His voice bitter, he glared at Mary.

"Oh please, Garrick. Please don't be angry. We didn't mean for it to happen. It just did."

Knowing Mary as he did, he knew she was telling the truth. He suddenly grew still and narrowed his eyes at her.

"Does he know the truth?"

"Yes." She nodded as a look of sorrow flitted across her features. "I told him everything. He loves me in spite of it all, and he wants us both. He loves Davy as if he were his own son."

The mention of his godson made his heart sink. Naturally, she'd take the boy with her, and the knowledge cut deep. Davy had become the son he'd never have. He'd been there at his birth, held him and loved him. Parting with the two of them would not be easy. Damn it, he didn't want things to change. He wanted everything to stay the way it was.

Guilt streaked its way through his veins. He'd made Mary into a whore in the eyes of others. For almost three years, he'd deliberately ignored that fact. The two of them knew the truth, but it didn't change the fact that in everyone's eyes, even the servants', she was a fallen woman. Remorse snagged at him like a piece of cloth ripping on a nail. Christ, he was a selfish bastard. He'd used her for the sole purpose of impressing on Society that he was something his uncle had continuously said he wasn't. A real man. Closing his eyes, he turned away from her.

"I regret ever offering you such a devil's bargain. It was self-serving of me." She was at his side in seconds to tug hard on his arm, forcing him to look at her.

"That's ridiculous, and you know it," she snapped. "As I recall, you were the one who found me after . . . after what happened. You offered me a safe harbor."

"It doesn't change the fact that I took advantage of you as well. You were vulnerable. I could have taken you to a different part of the country. Presented you as my recently widowed sister. I should have found some other way to protect you from Tremaine."

"He would have found me no matter where I went. He found me here." A flash of emotion flared in her blue eyes. "The only reason Tremaine never came back was your threat of having him thrown into prison."

The memory of finding Viscount Tremaine here in the house still made his gut clench. The libertine had threatened to take Davy from her in his attempt to get Mary to leave with him. The man had been lucky he'd not beaten him to an inch of his life. Instead, he'd dragged Tremaine down the stairs and thrown him out of the house with the warning that if he ever laid eyes on the man again, he'd kill him. But not even that excused his own selfish behavior. Almost as if she could read his mind, Mary gave him a slight shake.

"It didn't matter to others whether or not the bastard forced himself on me. I was soiled goods in the eyes of everyone who knew me. I had few options open to me. You saved me from a horrible existence. You saved Davy, too."

Perhaps she was right. They'd needed each other at the time, and the arrangement had given Mary a chance to heal emotionally and physically. Her resilience amazed him given what she'd gone through. And the fact that she'd insisted on keeping her baby despite the violence of the conception had made him admire her that much more.

"You're generous in your assessment of me."

"And *you* are far too hard on yourself. You're a good man, Garrick. The woman you marry will be a fortunate one."

Her words sent a chill through him. If she knew the full truth, she'd realize such a thing would never happen. Resigned to his fate, he walked across the floor to stare down into the fire in the hearth.

"How soon before the wedding?"

"We were hoping to be married this week. Jeremy accepted a headmaster position in America. A boys' school outside of Philadelphia, and he needs to be there in two weeks. They'll even take Davy as a student." She crossed the room to touch his arm. "I was hoping you . . . that you might give me away."

Anyone else might have thought it a strange request, but with her parents dead, she had no one. He actually found it touching that she thought so highly of him as to even ask. He glanced at her and nodded.

"It would be an honor to do so, Mary." His response elicited an impulsive hug and a kiss on his cheek as she smiled happily.

"Oh thank you, Garrick. You don't know what it means to have you say you'll give me away. It just wouldn't seem right to not have you there."

He released a sigh of resignation at her enthusiasm. While he was happy for her, he couldn't help but feel a touch of envy at the joy that made her face glow. It filled him with a longing for something he knew he'd never find. No woman would be able to accept him as he was, let alone his inability to sire children. Garrick squeezed Mary's hand and forced a smile.

"I'm happy for you my dear. I shall have to think of a suitable wedding present."

"But you've given me so much already."

"All the same, it would be remiss of me to let you run off and marry your Mr. Routh without a dowry. I'll have my solicitor see to it."

"You're far too generous, Garrick. I only wish you could find someone to make *you* happy."

"I'm quite content with my life the way it is, thank you." He suppressed a yawn.

"You're tired," she exclaimed softly. "I should have waited until this evening, but I—"

"It's all right, Mary. You expected me to be up early, not just coming home at this hour." He flinched. Home. This *was* home. More so than Chiddingstone House. This was where he came when he wanted peace and quiet. It was a place to gather his thoughts. Chiddingstone House, on the other hand, was a house of constant frenetic energy, and as much as he loved his siblings, he found it wearing on his soul. Now everything was going to change.

"I have an afternoon appointment, which shouldn't take long. Why not invite your Mr. Routh to dinner? I would like to ensure he intends to be good to you."

"I'm sure he'd be honored."

With a kiss to Mary's forehead, he left the salon and quietly closed the door behind him. He leaned against the hardness of the carved mahogany for a moment before he pushed himself away and climbed the main staircase. Now what was he going to do? It had always been difficult keeping his secret, but at least the illusion of a mistress had left everyone thinking that he wasn't ready for a wife yet.

He muttered a harsh oath of frustration, and the door to his bedroom crashed back into the wall before he slammed it shut. With a vicious movement, he removed his coat and threw it over the back of a nearby chair. Unlike his friends, he had no valet. Shame had taught him to do without a manservant. He jerked off his tie then unbuttoned the collar of his shirt, uncaring when a button popped off and flew across the room.

Stripped to his bare skin, he caught a glimpse of himself in the floor-length mirror he passed on his way to the bed. He paused at the sight of his reflection. A sense of revulsion rose up inside him.

His uncle was right. With only one ballock, he wasn't a real man at all. He abruptly turned away from the mirror.

He'd been eleven at the time of his father's suicide, when Beresford had assumed guardianship of him and his siblings. Not only had his uncle managed Garrick's home and inheritance as if they were his own, but for some twisted reason, the man had taken pleasure in tormenting him. His uncle had tried to do the same to his sisters and brother, but Garrick had managed to shield his siblings from the majority of the man's cruelty. And Beresford had excelled at it. A sliver of a memory taunted him, and he fought to push it back, but failed.

An image of Bertha flashed through his head, and he drew in a sharp breath. He closed his eyes as the painful past reared its ugly head. His uncle had routinely held parties, inviting the worst of the demimonde to the house. Bertha had been a pretty ballerina he'd stumbled across the first night of one of Beresford's decadent house parties. He'd been smitten with her from the moment he'd first laid eyes on her.

At seventeen, he'd thought himself in love. He'd courted her persistently, and when she'd asked him to visit her rooms, he'd been giddy with excitement. But what was supposed to have been a night of passion had turned into one of deep humiliation. It wasn't until he'd undressed in front of her that he'd realized his mistake. Bertha had been revolted by his physical deformity. Mere moments later, her revulsion had changed to mocking peals of laughter he could still hear in his head.

His hands curled into tight fists at the memory of his uncle barging into the room. At that moment, it had been evident the entire event had been staged by Beresford for his own sick amusement, which only sealed Garrick's mortification. His gut knotted viciously as he fought to bury the past deep in the back of his mind.

From that night forward, he'd done everything in his power to make people view him as a man who other men wanted to emulate. A man who could ride and hunt better than anyone else, an exceptional boxer, a man of discriminating taste in all things, even women. The illusion where women were concerned had been the most difficult one to create and preserve.

He'd made it a point to develop a skill for kissing, but had used it sparingly. On the one or two occasions when desire had actually become a problem, he'd quickly extricated himself from the situation. Mary agreeing to pose as his mistress had freed him from those types of problems. Now she was leaving, and with her his ability to keep up appearances.

He didn't begrudge Mary her happiness, but hearing that Wycombe had a wager to learn more about his mistress made the timing of her impending nuptials awkward. The mattress gave way slightly beneath his weight, and he pulled the covers over him. Well aware how hedonistic sleeping in the nude was viewed, he took a small amount of satisfaction in defying the social norm.

Arms tucked behind his head, he stared up at the ceiling as he tried to figure out what to do next. Where in the hell was he going to get a new mistress who wouldn't question why her patron refused to touch her? Ruth's face fluttered its way into his head. Absolutely not. He was far too attracted to the woman. And she was far too intelligent not to question his reasons for their relationship to remain platonic. A groan rolled out of him. Maybe he could go to Paris for a few months. No, he had responsibilities, and he wasn't about to walk away from those.

Perhaps he could say he was between mistresses at the moment. The thought was laughable. It had always been difficult to avoid the marriage-minded matriarchs who constantly pushed their daughters in front of him. The moment news circulated that he was no longer supporting a mistress the vultures would circle. Even the somewhat rakish reputation he'd worked hard to foster would do little to keep some mothers away.

Images of Ruth forced their way into his thoughts. She'd been a tantalizing vision in the gaslight with hints of gold in her chestnut hair. The dress she'd worn had highlighted every delicious curve of her, right down to the fullness of her breasts. His cock stirred to life as he recalled the sweet sensuality of her lips. She had a mouth begging to be kissed. Even more pervasive was the memory of her scent. A mysterious, exotic mix of jasmine with a touch of spicy citrus. Would she taste as delicious as she smelled?

The moment the question dashed through his head, he cast it aside. Christ Jesus, that fact was precisely *why* he needed to forget about Ruth as a replacement for Mary. He rolled over and punched at his pillow. All too aware of his growing erection, he groaned. He was exhausted, but his body was demanding something he couldn't give it.

What would it be like to have Ruth beneath him? To taste her throat, her breasts, and her nipples. He swallowed hard at the image. He wrapped his hand around his stiff rod and allowed himself the pleasure of visualizing her in every carnal position he could imagine as he worked his cock hard until he spilled his seed. It wasn't enough. He wanted something more. Something he could never have.

Even if he did the unthinkable and offered his protection to Ruth, this was the closest he'd ever get to being with her. He dragged in a deep breath as he cleaned himself up. God, he was tired. He yawned. His problems weren't going anywhere. They'd be here when he woke up. He closed his eyes and just before he drifted off, he thought he heard the sound of his uncle and Bertha laughing. It made his stomach lurch.

Through the black veil covering her face, Ruth slowly turned around to study every aspect of the parlor. Nothing about the room had changed since the last time she'd visited Crawley Hall. It was still as bright and cheery as she remembered. Behind her, Smythe waited impatiently in the doorway.

The man was beginning to become annoying. She wanted to take her time viewing the house. She'd already made up her mind to buy the estate, but she knew it was important to scrutinize it just in case her instincts were wrong. The only time she'd visited Crawley Hall had been shortly after she'd become involved with Marston. Their carriage had broken a wheel near the entrance to the Hall, and the owner had invited them to tea while repairs were made.

Although they'd never met before, Ruth had immediately recognized the woman as a former mistress of the Prince of Wales. She hadn't realized it at the time, but the older woman had been a prophetic sign of Ruth's future. Perhaps that was why she'd never forgotten Crawley Hall. Subconsciously, she'd known then that her own retirement was close at hand. When she'd heard the woman had died and the estate was for sale, she'd mentioned to Marston that she was considering buying the house.

He'd immediately offered to purchase the estate for her, but requested she wait a couple of months for some of his investments to mature. She released a soft noise of disgust. She should have pressed him about the estate weeks ago, although something told her the man would have put her off just as he had the first time.

The sound of a carriage rolling across the gravelly drive caught her attention, and she crossed the drawing room floor to peer out the window. Having removed her gloves earlier, the sheer curtains that lined the interior portion of the window brushed over her skin like a fine sandpaper as she pushed the material aside. The position of the carriage made it impossible to see who'd arrived. With a frown, she turned back toward the salon doorway to see that Smythe had disappeared.

Her chest tightened with fear. Damn, the little toad. This couldn't be a coincidence. The man knew she had limited funds. The sales agent was using her simply to extract a higher price from another potential buyer.

Perhaps the other bidder wouldn't like the house. It had been on the market for more than a year, and that meant Smythe might find it difficult to sell to this new prospective buyer. Male voices echoed in the hall, and she sighed with resignation as she moved toward the doorway. She'd taken only two steps into the foyer when she came to a dead stop.

Stratfield.

Almost as if he were expecting to see her, the man bowed in her direction, and as he straightened, a small smile curved his sensuous mouth. She clenched her teeth as she directed a sharp nod toward him.

"Lord Stratfield."

"Lady Ruth."

He moved toward her and she was forced to offer him her hand. The moment his mouth brushed across her skin, it was as if she'd been burned. She jerked her hand free of his to turn her attention toward the sales agent.

"I would like to see the upstairs now, Mr. Smythe."

"Of course, my lady." The sales agent bowed slightly, his manner hesitant. "Would you mind, if Lord Stratfield joins us?"

"Not at all," she bit out. Did she mind? Of course she did. She didn't want the bastard anywhere near her. *That wasn't exactly true.* Determined to ignore the small taunting voice in her head, she turned away from Lord Stratfield in a dismissive manner and pinned her gaze on the sales agent. "Might we continue, Mr. Smythe?"

"Certainly, my lady. If you'll both follow me." The sales agent, suddenly realizing she wasn't happy, bowed obsequiously to her as he headed toward the main staircase. At least the man finally understood that his efforts to provoke a bidding war might be in danger. But she already knew Crawley Hall was lost. She was certain Stratfield was far better off financially than she was, which meant the man could outbid her.

Muscles stiff with anger, she followed the balding sales agent toward the steps. It seemed pointless to see the remainder of the house, but perhaps Stratfield would decide the estate wasn't to his liking. Fingers sliding over a burnished oak railing, she climbed the stairs that rose up from the center of the foyer to branch off to the left and right at the first landing.

As they reached the second floor's main hall, she counted the number of doorways. Eight rooms. She entered the first bedroom and carefully assessed its dimensions. If the rest of the bedrooms were this size, she could easily accommodate more than twenty children on this floor alone, while still leaving two rooms for her and Dolores to use. The servants' quarters would no doubt allow for two or three more children. She moved toward the window to look out at the landscape.

The sunshine made the late winter snow on the ground glisten. It was lovely now, but in the spring it would be even more so. She whispered a silent prayer that her rival wouldn't want the house.

The children she brought from the orphanage would flourish here. Smythe's voice echoed in the corridor in an obvious attempt to capture Stratfield's attention. She turned back toward the door only to see her competition leaning against the doorjamb. There was something beautiful about him in the nonchalant position he'd assumed that stole her breath away.

Irritated that she could even *think* to find him attractive after last night, she gripped the stem of her umbrella so tightly she thought it might snap. Not bothering to speak, she crossed the floor and waited in silence for him to move. With a frown, he straightened and she quickly tried to pass him. As she drew abreast of him, his hand caught her upper arm to hold her in place.

"Let me go," she snapped.

"I'd like to explain about last night."

"There is *no* explanation necessary, my lord."

"I think there is," he said as he leaned into her. She immediately shrank back, aware of the heat spreading its way through her that was becoming all too familiar. Equally familiar was that steady gaze of his. "I danced with you because I wanted to, Ruth. *Not* because I pitied you."

Surprised by his fierce declaration, she stared at him in silence. In the deepest reaches of her mind, she acknowledged that she liked the way he'd said her name. There was a warm intimacy to the sound that threaded its way through her senses. She swallowed hard as she remembered the humiliation she'd felt last night as she walked away from him. Was it possible he was telling the truth?

The earnest expression on his face made her think he was. There was such an intensity about him that she could almost swear he was mentally willing her to believe him. The knowledge that he'd danced with her because he wanted to sent a warm rush of pleasure pulsing through her veins. Alarmed by her reaction, she gave him a quick nod and drew in a deep breath.

"I believe you."

"Thank you." The simplicity of his response made his confession all the more sincere. Rattled by the intensity of his gaze, she looked down at the hand wrapped around her arm.

"I'd like to see the remainder of the house, my lord."

"Garrick."

"I beg your pardon?" She knew exactly what he was doing, but the intimacy of using his first name frightened her. *Everything* about this man frightened her.

"My name is Garrick." A stubborn look crossed his handsome features, and she studied him for a minute before nodding.

"Very well. Garrick." She kept her tone crisp, expecting him to say something else, but he didn't. He just stared at her. She grew self-conscious under his gaze and nodded toward his hand one more time. "May we continue, my . . . Garrick."

"What? Yes. Of course."

He seemed almost dazed for a moment as she darted a glance in his direction. He quickly released her, and stepped back to give her access to the hallway. As she moved past him, a whiff of cologne teased her nostrils. It was a heady aroma of spice and cedar. The scent lingered on her senses as she put distance between them. Smythe appeared out of one of the other rooms down the hall.

"There you are. If you'll come this way, my lord, my lady, I'll show you the master suite."

Eager to finish viewing the property so she could escape, she hurried toward the sales agent, all too aware of Stratfield following close behind. As she entered the master bedroom, her first impression was that she'd entered a male domain. The furniture was heavy and masculine, while the drapes were a deep maroon brocade. She darted a look in Stratfield's direction as he strode to the window and flung the curtains back. The room was a perfect complement to his sinfully dark looks. He turned around and as he met her gaze, his mouth curled upward in a small smile as if he had a secret. She immediately looked away.

"Is the furniture included in the sale price, Mr. Smythe?" she asked quietly as she looked around the room. There was little here she could use.

The stocky sales agent nodded his head. "Everything is included, but if the buyer prefers, the furniture can be sold at auction prior to moving into the house. Of course, this room in particular was clearly made for the master of the house."

The reminder that she wasn't the only one considering the purchase of Crawley Hall renewed her sense of frustration. The Hall should have been hers. Now she was forced to bid on the house and hope that Garrick didn't offer more money.

"I'd like to see the dining room and kitchen if you please," she said with a brisk note in her voice. She quickly turned toward Garrick. She winced. How quickly she'd fallen into thinking of him by his first name. "That is, if you've seen enough on this floor, my lord."

He arched his eyebrow at her abrupt tone, but his only response was a brief nod and a slight bow. It was as if he was humoring her, and she didn't like it. Struggling to keep her irritation hidden, she turned around and headed toward the door.

"Smythe, do you know anything about the current owners of the estate?"

Garrick's question brought her to a halt as she turned and waited for the short, stocky sales agent to answer. To her surprise, Smythe suddenly appeared distinctly uncomfortable. He threw her a quick glance then averted his gaze.

"The owner died recently and her heirs wish to sell the Hall."

"And the lady who owned the house. Do you know anything about her?"

"Only that she was one of the Prince's . . . lady friends from his youth." Smythe's pained expression almost made her laugh, and her gaze met Garrick's, whose mouth was twitching with amusement.

"Ah, then that explains the mirror."

Puzzled, she watched Smythe swallow uncomfortably as the sales agent's gaze shifted toward her then back to Stratfield. "Mirror, my lord?"

"I'm disappointed, Smythe. Don't tell me you've not noticed it."

With a nod toward the bed, Garrick arched his eyebrows at the sales agent. Frowning, she crossed the floor and looked up at the underside of the canopy. Attached to the ceiling, the canopy hid a large mirror centered over the bed. Etched boldly into the glass was the inscription *For Queen and Country*.

"Good lord," she gasped, trying not to laugh.

The woman Ruth remembered from their only meeting had exhibited a wicked sense of humor, and she wondered if the Prince of Wales had actually slept in the bed. Somehow she was more inclined to believe Bertie's old mistress had commissioned the mirror long after her affair with the Prince had ended. It didn't really matter. She was certain Bertie wouldn't want anyone else to see the mirror, and she was certain Mr. Smythe knew it, too. No wonder the man looked so uncomfortable. "Forgive me, my lady. My lord." Smythe cleared his throat and one glance showed sweat milling on his forehead. "I apologize. I left word the mirror was to be removed this morning. Obviously my instructions were not followed."

"I trust you'll see to its removal soon," Garrick said with a hint of steel in his voice.

"Most assuredly, my lord. If word ever reached . . . well I'd be ruined." The sales agent eyed both of them with terror in his eyes.

"I have no desire to see your livelihood jeopardized, Mr. Smythe," she said with a sigh. Despite his annoying manner, the man wasn't to blame for the previous owner's decorating choices. "But I agree with Lord Stratfield that the mirror should be removed without delay."

"Yes, my lady. Thank you." The sales agent bowed his gratitude then hurried toward the bedroom doorway. "Now if you'll follow me, I'll show you the remainder of the house."

Ruth resisted the impulse to look in Garrick's direction as she turned to follow the sales agent out of the room. In the space of less than an hour, the man had forced her to completely redefine her opinion of him. It had been easy to keep her distance from him when she found him despicable. But now . . . now she was struggling hard not to like him.

Unable to help himself, Garrick was entranced by the gentle sway of Ruth's hips as she turned and walked toward the bedroom door. There was no artifice in her movements, and the sensual elegance with which she moved stirred his blood in a manner he'd not experienced since he was seventeen. But not even Bertha had created this strong of a reaction in him. He ran his finger just beneath his stiff collar in an effort to ease his breathing. Christ Jesus, the woman was a heady experience.

Just moments ago, she'd sent him reeling when he'd inhaled that sweetly tart scent of hers. It beckoned a man to see if she tasted as good as she smelled. It was a distinctly different fragrance from last night. Today she smelled crisp and fresh, while last night she'd been an exotic mystery for his senses. He suppressed a groan.

The minute he got Smythe alone, he was going to pummel the man for putting him in such a devilishly tight spot. He wanted Crawley Hall, but it was clear she did, too. And *that* was a problem he'd not had to consider on his way here. Although she didn't show it openly, he could tell by the way she touched the doors, the banisters, everything, she wanted the property badly.

She didn't just touch things. She caressed them. As gently as she might stroke a lover. He swallowed hard as his collar tightened around his neck again. He followed her out of the bedroom at a deliberate pace. He was walking a dangerous path with the woman. First last night, and now the proposition he'd seriously contemplated the entire ride to Crawley Hall.

It would have been best to just let sleeping dogs lie. Easier to let her think pity had been his motivation last night when he'd asked her to dance as opposed to his spontaneous desire to hold her. No, the only thing piteous about dancing with her last night had been his reaction to her. As he followed her down the corridor, his gaze dropped to the small of her back, where his hand had rested as he'd guided her around the dance floor. She'd been a soft heat in his arms, and he had no doubt she'd be a fiery creature in a man's bed.

He shook his head slightly as he obliterated the images beginning to take hold in his head. That was never going to happen. It couldn't. But if the woman could cloud his senses so easily in the company of others, what would it be like when he was finally alone with her? He clenched his jaw as they made their way downstairs.

Perhaps Smythe had done him a favor. In the light of day, he was seeing just how difficult things could be if he were to approach Ruth about being his lover in name only. It wouldn't be as cut-and-dried as it had seemed in the carriage this morning. In fact, he had the distinct feeling it would be one of the most difficult challenges he'd ever undertaken.

Despite the dimly lit hallway leading to the back of the house, the kitchen was bright and open. It was an enormous room with a large brick oven and a cookstove that was so shiny clean it could have easily been brand-new. Delight lit up Ruth's features as she carefully rolled her veil up onto the brim of her hat.

He couldn't remember ever having seen a more beautiful woman. Her cheeks had a slight blush to them, and a pair of widely set eyes offset her slender nose. He could think of no one he'd ever met who had eyes the color of hers. They were dark violet and filled with secrets. But it was the dark pink of her full, plump lips that made his mouth go dry.

Clasping his hands tightly behind his back, he jerked his gaze away from her animated features. His reaction to her was aggravating. He knew better than to let physical desire take command of his senses. If he had any intention of presenting his proposition to Ruth, he needed to make damn sure he could maintain control of himself when near her. It was the only way the arrangement would work between them. He needed to keep the relationship strictly platonic.

"Do you know if the flue is capable of supporting a second cookstove, Smythe?"

Startled by her question, he looked in her direction. What the devil did she need a second cookstove for? The sales agent seemed equally puzzled as he shook his head.

"I'm not certain, my lady. I would have to have the local blacksmith inspect it."

"Before I even consider making an offer, I would need that question and several others answered."

"Of course, my lady," Smythe said with a look of defeat.

"If you don't mind, I'd like to see some of the garden."

"But there's snow on the ground, my lady!"

"Thank you for that observation, Smythe, but all the same, I'd like to take a walk outside. I'm sure Lord Stratfield has questions, so there's no need to accompany me."

Before either of them could stop her, Ruth headed toward the door that led to a small mudroom and then outdoors. Smythe's dumbfounded look almost made Garrick laugh out loud. The agent had no idea how to react to her, but then he wasn't sure he would have had a response either. As she disappeared out the back door, Smythe turned to him with amazement.

"My lord, do you have—"

"I think I'll join the Lady Ruth for a stroll outside as well, Smythe. I suggest you wait for us in the main hall."

He grinned as he walked past the man on his way outside. For a second time the stocky sales agent was at a complete loss for words. The door to the kitchen closed behind him as he paused for a moment in the mudroom. Had Ruth actually gone out into the snow without overshoes? He rapidly donned a pair of the rubber coverings and followed her out into the snow.

From the size of her footprints, she'd foregone the galoshes, which meant she could easily fall if she wasn't careful. Concerned for her welfare, he moved quickly along the path she'd made in the snow. The garden was lifeless at the moment, small bits of dead plants pushing through the few inches of snow on the ground. Fruit trees, their bare branches like spider legs crooked in every direction, lined the rear of the garden, while a barren white arbor crossed the path he followed.

Ruth's footsteps led toward an orangery a short distance away, and he could see her shadowy figure through the steamed windows of the hothouse. He reached the building quickly and stepped into its humid warmth. The size of the indoor garden was larger than he expected. Someone had obviously been caring for it as he could see tomato plants bearing small fruit.

Ahead of him, he saw the top of Ruth's hat. He really needed his head examined for seeking the woman out. But something beyond his comprehension drove him forward. Worse, he knew whatever was compelling him onward would most likely bring him nothing but trouble. He rounded a corner to find Ruth examining an ornamental pear tree. Whether she'd been so preoccupied inspecting the hothouse or his tread had been lighter than he expected, she cried out in surprise the moment she turned and saw him standing behind her.

"Good lord," she gasped as her eyes flashed with anger. "You scared me half out of my wits."

"Forgive me. I thought you heard me come into the building."

"*No.* I didn't."

She turned away from him to continue along the pebble-lined path in silence. With a frown, he followed her. After several steps, she whirled around to face him.

"Is there something I can help you with, my lord?"

"I thought we'd settled on you calling me Garrick."

"Oh for heaven's sake. Is there something you want, *Garrick*?"

He ignored the lustful images that immediately flooded his head at her words. Folding his arms across his chest, he eyed her cautiously. "Why do you want Crawley Hall?"

"*What?*" Shocked, she took a step back from him and shook her head as she stared at him in mute surprise.

"I asked you *why* you want Crawley Hall."

"I . . . it's an investment," she snapped.

"No. It's more than that." He frowned at the way she blanched. "You want this estate. Badly."

"I don't know what you're talking about."

"Yes you do. You show it with every thing you touch in the house, even with these plants. A man could easily die of pleasure in your arms if you were to stroke him the same way." He stiffened as he saw her eyes widen, and he realized he'd said too much.

"Don't be ridiculous." She sniffed, her cheeks flushed with color. "It's a house, nothing more."

"If that's true, then why don't you answer my question, Ruth?"

He saw her swallow hard the moment he said her name, and the flash of emotion in her eyes propelled him forward until there was little more than an inch between them. She was breathing rapidly, and her scent filled his nostrils as he concentrated on the lushness of her lower lip. He stood there breathing her in, feeling her heat press into him despite the fact that he wasn't touching her.

What the devil was wrong with him? At the first sensation of desire, he'd always managed to put distance between himself and a woman. But not this time. Christ Jesus he knew it was a mistake, but he wanted to taste her. He lowered his head toward her, but she suddenly darted out of reach.

"You must excuse me, my lord. I must return to London now in order not to be late for a supper engagement." Clearly agitated, she started to move past him, but he blocked her path.

"Not until you tell me why you want Crawley Hall." His persistence puzzled him. Why was it so important to him to know her reasons for wanting the Hall? The answer to that question eluded him. He simply knew he had to know.

"Step aside please, *my lord*. Your tenacity is most annoying particularly when I'm not obliged to tell you anything."

"True," he said quietly. "But I would like to know why it's so important to you."

She stared at him for a long moment, her gaze filled with a wariness that made him frown. He wanted her to trust him as she might a friend. The thought made him question his sanity again. Resignation furrowed her brow as she released a sharp sigh.

"Very well. I wish to retire here." Another emotion darkened her gaze as he stared at her. He was certain she was telling him the truth as to why she wanted the estate, just not the whole truth. She didn't need a house as big as Crawley Hall. It was meant for a large family, or as in his case, as a home for orphans. He clasped his hands behind his back and arched his eyebrow.

"Retirement? You're far too young for that." It was a sincere observation, but it made her eyes open wide with amazement. Suddenly, she laughed out loud. It was a melodious sound that generated a bolt of pleasure inside him. He liked the sound of her laughter.

"I thank you for the compliment, but I'm forty-one. And for a woman in my position, that makes my prospects shall we say . . . limited."

"I think you underestimate your charms, Ruth. There are plenty of men who would eagerly seek out your company. You're a beautiful woman." And younger looking than she gave herself credit for. The woman could have easily passed for little more than a few years older than him instead of the twelve that was between them.

"You flatter me, but you have the blindness that comes with youth, something I lost a long time ago." She sent him a wry smile. It irritated him that she could dismiss his compliment so easily. She was more desirable than she realized. He ignored the alarm ringing in his head.

"You seem to think me a callow youth attempting to gain your favor with flattery," he snapped. "I'm not in the habit of saying something I don't mean."

Her violet eyes turned a stormy hue as she stared at him in surprise before she tipped her head in his direction.

"Forgive me. I've clearly forgotten how to accept a compliment."

Despite her quiet apology, he was still annoyed. There might be a substantial gap in age between them, but it wasn't as if he was fresh out of the schoolroom. Nor had she captivated him so completely that he'd lost his senses. An unconvincing lie, but one he could live with at the moment. He might not have the experience of a woman's bed, but he was far from innocent as to what happened between a man and woman. More importantly, he wasn't the kind of man who would unceremoniously discard a mistress simply because of her age.

And Marston had made that point brutally clear by his comments and current relationship with a woman half Ruth's age. What the bastard had done to Ruth was reminiscent of the humiliation he'd suffered more than ten years ago. He'd lost his youth and innocence in one fell swoop the night his uncle and Bertha had deliberately humiliated him. He understood more than she'd ever know how deeply insults could cut.

The thick silence between them obviously made her uncomfortable, and he saw her fingers fidget with the handle of her umbrella. A ridiculous thing to be carrying out here in the snow. Of all the things about women, their fashions and need for fripperies was the one thing he'd never understood.

"If you'll excuse me, my lor . . . Garrick, I think I'll return to the house."

"You continue to have difficulty with my name. Do I make you nervous?" He narrowed his eyes as he saw color flush her cheeks.

"It . . . it denotes an intimacy that doesn't exist between us."

"There are various forms of intimacy, Ruth. Could we not at least be friends?"

"I'm afraid that's not possible."

"Because there are a couple of years difference between us?" He saw her flinch at the question. The devil take it, he would have to remember how sensitive she was about her age.

"*No,* of course not." The tone of her voice told him the age difference between them was precisely the reason why she'd refused his offer of friendship.

"And if I bought Crawley Hall for you? Would that change the way you feel?"

Bloody hell, had he lost his mind? This was the largest place he'd found in months that would house more children, while allowing for the expansion he knew would be needed in the future. And here he was offering it up to her on a silver platter. He frowned as she glared at him.

"A generous offer, my lord, but I must refuse. I'm not ashamed of how I make my living, but I am not so desperate as to sell myself off to the first man who comes calling after another breaks with me."

With a scornful nod, she spun away from him and left him to stare after her with what he could only define as intense remorse. A feeling he didn't like at all. Not only had he jeopardized his own plans where she was concerned, he'd proven her right. His inexperience in securing the services of a mistress was more than evident and only served to emphasize his youth all the more.

Irritated by his lack of finesse, he clenched his teeth in self-disgust. He'd insulted her. It wasn't his habit to insult people he liked. And he definitely liked Ruth. He grunted with anger. There was definitely a protocol involved in these types of matters, but in his ignorance, he'd blundered badly.

Worse, his treatment of her, whether intentional or not, differed little from the contempt Marston had shown her. The sound of the hothouse door slamming shut jerked him out of his stupor, and he ran after her. As he stepped out into the snow, he saw her making her way quickly, yet cautiously, down the slight hill toward the garden. He easily caught up with her before she could reach the barren rose trellis.

"Ruth . . . I'm an ass."

"Of that I have no doubt," she bit out viciously.

He touched her elbow only to have her yank herself free of his grip to continue toward the garden. She'd only taken two steps when her feet went out from under her. Her soft cry made him leap forward, and he caught her in his arms as she fell. The scent of her swept over him as a soft shoulder pressed into his chest. He'd never realized a woman could smell so delicious all in one breath. The sound of her ragged breathing stirred something deep inside him.

It was a predatory response on his part. He knew it wasn't the fall that had affected her breathing, and it excited him. A tremor shook her body, which only heightened the sensation. Desire barreled its way through him as he glanced down to see his fingers splayed against her stomach, mere inches from the lush fullness of her breasts.

An image of her naked, her nipples stiff and begging to be licked, flashed through his head. Almost immediately, his cock swelled in his pants. Christ Jesus, the woman was temptation personified. Her head was slightly turned away from him, exposing a delectable neck he wanted to nibble on. Without thinking, he bent his head toward her, his mouth barely brushing across her skin.

Her sharp gasp made him jerk his head up. Where the hell was the control he'd always managed to maintain with other women and the desire they'd aroused in him? He'd already erred with her twice and had no wish to repeat his mistake. He immediately pulled back and helped her straighten upright. The minute she pulled away from him, his body protested with a strength that tightened every muscle in his body. A stark hunger gripped his insides as he noted the slight flutter on the side of her neck. He crushed his urge to reach out and drag his finger across the spot. Instead, he took a step back from her.

"I made a mistake."

"More than one," she snapped.

"Perhaps we might start over."

His gaze met her wary one as he watched her mulling his suggestion over. Her violet eyes darkened suddenly, and a composed mask settled over her features.

"I see no point in doing so, my lord. I have no wish to enter into a new liaison with any man. Particularly one who thinks gaining access to my bed is little more than a simple monetary transaction.

I'm not ashamed of the way I make my living, but I offer a great deal more than the ordinary whore you mistake me for. Even Marston, for all his faults, knew that much."

Without giving him a chance to respond, she turned away and proceeded to make her way to the house. He stood there watching her walk away, her back ramrod straight with what he was certain could only be indignation. The idea that she'd placed him on a rung lower than Marston made him stiffen with anger. He wasn't sure if his irritation was rooted in self-disgust or if it was the fact that Ruth didn't like him. Either way, it was best that he stayed away from her, and the idea he'd even thought of asking her to be his mistress in name only was laughable. Unfortunately, he was far from amused.

Ruth frowned as she struggled to focus her attention on the book she held. For the third time, she reread the paragraph on the page before closing the book with a noise of disgust. It had been a week since her visit to Crawley Hall, and she didn't like the way she jumped every time the front doorbell rang.

There was no reason for Lord Stratfield—Garrick—to call on her. No reason except his obvious attraction to her. An attraction that she couldn't deny feeling, too. Or at least in the darkness of her bedroom she couldn't. Her heart skipped a beat at the memory of the dream she'd had last night. Images of Garrick pleasuring every inch of her with his mouth until she screamed out his name and her body convulsed in one orgasm after another.

She quickly stood up and dropped her book onto the side table next to the chair. The leather-bound volume cracked loudly against the walnut surface. Crossing the room to the window, she pushed aside the curtains to look out on the busy street. She couldn't remember the last time she'd felt so confused about what she wanted or so lost as to what to do.

The sun was brilliant, and for a change the sky wasn't cloudy with smoke from chimneys spewing out the residue of heat-producing coal. It was a perfect day for a ride in the park, and yet it was the last thing she wanted to do. The heat of the sun penetrated the glass and warmed her face as she closed her eyes for a long moment.

Why couldn't she shake this listlessness? She opened her eyes as she let the curtains fall back into place. Her life wasn't over simply because Marston had ended their liaison. There were the children to look after. She bit down on her lip. Although she hadn't heard back from Smythe about Crawley Hall, she was certain the offer she'd made yesterday wasn't high enough. She would have to search for another property soon. St. Agnes's was bursting at the seams.

The doorbell jangled in the front hall, and her heart skipped a beat. Had Garrick—she brushed the thought aside before it could even take hold in her head. Simmons quietly entered the salon.

"Yes, Simmons?"

"A note from Mr. Smythe, my lady." Simmons offered her an envelope, which Ruth accepted with resignation.

"Thank you."

She stared down at the envelope then released a sigh of annoyance. There was little use in putting off opening the bloody thing when she already knew what it said. With a vicious tug, she tore the envelope as she yanked the letter out. Quickly unfolding the paper, she skimmed the words on the page, her body growing rigid as she read the message then read it again.

Crawley Hall was hers.

Stunned, she stared at the letter and the words saying her offer had been accepted. She closed her eyes in a brief prayer of gratitude. Dazed, she stared at the letter's content with disbelief as she tried to comprehend the fact that the Hall was hers. Had her offer actually been higher than Garrick's? Her eyes scanned the contents again for the line she'd skimmed over the first time. As she was the only bidder on the property, the owners had decided to accept her offer rather than wait for another buyer.

The only bidder on the property.

Garrick hadn't bid on the property? If so, why not? She was certain he'd wanted the Hall. She frowned, uncertain whether to feel elation that Crawley Hall was hers or irritation at the notion that Garrick might have been feeling magnanimous by not bidding. There was no doubt in her mind that he'd wanted the Hall almost as badly as she had. With a sharp exhalation, she shrugged slightly. It didn't matter why he'd failed to make an offer. The Hall was hers. The front door rang again, and tension immediately tugged at her muscles. She wasn't expecting any callers. Perhaps Garrick had come by to accept her gratitude for not bidding against her. She dismissed the idea as being ridiculous. A moment later, Simmons entered with a medium-sized box.

"A delivery for you, my lady."

"Was there a card?"

"No, my lady. A boy made the delivery." At the butler's reply, she nodded her head.

"Thank you."

As Simmons left the salon, she stared down at the jeweler's box the servant had given her. Despite the lack of a card, she was certain it was from Garrick. Anticipation made her throat tighten in its effort to rush through her. She squashed the sensation immediately. Determined to remain detached, she slowly opened the box.

The name Garrard was imprinted on the white linen interior of the lid. It had been a long time since a suitor had sent her jewels from the Crown Jeweler. There were two smaller boxes inside, and the first one she opened contained a crystal paperweight in the form of a jackass. She laughed softly. Not only did Lord Stratfield have a sense of humor, he could laugh at himself as well.

She set aside the paperweight to open the second box. Nestled in the silk-lined interior was a delicate tulip made of small diamonds. She smiled. A paperweight that said he believed he'd behaved like an ass and a white tulip brooch that represented a request for forgiveness.

But had he really said or done anything terrible? He'd insulted her, and yet she didn't believe he'd meant to do so. If anything he'd been quite complimentary, and in a manner that had made her feel young again. And his comment that she could pleasure a man with a simple stroke of her hand had stirred a dangerous excitement in her. Her skin grew warm as she remembered his provocative words. It *had* been a scandalous observation, but it had made her feel desired. She suddenly realized it was a sensation she'd not experienced for a very long time. Her fingertips trailed across the cool metal and precious stones.

It was obvious the man was apologizing. She just didn't know whether she wanted to encourage him. And keeping the brooch, as lovely as it was, would do just that. Accepting his gift would indicate she'd forgiven his clumsy attempt to gain entry into her bed. She sighed. Garrick Stratfield's attentions were flattering, but the gap in their ages made her hesitant to allow him to court her.

She had no doubt he would make her feel young again. At least until that moment when he left her for a woman his own age, someone younger than her. It would be devastating. Even more so than when Marston, or Grenville before him, had parted with her. She looked down at the brooch again.

It was clearly worth a substantial amount of money. But what would she gain if she accepted his gift? She'd be signaling that she would accept him as a suitor, and a liaison with him was certain to be short-lived with a painful ending. Still, he'd offered to buy Crawley Hall for her, which meant he was not without funds. Could she really afford to say no? If he were older—she bit down on her lip. It was impractical not to accept his gift, and she would no doubt come to regret it, but something told her she'd regret it even more if she accepted Garrick's gift.

She returned the paperweight and brooch to the box, snapping it closed. Quickly crossing the floor, she sat down at the secretary to pen a brief note of refusal to accompany the jewelry back to the merchant. Just as she rang for Simmons, the front doorbell sounded again. She frowned as she slipped her note into an envelope. What now? Surely the man hadn't sent another present. A quiet knock echoed in the parlor, and she stood up at the same moment that Simmons opened the door.

"Lord Stratfield, my lady."

Caught by surprise, the note she'd written to the jeweler fell from her hand onto the desk as she stared in amazement at the sight of Garrick entering the room. She rarely was at a loss for words, but his unexpected appearance made her feel like an awkward, ungainly girl again. Her fingertips pressing hard against the cherry desktop of the secretary, she struggled to regain her equilibrium. He was just one man. She was more than capable of handling him as she had so many others. The lie incited mocking laughter in the back of her head. She silenced it with the iron will she'd developed at the age of seventeen. When one was hungry, one could endure almost anything for a meal.

"Lord Stratfield, this is a surprise." Her fingers toyed nervously with the lace at the base of her throat at the frown on his face. She should never have agreed to call him by his first name. When she realized she was still fingering the lace, she immediately dropped her hand to her side.

"I see you received my gift." His gaze dropped pointedly to the jeweler's box on her desk then returned to her face.

"Yes." She glanced away from him. "I just finished writing a note to accompany its return to the jeweler's."

"It's not to your liking?"

"On the contrary, the paperweight is quite amusing, and the brooch is beautiful, but—"

"Then there's no reason not to keep them."

"Lord Strat—" She saw his frown grow darker and relented. "Garrick. While your gift is generous, I cannot accept."

"Why not?" The blunt question left her floundering for a response.

"It's far too extravagant."

"Somehow I don't think that's the real reason, Ruth." He gestured toward a nearby chair. "May I?"

When she hesitated, a small smile of wicked amusement curved his sensual mouth. It disconcerted her even more than she already was. Heat skimmed its way through her body, and she tried to wet her lips with the tip of her tongue. The moment she did so, she saw Garrick's eyes narrowed on her, and her mouth went dry. She suppressed her nervousness and sent him what she hoped was a serene nod.

"Of course." As she gave her blessing, he seated himself in the chair with a casual air that reflected all the grace and power of a sleek panther. Even his gaze reminded her of a predator assessing its prey.

"I'm under the distinct impression you don't like me, Ruth." The casual tone of his voice didn't deceive her. The man was about to pounce.

"I don't recall ever saying such a thing."

"No, but you clearly showed a distinct aversion for my company at Crawley Hall. Even after I explained my actions at the Somerset ball. You bristled every time I came near you. Except one." His last words were a low murmur as if he was talking to himself.

"I do *not* bristle," she snapped, her tone immediately contradicting the words. She clasped her hands to keep from balling them up into fists. "Any aversion for your company was because you were a threat."

"A threat?" The way he arched his eyebrows in amusement only agitated her more. This time with irritation.

"Yes, a threat. I wanted Crawley Hall in the worst way, and when you arrived, I saw it slipping through my fingers. You were the competition, and I couldn't afford to like you."

"So you *do* like me then?" He slammed the cage door shut.

"I . . ." Her skill at witty repartee deserted her when she needed it most. "I don't know you well enough to say one way or the other."

"Then tell me why you really don't want to accept my gift."

"It would offer up . . . the wrong impression."

"Wrong impression?"

"That I'm interested in pursuing a relationship with you."

"I see." He lifted up the cane he carried to examine its silver head. "And what type of liaison do you think I want from you, Ruth?"

"I . . . I was under the impression that you . . . that . . ." Irritated by her inability to remain calm and serene in his presence, she drew in a sharp breath of frustration.

"That I want you for my mistress?"

The question made her heart sink with fear and unexpected disappointment. Of course he wouldn't want a woman of her significant age as a mistress. Even worse was the small voice inside that mocked her for even considering the idea of a liaison with him, let alone wanting one. She shoved the thought into a dark crevice in her head to silence it, but it was still there taunting her. Unable to trust her voice to remain steady, she didn't respond. His dark eyes studied her for a moment, his expression revealing little.

"I wonder if you would even *allow* me to be your patron, Ruth."

"Of course not."

Her quick response brought him to his feet in one powerful movement, and she instinctively took a step back and averted her gaze the moment he stepped forward to tower over her. Another smile tipped the corners of his mouth as his forefinger trailed its way lazily along her jawline until he forced her chin up so she had little choice but to look at him.

The banked fire in his blue-eyed gaze alarmed her. It displayed his ease of self-control—a discipline she didn't possess at the moment. Worse, his look created a stark hunger inside her, one she wasn't accustomed to feeling. Lust was a requirement of any intimate relationship she entered into, but this man was different. The intensity of the emotion he aroused in her was far too dangerous. She drew in a sharp breath as his thumb brushed across her lower lip.

"I wonder why you're so resistant to the idea, Ruth." He leaned into her, his breath warming her lips as his gaze locked with hers.

"I simply have no wish to enter into another liaison so soon after Marston," she snapped, irritated that she couldn't control her attraction to the man.

"What if it were your friendship I wanted?"

The quiet question was so unexpected she simply stared at him in bewilderment. She'd never had a man ask for her friendship. Although there was the occasional past lover she'd remained good friends with, such as Westleah, there were few men she could call her friend. Even her circle of women friends was limited to a small number.

When she didn't respond immediately, she saw a flash of indecision cross his features and it surprised her. The idea that he was uncertain about anything was at odds with the impression she had of him. Lord Stratfield was not the type of man to lack confidence in anything he did.

He stepped back from her, and she immediately regretted the loss of his heat and the way it had warmed her body. As her eyes met his, she saw a glint of something she recognized in herself. A need to keep a distance between him and whatever might be a threat. But why would he think her a threat? He'd been the one to seek *her* out.

"Why?" She shook her head slightly as he watched her with a quizzical expression. "Why do you want to be my friend?"

"Because I like you."

"You don't even know me."

"I know that you've an immense amount of courage. You displayed it when you entered the Somerset ballroom the night we met. Marston had just broken with you and yet you found the wherewithal to enter that room with your head high. You also have a good sense of humor."

"And exactly how do you know that?"

"For Queen and country?"

There was mischief in his voice, and his wicked smile made amusement tug at her own mouth as she remembered the mirror in the master bedroom at Crawley Hall. Her good humor subsided slightly as she wondered what had made him not bid on the property. She wanted to ask him, but was afraid of what his answer would be. She wanted to believe it was because the property didn't suit him. Otherwise, why ask for nothing more from her than friendship?

The sudden sliver of disappointment she experienced that he'd not asked for something more alarmed her. It was a preposterous idea to even imagine becoming his mistress. It was the last thing she wanted. *Liar.* Her inner voice was quick to denounce her, but she ignored it. She glanced across the room to where the jeweler's box sat on her desk.

What would it be like to be friends with a man who expected nothing but friendship in return? Was it even possible? She turned and quickly crossed the floor to the secretary. The moment her fingers wrapped around the jeweler's box, she wondered if she was in her right mind.

"My friendship isn't for sale," she said as she looked down at the small package.

"I see."

His words were like ice cracking in the room, and she looked up to see that his features resembled the unemotional façade of a statue. Her heart thudded wildly in her chest as she drank in a deep breath.

"But as a friend, I would never refuse such a lovely apology as this. Thank you."

Silence filled the room as she stood there in front of him with the jeweler's box in her hands. He didn't say anything. Instead, he found himself debating what her words really meant. Had she just accepted his friendship or had she just agreed to be his mistress? The mere fact that he was even questioning himself over the matter irritated him.

It was true she was far more skilled than him in the intricacies that existed between a man and his mistress, but he didn't like feeling as if she was the one in control. Now what the hell was he supposed to do? His fingers curled tightly around the silver wolf that capped the top of his cane. The sooner he was back in charge the better. He cleared his throat and offered her a slight bow.

"I'm delighted to know you intend to keep my . . . apology. If you like, I can offend you more often so as to ensure that my apologies are equally pleasant." He deliberately kept his tone light and teasing.

"No. If I accept gifts from you it changes everything between us."

Her quick response put him back on a balanced footing. So she really didn't want to be his mistress. The disappointment nailed into him with surprising force. What the devil was wrong with him? This arrangement was far better than making her a mistress in name only. It would make things much easier.

The Set would automatically assume Ruth was engaged in a liaison with him whenever they appeared in public, and it would immediately put to rest any unpleasant rumors. It would also hold the mothers with marriageable daughters at bay. It was the perfect solution. Better still, he didn't have to explain why he wouldn't touch Ruth.

Touch her? Bloody hell. He'd been itching to do more than that since he first walked into the room. And given he'd never actually performed the deed, that would be a joke of magnificent proportions, especially since his first and only attempt had resulted in humiliation and disaster. His hand pressed painfully into the snout of the wolf cane head. No, this wasn't the direction he'd planned to follow at all where she was concerned.

Now he'd agreed to an arrangement that was far different than the one he'd envisioned. Were she his mistress, he could have kept his distance. The entire affair would have been a financial arrangement, nothing more. He ignored the mocking laughter echoing in the back of his head. A friendship on the other hand put them on a far more intimate footing.

He'd walked into a trap of his own making. And instinct told him it had the possibility of sending him straight to hell if he wasn't careful. It wasn't his habit to be at a loss for words, but at the moment, he wasn't certain what to say. Even Ruth seemed disconcerted. Her violet eyes had darkened significantly, and he saw a small tremor pass through her.

Perhaps he wasn't the only one uncertain as to how to proceed. She looked like a vulnerable young girl. How she could think herself old was unimaginable. He wanted to pull her into his arms and reassure her there was nothing to fear from him or anything else. The thought made him wince inwardly.

If anyone should be afraid, it was him. His throat tightened at the erotic images in his head. To break the awkwardness of the moment, he pulled his pocket watch from his waistcoat and flipped open the lid. It was past two, and he'd promised to meet Lily at Caring Hearts Home to review the orphanage's financials.

"You have an appointment?" Her voice was a soft breeze in his ears.

"Yes. I promised to meet my sister. But if I may, I'd like to escort you to the opera tonight."

"I would like that very much." There was a breathless quality to her voice that sent a rush of heat through him. He immediately crushed the sensation.

"I'll call for you at, shall we say, seven?"

He stepped forward and accepted her outstretched hand. The instant he wrapped her hand in his, an electric shock raced up his arm. He bowed slightly, his mouth lingering against her skin. The crisp scent of lemon brushed against his nose. It did things to his insides he'd not experienced since he'd thought himself in love with Bertha.

The sobering thought was the same as if someone had doused him in icy water. Desire was an animal reaction, nothing more. He'd managed to control his physical needs where other women were concerned. Ruth would be no different. The mocking laughter he'd heard earlier echoed in his head again.

He straightened upright, his eyes meeting hers. The sudden warmth in her gaze made his chest seize up with an emotion he annihilated before he could even define it. With a quick nod, he left the salon and charged out of her house as if the hounds of hell were snapping at his heels. He wasn't able to outrun the demons as he threw himself into his carriage.

"*Damnation.*" He slammed his cane against the seat opposite him in a vicious blow. "Friendship. You offered the woman *friendship*. You're insane, Stratfield, goddamn insane."

A groan rolled out of him as he closed his eyes. Why the devil did he care so much what anyone thought of him? He didn't need the approval of people like Wycombe or Marston, so why did he bother to keep up this ridiculous farce? An image of his uncle filled his head, and he flinched. The man had hated him and his siblings. They'd stood in Beresford's way to a small fortune and a profitable estate. A fortune and livelihood his uncle had almost bankrupted.

The past threatened to push its way up over the wall he'd built around it, and he breathed a sigh of relief as the carriage came to a stop in front of the orphanage. Here was a place where his troubles always seemed negligible. A great many of the children at Caring Hearts Home had endured much darker woes than he or his siblings. He didn't wait for his driver to open the door for him, and in seconds he'd crossed the threshold of the orphanage.

Despite the gray stone exterior, the inside of the home was warm and cheerful. There was no resemblance between it and the atmosphere he'd grown up in. Laughter echoed out of a room just down the main hallway, and he moved toward the sound.

He came to a stop in the doorway of what was the home's primary classroom. The sight of Lily blindfolded, her hands outstretched in an attempt to find one of the giggling children surrounding her, made him chuckle. His sister immediately placed her hands on her hips and tilted her head in his direction.

"Children, is Lord Stratfield here?" she asked with the blindfold still over her eyes.

"Yes, Miss Lily. 'Is lordship's—" The boy who'd piped up groaned loudly as Lily darted forward to wrap him in her arms. Squirming like an eel, he slipped free of Lily's embrace. "Aww, that's not fair, miss."

"It's perfectly fair, young master Alfred, and you know it," Lily said with a laugh as she tugged off her blindfold and handed it to the boy. "You didn't have to answer me until you were out of reach."

With a begrudging look of resignation, the boy accepted the blindfold and proceeded to become *It*. Wading her way through the children, Lily stopped at Garrick's side to kiss his cheek.

"I was beginning to think you'd forgotten our appointment."

"I'm not that late."

"No, but usually you're early when it has to do with Caring Hearts." Lily linked her arm with his and pulled him down the hallway to the office. "Is something troubling you?"

"No. Why would you ask?"

"Vincent mentioned you've spent every night at Chiddingstone House for the past week. It makes me wonder if you've perhaps parted ways with your mistress."

"Blast it, Lily. That's not the sort of thing you should be asking me." He frowned at his sister, who rolled her eyes at him.

"Why? I care about you. Vincent and Grace do as well. We want you to be happy, and if you've broken with your mistress, then perhaps you're finally considering marriage."

"*Marriage.*" He came to an abrupt halt and looked at his sister in stupefaction. "What in God's name would make you think such a thing?"

"Well, you can't woo a potential bride if you're still keeping a mistress on the side."

"I can assure you, I'm not considering marriage now or in the near future," he snapped. "And any further discussions of my personal affairs are off limits."

"So you *have* broken with your elusive Mary. I thought as much when I heard you were seen dancing with the Lady Ruth at the Somerset ball."

"Damn it, Lily. This isn't a suitable discussion topic. We both know what can happen when gossip runs its course. Particularly where love affairs are concerned." The moment the words were out of his mouth, he regretted it. A blank look quickly replaced Lily's teasing expression.

"You're right. Forgive me. After all, we both know I'm too much like our mother. Fickle to a fault." There was a bitter note in her voice, and he grimaced.

He hadn't meant to call forth sensitive memories where Lily was concerned. Their mother was a vain, selfish woman who had run off with her lover just before he turned fifteen. Her actions had driven his father to take his own life, leaving Garrick's uncle in control of the estate until Garrick had come of age. Lily didn't have it in her to do what their mother had done. For that matter, none of his siblings had that kind of callous nature.

"You're nothing like her," he said quietly as they entered the orphanage's small office.

"No? In case you've forgotten, I left my husband, too."

"The circumstances aren't the same."

"True." Lily shrugged with detachment. "But it doesn't make me any less my mother's daughter. If anything it confirms it."

"You didn't run off with a lover and leave your children behind," he bit out in a vicious tone. He despised his mother for what she'd done to him and his siblings. It was unconscionable.

"Perhaps, but an apple never falls far from the tree." Lily seated herself at the desk and opened up one of the ledgers. He frowned at her cynicism. It wasn't natural for a young woman to have such a jaundiced view of the world.

"One day, you'll find love again, Lily." He heard the conviction in his voice, but the slight shrug his sister made said he'd not convinced her.

"The day *you* change your mind about marriage will be the day you can lecture me on the matter. Until then, I'm content to work here at Caring Hearts or Crawley Hall."

At the mention of the Hall, he winced. Exactly how was he going to explain that he'd not even bid on the property, let alone secured it? He knew how much Lily preferred it over the others. She'd been the one to insist he bid on it in the first place after she'd visited the property without him. He walked toward the window and stood there staring out at the small garden at the back of the house. It wasn't large, but it served as a place for the children to play when the weather accommodated.

"I'm afraid I wasn't able to acquire Crawley Hall."

"*What?*" Lily jerked her head up to stare at him in amazement. "You said it was as good as ours. I've already spoken with a contractor about the improvements needed."

"It sold to another bidder." Hands clasped behind his back, he shrugged, deliberately keeping his expression neutral. He didn't elaborate that he knew the other bidder. The last thing he wanted was Lily asking him questions about Ruth. "There are other properties equally suitable for our needs. I've already arranged with Smythe to view two of them tomorrow. I'll have something finalized by next week."

"Are you telling me that someone actually outbid you?" His sister's incredulous tone made him frown as she completely ignored his reassurance that he would find a replacement for the Hall in a few days.

"I always have a price I'm not willing to exceed."

It was only a slight deviation from the truth. He set limits in everything he did. But in this case, he'd not even bothered to bid on Crawley Hall. A fact that said his interest in Ruth was far more reaching than it should be. He'd practically given the estate to her. No, he'd tried that and she'd refused. He hadn't realized it until now, but that day in the hothouse, he would have willingly bought the Hall and presented it to Ruth as a gift.

He'd never been that extravagant with any woman, not even when he'd settled a sizeable dowry on Mary as a wedding gift. The knowledge made him resolve to strengthen his self-control when it came to Ruth. The mocking laughter resounding in his head made him wince. Even his subconscious found it easy to scoff at him.

"*Blast.*" Lily's disappointment pulled him out of his thoughts. At least she didn't probe further. He inhaled a deep breath then released it as his sister turned to a spot in the ledger. "Well, if we have to put off moving the children another few months, I suppose we could consider Doctor Lawrence's suggestion about bunk beds."

"Bunk beds?" This wasn't the first suggestion the good doctor had made, and it was a good one. Even more impressive was Lily's willingness to consider the man's recommendation.

"Yes, he said we could increase the number of children we take in and that the boys would vie for a top bunk. We could free up at least two rooms for the girls, while adding more beds for the boys."

"The cost?"

"It's a rather small amount, but unless we receive a sizeable donation in the future, it's not the cost of the beds that concerns me. The more children we take in, the larger our food bill. At this rate, we might be forced into drawing from the foundation's savings before the end of the year."

"I don't think that will be a problem. The dairy in Grantham is beginning to show a profit, and the cotton mill in Northwick will be operational at the end of the month. The profits from both properties are designated strictly for the foundation."

"I'm worried we might also have to reduce the apprenticeship age down to twelve to make room for more children. Mrs. McGrath took in two more babies this week that we really don't have room for, but how could she say no? How could I?"

"If it comes to that, then we'll hire a teacher for each of the properties. The children will continue their schooling as they learn their trade. We'll care for the children as we always have."

"I couldn't bear it if the younger children were sent away from the home too soon."

Lily's worried expression prompted him to cross the room and place his hand on her shoulder. All of his siblings took an interest in Caring Hearts Home, but Lily was the one who'd invested her entire being into the orphanage. She'd been almost thirteen when their mother had abandoned them, and she'd taken it hard.

Worse, she'd been born a beauty and suffered for it. Their uncle had made her marriage to the Earl of Lynmouth doomed from the start. Beresford had more to pay for than the humiliation Garrick had suffered at his hands. The pain and trauma he and his siblings had endured had driven him to open the orphanage. Not only had he wanted to protect other children from men like his uncle, he'd wanted them to have a chance at a better life by learning a trade.

Over the past eight years, the orphanage had ensured that every child it took in had a basic education and didn't start working until the age of thirteen. An age that was higher than the current child labor laws allowed. The children were taught a trade and paid from the proceeds of the businesses where they worked.

"You worry too much, Lily. The children will be fine." He squeezed his sister's shoulder. "Now show me the financials you've prepared. I'm sure the picture isn't quite the doom and gloom you're convinced it is."

As he bent over her shoulder, he reviewed the meticulously kept ledger, pointing out where concessions could be made to address needs elsewhere. After more than an hour, Lily closed the book and smiled up at him.

"All right. I concede things aren't as bad as I made them out to be."

"You're a worrywart," he teased as he bent and kissed her brow. "But the best kind. You worry about others."

She squeezed his hand in sisterly affection as she got to her feet and looked at the small watch pinned to her dress. "Good heavens. I didn't realize it was so late. I've a dozen things to do before I leave here today. Shall I tell Cook that you'll be with us for supper? The Hamiltons are joining us."

"No. I've other plans this evening."

"The Lady Ruth?" The sly question caught him off guard as he met his sister's curious gaze.

"And if I said yes, would that matter?" he asked in a neutral tone.

"She's hardly marriage material, and isn't she a bit old for you?" There was just a hint of scorn in Lily's voice, and he sent her a harsh look.

"That's the sort of comment I would expect from others of a less generous nature, Lily. You don't even know the Lady Ruth."

"I know that she seems interested in making you her latest conquest." Cheeks flushed from his disapproval, his sister tipped her head upward in a stubborn pose. He looked at her in disbelief before laughing out loud. When Lily's mouth fell open in surprise, he laughed harder.

"Up until this morning, the lady in question found my company less than amenable. I can assure you that she's not set her cap for me by any means."

"We'll see," his sister muttered. "You're a good catch, and there are dozens of women who would be happy to have you pay them attention."

"I am quite content with my life as it is." He sent Lily a warning look. "And I like the Lady Ruth."

"How *much* do you like her?" Lily eyed him pensively. It was a question he wasn't sure he wanted to answer. Not because he didn't want to talk about Ruth, but because he didn't want to think about how easily he'd become enamored with the woman. He averted his gaze.

"I like her enough," he replied. "Now I have other business to attend to, and I believe you do as well."

He quickly moved toward the office door in his desire to escape his sister's inquisition. Behind him, Lily released an unladylike snort.

"You like her a lot more than you want to admit, and if she knows what's good for her, she'd better be kind to you."

"As I said before, you're a worrywart," he said as he tugged the door open and left her standing alone in the office. He frowned as he strode down the hallway to the orphanage's front door. Maybe Lily had good reason to worry about him. Ruth was beginning to present some unexpected problems for him, and for the life of him, he didn't seem capable of staying away from her.

The stairs leading to the exit of the Royal Opera House were crowded as Garrick guided Ruth downward from the balcony above the Grand Tier. He'd always enjoyed the opera, but tonight was the first time he'd found himself watching the woman he was with more than he had the stage. Seeing her enjoyment had given him more pleasure than he cared to admit. Then there had been the occasional glance she spared him at different points during the performance. Over the course of the evening, it had created an unexpected intimacy between them as she silently signaled her appreciation of the music.

They reached the wide landing of the Grand Tier to join the rest of the Marlborough Set making their way out of the theater. A flurry of activity in front of them signaled the departure of the Prince and Princess of Wales from the royal box. The crush of people forced Ruth into his side, and he unconsciously wrapped his arm around her waist in an effort to protect her.

As the crowd parted for the royal couple and their entourage, he felt Ruth go rigid against him. Puzzled, he turned his head to see a look of distress on her features. His gaze followed hers, and he saw an elderly gentleman with the royals staring back at her. Disgust darkened the man's features before he quickly dismissed her without another glance.

Garrick turned back to Ruth to see a smooth mask of composure fall over her face, but her violet eyes were dark with a pain he immediately wanted to ease. When the crowd around them began to surge forward again, she didn't move until he gently pushed her toward the stairs leading to the lobby.

"Are you all right?" he whispered in her ear as they followed the royals and their entourage.

"What?" She turned her head, and immediately closed herself off to him as she met his gaze. With a shake of her head, she looked away. "No. Not really, I've the beginnings of a headache."

"Then the sooner we're out of this noise, the better."

He knew damn well it wasn't a headache that had her out of sorts. Whoever the gentleman was who'd dismissed Ruth so coldly, he had upset her deeply. An old lover perhaps? His icy behavior had struck Ruth to the core, and Garrick didn't like that someone had hurt her. He ignored the warning that echoed in his head at this possessive thought.

With his hand at Ruth's elbow, they made their way through the crowd toward the first flight of steps. Behind him, a feminine voice commented about the scandal of older women and younger men. If he hadn't been so close to Ruth, he wouldn't have noticed the small stumble she made. A quick glance in her direction showed she'd heard the observation.

She'd been insulted twice in the span of minutes, and despite her obvious effort to ignore the slights, they were taking their toll on her composure. The need to protect her swelled inside him, and he leaned into her.

"Should I be worried?" he murmured. At the startled expression on her face, he arched his eyebrow at her in mock irritation. "My vanity would be deeply insulted if I discovered I was vying with a younger man for your attentions."

For a moment, she simply stared at him in amazement before she laughed. It was a vibrant sound that said he'd managed to ease the pain others had caused her. Amusement sparkled in her eyes, and her mouth curled upward in sweet temptation.

"You sound like a jealous suitor rather than a friend," she said with a smile. It irritated him that she could discount him so easily.

"Perhaps I'd prefer something more than just friendship."

It was a ridiculous thing to say, especially when he knew nothing of the kind would ever happen between them, no matter how much he might desire her. And he did desire her. It wasn't a fact he enjoyed admitting. But it didn't keep the tension between them from accelerating until a primitive rhythm pounded its way through his veins.

As her mouth formed a small *oh* of surprise, he suddenly wished they were alone so he could kiss her. The dangerous thought didn't stop him from noting the telltale sign of her excitement in the fluttering pulse on the side of her neck. She wasn't immune to him. His gaze moved back to her mouth, and he watched in fascination as the tip of her tongue darted out to wet her lips. The sudden stirring of his cock inside his trousers immediately set him on edge.

He recognized the treacherous ledge he was standing on, but it didn't stop him from imagining Ruth in his bed. Tension ricocheted through him as he realized how easily she was drawing him to her without even trying. God help him if she ever decided to actually try and seduce him. His jaw tightening with self-control, he forced a smile to his lips and continued to guide Ruth down to the lobby where he recovered her wrap for her.

Outside, the night air was unseasonably warm for the beginning of April. As they reached the sidewalk, he looked down the row of carriages in search of his driver. When he failed to see Jasper, he frowned. He would have to leave Ruth in front of the opera house to search for his carriage.

"It appears that my driver had difficulty securing a spot close to the theater. Wait here and I'll be back in a few moments."

"Should I come with you?"

"No," he said firmly. "You'll be safer here."

"Are you saying I won't be safe with you?" The mischievous smile on her face sent a jolt of electricity through him. The ambiguity of her statement made him search her face intently for a long moment. She blushed in the soft yellow glow of the gaslight and quickly clarified her comment. "As I understand it, you're an excellent pugilist."

"And I think you were implying that you wouldn't be safe with me for an entirely different reason."

"Then you're mistaken." There was the slightest note of panic in her voice that convinced him otherwise. Arching his eyebrow, he saw her blush deepen, but he refrained from arguing with her.

"I'll return in a moment."

His stride quick, he moved along the long line of carriages looking for Jasper and his Berline carriage. He'd passed more than ten vehicles before he saw his driver standing on the sidewalk straining his neck in an attempt to see over the crowd. The moment he caught Jasper's eye, he waved to the man then turned back to collect Ruth.

The return trip to the Opera House steps was quick, and as he approached the theater's entrance, he saw Wycombe talking to Ruth. He couldn't be sure, but from the rigid line of Ruth's back, he knew it was a strong bet that she wanted nothing to do with the bastard. The moment Wycombe saw him approaching, a nasty smile curled the man's lips. As he reached Ruth's side, he sent his nemesis an icy glare and gently gripped her elbow.

"I'm surprised to see you here, Wycombe. I thought your entertainment preferences ran to less sophisticated tastes, such as—brawling." His comment made the other man narrow his eyes at him.

"Hardly, my dear *boy*. I find the opera quite stimulating when in the company of a woman. Particularly one as lovely as the Lady Ruth, although what possessed her to accept your escort is a mystery to me." Wycombe nodded toward Ruth with a charming smile.

If it were any other man, he would have taken the earl's comments as good-natured rivalry. But this was Wycombe, and the man was being deliberately insulting. Few people could anger him to the point of losing control, but this man could. There was no love lost between them, and they both knew it, along with everyone else in the Set. The earl's attempt to charm Ruth simply deepened his antipathy for the man. Suddenly, he wanted to give Wycombe another pounding, just as he had in school years ago. Tension rolled through his limbs as he eyed the man coldly.

"Why don't you run along and find sport elsewhere, Wycombe."

"Perhaps we should allow the lady to choose whether she prefers my company or yours, Stratfield." The earl looked at Ruth with a confident expression. "My dear Lady Ruth. Might I have the pleasure of calling on you tomorrow?"

"I . . . I'm afraid I have—"

"She's already agreed to accompany me on a drive out of the city tomorrow, Wycombe."

"Then the day after perhaps?"

The earl persisted as he took Ruth's hand in his and sent her a confident look. Wycombe's arrogance sent a blast of fury through him. The bastard simply wanted Ruth because she was with him. The moment Wycombe secured her attention he'd discard her without a second thought.

"The lady will be occupied for quite some time to come, Wycombe," he said between clenched teeth.

"You seem quite certain of her, Stratfield."

"Ruth is an intelligent woman. Even if her time wasn't going to be occupied, I am confident she'd have the good sense God gave her not to accept the attentions of a *buffoon*."

Garrick immediately regretted losing his temper. Despite the fact that he'd kept his voice low, he was suddenly aware of the curious eyes watching them. *Bloody hell, the Set will be rife with gossip by morning.* Outrage darkened Wycombe's face. Either the earl didn't realize they were being watched or he didn't care.

"If the woman were intelligent, she'd know she was being used by you to make everyone think you a womanizer, when we both know you're something else entirely," Wycombe sneered with contempt.

He barely heard Ruth's gasp of shock as a lethal fury blazed through him at Wycombe's insult and its veiled implication. It didn't matter that the bastard hadn't outright denounced him as a sodomite. It was enough to seed doubt, and the man had said it within hearing distance of at least a dozen people. The bastard had also insulted Ruth. He took a quick step toward the earl, who went rigid with surprise and more than a hint of fear.

"Apologize, Wycombe, or God help me, I'll make you regret your words in the worst way possible," he said in a deadly tone that made the man blanch. Despite his evident fear, the man hesitated and Garrick released a low growl of fury. "*Now.*"

The earl turned to Ruth and gave her a slight bow. "My apologies, my lady. I allowed my temper to get out of hand and insulted you unintentionally."

Then with a defiant look in Garrick's direction, the earl whirled around and stalked away without expressing any regret for the innuendo he'd openly made in public. Garrick watched him retreat with an icy rage he'd not experienced since the day he'd found Tremaine threatening Mary. He wanted to kill Wycombe. The bastard hadn't apologized for implying he was a sodomite, and the speculation and curiosity on the faces of the small crowd that had observed the altercation angered him even more. His fingers tightened on Ruth's elbow as he caught the eye of an acquaintance from the Marlborough Club. The man gave him a nod of greeting, but the obvious support did little to ease his fury.

"Come," he said in a curt voice.

Ruth didn't argue and kept pace with him as his angry strides ate up the distance between them and the small, intimate carriage. When they reached it, he helped her up into the enclosed vehicle then joined her. Seconds later, the Berline moved out into the heavy after-theatre traffic.

Wycombe's words swirled in his head in an insidious serpentine manner that only kept his rage flowing hot through his blood. As he stared out the window of the carriage, the earl's veiled accusation reverberated in his head. Following close on the heels of that memory was the man's statement that he was merely using Ruth for his own ends.

There was a measure of truth in those words, and it wasn't sitting well with Garrick's conscience. It wasn't his habit to use others like he was using Ruth. Even with Wycombe's malicious insinuation, he was well aware that his appearance with Ruth tonight would go a long way toward discrediting the earl's comments. The fact didn't bring him much satisfaction.

In truth, it only increased his anger. He was a bastard. At least if she were his mistress in name only she would be receiving a monthly stipend from him. It would ease his conscience. He jerked with surprise as Ruth leaned forward to gently touch his knee, a concerned frown on her face.

"He's an odious man. For him to insinuate something of that nature is appalling, let alone to do it in public." There was a soothing quality to her voice, but it didn't erase the angry tension holding his limbs hostage. The thought that she might believe Wycombe made him even more outraged.

"Do you believe him?" he growled.

"Of course not," she exclaimed as she pulled back from him in surprise.

"Why?" He bit out the question in a fierce tone. He narrowed his gaze at her and saw a blush rise to her cheeks as she looked away from him. "Tell me why you don't believe him."

The moment he leaned toward her, she jerked her head back to look at him. The color in her cheeks darkened even more in the shadows of the carriage as she met his gaze. He reached out to touch the pulse beating wildly on the side of her neck without looking away from her.

"Tell me."

"Because I know when a man desires me," she whispered. "And you want me."

Her reply was straightforward and without any hint of seduction. If anything, there was a note of trepidation in her voice. And yet her words burned their way through him. She was right. He did want her. He wanted her in the worst possible way. Alarms were going off inside him, but they were quickly silenced by an overwhelming need to touch her. To prove to her that he wasn't the man Wycombe alleged him to be. His hand cupped the nape of her neck, and he tugged her against him.

A small gasp escaped her, but she didn't resist. His mouth brushed over hers in a light caress as he savored the first taste of her. The faintest hint of citrus lingered on her lips from the lemonade she'd had at the opera. It made the sweetness of her mouth slightly tart and even more tempting than he'd expected. He deepened the kiss, enticing her to part her lips beneath his. Seconds later, his tongue slipped its way into the heat of her mouth.

She responded to his caress with practiced skill, but there was an eagerness about her kiss that excited him. This wasn't just the kiss of a courtesan. This was the delicious taste of desire. She wanted him. It was in every sweet swirl of her tongue. His tongue mated with hers in a blind, feverish need that left him thirsty for more. Suddenly the kiss changed, and she was the one in control. Her mouth demanded and teased his with a skill that was beyond his experience.

With each honeyed stroke of her tongue, she stoked a raging river of fire in his blood that tugged and pulled at him until his cock was thick and hard inside his trousers. A deep groan rumbled out of his chest as his entire body demanded satisfaction. Christ Jesus, he'd never been so close to falling over the edge like this before. A gentle hand touched his thigh then softly brushed across his rigid staff with an expertise that sent him reeling.

What the hell was he doing? He grabbed her hand and roughly shoved it away as he threw himself backward into the leather squabs of the seat. He drank in several gulps of air in an attempt to control the heat still pounding through his limbs. The startled expression on her face made him grimace, but there was another emotion on her face that twisted his gut with regret.

He quickly looked away from her, unable to stomach the humiliation he was certain he'd caused her. Marston's breaking with her had affected her a great deal more than she ever showed in public, but he'd seen the mortification in those beautiful violet eyes the night they first met. Now he'd rejected her. It *had* to have an effect on her.

How was he supposed to explain why? What was he supposed to tell her that would make her understand that *he* was the problem not her? He closed his eyes against the memory of her kiss. Sweet Jesus, he'd kissed women in his past. Not a great many, but enough to perfect his ability to control his desire while convincing the women he'd kissed that he was a skilled lover.

In the past, he'd always found the right excuse to avoid the ultimate intimacy of the bedroom. More importantly, he'd deliberately chosen women whose vanity was such that they would never admit their failure to warm his bed. But Ruth's kiss had been beyond anything he'd ever experienced in his life.

And the way his body ached. It was crying out for something he'd never had before, and he wanted it badly. The problem was he couldn't have her. The sudden realization that his hands were trembling made him quickly fold his arms against his chest.

If he gave in to this raw, base desire, he'd only end up either earning her pity or her amusement the moment he stood naked in front of her. Her pity would be difficult to bear, but her laughter would be excruciating. Never again would he allow himself to experience the vicious humiliation Bertha and his uncle had heaped on him.

Fuck.

He cleared his throat and continued to stare out the window, uncertain of what to say. The silence in the carriage was a heavy weight bearing down on him as he struggled to find words that would protect his secret and reassure her that she was desirable. And the look he'd seen on her face told him she was questioning her worth as a woman.

The urge to pull her back into his arms and reassure her that she was the most desirable woman he'd ever met plowed through him. The thought made him break out in a cold sweat. A mistake like that would cost him dearly. He ruthlessly crushed the desire still bubbling close to the surface, desperately fighting to compose himself enough to look at her.

"My apologies," he croaked. The strangled sound passing his lips said he was far from being in control of his senses.

"It's unnecessary." The cool note in her voice made him jerk his head toward her. She was staring out the window with a serene expression on her face, but the tension in her was almost a tactile sensation.

"It is. I lost my head." The moment he said the words, he knew exactly how to heal the breach between them. "You made it clear you weren't interested in a liaison, and I betrayed your trust by allowing myself to lose control. I'm sorry."

"As I recall, I didn't protest," she said with a throb of emotion in her quiet voice. "Your pride was injured, and it was natural for you to feel compelled to demonstrate you weren't anything like Wycombe suggested."

"*No.*" He glared at her, barely holding himself in place to keep from pulling her toward him to show her just how wrong she was. "I kissed you because I wanted to. You're the most desirable woman I've ever met. If you could see yourself as I see you, you'd understand why my body is torturing me right now."

He suppressed the groan of dismay rising up in his throat. He'd gone stark raving mad to admit such a thing to her. What if she were to change her mind where he was concerned? What would he do if she decided to seduce him? He'd be damned for sure. The uncertainty in her eyes reflected her struggle to determine whether or not he was telling the truth. She turned her head away from him.

"Wycombe is a bully, and while it was unnecessary, I appreciate your coming to my defense," Ruth said quietly.

It was a silent acceptance of his apology, yet left their relationship unchanged. A part of him cried out a vehement protest, while the rest of him breathed a sigh of relief. He ran his damp palms along the top of his trousers in an attempt to make his body relax. He grimaced as he accepted that none of what had just transpired between them would have happened if he'd not allowed Wycombe to provoke him.

"It wouldn't have been necessary if I'd simply walked away instead of confronting him. He thrives on conflict."

"A conflict which he would have escalated even if you had walked away. You might dislike the man, but he detests you. It was obvious he wanted to do what he could to humiliate you." The unspoken question in her voice brought back the unpleasant memories of what life had been like after his father had killed himself.

"Wycombe and I have been enemies for a long time."

"A woman?"

The curiosity in her question made him wince at the irony of it. Garrick could see where the man had formed an opinion about his sexual preferences. The earl's incessant bullying at school had started because the headmaster had taken an interest in Garrick. Wycombe had been on bad terms with the academician and became outraged that a mere baron was favored over him. It made sense that the earl had formed his opinion of Garrick a long time ago. He shook his head.

"No. Wycombe thought I was receiving preferential treatment from the headmaster. It made the only refuge I had rather unpleasant."

"Refuge?"

The quiet invitation in her voice said her question was simply an offer to listen. He hesitated. How much did he really want to share? He looked away from her sympathetic gaze to stare out at the dark street.

"My mother left my father for another man when I was fifteen years old. Shortly afterwards, I found my father dead in his study. He'd taken his own life."

"Dear God," Ruth gasped with horror.

Garrick clenched his jaw as he recalled those first moments when he'd found his father's body. The panic when he'd tried to wake his father then the fear when he'd seen the blood. But it was the anger he remembered most. He'd been furious with his father for taking his life. He had left Garrick and his siblings in the hands of a man who would have drowned the lot of them if he'd thought he could get away with it.

"Did your mother come back when she learned of your father's death?"

"No," he said in a clipped tone. "She left my siblings and me in the care of my father's brother."

"Then you had someone who cared for you."

"*Cared* for us?" Disgust lanced through him as he recalled those first few days when his uncle had arrived at the hall. "The bastard hated us. He took great satisfaction in pointing out to all of us that neither of our parents had wanted us or they wouldn't have left us the way they did."

"Surely not," Ruth said quietly. "What reason would he have to despise you?"

"We stood in his way. The estate my father left was quite sizeable, and my uncle was deep in debt until he took over the management of the family's holdings. By the time I came of age, the man had gone through a sizeable portion of the estate."

"It must have been very difficult for you to watch him go through your inheritance."

"Not nearly as bad as it was to watch him look at my sister the way he did," he rasped softly.

"Dear lord, he didn't—"

"No. He never got the chance after I caught him attempting to enter her bedroom one night."

He didn't elaborate on how close he'd come to killing his uncle the night he'd caught the man about to enter Lily's bedroom. It was the first time his uncle had shown any other emotion for him except hate. That night the man had been afraid.

"And your sister? Did she know about your uncle's . . . fascination with her?" There was a note of disgust in Ruth's voice that said she found his uncle's behavior just as abhorrent as he did.

"Yes," he ground out with restrained fury as he looked out the carriage window. "I didn't know it at the time, but the bastard had caught her alone several times, but she'd always managed to elude him. I'm not sure she would have escaped him that night if I'd not stopped him."

"Providence has a way of saving those we love." At her quiet observation, he allowed himself a small smile of bitter satisfaction.

"When I came of age a few months later, I had the servants drag the bastard out of bed shortly after midnight and throw him from the house."

"I would have done the same thing."

Ruth's quiet statement made him look directly at her, and the empathy in her expression made him realize he'd not shared this much of his past with anyone except his siblings. And even they didn't know everything. He winced at the memory of standing naked in front of Bertha just as his uncle burst into the room. The echo of their laughter was a sound he'd never forgotten, and the humiliation of that moment still stung like a razor cutting into his skin.

"I find it hard to believe you capable of such an act," he said as he met her compassionate gaze.

"I can think of several instances where I would have been happy to have done something similar to those who've hurt my loved ones." She looked away from him to stare out the window. "What happened to your uncle?"

"He receives an annual stipend to stay away from my family." Garrick's mouth tightened with anger.

The annual income had been attractive enough to entice Beresford to comply, but he'd included the threat of complete financial ruin if the man refused. Garrick had made it clear that there would be no contact with him or his siblings, and that any family secrets divulged would bring a fiery hell storm down on the man's head.

"A generous gesture on your part. It shows you are the better man."

"It was a necessary evil," he ground out between clenched teeth. More like self-preservation. For the first year, he'd lived with the fear that the bastard would still find a way to reveal his shameful deformity. "Fortunately, my uncle's need for money and a position on the fringes of Society has helped ensure he doesn't contact my family."

Over the years, it had become clear that Beresford found his lifestyle far more attractive than any desire to bring humiliation down on Garrick's head. While the fear never went away, each passing year made him less uneasy that his uncle would betray his secret. A deception he'd perfected with the reputation he'd so painstakingly crafted for himself. The entire house of cards would tumble if just one woman confessed she'd never actually been in Garrick's bed.

It was why he'd taken Mary as a mistress in name only. The thought made him wince in self-disgust. Deep inside he'd known Mary's interests weren't the only thing that had driven him to propose their agreement. It had sustained the image he'd wanted to project for more than two years, but now Mary was in America with her new husband, along with Davy. His heart clenched at the thought of his godson. He missed the boy.

"It sounds as though he doesn't move in the same social circle as your family. That must surely make it easier for you." Her observation made him grunt in agreement.

"While there are the occasional encounters at the larger venues, it's something my family and I have learned to adapt to," he said tightly.

He hated those rare moments when he came face-to-face with Beresford in public. Despite the fact that his uncle had abided by their agreement, he was always on edge whenever the man was near. The sight of him always managed to bring back that humiliating night.

It drove his fear that the bastard would blurt out his secret, telling everyone that he was only half a man. He could only hope Beresford, like the rest of the Set, had been deceived into thinking Garrick's reputation with the ladies was more than an elaborate ruse.

He caught the compassionate look in Ruth's eyes and glanced away from her. She was far too easy to talk to, and he'd told her far too much about himself. The thought did little to brighten his mood. Perhaps the easiest thing to do would be to keep their conversation on a less personal footing. Hopefully it would keep him from touching her again. Eager to change the subject, he forced a smile to his lips.

"Did you enjoy the opera tonight?"

"The music was wonderful," she said with a smile. "Mozart is always a delight for the ears even if the story depicted women in a less than flattering light."

"An interesting observation." The past drifted away as he frowned at her statement. "My impression was that *Così fan tutte* was about the nature of love, fidelity, and betrayal."

"It is, but at the expense of all women."

"So you disagree that women's hearts are fickle." He thought of his mother and the way she'd left her family so easily.

"I think a woman's heart is no less likely to be fickle than a man's." Moonlight streaming through the carriage window illuminated the lovely curve of Ruth's shoulder. He crushed the need threatening his consciousness as she shrugged slightly. "My objection is to Don Alfonso's use of deceit to prove the women were unfaithful."

"Betrayals are always about deceit."

"*But*, without Don Alfonso's guidance, there's no guarantee the two women would have betrayed their lovers, because the two men would not have wooed them in disguise."

"And yet the women *did* succumb to temptation."

"Yes, but only when their lovers proved equally deceitful. The men chose to let Don Alfonso manipulate them into betraying the trust of their lovers."

"Interesting," he said with a smile. He was beginning to enjoy their debate on the morals of the opera. "You're portraying the Don as the villain in the piece."

"Isn't he? Don Alfonso manipulated everyone until he achieved the result he wanted. He needed to prove his belief that *all* women are untrustworthy. But all he proved was that somewhere in his past a woman had betrayed him."

"But it still doesn't absolve the women of their own betrayal."

"Nor does it pardon the men for deceiving their sweethearts."

"Which doesn't change the fact that in the end, temptation won out."

He grinned as he met her look of exasperation. It was clear to him that Ruth didn't like losing. Her eyes narrowed as if she could read his mind. Suddenly, a mischievous look crossed her face and she smiled back at him. How in the hell could the woman think herself old when she looked the way she did right now? The effect she had on him was like a kick in the gut.

"The only reason temptation won out was because Don Alfonso resorted to trickery, and without that there wouldn't have been an opera." Her observation made him laugh out loud.

"Agreed."

"And I'm sure you'll agree that if a *woman* had written the same opera to point out that men are equally unfaithful, it would never have seen the stage."

"You're as cynical as Don Alfonso," he said with a chuckle.

"More a pragmatist I think, but you don't disagree that I'm right."

"No, I don't disagree." He laughed again at the complacent look on her lovely features. "The opera would never have been produced if a woman had written it."

"But you've evaded the original point of the conversation. Do you think a woman's heart is more easily swayed than a man's?"

"I lose, no matter what my answer. If I agree with you, I betray my fellow brethren, and yet if I disagree, you will be annoyed with me, something I have no wish to see happen."

"A diplomatic answer, which makes me think you believe a woman's heart is more fickle than a man's."

The look she sent him made him laugh again. She was annoyed with him for disagreeing, but her expression said she wouldn't hold the fact against him. She was a good sport, and he liked her all the more for it. He also liked the fact that she could make him laugh.

"But you're not completely sure, are you?" he said with a smile.

"I'm not sure *what* to think where you're concerned." She studied him for a long moment before her gaze narrowed to one of assessment, and he stiffened. "Why didn't you bid on Crawley Hall?"

He grimaced at the question. It was an unexpected shot out of the blue. He'd known the topic would arise eventually, just not quite this soon. He should have prepared a reason before this. He'd not known her long, but he'd already seen how independent she was. Somehow he didn't think she'd be pleased if he told her he'd not bid on the property simply because he'd not had the heart to take it from her.

While there had been other properties just as suitable, Crawley Hall had been the better bargain. If she were to discover that he'd passed over the Hall simply because of her, he was certain she wouldn't be happy with him. She'd see it as an attempt to gain her favor. Wasn't it? He clenched his teeth at the thought.

"Well?" Her clipped tone indicated her impatience and perhaps a note of dismay.

"The property didn't have enough land to suit my needs." A lie, but a necessary one if he wanted to ensure she didn't refuse to see him in the future. And despite the fact that it went against his better judgment he wanted to see her often.

"I see." She drew in a deep breath and released it. The sound was one of relief, but it was the note of disappointment he heard that startled him.

"You sound relieved."

"I am. I thought you might . . ."

"What? Refrain from bidding because I offered to buy you Crawley Hall?"

"Yes." She nodded and met his gaze steadily.

"Yet you accepted the gifts I sent earlier."

"That isn't the same thing. You sent the paperweight and brooch as means of an apology, and the only reason I didn't send them back to the jewelers is because you arrived and persuaded me not to."

Her fingers reached up to touch the diamond encrusted tulip she wore at the vee of her bodice. The movement caused her arm to brush across her breast, and she drew in a sharp, silent breath of awareness. Ever since Garrick's kiss, she'd been on fire.

Every part of her body ached with a need she'd not experienced in years. The desire assaulting her was stronger than anything she'd ever felt for a man. It made her long for him to kiss her one more time. He'd made her feel young and alive again. But the way he'd pushed her aside had been more devastating than she cared to admit, although his explanation had taken the sting out of his rejection.

His refusal to push his advantage had been an honorable one. She was the one who'd laid out the terms of their relationship, and he wouldn't step across the line she'd drawn between them. But she was certain he wanted to. She'd seen the way his hands had been trembling moments ago. If she'd not been aware of his attraction to her before, his reaction just now would have spoken volumes.

No man she'd ever been with had demonstrated the kind of steely self-control Garrick had displayed. She could only imagine the explosion of passion that would have occurred if he'd not obeyed the limits she'd set. What would he say once they reached her town house if she suggested he come inside to enjoy a brandy? Her heart slammed into her breast with a vicious thud. Now *she* was being ridiculous.

She was far too old to be seducing a man so much younger than her. *Only a few years.* She tried to ignore the tempting thought. Would it be so bad to allow herself the pleasure of his touch simply because he was younger than her? *No.* That wasn't what frightened her. Somehow she was certain Marston's breaking with her would seem trivial in comparison to the end of any relationship she had with Garrick. And it would eventually end whether he grew tired of her or sought to marry.

"Ruth, did you hear me?"

"I'm sorry. You were saying?" She met his gaze with a blank look. She'd been so deep in thought she'd not heard a word Garrick had said.

"I said, that since I was able to persuade you to keep my gift, I should have no trouble convincing you to take that drive with me that I mentioned to Wycombe."

"I'm sorry, but I already have an engagement."

"Supper then." His mouth tightened as if her refusal displeased him. She frowned. Supper invitations could mean so many things. It could be in the company of a few select friends or something much more intimate—dangerous. The way she was feeling at this point in time, she wasn't prepared to risk having an intimate meal with him.

"It will be a busy day for me tomorrow, so you'll forgive me if I decline your offer." At her answer, he jerked forward then immediately reclined back in his seat.

"Very well. Perhaps later this week."

"I'd like that."

She meant it. She did want to see him again. It might be a foolish thing to do, but he was a pleasant companion, someone she enjoyed talking with. There was great freedom in not having to cater to a man's needs for a change. In fact, he seemed more than eager to indulge her every desire. Her mouth went dry at the thought. Deep down inside she knew exactly what she wanted from him, and she knew better than to express that need.

The Berline rocked to a halt, and Garrick immediately exited the vehicle then turned to assist her out of the carriage. She hesitated to take his hand, but when her gaze met his, the challenge in his dark eyes made her slip her fingers in his palm. Seconds later, she was on the stoop of her town house. As the front door opened, she smiled at Garrick, who stood beside her on the expansive top step.

"Good night," he murmured as he raised her hand to his mouth.

The heat of his touch penetrated the silk of her evening glove and sent a flush of warmth across her skin until it sank into every one of her pores. She trembled slightly at the sensation, her heart pounding a frantic rhythm. His gaze narrowed at her, and she was certain he could tell how affected she was by his touch.

Desire flared in his eyes, but he didn't say a word. He simply turned away and returned to his carriage as she entered the house. As Simmons closed the front door behind her and took her wrap, Ruth closed her eyes for a brief moment. She had a problem on her hands in the form of the Baron Stratfield, and she wasn't exactly sure what to do about it.

Ruth used her forearm to rub the damp heat off her brow then returned her attention to the dishes in the orphanage's large porcelain sink. The warmth of the kitchen was pleasant when one wasn't exerting herself. She'd long ago removed her jacket and hung it on the coatrack in the mudroom.

The shirtwaist and skirt she wore now were serviceable and infinitely cooler than what she'd been wearing two days ago when she arrived at St. Agnes's to find the orphanage's cook, Mrs. Beardsley, looking pale and fragile. Ruth had immediately ordered the usually hale and hearty woman to bed and sent one of the older boys to fetch the doctor.

Sarah, the kitchen maid, had taken responsibility for preparing the meals, while Ruth did what she could to help, including washing dishes. Plunging her hands back into the sudsy water, Ruth scrubbed a plate, rinsed it in the adjoining sink, then set the dish onto a wooden rack to dry. Through the window over the sink, she looked out on the small garden where several students were receiving a botany lesson from Reverend Shelton, who volunteered one day a week at the orphanage.

It was a beautiful day. There was a hint of spring in the air and the cloudless sky reminded her of Crawley Hall and its wide-open spaces where the children would grow healthy and strong. The sky's vivid blue color reminded her of a different hue—the intense blue of Garrick's eyes.

She dropped her gaze back to the dish in her hand and resumed scrubbing. Despite her best effort to push the memory of Garrick out of her head, her skin grew hot as she remembered the way he'd kissed her in the carriage three nights ago. It wasn't the first time she'd thought about the way his mouth had caressed hers. In fact, she'd recalled that kiss many times.

The memory of his touch was most vivid in the early morning hours with her body crying out for him—aching for him with a strength that alarmed her. It was one of the reasons she'd stayed here at the orphanage for the past two nights. Simmons had sent word that Garrick had called twice the day after they went to the opera and three times yesterday.

It might have been cowardly, but seeing him meant testing her fragile control over the desire he'd ignited inside her. God help her if he tried to kiss her again. She wasn't sure she'd have the strength to resist. The scent of him still tantalized her senses. He'd smelled of cognac and a hint of sweet tobacco.

Even now she could still feel the strength of his hand on the back of her neck. The way it had gently, yet firmly, pulled her toward him. His kiss had been the touch of a man who was well skilled in pleasuring a woman, and yet there had been something different—unexpected—about the caress.

He'd explored her mouth with a slight touch of uncertainty. Almost as if he wasn't sure of himself. It had only made his kiss that much more arousing. She swallowed hard at the sudden rush of heat between her legs. His touch had made her feel like a girl again. It was a dangerous sensation when she knew her age was a barrier between them that was impenetrable.

Nevertheless, that fact didn't stop her body from begging for the satisfaction of his touch. She'd resorted to pleasuring herself, but had failed to gratify the craving her body demanded. It was a taste she was certain only Garrick could assuage, but allowing herself to even think about the possibilities was a terrible mistake.

If only she were younger. She pulled her hand out of the dishwater and stared at it. Although red and chafed from the harsh soap, the skin still looked firm and supple with only a few fine lines across the back of her hand. A quiet gasp jerked her out of her thoughts.

"Oh, my lady, it's not right, you washing dishes, you being a lady and all. Let me do it for you." Annie, one of the older girls who'd been at the home for more than a year, joined her at the sink.

"I don't think a little dishwater will hurt me, Annie. Mrs. Beardsley should be able to resume her duties by tomorrow, which means things will go back to normal."

"Well, it's just not befitting I'm saying, it ain't."

"Nonsense. As a girl, I washed my fair share of dirty dishes." She laughed as Annie eyed her with skepticism. "You need to go help Emmie with the little ones."

"I still think you should let me do the dishes, my lady." The stubborn expression on the girl's face made Ruth shake her head in gentle rebuke.

"We all have a job to do, Annie. Yours is to help Emmie. Go on now."

Her expression still one of reluctance, the child frowned and turned away to do as she was told. As the girl headed out of the kitchen, Ruth heard her mutter something under her breath. She stifled a laugh at Annie's obvious disgust. She looked back at the dirty dishes beside the sink and sighed.

When she'd told Annie that she'd washed dishes before, it had been the truth. Her childhood had not been the luxurious one the children all thought she'd enjoyed. Far from it. In fact, if not for the small annual stipend her mother had received from her maternal grandmother, things could have been much worse.

Despite the hardship that accompanied the lack of funds, there had always been love and laughter in the small two-room cottage they'd lived in. Her mother had done her best to see to it that Ruth had the benefit of an education by teaching her all she knew. When Ruth was little, she'd learned how to do needlepoint for the thread-bare chairs they used and for their bed linens.

Her mother had insisted she learn to speak French and Italian fluently, and often demanded they converse only in one language or another to hone her skill at speaking both. Then there had been the daily lessons. There had been no money for books, so her mother had borrowed them from the local rectory. Her mother had made learning fun, and she'd spent many a happy hour working hard to please her.

"Good God."

The deep baritone exclamation made her jump with surprise, and the piece of crockery in her hand splashed back into the dishwater. She turned her head and saw Carter Millstadt, a member of St. Agnes's Home's board of directors, standing just inside the kitchen doorway with an appalled expression on his face.

"Mr. Millstadt," she said in bewilderment. "This is a surprise. I've not forgotten an appointment, have I?"

"No, not at all, my dear lady. Where is Mrs. Beardsley? And why the devil are you washing dishes?" The note of deep dismay in his voice made her smile.

"I'm afraid she's been under the weather for the last three days. The doctor says she should be fit for duty tomorrow."

Ruth reached for a dishtowel as a woman followed the board member into the large kitchen. Quickly smoothing the front of her skirt, she smiled at the man as if his finding her washing dishes was an everyday occurrence. Her aplomb only seemed to distress him further.

"You should have sent word to me, my lady. I would have arranged for a member of my staff to assist you," Mr. Millstadt said with frustration.

A wealthy merchant, the man was one of the orphanage's strongest supporters, but she didn't want to be beholden to him any more than necessary. It might encourage the man, and she didn't wish to do that. Her gaze shifted to the woman with the chairman, and Ruth frowned in puzzlement. Why did she look so familiar? The lady coughed softly, and a red flush flooded Millstadt's features.

"Forgive me. Lady Ruth, may I introduce the Countess of Lynmouth." The director looked from one woman to the other. At the introduction, the young woman nodded her head in Ruth's direction. While the woman's smile was polite, she studied Ruth with an intense look that made her feel lacking in some way.

"How do you do, Lady Ruth. Mr. Millstadt has sung your praises ever since we first met. I hope you'll forgive the intrusion, but I convinced him to bring me here so we might talk."

"Mr. Millstadt is too kind," she murmured as she smiled and gestured toward the door. "Perhaps it would be best if we went to the office."

Ruth gestured toward the door and without waiting for a response, walked past the two guests and down the hall. As she headed toward the office, she rolled her sleeves down and buttoned them at her wrists. Perhaps seeing her more presentable would allay some of Mr. Millstadt's dismay at having seen her doing menial work.

The man had taken far too much interest in her of late, and the knowledge that he'd been singing her praises did little to comfort her. He was a nice man, but she had no desire to extend their acquaintance past his involvement with St. Agnes's. She sat behind the room's large desk and invited her guests to sit in the chairs facing her. She directed her gaze at the woman opposite her.

"Well now, Lady Lynmouth, what may I do for you?"

"I am . . . that is my brother and I . . . are the primary patrons of Caring Hearts Home. Perhaps you've heard of it?"

"Yes, of course. You're near the East End, correct?"

"In Bethnal Green actually," Lady Lynmouth said with a nod, then hesitated slightly, almost as if she didn't know how to continue. "Mr. Millstadt and I met at a charitable event where he generously donated to Caring Hearts."

Ruth glanced at the man, who was beaming with pleasure at the recognition. She looked back at the countess, who was studying her with something akin to distrust and hostility. Ruth frowned as her gaze locked with the other woman's. She wanted something, but either the woman didn't know how to ask or it was more a question of not wanting to ask it of Ruth.

"Mr. Millstadt has been most generous to St. Agnes's, too," she said quietly as she met Lady Lynmouth's eyes with a steady gaze.

"And it's because of his generosity that I asked him to bring me here. I am hoping that you and the board of directors for St. Agnes's will consider a joint venture with Caring Hearts."

"A partnership?" Ruth asked quietly.

"Precisely," Lady Lynmouth said with a bit more enthusiasm. "Once I explain myself, I hope you'll encourage your board to agree to my proposal."

"If St. Agnes's and its board of directors can assist you then we'll be happy to do so."

"Thank you, my lady." The countess folded her hands in her lap, and her wariness eased somewhat, although there was still critical assessment in her gaze. "All the children at Caring Hearts are given a general education and at the age of thirteen, they're apprenticed at one of several farms or manufacturing businesses throughout England."

"That's extraordinary. How did you convince the owners to take on your children as apprentices?" Ruth asked with amazement. Why in heaven's name hadn't she thought of something so simple?

"My brother owns numerous properties and arranges the apprenticeships with local businesses." Lady Lynmouth's response made Ruth frown. Was the woman's brother exploiting the orphanage's children? She would never be a party to such a scheme.

"That sounds like a . . . profitable venture."

"Good heavens, no."

The woman looked mortified and glanced at Millstadt, who quickly straightened in his chair. He stretched out his hand in the countess's direction in a comforting manner as he looked at Ruth.

"The properties are indeed profitable, but the monies are used to pay the children who work there," Millstadt said as he shifted positions in his chair as he warmed to his topic. It was clear the orphanage's operation had impressed him. "Once the child's apprenticeship is complete, they have the option to seek employment elsewhere or stay. Any extra monies not used to maintain the property or pay the workers are returned to the orphanage. A remarkable setup, actually."

The man was right. It was an impressive feat to care for children while creating an environment for them where they could become self-supporting. Something told her Millstadt would be making a proposal at the next meeting of the board of directors that a similar plan be put into place at St. Agnes's. It was a proposal she'd be more than happy to endorse, but this didn't explain why the countess had come to see her.

"I admit that I'm most impressed with the operations of your home, Lady Lynmouth, but what could I possibly offer you in a joint venture?"

"At the moment, Caring Hearts is bursting at the seams. Although my brother just purchased a new property this morning, the improvements to make it suitable for children will take several weeks. I was hoping to find a safe haven for some of my older children until we can place them in an apprenticeship or until the new property is ready for use."

"Although we're also crowded here, I'm sure we can find a way to take in a few more children. And I'm certain St. Agnes's board of directors would be more than happy to be of assistance," Ruth said, her mind already calculating how many more children the orphanage could handle.

"Thank you." The woman leaned forward, gratitude lighting her beautiful face. "In return I would be more than happy to arrange apprenticeships for the older children here at St. Agnes's."

"That would be most kind," Ruth said as she smiled at the woman across the desk from her. "As it so happens, I also just purchased a new piece of property—a small estate in West Sussex. I expect to finalize the sale tomorrow. Improvements are already underway, so Crawley Hall should be ready by the end of the month."

"Crawley Hall?" The countess's voice was a choked gasp, her expression one of astonishment.

"Lady Lynmouth, are you all right?" Millstadt asked with concern, and the woman gently waved aside her escort's attentive manner.

"*You* bought Crawley Hall?" Disbelief echoed in the woman's voice as she stared at Ruth.

"Yes. Do you know the property?" Ruth frowned as she studied the other woman's bemusement.

"Quite well. It was one of three we'd been considering," the woman said with a frown, as if working through a problem. "But, your offer was higher than the bid my brother Garrick made on the estate."

"Your brother?" Startled, she stared at the countess.

"Yes, I believe you know him, the Baron Stratfield. He's spoken of you to me, and I am under the impression that he holds you in the highest regard."

The woman's response sent Ruth's head spinning. Lady Lynmouth was Garrick's sister. It explained why the woman had looked so familiar to her. The two siblings looked very much alike.

"I'm flattered that your brother thinks me worthy of his admiration," Ruth said quietly as she studied Lady Lynmouth's unreadable expression. Something in the woman's voice said she wasn't happy that Garrick even knew her. It wasn't unexpected that Garrick's sister would disapprove of her, but for him to discuss her with his sister left her feeling exposed. Prompted by the sudden need to escape any further conversation until she'd gathered herself, Ruth stood up and circled the desk in a clear signal that the meeting was concluded. She offered her hand to the board member sitting across from her.

"Mr. Millstadt, I believe we should call a meeting of the board to secure their approval of her ladyship's request."

"Of course, my lady. I'll see to it as soon as I've seen the countess safely home." Millstadt got to his feet and kissed her hand then turned to the woman still seated in front of the desk. "Shall we, Lady Lynmouth?"

Garrick's sister frowned and shook her head. "Mr. Millstadt, would you mind giving me a moment alone with her ladyship?"

"Why . . . of course . . . certainly, my lady," the man said with surprise as he looked from Lady Lynmouth to Ruth and then back again.

With a slight bow to them both, he left the office, closing the door behind him. Ruth had a strong inkling as to what was to come. She'd had visits from mothers in the past, demanding that she stop seeing their sons. No doubt, Garrick's sister would do the same. She returned to her seat behind the desk, but didn't sit down. The furniture would provide a sufficient barrier to help distance herself from the woman. Not willing to wait for the attack that was certain to come, she held herself rigid and straight with her fingertips pressing into the mahogany desk.

"I'm sorry for your distress at hearing I am the new owner of Crawley Hall." She drew in a deep breath and released it. "I hope for the sake of the children you will see fit to continue with this joint venture between our two orphanages."

"I wouldn't think of refusing your generosity. I was merely surprised to hear that *you* were the one who'd outbid Garrick. It's the first time he's ever failed to buy a property he wanted."

Ruth's muscles grew taut. Property *he* wanted. The other night he'd told her the exact opposite. He'd said Crawley Hall didn't suit his needs, and yet his sister was saying something different. One of them was lying. Then there was the woman's surprise that Ruth had been the one who supposedly outbid Garrick.

The countess must assume she was poor as a church mouse. The assumption wasn't far from the truth. She'd had to sell all of her jewels and the house near Bath to pay for the Hall. Although she still had the town house, she would eventually have to rent it to subsidize her income from her other investments. She would have enough to live on, but she would always have to be careful with money.

She frowned as she questioned why Garrick would tell his sister he'd bid on Crawley Hall when he'd done nothing of the sort. Then there was the question of why he would tell her the property didn't suit him when his sister said otherwise. Lady Lynmouth eyed her intently, and Ruth tried to recall what the countess had just said. Something about her reason for buying the Hall. The woman was as inquisitive as her brother.

"It would seem that Lord Stratfield and I have been working at cross-purposes. I bought Crawley Hall so that I might send the more sickly children out into the country."

"Ah, I see." Lady Lynmouth narrowed her eyes at her. "So you don't intend to retreat to the country . . . permanently."

Ruth sucked in a sharp breath. The woman's words created a sinking sensation in the pit of her stomach, leaving her queasy. Why would Lady Lynmouth ask if she planned to retire to Crawley Hall? Something Ruth had revealed *only* to Garrick, when he'd pressured her for her reasons for purchasing the Hall.

What in heaven's name had made her tell him she planned to retire at Crawley Hall? She could have told him the real reason why she wanted the house, but most of the men in her life had always had an aversion to children. Men didn't like to talk about children, even their own. Why should she have thought him any different? Telling him anything at all had been against her better judgment, but he'd been so damned persistent. Now the bastard had told his sister that Ruth planned to retire to the country.

She stiffened with horror. Oh God, if the real reason he'd not placed a bid on the property was because he felt sorry for her . . . she swallowed the bile rising in her throat. Suddenly, she felt older than ever before. It was a deep, gnawing ache that twisted its way through her body until she could have sworn she'd aged twenty years in less than a few moments.

Not even when Marston had left her less than a month ago had she ever felt so desperate to be young again. Determined not to reveal how devastating Lady Lynmouth's observation had been, she straightened her shoulders as she looked at the woman.

"My plans are focused on St. Agnes's and the children."

"I admire your devotion to the children, but it is my brother I am really concerned about."

"I think your fears warrantless in that direction." The woman was assuming Ruth's influence over Garrick was one of great substance. It was anything but.

"Perhaps. Then again, you might underestimate your charms. My brother has only had one mistress, who he just parted with a short time ago. I'm certain he would find your . . . experience . . . a strong attraction."

Lady Lynmouth's statement sliced through Ruth with the precision of a finely sharpened blade. The word *experience* suddenly took on new meaning, and she could feel the wood giving way beneath her fingers as she fought to control her emotions. Insults were something a woman in her position dealt with fairly regularly, but Lady Lynmouth had chosen to highlight the fact that Ruth was a mature woman with a younger man. In other words, she was old.

"As I said a moment ago, your fears are misplaced." The terse note in her voice made Lady Lynmouth have the decency to appear contrite.

"Forgive me, my lady. I love my brother very much. Garrick looked after me, my sister, and my younger brother when we were growing up. His happiness is all that matters to us."

"An admirable sentiment, but your brother and I are little more than acquaintances."

Did acquaintances kiss in a carriage with the heat and intensity that Garrick had kissed her with the other night? The memory created a languid coil of heat in her belly. It did so with a speed that alarmed her, forcing her to realize that there might be more truth to Lady Lynmouth's fears than Ruth had thought.

"Acquaintances at the moment, but I saw the way Garrick looked when he talked about you. His heart is not lost yet, but if you continue to see him . . . I simply do not wish to see him hurt."

An abrupt blaze of anger lashed through her at the woman's words. While she could understand Lady Lynmouth's desire to protect her brother, to imply that Ruth was somehow responsible for Garrick's pursuit of her infuriated her.

"Lord Stratfield is more than capable of making his own decisions, and to imply that I am responsible for his continued association with me is not only insulting, but ludicrous," she bit out in a freezing tone. "I am *not* pursuing your brother, as you have suggested, Lady Lynmouth. In fact, I have done everything to dissuade him from furthering our acquaintance. To suggest that I have encouraged him tells me it's either my reputation or *maturity* that you find so threatening where your brother is concerned."

"I am only—"

"Yes. I know. You're only concerned for your brother's heart." The caustic tone of her voice made Lady Lynmouth frown with what almost looked like regret. Ruth didn't care as she sent the woman a cold stare of anger. "I think it's time you left, Lady Lynmouth, before I do something rash and penalize others for your rude, offensive behavior."

The woman appeared on the verge of speaking, and Ruth uttered a noise of outrage as she circled the desk to move toward the office door.

"Lady Ruth—"

"Spare me the obligatory apologies, please. We both know they're not sincere," Ruth said coldly as she jerked the office door open. "I think you can see yourself out, *Lady* Lynmouth."

The sarcastic emphasis on the woman's title made it clear that Ruth didn't find Lady Lynmouth's behavior noble in any way, and she allowed herself a small nugget of satisfaction at the woman's quiet gasp. Good, the barb had hit home. Maybe the woman would think twice before insulting someone else in the future. Her stride filled with anger, she charged out of the office and down the hall toward the kitchen.

She couldn't remember the last time she'd been so angry. Not since the day she'd seen one of the local pickpockets slapping little Jenny Chapman in the face had she been this furious. She'd not encouraged Garrick in any way since their initial meeting. *You accepted his friendship.* She ignored the voice in the back of her head.

The man had been so insistent, it had been impossible to refuse him. *Not impossible.* She released a small noise of frustration at the nagging voice that hammered away at her. *She* wasn't the one who'd asked for jewelry. *He'd* sent it without any encouragement from her. *You kept it.* She shoved the silent accusation aside.

The man had been attempting to apologize, and with a great deal more imagination than any other suitor she'd ever had. No. Garrick wasn't a suitor—he was a friend. Not even that. Friends didn't discuss her with others, not even family. She could just imagine what the man had said about her.

When Lady Lynmouth had asked whether she was going to retire to the country, it had made her ill. It could be a coincidence that the woman might think Crawley Hall was a place for Ruth to live out her remaining years, but it all seemed a bit too convenient. Worse, it meant she was an object of pity, and that was something she wouldn't tolerate.

She'd had no choice in the life she'd chosen. Her father had seen to that. When he'd abandoned her mother, he'd abandoned her, too. She'd done what she had to to survive. Now that she was teetering on the edge of retirement, she didn't want anyone's pity, least of all Baron Stratfield's. She rubbed her fingers across her forehead in an effort to stave off the headache threatening to overpower her. There were still dishes to do, and worrying herself silly over either Garrick or his sister's visit was pointless.

Hours later, she'd finished helping with putting the younger children to bed and was debating whether to stay another night at St. Agnes's. She had a sudden longing for a long soak in a hot tub of scented bath salts. Her fingers undid the knot at the back of her apron as she descended the back staircase of the orphanage into the kitchen.

Candles were the room's only light, as the sun had set more than an hour ago. She smiled as she saw Annie sitting by the fire warily eyeing Simmons, who was sitting in a chair by the back door. Dolores had decided it was time she came home, and her friend had sent reinforcements to ensure that outcome. The moment he saw her, the man quickly stood up, his derby hat in his hand.

"I've come to fetch you home, my lady."

"Yes, thank you, Simmons."

She removed her apron and dropped it into the laundry basket in the far corner of the room then accepted her cape from her butler.

"Annie, come lock the door behind us, and make sure Thomas locked the front door as well. He's a good boy, but can be forgetful."

"Yes, m'lady. I'll make sure he does. Do you want me to tell Mrs. Beardsley anything?"

"Just that I'll resume my normal visits next week, and if she has need of me to send me word."

"I'll make sure she knows, m'lady. I'm glad to see you going home to get a proper night's sleep."

Annie's dismay that Ruth had spent two nights in the orphanage was evident in her voice, but Ruth didn't respond. It was impossible to argue with Annie once she'd made up her mind about something. And the girl was convinced Ruth was doing things unfitting to her station in life. Instead she simply smiled and allowed Simmons to usher her out into the night.

As the carriage rattled through the still busy streets toward her town house on Carlisle Street, her thoughts drifted back to Lady Lynmouth's visit earlier that afternoon. She'd thought her anger had vanished, but it hadn't. The woman's audacity in lecturing her about how she was an older woman leading on an innocent young man infuriated her.

The idea was ridiculous, but the woman's scandalized tone had been a stinging reminder of the other night when Garrick had taken her to the opera. Everyone who'd seen them together had reacted the same way as Lady Lynmouth. Horrified to see her in public with a younger man. She should have known better when she agreed to his offer of friendship. Well, the sooner he was out of her life, the better. The man was proving to be nothing but trouble. She ignored the rebellious voice crying out a protest.

The vehicle rocked to a gentle stop and less than a minute later she was climbing the steps to her house as Simmons saw to the business of returning the carriage to the mews. As she walked through the front door, Dolores came running down the hallway to greet her, a worried expression on her face.

"Oh my lady, I'm so sorry—"

"Where the devil have you been for the past two nights?"

Garrick's voice made her jump as she whirled around to see him standing in the doorway of the salon. Her initial impression of him was that he looked tired. Almost as if he'd not been sleeping. A frown furrowed his brow, and his expression wavered between deep worry and another emotion she hesitated to name. For a moment, she felt the need to go to him and ease his concerns. She stopped herself as the memory of his sister's visit shoved its way into her thoughts. She longed to race upstairs and away from a confrontation, but it would only put off the inevitable.

"I wasn't aware that I answered to you as to where I spend my nights, my lord." She undid the frog loops of her cape, and as it slid from her shoulders, she handed it to Dolores.

"You *don't* answer to me. I'm simply saying I was worried," he said fiercely, his posture revealing his tension.

With a light touch of reassurance to Dolores's arm, she moved toward the salon doorway. Bergamot mixed with spice wafted beneath her nostrils as she brushed past him, and she crushed the emotions the scent stirred inside her. When she reached the center of the room, she turned to face him.

Her heart skipped a beat as he slowly closed the salon door to lean against it. Arms folded across his chest, he studied her with a watchful gaze. His silence didn't make her nervous, but the predatory tension in his tall frame did. Despite the distance between them, her awareness of him was heightened to a fevered pitch that made every inch of her tingle. Even from several feet away he was the one in control. She drew in a quick breath then released it as she cleared her throat.

"I met your sister today."

He didn't move, but the sudden tic in his cheek said her statement had thrown him slightly off balance. However, it wasn't the startled reaction she was looking for. Had he talked with Lady Lynmouth already? Was that why he didn't appear surprised?

"Which sister? I have two." His cool response reminded her of his sister.

"Lady Lynmouth. An acquaintance introduced us." Ruth clenched her teeth as she remembered the private conversation that had followed Mr. Millstadt's introduction. "She appears to be under the impression that I'm pursuing you."

"I see." He pushed himself away from the door and slowly closed the distance between them. "I can assume you corrected her on that issue."

"I tried, but she's determined to believe that I'm the older woman leading you into hell and damnation."

Ruth glanced away from him as she remembered the way his sister had emphasized her age for the majority of their conversation. She didn't need anyone to remind her that time was her enemy or that becoming involved with a younger man was a desperate attempt to cling to her youth—friendship or love affair aside. She tensed as he stopped less than a foot away from her.

"We both know you're not." The soft caress in his voice made her heart skip a beat, and she stiffened at the traitorous way her body reacted to him.

"You lied to me," she bit out in a tight voice. He jerked his head back in surprise.

"Come again?"

"You told me you didn't want Crawley Hall, but that's not what your sister said." Her sharp tone made him frown with exasperation.

"My sister needs to learn her place and not interfere in my affairs," he growled as a frown of annoyance creased his brow. "If I had told you the truth, you would have been as angry with me then as you are now."

"Angry?" She shook her head sharply, the strength of her emotions surprising her. "I'm furious. First you offer to buy the Hall for me. When I refuse, you decide to take pity on me and help me acquire the estate by *not* bidding against me."

"I did not do what I did out of pity," he growled.

"No? Then why did your sister think I was planning on retiring to the country—*permanently*?" She flinched as she remembered the countess saying they'd discussed her. "Don't bother answering the question. I already know. You told her all about me. She said so herself."

"You seem to know quite a bit about my motivations and actions after just one conversation with my sister." His voice was a menacing rumble as fury made his eyes a piercing blue.

"Don't try to deny the fact that you discussed me with your sister," she snapped.

"I won't deny that your name was mentioned. But I said nothing about the conversation you and I had at Crawley Hall." He scowled as he leaned into her. "I simply told Lily that we were friends."

"She didn't believe you." Ruth held her ground, unwilling to let him see he was intimidating her. Her heart slammed into her chest as an odd expression crossed Garrick's face.

"I don't give a damn what she believes. What do *you* believe?"

"I . . . I don't know what you mean," Ruth gasped as she stared up at Garrick's suddenly inscrutable features.

"You know exactly what I mean, Ruth. You've balked at having anything to do with me from the beginning. I'd like to know why."

"I have not *balked*, as you call it, at an association with you," she snapped. "I accepted your friendship, and yet I'm still not sure that's what you really want from me."

"Why is it so difficult for you to believe that a man could enjoy the pleasure of your company without any expectations on his part?" he asked with harsh frustration. She stared at him, disconcerted by her sudden, fervent wish that he ask her for something more than just friendship.

"Because I've learned over time that *everyone* has expectations—even young men who offer me friendship." Her body tensed as an odd expression crossed his face.

"Emphasizing that I'm younger than you doesn't change the fact that I find you witty, intelligent, and in possession of the extraordinary ability to make me laugh," he said as he shoved his hand through his hair in an exasperated manner.

"Required traits of my position in Society."

"Christ Jesus, you're a stubborn little mule. I don't believe for one minute that those *so-called* traits aren't a part of the woman you really are. If anything, you've honed them well simply to keep people at a distance."

"Don't be ridiculous. I am what I am."

"I don't think so. There's a great deal more to you than you're willing to share with me." His eyes narrowed as he pinned her with his gaze. "For instance, you're reluctant to tell me where you've been for the past three days. Why? My question earlier wasn't that of a jealous lover, I asked out of concern for your well-being."

"Oh for heaven's sake, you are the most tenacious man I've ever met. If you must know, I was at St. Agnes's orphanage. Mrs. Beardsley, the cook and housekeeper, was ill."

She swallowed hard as he grasped her hand to study the chafed skin of her knuckles. When his gaze met hers, she saw a deep respect in his blue eyes that warmed her heart. He approved of her actions. Her mouth went dry. The fact that his approval meant so much to her was a warning sign she found far too easy to ignore when he was holding her hand.

"You worked as a maid." The gentle note of admiration in his voice made her cheeks grow hot.

"It was necessary. There wasn't anyone else to help." She quickly tugged her hand free of his then put some distance between them as she massaged the side of her neck with her fingers.

"When was the last time you ate?" It wasn't so much a question as it was a demand, and she shot him a quick look. The frown on his face made her realize he wasn't lying when he'd said he was concerned for her. She shrugged.

"I don't remember. Lunch I suppose."

He immediately turned away from her, and went to the salon door. Startled by his abrupt manner, she watched as he vanished into the main hall. When he returned a moment later, there was a determined look on his face that said he was going to insist on having his way. At the moment, she was too tired to continue arguing with him.

"Dolores has prepared you a bath. When you've finished soaking, you're going to eat then go to bed."

Despite the autocratic note in his voice, a rush of warmth flooded her veins. It was the first time in memory that a man had put her needs ahead of his own. She liked the way it made her feel, and she was too tired to question why that was. With a weary nod of her head, she moved toward the doorway and didn't object as his hand pressed into the small of her back as he guided her out into the hall. At the foot of the stairs, he gently pushed her forward. She looked up at him and offered him a small smile.

"Thank you, Garrick."

"You're welcome," he said as he carried her hand to his mouth to tenderly kiss the roughened skin of her knuckles. She sucked in a sharp breath.

The moment he released her hand, she stared up at him, unable to tell what he was thinking. The back of her hand was hot from his touch, and she wasn't sure what to make of the tender caress. Suddenly feeling embarrassed, she turned away from him to climb the stairs, all too aware of his gaze on her back.

When she reached the second floor hallway, she looked down, only to see he was no longer standing at the foot of the stairs. The quiet sound of a door closing told her that he'd gone. Disappointment skimmed through her, and she quickly banished it from her thoughts. She couldn't afford such an emotion where Garrick was concerned.

All the way home from St. Agnes's, she'd devised first one plan and then another for breaking her ties with the man. Now, all she'd done was reinforce their friendship by letting him take charge of her well-being. Something she'd never allowed any other man to do before, yet with Garrick she hadn't argued. In fact, as much as she hated to admit it, she liked how he'd ordered her to take care of herself.

With a small noise of disgust, she mentally shook her head. His behavior had been that of a concerned friend. She was reading more into things than was there. The thought was a double-edged sword, and she didn't like the opposite side of the blade. She frowned as she entered the small bath off her bedroom, steam rising off the water in her modern tub with its brass faucet. The decision to install plumbing and its fixtures in the house last year was one of the best decisions she'd ever made.

The convenience and amenity of her new bath had made her adamant that St. Agnes's receive similar improvements. It had been a major expense that many on the board of directors had protested, but it had been worth it. She was certain that it had made a difference in keeping the children healthy.

She undressed quickly, and the moment she sank into the heat of the water, she closed her eyes from the pleasure. With her head back against the rim of the tub, she relished the soft scent of the bath salts Dolores had added. Time ceased to exist, and a delicious lethargy settled into her limbs as she luxuriated in the fragrant water.

A short time later, she heard the rattle of dishes through the open door leading into her bedroom. Dolores had brought her supper. Aware that the water had grown tepid, she reluctantly reached for the lemongrass soap she used when bathing. When she finally stepped out of the tub, she dried herself off then pulled a thin wrapper on over her shoulders and padded barefoot across the floor.

The scent of bay leaves teased her nostrils as she reached the door of her bedroom. Dolores had made beef stew, and the aroma made her stomach growl. She hadn't realized how hungry she was until now. Her head slightly bent, she reached up with both hands to pull the pins out of her hair. She shook her head so the wavy locks could tumble down onto her shoulders.

Her fingers massaging her scalp in a careless fashion, she moved deeper into the bedroom, and the quiet noise that greeted her made her jerk her head up in surprise. Stunned, she met Garrick's intense gaze. Dear Lord, what was he doing here? Her heart skipped several beats as she saw the hungry expression on his face. It was a look she recognized, but she couldn't remember ever having been aroused so easily by any other man's stare.

She stood frozen as she saw his gaze roam downward, and she suddenly realized she'd not tied her wrapper closed. Heat seared her cheeks with embarrassment, and she tugged on the edges of the garment and tied it shut with the belt sewn into the seam. As if suddenly realizing he was staring, Garrick jerked his gaze away from her, and to her surprise, she saw a tinge of color darken his cheeks. Was the man blushing? Impossible.

"Remind me not to bring you supper again until I know you're suitably dressed," he said in a strangled voice as he cleared his throat.

Still disconcerted by his presence, her gaze shifted toward the fireplace. The large, comfortable chairs she often used when she wanted to warm herself in front of the fire had been pulled closer together. In between the chairs, Garrick had placed a small table with two bowls of steaming stew and a plate of fresh hot bread.

Completing the scene was a small fire that crackled softly in the hearth and cast a warm glow over the table and chairs. The intimate atmosphere should have alarmed her, but at the moment she was too tired and hungry to care. Yet despite how exhausted she was, a frisson raced along her skin to every part of her body as she stared at him. It was the first time in years that she'd felt so nervous and yet exhilarated.

"I thought you'd gone home," she breathed as her usual confidence fled.

"I decided to stay and make sure you ate supper. Not to mention I was hungry myself." He gestured toward the chair opposite where he stood. "Come. You need to eat."

The quiet command made her sweep her hair off her shoulders as she prepared to gather it up into a hasty bun. Garrick immediately stepped toward her, causing her to start with surprise. His expression was unreadable as he closed the distance between them. Slowly, he reached out to grasp her hand and forced her to let go of her hair.

"Don't. I like seeing you with your hair down." His hand warmed hers as he pulled her toward the fire. When she was seated, he sat down opposite her and smiled as he picked up his spoon. "This stew smells delicious."

"It's one of Dolores's specialties," she said as she blew on a hot spoonful of the hearty concoction.

The stew quickly warmed her belly and made her even more lethargic than her bath had done. When she'd finished her bowl, Garrick raised an eyebrow as he smiled at her.

"Shall I go down and get you more stew?"

"No, thank you." She shook her head. "It was just enough to ease my hunger."

He nodded, his face darkening with an emotion she couldn't identify. In an instant it was gone, and he took another bite of his meal. Without looking at her, he buttered a piece of bread and cleared his throat.

"Tell me about St. Agnes's. Are you a sponsor?"

"I started the orphanage." Her answer made him jerk his head in surprise toward her.

"*You* did?"

"Why is that so hard to believe?" she said with a touch of annoyance. "Women are just as capable as men when it comes to business or charitable work."

"You misunderstand my surprise," he said. "It didn't occur to me that you might be the primary benefactor of the institution. When did you first start the orphanage?"

"More than fifteen years ago." She winced as she realized how quickly time could pass one by.

"What prompted you to establish the home?" His gaze was steady as he asked the question. She nibbled at her lip, wondering exactly how much she should tell him. It didn't help matters that he was so easy to talk to.

"I know what it's like to have nowhere to go, and I wanted to prevent that from happening to others."

"And so you created St. Agnes's." He reached for his napkin and pressed it against his mouth before tossing it carelessly back onto the table. "Tell me why you know what it's like to have no place to go."

"It's of no importance." She shivered as she turned her head away from his penetrating gaze to stare into the yellow and blue flames in the hearth. It was a lie. Despite the length of time separating her from the day her mother died, it was still painful.

"I don't believe that."

"Why not?" Her gaze jerked back to him in surprise.

"Because I can hear the pain in your voice." The astute look he sent her made her turn back toward the crackling fire. Suddenly leaning forward, he touched the hand that she'd subconsciously balled up into a tight fist. "I'm a good listener."

She stared down at his long fingers lightly resting on her hand. In the back of her mind, she noted the muscular strength of his hand and the fine dusting of dark hair that disappeared up under the sleeve of his shirt and coat. She'd always enjoyed looking at the beauty of a man's hands. The moment she looked up to meet his gaze she knew she would tell him her story.

While most of the Set knew she claimed her title as the Marquess of Halethorpe's daughter, most of them believed she was another man's child. Her father believed it, too. She turned back toward the fire. It had been a long time since she'd thought about the reasons why she'd come to follow her particular path in life. And for the past few months, she'd found herself longing for what might have been.

"The other night at the opera, do you remember the elderly gentleman who was part of the Prince and Princess's entourage?" she asked quietly.

"The one who didn't seem particularly happy."

"Unhappy to see *me*, is what you mean." Ruth nodded as the old ache spread through her. "He is the Marquess of Halethorpe . . . and my father."

"Your father." It wasn't a question so much as a puzzled observation.

"My father," she repeated the words. Despite her best efforts to disguise the bitterness in her voice, it resounded loudly in her ears. "He gave up a lifetime of happiness because he chose to believe the word of another man over his own wife's."

She paused as she watched the logs burning in the brick hearth. An ember popped loudly and the unexpected sound made her jump. The gentle touch of his hand prompted her to look at Garrick. He didn't say a word. It was simply a gesture of comfort, and it warmed her, encouraging her to go on. Leaning back into her chair, Ruth drew in a deep breath.

"My parents were unusual in that they were a love match. Although my mother rarely spoke of the incident that made my father throw her out of Halethorpe Manor, I managed to piece together the story over a period of years." A shiver rippled through her as she remembered the pain her mother had suffered. Yet in spite of her husband's cruelty she'd never stopped loving him. "My parents had only been married a short time, and my father was very jealous of anything that occupied my mother's time, aside from him. They hosted a house party where one of the guests tried to assault my mother in the middle of the night. My father interrupted and assumed the worst."

"Christ Jesus," Garrick said softly. The outrage in his voice mimicked her own.

"The man knew my father was more than capable of destroying him socially and financially, and the bastard immediately blamed my mother for the entire incident. My mother protested, but blind with jealousy, my father believed Lord Tremaine."

"Tremaine?" The harsh question made her look at him in surprise.

"Not the current viscount, his father."

"The apple never falls far from the tree," Garrick said fiercely.

His obvious disgust told her that he held the current Lord Tremaine in the same regard as she had the elder viscount who'd died several years ago. The old anger sliced through again at the heartache the elder Tremaine had inflicted on her and her mother.

"My father ordered my mother out of the house. A vicar's daughter, she had no place to go, as my grandparents were dead. It was a childhood friend who arranged a small cottage for her use. When she realized she was with child, she went to my father to plead her case with him, but he said he had no intention of raising a bastard."

Ruth clenched her jaw at the memory of him using similar words the day she'd sought his help when her mother was dying. It was the first time she'd ever hated someone. She pushed the memory aside and continued with her parents' story.

"My mother used to tell me how wonderful my father was, and I believed her up until I turned ten. That's when she took me to meet him. At the time, I looked very much like he had as a child. My mother was convinced he'd see the resemblance and realize the truth."

"But he didn't," Garrick said quietly.

"No. Tremaine had spread rumors that he'd cuckolded my father, which only hardened my father's heart against my mother. The argument they had that day was terrible. My mother made me leave the room, but she remained behind."

She paused as she remembered the shouts that had echoed behind the door of her father's study. It had been impossible to hear everything, but she'd heard enough to know how cruel the marquess could be. The wood in the fireplace popped and she watched a spurt of blue flame race across the surface of one of the burning logs. She frowned and continued her story.

"They argued terribly for several minutes, and when my mother came out of the study, she looked as though she'd aged years. She was never the same after that."

"And yet he didn't divorce her," Garrick said with a thoughtful frown. "Is it possible your father still loved your mother in spite of what he believed?"

It was a question she'd often asked herself. She knew her father was a proud man, and the idea that his wife had betrayed him was something he would find impossible to forgive. She met Garrick's curious gaze.

"It's possible he still loved her, but I think revenge might have been his real reason. He knew my mother would be free to marry if he divorced her. It would be the final humiliation for him. In his mind, his wife would have cuckolded him twice."

"Yet the possibility exists that he loved her in spite of what he believed was the truth," he said, and she contemplated the suggestion for a moment. What Garrick suggested couldn't be true. She shook her head.

"After that terrible fight with my father, my mother's health declined over the next eight years. I'm convinced she gave up the will to live. When she was dying, I went to my father at her request. She wanted to see him one last time." Her voice choked on the last few words.

"He refused." Garrick uttered a small noise of appalled anger.

"Yes. The bastard told me she could rot in hell, and ordered me out of his house and said he never wanted to see me again. My mother died a few days later still calling his name." This time she didn't bother to hide her bitterness. "I tried to find work, but I had no skills. The one job I did manage to find as a downstairs maid ended a week later when the mistress of the house caught her husband trying to kiss me. She refused to give me a reference and finding work became impossible. Then, three weeks after I buried my mother, the Viscount Chippenham paid me a visit. He'd seen me visit my father, and had apparently become enamored with me. He offered me a home in exchange for . . . in exchange for me in his bed. There are many things one will do when one is hungry, particularly when one has nowhere left to turn. Without hope of gainful employment and my mother's stipend gone, there was nothing to fall back on, so I accepted his offer."

"The bastard," Garrick growled.

"On that we both agree, my father had a wife who adored him—"

"I'm not talking about the marquess and his wretched behavior. I'm talking about Chippenham and how he took advantage of your situation." The heated words made her look at him in surprise.

"Perhaps—but if he hadn't, I could have just as easily ended up in a brothel simply to feed myself. Being Chippenham's mistress was infinitely preferable to the life I might have led." She rolled her shoulders in a small shrug as she saw Garrick frown. "Since my father never divorced my mother, I chose to make good use of my title. It gave me an air of respectability so many of the other professional beauties enjoyed. *And* it infuriated my father."

She allowed herself a tight smile as she recalled the first time she'd stumbled into her father's presence at an event Chippenham had taken her to. He'd pulled her aside away from anyone's hearing to demand she stop using her title. She'd taken great pleasure in pointing out that because he'd never divorced her mother, she was for all intents and purposes his daughter. Her words had only made him more livid as he'd accepted the truth of what she'd said.

That had been the moment she'd realized he would never openly acknowledge her, any more than he would denounce her as an imposter. To denounce her meant not only proceedings in a court of law, but public opinion as well. She was certain her father never concerned himself with public opinion. If he'd cared, he would never have discarded her mother so cruelly. But they both knew that if he acknowledged her or the courts declared her his child, it would change everything. And *that* would be the ultimate humiliation for him. Acknowledging a child he believed wasn't his own. It was why she'd never been afraid to use her title, despite the lifestyle she'd led.

"You risked a great deal standing up to Halethorpe." His comment made her shake her head.

"I had nothing to lose. Any legal action might have forced him to recognize me as his daughter. He'd never risk admitting that my mother had told him the truth. Either he couldn't bear the guilt of it or the idea of being wrong is even more uncomfortable for him."

Reclined in his chair, Garrick studied her over the top of his steepled fingers. The sympathetic look on his face made her shiver. She closed her eyes against his intense gaze. What in heaven's name had possessed her to share her story with him? She didn't need his pity, or anyone else's for that matter. She'd made a life for herself despite her father's rejection. It might not be the life her mother had envisioned for her, but it was better than the alternatives.

"Nonetheless, standing up to your father took a lot of courage," he argued. "Your mother would be proud of you."

The sudden image of her mother's face flashed through her head, and the dull ache that had been pressing on her heart sharpened. What would her life have been like if her mother had been able to convince her father of the truth? It was a useless question to ask. Her father had abandoned her just as he had her mother, and nothing she did could change that. But accepting the truth didn't make the pain go away.

On the verge of tears, she closed her eyes and turned her face away from Garrick in an attempt to regain her composure. It had been years since she cried over her father's abandonment. The man had made his choice, forcing her to make hers. That was the one thing she would never be able to forgive her father for.

He'd thrown his own flesh and blood to the wolves, and she hated him for it. Tears pressed against her eyelids as she swallowed hard. A soft rustle of movement echoed in the vicinity of where Garrick was sitting, but she couldn't look at him. He'd be able to tell she was about to cry, and she didn't want his pity.

Strong arms lifted her up out of her chair as Garrick sat back down with her cradled in his lap. The last time she'd been this close to him, he'd kissed her. Bemused by his behavior, she swallowed her tears and stared up at him in bewilderment.

"You look like you need a strong shoulder to cry on," he said in a gruff voice. "So use mine."

It was one of the kindest things a man had ever done for her, and like a dam breaking, tears rolled down her cheeks. She cried softly while Garrick held her in his arms with the quiet strength of an oak tree. When her sobs faded, she lay exhausted against him with her head on his shoulder. A crisp white handkerchief appeared out of nowhere, and she took the linen from him to blow her nose.

"I'm sorry," she choked out with embarrassment, unable to look up at him.

"For what? Feeling hurt and betrayed because your father abandoned first your mother and then you?" There was a fierceness to his words that showed how contemptible he thought the marquess was. "It's the real reason why you started St. Agnes's. You wanted to give children what your father refused to give you. A safe harbor."

His arms tightened around her just a bit, which reinforced his strength and the protection his embrace offered. It made her relax wearily against him. The fact that he'd seen a side of her she'd never shared with any other man alarmed her, but as she tried to think of something to say, her thoughts all ran together like a stampede of wild animals racing away from danger. She was too tired to think straight and form a plan to distance herself from him.

She yawned, and the earth suddenly shifted as Garrick stood up with her still in his arms and carried her toward the bed. She immediately stiffened, her heartbeat accelerating at a furious pace.

"You need to sleep. You're exhausted."

He didn't look at her, but there were fine lines of tension at the corners of his mouth. The softness of the mattress welcomed her weary body, and as his arms slid out from underneath her, the wrapper she wore fell open to reveal one of her breasts.

The exposed nipple immediately hardened the moment he sucked in a sharp breath. It was the sound of desire, and it made her blood run hot. She fought hard not to look at him, but failed. The desire darkening his expression made her mouth go dry as he sank down onto the bed beside her.

How in God's name had she gotten herself into this situation? Blue eyes dark with a fierce hunger, he lightly traced the line of her bared shoulder then downward. The touch pulled a shudder from her then sent fire streaking through her veins to warm every inch of her. This was trouble of the first order. She wouldn't be able to refuse him if he were to push his advantage. Refuse him? She was praying he wouldn't stop touching her.

"You have no idea how breathtaking you are, do you?" The roughly spoken words were soft, almost as if he were thinking out loud as he studied her as if she were a precious piece of art.

"Garrick . . . I . . ." She whimpered as his hand cupped her breast and he ran his thumb across her nipple.

"I want to know every inch of you," he rasped.

With almost a slow precision, he lowered his head and took her nipple into his hot mouth. The heat of the touch sent her arching upward against him as she released a soft cry of pleasure. Dear Lord, she knew this was a mistake, but at the moment she didn't care. The time for repenting could come later.

Her fingers threaded through his dark silky hair as his tongue swirled around the peak of her breast. The seductive touch sent a shudder through her as his mouth teased and tempted. It had been such a long time since a man had ignited this kind of fire in her. The desire spiraling through her made her ache with need, and she longed for him to taste every part of her, particularly the sensitive spot between her legs. The image of him using his tongue to bring her to a climax was a delicious thought, and she pushed her bottom up off the bed in a silent cry for him to explore her sex.

The moment his mouth released her, she wanted to whimper with disappointment at the loss of pleasure. An instant later, he captured her lips in a hard, passionate kiss. She welcomed his caress, her arms wrapping around his neck to pull him down to her. He responded by pushing aside the other half of her thin robe and thrumming her nipples with his thumbs.

The touch was exquisite torture. She wanted him now—this instant. The difference in their ages she could face in the morning. Right now, the only thing she craved was the heat of his touch. Desire spread its cloak over every inch of her, pushing her toward a peak that promised a fiery completion. It dragged her forward until she was beyond thought of anything but the need for his touch.

Caught up in the strength of her desire, she responded to his kiss fervently. Her fingers wrapped around the lapels of his coat to push the garment off his shoulders. She wanted to feel his hard, muscular body pressed into hers. It had been such a long time since her blood had burned so feverishly.

A dark growl rumbled out of his chest at her efforts, and he suddenly jerked away from her in an explosive movement. Stunned, she stared at his back, her body screaming in protest as he walked away from the bed. The fierce sting of his retreat lashed through her as she slowly comprehended the fact that the satisfaction she craved was not going to be assuaged.

The powerful ache inside her slowly ebbed, replaced by a sickening dread that made her stomach churn. The stark silence in the room didn't ease her apprehension as he had yet to turn and face her. Fear slithered through her. She didn't know what to do. Had she offended him with the uninhibited demonstration of her desire?

There were men who preferred to be in control in the bedroom, but Garrick had never struck her as that type. She pulled her wrapper closed as she got out of bed. The rigid line of his body revealed his tension, and she took a hesitant step toward him.

"Garrick—"

"I can't do this, Ruth."

The words were like pieces of ice that hit her skin and spread their chill all over her body. He didn't want her. With a mental shake of her head, she denied the thought. She knew the touch of a man eager to bed her, and Garrick had wanted her just as much tonight as he had that night in the carriage. He'd refused her then because he hadn't wanted to jeopardize their friendship.

That had to be why he'd rejected her just now. Deep in the recesses of her mind, a mocking voice told her something different. She refused to consider the alternative reason for the way he'd pulled away from her. She took another tentative step toward him.

"If it's our agreement that we be friends only—"

"No," he rasped. "It's the difference in our . . . our years of experience."

A lightning strike could not have hurt more. *Years of experience.*

He was saying the age difference between them was too great. She'd been right all along. He thought her too old. A woman past her prime with nothing to offer a man in the bedroom. Her gaze met his, and she vaguely wondered at the frustration darkening his eyes. A part of her wanted to demand an explanation from him, but derisive laughter floated through her head. It was all too clear why he'd rejected her. She turned and walked woodenly toward the bedroom door and opened it.

"Please leave."

"Ruth, I need to explain—"

"I don't want an explanation. I just want you gone," she said flatly as she stared at the wall.

The violent noise he made broke through the numbness settling into her to make her jump, but she didn't look at him. She couldn't. The pain slashing through her made it impossible to do so, a pain that was quickly outweighing the humiliation she was feeling. With a vicious oath he bolted from the room as if he had suddenly been saved from making a terrible mistake. She closed the door behind him then turned the key in the lock. Not that it was necessary. She knew he wouldn't be back—ever.

The thought made her entire body feel as if someone had bludgeoned her. She stumbled her way toward the bed, where she fell onto the mattress and curled up into herself. A deep, penetrating ache assaulted every inch of her. Age wasn't just a mental state. It was physical, too, and she'd never felt so physically and emotionally worn-out.

If she had ever needed instruction as to how old she was, tonight had been that lesson. What had possessed her not to order Garrick out of her bedroom when she'd found him waiting for her? That had been her first error in judgment. Her second mistake had been to let him coax her into talking about her father.

She never would have even considered sharing such intimate details of her life if she'd not been so tired. And she *was* tired—exhausted. Eyes closed, a tear squeezed itself out of the corner of her eye. The fact that she was crying over a man was bad enough. Even worse was the fact that it was a man she'd never been intimate with.

No, that wasn't accurate. She simply hadn't felt him sliding between her legs. And dear lord how badly she ached for him now. The image of him on top of her stroking her with his hard length was one that refused to leave her mind. It made her long for a release that, even in spite of her exhaustion, was assaulting her body. Just as bad was the way her skin still burned in every spot his tongue had touched.

Another tear pushed its way out from behind her eyelids to slide down her cheek. It was an indication of how deeply he'd affected her. She should never have agreed to be Garrick's friend. It had been her ego that had allowed him to persuade her that they could have a platonic relationship.

She'd recognized her attraction to him, but thought she could put it aside simply for the pleasure of his company. It had been ridiculous to even think friendship between them was possible. Where had her age and experience been when she made that decision? They had been nonexistent because she'd allowed desire to control her head. Desire for a younger man and the way her body reacted to him every time he was near. A man who hadn't bothered to hide his attraction to her, despite the difference in their ages.

As painful as it was to accept, she'd agreed to the relationship because she'd been flattered by his obvious desire for her. She recognized her decision now for what it was. It had been a desperate cry for attention by a woman who couldn't accept the fact that she was past her prime. Oh God, she should have sent him away, gifts and all, the day he'd asked for her friendship.

It was all too clear now that her decision to pursue a relationship of any kind with him had been a mistake of colossal proportions. They couldn't be friends, any more than they could be lovers. The notion sent another tear rolling down her cheek. She'd never thought growing old could be so lonely.

Garrick threw himself into one of the Marlborough Club's roomy leather chairs. What the hell had he been thinking? He'd almost bared himself completely to the woman, and not just physically. The thought of her staring at him with either disgust or amusement made his stomach knot with that sickening sensation he remembered all too well.

He buried the ugly memory of his uncle's and Bertha's laughter back in the deep hole it had emerged from. He should never have insisted on Dolores allowing him to take Ruth's supper up to her room. If he'd simply gone home, he never would have touched her. Christ Jesus, what a mess he'd made of things.

Out of the corner of his eye, he saw Jenkins, one of the Club's menservants, suddenly appear at his side. The man bowed slightly, a solicitous expression on his face.

"Good evening, Lord Stratfield. May I bring you something?"

"A bottle of Hennessy."

"A bottle, my lord?" The small element of surprise in the manservant's voice made Garrick lift his head up to send the man a hard stare.

"*Unopened*," he growled.

As the man scurried away, Garrick rested his head on the back of the firm leather chair and closed his eyes. He'd not even had the ballocks to face Ruth when he'd pulled away from her so abruptly. His gut churned with disgust. That was a laughable thought when he only had *one*. It only emphasized the fact that he was less of a man for not explaining his reasons for rejecting her.

And it *had* cost him dearly to push himself away from her. God help him, not since Bertha's ridicule had a woman tempted him so much that he'd been on the verge of opening himself up to another humiliation. The fact that he'd come so close to exposing his secret scared the hell out of him. The soft clink of crystal on metal forced his eyes open. Jenkins set a silver tray on the table in between his chair and the empty seat on the other side. The manservant opened the bottle, but Garrick waved him aside.

"I'll pour it myself, Jenkins."

"Of course, my lord." The man hesitated, then left him alone.

With a heavy hand, he splashed the cognac into his snifter. He downed the liquor in one quick gulp then poured himself another draught of the strong, select drink. It, too, followed the first. Somewhere in the back of his head a small voice reminded him the premium liquor was to be savored, not tossed down like swill from a back alley pub. He ignored the internal chastisement.

More liquid splashed its way into the glass, and he drank it just as quickly as the previous draughts. As the smooth-tasting liquid slid down his throat, he refilled his glass again then lifted it to study the contents. The amber-colored drink reminded him of the hints of gold in Ruth's hair. Eyes closed again, he reclined deeper into the chair as her image took form in his head. How he'd ever found Bertha enticing mystified him. The bitch couldn't hold a candle to Ruth.

The memory of her emerging from her bathroom with her robe billowing open made his mouth go dry. Water beads still clinging to her skin, she'd looked like a beautiful water nymph. Her breasts were full and lush with dusky pink nipples, while her waist had curved sweetly inward above a shapely thigh.

She'd been exquisite. The one surprise had been the smooth, hairless skin at the apex of her thighs. Despite his lack of experience in the bedroom, he wasn't completely unacquainted with the female form. But he'd never seen a woman who'd shaved her sex before. It had only strengthened the tangible force of his desire for her. A need he'd barely kept under control when he'd stopped her from hiding the luxurious length of her hair from him.

The moment his hand had touched hers, he'd wanted to pull her into his arms. But sanity had prevailed. Having supper with her in such an intimate setting had aroused something other than desire in him. There had been a quiet, comfortable intimacy in sharing a meal with her. The familiarity of it was of the nature that only happened between good friends.

That feeling had strengthened when she'd shared the story of her childhood and her father's reprehensible behavior. It had been a display of trust that he instinctively knew she'd not shown with many. And God help him, when she'd been fighting back those tears, he'd not been able to keep from offering her comfort. It had been a spontaneous action, which had led to something much more dangerous.

He tossed down his cognac and poured another glass of the liquor. Cradling her in his arms had aroused his protective instincts where she was concerned. She'd been hurt, and he'd experienced an urge to charge out into the night and find the men responsible for her pain. Instead, he'd simply held her and allowed her to weep.

He was accustomed to his sisters weeping, and although seeing a woman in distress was never comfortable, he'd learned to just offer his shoulder for them to cry on. That had been the mistake he'd made tonight. He should have simply held her hand. Holding her in his arms had made it difficult to let her go. And Sweet Jesus, when her robe had fallen open as he put her to bed . . . it had been impossible to turn away. The desire he'd barely had under control all through supper had erupted with a force unlike anything he'd ever experienced.

It had pushed him to touch her, explore her, and make her his. The taste of her had been deliciously sweet, almost as if she'd bathed herself in citrus oil. His cock stirred in his trousers as he remembered the scent of her. Warm and exotic against his senses. Even the satiny smoothness of her skin had been an intoxicating sensation beneath his fingers.

And the way she'd responded to him. His body tightened at the memory of her small whimper of desire. She'd wanted him. He had no doubts she'd been more than willing to open herself up to him. Just the way she'd responded to him had said how eager she was to welcome him into her bed.

It had been her ardor that had awakened him to the danger he was in, making him jerk away the instant he recognized how close to the precipice he was. But the way he'd pulled away from her had been cruel. The pain and humiliation in her voice had been like a sharp blade cutting into him.

He choked out a sound of self-disgust then gulped down the remaining liquor in his snifter to pour himself another stiff drink. Drunk. That's what he wanted to be. Drunk to the point of forgetting how he'd not had the courage to look at her before leaving her bedroom. He was a bastard—a worthless son of a bitch who didn't deserve the trust Ruth had placed in him tonight. Loud voices bellowed into the room behind him, but he didn't bother to turn and inspect the new arrivals. Instead, he poured himself more Hennessy.

"Well, well . . . look who's here, Marston. If it isn't the little runt who took up with your antiquated leavings." Mockery filled Wycombe's voice as the man paused near Garrick's chair.

The cognac flowing freely in Garrick's veins ignited a fire in his blood at Wycombe's insulting comment. He could care less what Wycombe thought of him, but when it came to Ruth, that was another matter all together. Ruth was far from old. She was a vibrant, youthful woman. His eyes, hands, and mouth were testimony to that. Marston had been a fool to give Ruth up for an addle-brained strumpet.

Slowly, he turned his head to study the contempt on Wycombe's face before he returned his attention to the cognac bottle in his hand and set it down on the silver salver. In a deliberate movement, he looked away from the man standing over him and picked up his glass to take a drink of the premium liquor.

"Why is it, Wycombe, that whenever you open your mouth, you bray just like the jackass you are," he said in a bored manner. His nemesis released a sharp hiss of anger, and Garrick's mouth curled in a tight smile of satisfaction. Good. His insult had drawn blood.

"This coming from a man who pretends to be something he isn't," Wycombe said with malicious amusement.

"Your point, Wycombe? That is if you even have one in that half-wit brain of yours."

"My point is that there's some question as to whether your recently departed mistress was really your mistress at all."

The hair on the back of Garrick's neck rose as he struggled not to launch himself out of his chair and beat the man to within an inch of his life. Instead, he slowly set his snifter glass next to the cognac bottle and sent the man a cold look.

"You clearly don't remember the lesson I taught you a few years ago, do you Wycombe?"

"Are you threatening me?" The earl's voice rose a notch, and Garrick leaned forward in his chair to glance around the room. The interest their altercation was drawing pierced the alcohol-induced fog suddenly thickening his head.

"You're far too insignificant to warrant a threat, Wycombe." With a rude snort Garrick looked away from him and retrieved his drink from the salver. He refused to let Wycombe bait him, even if it meant denying himself the pleasure of beating the man into the ground.

"You always were an arrogant prick, Stratfield. The question is, are you really able to use it on a woman?" Wycombe sneered.

Ice slugged its way through Garrick's veins. The man spoke as if he knew something . . . had spoken to someone. A dark fury dug its vicious claws into his body and drew him up tight with tension. If his uncle had broken his silence . . . he didn't allow himself to finish the thought as he set his glass down.

His fingers digging deep into the leather arms of the chair, he slowly rose to his feet and turned to face the man. He'd expected to see the Earl of Marston, but the man standing next to him was a surprise. What the hell was Tremaine doing here? His gaze narrowed at the man, and the viscount sent him a contemptuous smile. The alcohol in his body was quickly making his brain sluggish, and he found himself regretting his decision to imbibe so freely. He jerked his gaze back to Wycombe, whose expression had become one of loathing.

"You see, gentlemen"—the earl directed a gloating smile at his companions—"the man doesn't know how to answer me, which leads me to conclude that he's not half the man he claims to be."

Christ Jesus, either Wycombe's words were sheer coincidence or his uncle *had* revealed his secret and Wycombe was privy to it. His temper on a thinly stretched leash, Garrick narrowed his eyes at the earl. The only way out of this quagmire was to turn the tables on the bastard. With a cold smile he arched his eyebrows at the man.

"Your preoccupation with my sexual prowess, Wycombe, makes me think that either one of *my* leavings has found you lacking in the bedroom or you're an acolyte of buggery. If the former, you've my pity. If the latter, you'll need to look elsewhere as I have no stomach for the sport."

Wycombe sputtered with fury before he swung his fist in Garrick's direction. Despite the amount of liquor he'd consumed, Garrick easily dodged the earl's vicious jab. As he darted to one side, there was a surge of movement throughout the room. Somewhere in the back of his brain, he noticed two gentlemen springing from their seats to move quickly in their direction. Marston and Tremaine had a strong grip on the earl, but Wycombe was still fighting hard to be free.

"I'll make you pay for this, Stratfield," he snarled.

"You may certainly try." A mist of alcohol still clouding his senses, Garrick fought to maintain his balance as he scowled at the earl. "But I'll see you dead first."

Someone off to his side grasped his arm with a light squeeze as a silent signal that he'd already said too much. He turned his head to see Baron Rothschild standing beside him with the financier Ernest Cassel.

"Might we be of assistance, Lord Stratfield?" Rothschild's voice was low, but the note of warning in his voice was unmistakable as the baron sent Wycombe and the other two men a cold stare.

"Thank you, my lord, but Wycombe, Marston, and their *guest* were just leaving."

Garrick studied Tremaine with a look of contempt as the man offered him a feral smile. Wycombe shook off his friends' grasp and tugged at his clothes in an effort to straighten them. As he pulled at the cuffs of his shirt, the earl eyed Garrick with a menacing look. Behind him, Marston's expression was one of worried pacification.

"Actually, we've yet to have the drink we promised our friend here," Marston said, his mannerism one of forced joviality that indicated how uncomfortable he was at the moment.

"I think it best if you perhaps found another establishment in which to entertain Lord Tremaine." Despite the pleasant tone of the baron's voice, there was a hard note of steel layered beneath his words. "It would be most unfortunate if his Royal Highness arrived this evening to find the atmosphere in the Club less than harmonious."

"Now see here, Rothschild, I've no quarrel with you—" Wycombe blustered, his expression a mixture of humiliation and anger.

"Nor I with you, my lord." Rothschild tilted his head in an appeasing manner as he interrupted the earl. "But I *am* well-acquainted with his Royal Highness's likes and dislikes. And indiscreet behavior is something he abhors."

Wycombe paled at the baron's quiet statement, his expression one of trepidation. Banishment from the Marlborough Club was akin to social ruin. The man swallowed hard and offered them a stilted bow.

"My lords," he said in a vicious tone then whirled around to stalk out of the Club's lounge. Marston hurried after the earl like a puppy chasing its master, but Tremaine paused for a moment in open defiance of Baron Rothschild's obvious disapproval. The viscount smiled with more than a trace of insolence as he met Garrick's gaze.

"I must say, Stratfield, I'm puzzled that you've not considered having that sweet little Mary of yours or even the Lady Ruth dispute Wycombe's speculations." The man shrugged as if entertained by some private joke. He seemed on the verge of leaving, when he suddenly paused and eyed Garrick with growing amusement. "By the way, I'll be certain to give your regards to your uncle, Stratfield."

The man's comment was like a punch to Garrick's gut as he went rigid with a combination of dread and foreboding. Satisfaction tipped the viscount's mouth up into a derisive smile as he nodded his head and walked away. Rage rushed through Garrick as he made to follow the bastard, but a strong hand held him back.

"Another time, Stratfield. When your head is clear," Rothschild said quietly.

Garrick jerked his head in a hard nod of agreement as he watched Tremaine disappear from the lounge. The ache in his jaw didn't ease when the man was gone. He wanted to roar with anger, but locked his lips to keep the sound inside him. Between Wycombe's and Tremaine's innuendos, he was willing to lay odds that his uncle had betrayed his secret. And Tremaine was waiting for the right moment to use the knowledge against him. The sharp thrust of humiliation pierced his chest like an axe, and he forced himself to turn away from the entrance to the lounge.

"That man is a blighter," Cassel said with a snort of disgust. "Never have liked him."

"I agree. A most disagreeable fellow." A look of assessment on his face, Rothschild looked at Garrick as he nodded his agreement with Cassel's observation.

"Then the three of us are in complete agreement," Garrick bit out as he looked down at his drink on the table.

More than ever he wanted to return to his drinking. Anything to blot out the knowledge of what was on the horizon. It was like seeing a storm approaching and being helpless to stop it from destroying everything he'd built.

The moment he heard Rothschild clear his throat, he lifted his head to meet the man's gaze. There was no censure in the baron's eyes, simply curiosity, but he had no intention of satisfying the man's inquisitive nature. The drink he'd already had strengthened its grip on him, and he swallowed hard as he realized he'd not expressed his appreciation for the man's intervention.

"I am obliged to you for your assistance with Wycombe and the others."

"Don't mention it. Cassel and I never have cared much for the man."

"You've a mortal enemy there," Cassel observed quietly. He shrugged with resignation at the financier's comment.

"There's been no love lost between Wycombe and me since our school days, but he's more bluster than action."

"Not him. Tremaine," Rothschild said as he nodded at Cassel before looking back at Garrick. "I'd watch your back with that one."

"I shall. Thank you," he said as he cleared his throat and glanced down with longing at the Hennessy before raising his head to look at the two men. "I believe I'll find my way home. It's been an eventful evening."

"Certainly," Rothschild said with a smile of approval. "By the by, why don't you join the baroness and me for a small dinner party we're giving for His Royal Highness next month?"

Startled by the unexpected invitation, Garrick tried to think of a coherent response. What Rothschild had just offered was a highly coveted honor in the Set. He didn't speak. He simply nodded his acceptance. The baron's smile was friendly as he extended his hand to Garrick. Even if he'd not been drinking, he would have been just as sluggish at accepting the man's hand. As Rothschild turned with Cassel to walk away, he suddenly paused to look back at him.

"And bring the lovely Lady Ruth with you. My wife has a fondness for her. The baroness serves on several charitable boards with the lady."

As Rothschild and Cassel walked away, Garrick stood staring after them for a long moment. Bring Lady Ruth the man had said. He released a vicious growl of disgust. The odds of that happening were almost nonexistent. He'd humiliated the woman this evening. She wasn't likely to let him within fifty feet of her.

"*Damn it to hell*," he snarled beneath his breath.

With a sharp jerk, he wheeled about on his heel and headed out of the Club. Outside, Jasper was waiting for him across the street with the Berline. As he grabbed the carriage's door handle, he hesitated.

The thought of going home to Chiddingstone House was unappealing. Lily and Grace were beginning to take far more interest in his social life than he liked. If they learned he'd come home early, they'd seize it as a weapon in their newest campaign to find him a wife. He closed his eyes for a brief second. There was only one place to go—Seymour Square. Even though Mary and Davy were gone, it still felt like home. Not to mention it would be peaceful.

In less than fifteen minutes, the carriage pulled up at the steps of one eleven Seymour Square, and he used his key to enter the house. The door closing behind him, he turned to find Carstairs emerging from the back of the house with an expression of concern.

"My lord, I see you got my note."

"Note?"

"Yes, sir, I sent one to Chiddingstone House. I thought your arrival . . ." Carstairs frowned as if realizing Garrick hadn't received any message. "I'm afraid there's a bit of a problem."

"What sort of problem?"

"It's Willie, my lord. He's brought home a stray."

"He's no stray, my lord."

The defiant words made Garrick lean slightly to the right to see Willie emerging from the back hall with a smaller boy at his side. The young footman had appeared at the door of Caring Hearts early one morning more than a year ago asking for nothing more than a meal in exchange for some type of work. Lily had immediately assigned Garrick the task of finding him some.

Willie had been little more than skin and bones then, which made it difficult to find the lad a position, so he'd brought him home to Seymour Square and employed him as a footman. With the help of Mary and Carstairs, the boy had exceeded everyone's expectations, even those of Carstairs, who was an exacting taskmaster. But at the moment, it was obvious the butler was far from happy with the strapping young footman. Rubbing the back of his neck, Garrick heaved a sigh.

"Carstairs. A glass of whiskey. Willie, you and your friend, come with me."

As he entered the salon, there was a vague sense of something being off kilter. It feathered its way through his cluttered brain until he suddenly realized what it was. He'd never really taken notice of Mary's decorating before, but the difference in this room and Ruth's salon was like night and day.

Here, everything was cool and sedate, whereas Ruth's home had a passionate warmth that made him wish he were there now. He suppressed a groan at the way his mind kept returning to Ruth and the way he'd left her. With a grunt, he dropped down into one of the chairs and waved his hand abruptly at his footman.

"Explain."

"This is Samuel, my lord, and I told him that if anyone can help him, you can." Willie straightened to his full height, which was considerable.

"And what makes you think I can help your friend?" He shifted his gaze to the young boy standing in his footman's shadow.

"Because you helped me, my lord."

The unadulterated hero worship in Willie's voice made Garrick wince. If his footman had witnessed the way he'd treated Ruth tonight the man would realize he was bowing at the wrong altar. He was nothing like the man his footman thought he was. His gaze shifted to Samuel.

The lad couldn't have been more than ten or eleven at best. Tall, but scrawny, his cut lip and black eye made him look as though someone had beaten him severely several days ago. His jaw tightened with anger. As he stared into the boy's eyes, the look of hopelessness he saw there enraged him. He despised anyone who thought it acceptable to beat a child. Whoever had battered the boy deserved to be horsewhipped. Carstairs entered the room and handed him his drink. He took a stiff gulp of the whiskey then set it on the table next to his chair. His gaze pinned on the boy, he frowned.

"Well, Samuel. Can you speak for yourself?"

"Aye, me lord." There was a false bravado to the boy's response as he took a step closer to Willie's side.

"Where are your parents?"

"Me mum's dead, and I don't know who me sire is, me lord." The boy met his gaze with a good show of confidence, but he failed to completely disguise his apprehension. "It's just me, and Lucy."

"Lucy?" Garrick's gaze shifted from the boy's face to Willie's sudden look of chagrin.

"Me baby sister, me lord. We ain't got no one else, and I take care of her the best I can."

There was a protective note in the boy's voice, and Garrick immediately recognized a part of himself in the boy's defiance in the face of what had to be immeasurable odds. Life on the streets was difficult enough for a boy, but for girls it was almost always a death sentence. An image of his uncle testing Lily's bedroom door sent ice through his veins.

"Where is she now?" he bit out in a tight voice. At his question, Carstairs, who was observing the small drama from a short distance away, coughed softly.

"She's with Cook, my lord."

Garrick shot the butler a sharp glance then closed his eyes in an attempt to clear his cloudy head. Damnation, the boy had a sister. Fingers pressed into his temple, he reached for his whiskey and tossed down the rest of the liquor. In a silent command for more, he extended his glass to Carstairs and didn't look at the man as the butler took the crystal from him. Christ Jesus, this was turning out to be a hell of a night. He looked at Samuel again and frowned.

"Who beat you?" Garrick's question sent a shudder through the child as he looked up at Willie. The footman nodded with encouragement.

"It's all right, Samuel. His lordship's going to help. You can trust him."

The confidence in his footman's voice made Garrick wince. *Trust.* Something Ruth could enlighten the young man about when it came to him. His head suddenly began to throb as the echoes of Ruth's humiliation reverberated through his head. He frowned as he waited for Samuel to answer.

"His name is Billings, me lord. He said he'd give me food and a place to sleep if I worked for him."

"What kind of work?"

"He told me he needed someone who could run fast and deliver messages."

"And why did he beat you?"

"Because the last bloke I delivered a message to refused to pay. Said I was too late. That the message didn't do him any good if it was late."

Garrick clenched his jaw. His uncle had rarely laid a hand on him, but Beresford's treatment of him and his siblings had been as harmful as what Samuel had suffered at the hands of this Billings. Abuse was abuse. It was what drove him to help those who couldn't help themselves.

As he studied Samuel, he remembered what it was like to feel alone in the world with no one to turn to. He swallowed hard at the memory. Despite the difference in their stations in life, Samuel could have been him. Well, he'd be damned if he was going to let this bastard Billings touch the lad again. He'd been thinking of finding a boy to help Jasper in the stables for a number of weeks, but hadn't done anything about it. Now he wouldn't have to look elsewhere. He steadily met the boy's wary gaze.

"Do you like horses, Samuel?"

"Don't know much about 'em, me lord." The boy paused for a moment, his face lightened slightly. "But I suppose I do, like 'em that is."

"Would you like to learn how to care for them? My driver could use some help in my stables if you're willing to work hard." Garrick spoke quietly, watching as Samuel's face brightened with hope then grew suspicious again. The boy looked up at Willie, who nodded his head. Looking back at Garrick, the child straightened to his full height.

"Yes, please, me lord. I'm a hard worker, too." Samuel eyed him with a mixture of optimism and fear. "And Lucy? We're a bundle, me lord. I don't go nowhere without 'er."

"For the time being the two of you will stay here until I can make other arrangements." The boy opened his mouth as if to protest and Garrick waved his hand at him. "I have no intention of separating the two of you, but she'll need someone to look after her."

"I look after Lucy, me lord. She needs me, an' I don't like leaving 'er with strangers." Samuel's stubborn stance said his sister's fate was nonnegotiable, and Garrick nodded his agreement.

"All right, but we'll discuss it tomorrow. For now, you look like you could use a bath and some supper." The words immediately threw his thoughts back to Ruth and everything that had followed after she'd emerged from her bath.

"Thank ye, me lord," Samuel said. "I'll work 'ard. I promise."

"I imagine your sister needs a bath and supper as well. See to it, Willie," he grunted.

"Thank you, my lord. I knew you'd be able to help."

Willie shot him another one of those heroic looks that only served to make Garrick grimace with self-disgust. As the footman led Samuel out of the room, Carstairs returned with another glass of whiskey. He noted the butler had filled the glass almost to the brim, and he arched an eyebrow at the man before taking a drink. His elbows resting on the arms of the chair, he leaned back and closed his eyes with a weary sigh.

"Is there anything else I need to be made aware of, Carstairs?"

"No, my lord. I believe that is the last of the excitement for the evening." A touch of relief accompanied the butler's response. "Do you require anything else this evening?"

"Nothing other than a little peace and quiet."

"Very good, my lord."

The butler's soft tread and the salon door closing told Garrick he was alone once more. He opened his eyes to stare at the full glass of whiskey. Although his head was a bit fuzzy, the amount of liquor he'd consumed had done little to wipe away the remnants of the evening's disastrous events.

Ruth. He should be happy that she'd thrown him out. He'd caressed her like a lover then rejected her in a humiliating manner. How was he supposed to explain himself without sharing his secret? The internal question lanced through him like a sharp, poisonous spear. *Secret.* Whatever secret he thought he had, there was a very strong chance his uncle had divulged it.

A vicious hatred welled up inside him as he took another drink of his whiskey. He'd destroy the man. Beresford would have nothing left when he got done with the bastard. Deep down, he'd always known his uncle would one day break their contract. But he'd prepared for that. His solicitor had been keeping track of his uncle's financial matters over the years.

Every time Beresford had invested his finances, Garrick had reviewed the venture. If it was a sound investment, he'd bought a higher stake in the business for the sole purpose of destroying Beresford if the time ever came. Wycombe's persistence in attempting to learn more about his personal affairs had been more of an inconvenience than a threat. But his appearance at the Club with Tremaine in tow had changed all that, particularly with Tremaine's reference to Beresford.

Just the way the bastard had smiled at him when he'd mentioned his uncle had been enough to make Garrick believe the worst. It was possible his uncle hadn't revealed the specifics of his secret, but whatever Tremaine knew or had deduced, the son of a bitch would use it against him. He released a groan and leaned forward in his chair with his head bowed.

Bloody hell, what was he going to do? He didn't want Ruth to look at him with the same amusement Bertha had that night so long ago. He snorted with disgust. Look at him? Ruth wasn't going to have a thing to do with him after tonight. The knowledge should have made him happy, but it didn't.

Whenever he was with her, it felt right. There was something about her that made him trust her. *But you don't trust her enough to tell her your secret, do you?* He growled with anger. Tonight should never have happened. Thank God he'd come to his senses before things had gotten out of hand. He tossed down the last of the drink and stared at his empty glass. When the hell was this stuff going to numb his senses to the fact that he'd hurt her?

He didn't like the answer that came back. The idea that nothing could alleviate his guilt only made thinking about it that much worse. All of this could have been avoided if he'd just stayed away from the woman from the start. But he hadn't. The compulsion to pursue her was something he didn't understand, but he knew the need wasn't going to go away.

God help him, but he wanted to see her again. Wanted the opportunity to try and explain why he'd touched her and then rejected her. Even if he could form a rational explanation for her to believe, he wasn't very confident she'd even give him the chance to explain himself. It didn't matter. He had to try, if only to make sure she understood how desirable she was.

That was paramount. He wanted to make sure she knew his

rejection had been because of his own inadequacies. Not hers. He was the one with the flaws. Damaged goods. His uncle and Bertha had made him understand that so many years ago. Christ Jesus, his head ached. Closing his eyes, he rubbed his fingers against one temple. He needed to go to bed, but he was feeling too damned drunk to bother getting up out of his chair. It was much easier to simply stay where he was. The liquor was doing exactly what he'd intended all along. It tugged him downward into the darkness where he could forget all the pain. His glass slipped from his fingers to fall to the floor as he slid deeper into the alcohol-induced shadows. The tinkling sound of crystal shattering against wood was a distant sound, and he vaguely wondered where it was coming from.

She had a beautiful laugh. Everything about Bertha was beautiful. From the first minute he'd seen her, he'd known he was in love with her. It was impossible not to take pleasure in watching her. Every movement she made was poetry in motion. A ballerina, it was natural for her to be graceful, but Bertha was ethereal in her movements.

It was as if the angels had given her wings when she'd danced for his uncle's houseguests. For the first time in more than two years, he'd not minded his uncle entertaining friends. If not for Beresford, he'd never have met Bertha. For the past three days, he'd courted her—wooed her. Then this morning she'd invited him to her room after everyone had retired for the evening.

The day had dragged on interminably, but the evening even more so. During supper, his uncle had paid a great deal of attention to Bertha. The fact that she'd laughed at Beresford's jokes had made him want to pull her away from his uncle. He didn't want her talking to that bastard. She was meant for him.

Instead, he'd simply sat back and watched, keeping a tight leash on his jealous anger. He was the one she intended to welcome into his bed, not that son of a bitch. It was best to remain silent. If his uncle were to learn how he felt about Bertha, the man would torment him with the knowledge—possibly even turn Bertha against him.

The bastard enjoyed cruel jokes like that. He looked out on the lawn of Chiddingstone Manor. The pale moonlight was translucent as it illuminated the flower garden. The entire scene was reminiscent of Bertha's fragile beauty. The bluish black of the night sky was the same color as her hair, and the moonlight resembled her beautiful ivory skin.

The mantel clock chimed the hour, and he quickly left his room to move silently through the manor's hallway to Bertha's room. In front of her door, he hesitated. What if he didn't please her? He knew nothing of women other than the crude comments of his uncle and his friends. The memory of Bertha's inviting smile made him rap softly on the door.

She wouldn't mind. She cared about him and wouldn't have asked him to come to her otherwise. The door opened to reveal her in a sheer nightgown, and the air left his lungs at the sight of her. She quickly pulled him through the open doorway, and an instant later, she was in his arms.

Her lips tasted of wine, and he grew rigid as her hand caressed his erection. The minute she pulled back from him a shudder wracked his body. A mysterious smile curving her mouth upward, she tilted her head in a provocative manner.

"Are you all right, my darling?"

The bewitching sound of her voice tugged at his cock until he was ready to spill his seed. He nodded as he fought not to explode and embarrass himself. He knew she could have had any man she wanted this weekend, but she'd chosen him.

"I'm fine, sweetheart. I just can't believe I'm here with you. That you're mine."

"Why wouldn't I be," she whispered as she stepped away from him and moved toward the bed.

With a seductive sureness that made his mouth water with need, she slipped her gown off her shoulders. In the candlelight, she looked like a beautiful angel condescending to grant him access to her body. She stepped backward and sat down on the bed, her hand capturing his to pull him forward. He went willingly and cupped her breast. It was plump and firm in his hand.

"You're the most beautiful woman I've ever seen."

"Am I?" She smiled with pleasure at the compliment. "Do you want me, darling?"

Her question was a heated invitation that made his blood run hot. Unable to speak, he simply nodded his head and quickly started to undress. His eyes didn't leave her sylphlike form as he disrobed.

In seconds, he stood naked in front of her. She eyed him with calculation. The thought that she might find him lacking vanished from his head the minute she smiled up at him. Bertha stretched out her hand to drag her fingers down his chest toward where his erection was jutting outward. He trembled as her thumb brushed over him, and she laughed lightly.

"You like that don't you, dear boy." She laughed again when he nodded. "Am I your first woman?"

"Yes," he choked out.

"Then what are you waiting for? Isn't it time you gave me a little poke?" Clearly amused, Bertha leaned forward to blow on his cock, then jerked back from him. "Good lord."

"What?" he exclaimed at the repugnance in her voice.

"You only have one ballock."

Revulsion and shock filled her voice. The sound immediately made him go still. He'd never dreamed she might find his birth defect repugnant. Aside from his parents, only his old nursemaid had known of his physical defect, and she'd died more than a year ago.

His condition had never bothered him, although he'd instinctively kept the knowledge to himself. Somehow he'd always known it might be a source of entertainment for his uncle. A chill scraped down his spine as he studied her expression of disgust.

His mouth dry with fear, it was suddenly impossible to swallow. Didn't she care enough about him to accept him in spite of an imperfect body? His heart thudding violently against his chest, he told himself it would be all right. She loved him. Didn't she? A sickening sensation twisted his gut. Desperate to reassure her, he reached out to her only to have her recoil from him.

"You can't possibly think I'd let you fuck me now," she said with a sneer. "Not that you were going to get the chance to anyway."

Her words slammed into him as if someone had hit him with a pile of bricks. Why had she asked him to come to her tonight if she hadn't meant to give herself to him? Alarm bells went off in his head as he met her gaze. The malicious amusement curling her lips upward coated every bare inch of him with a blast of ice.

"But you . . . I . . ."

"Beresford," she shouted. "You were right. The boy actually believed I'd part my legs for him."

The moment she cried out, Bertha's bedroom door flew open. Panic lashed through him as he whirled around. His uncle stood swaying in the doorway, obviously intoxicated from a night of drinking and card playing. Garrick suddenly understood what a hunted animal felt like as his uncle staggered into the room and all he could do was stand frozen in front of the man.

"Didn't I tell you, Bertha?" His uncle sneered with a mocking laugh. "The boy's infatuated with you. I knew he'd fall for that act of yours."

"Well, I thought about making him a man, but you don't have enough money for me to do that. The boy's a freak. He only has one ballock." Bertha leaned forward to jiggle the only ballock he possessed with her fingers, and Garrick jerked back from her insolent touch. "What?" Beresford laughed uproariously. "Let me see, boy."

His uncle stumbled forward to grip his shoulder, and Garrick shoved the man's hand aside. Quickly grabbing his trousers from the floor, he struggled to get dressed. As he tried to force one leg into the pants, he collapsed in a heap, his legs twisted up in the clothing.

Bertha was laughing loudly now, the sound not the delicate one he remembered. Now it rang out brash and shrill in his ears. Physically ill from the sound of their laughter, he managed to get his trousers on then staggered to his feet.

"That's it boy, hide the fact that you're only half a man. Women want a real man in their bed, not a freak of nature," Beresford said cruelly. "Remember that the next time a woman asks you to her room."

"Half a man," Bertha squealed with laughter. He flinched at the sound. "It's surprising he could get that little prick of his to stand up so well."

Bile rose in Garrick's throat at her words, and he fought desperately not to throw up. He scooped up the rest of his clothing from the floor then dashed out of the room with their laughter following him down the hall.

The sound didn't leave him no matter how much distance he put between them and himself. It was like a swarm of bees engulfing him, stinging him until his body ached from the pain of it. Never again. He would never expose himself like that to any woman again. Not ever. He stumbled into his room and lurched toward the washstand, where he threw up.

Fingers digging into the wooden frame of the furniture, he fought to remain standing. What would his uncle do? The bastard would take pleasure in humiliating him again and again. That's what the son of a bitch would do. And he'd do it in front of others or at the very least threaten Garrick with the possibility. The knowledge renewed his vomiting.

When he was done, he pressed his back to the wall in an effort to remain on his feet. He was trembling so badly it was difficult to keep standing. He gave up the battle and curled up in a ball on the floor. He'd not cried since he'd found his father dead in the study and wouldn't cry now. He buried his head in his knees, fighting to control the shudders wracking his body. Never again. Never again. Never again.

The sound of someone muttering a desperate prayer in his ears jerked Garrick awake. As he shot upright, he glanced around the room half expecting to see his younger self curled up on the floor against the wall. Christ Jesus. He'd not remembered that night with Bertha so vividly for years.

Desperately, he shoved the past into the recesses of his mind, but it refused to stay there as the liquor he'd consumed stripped him of his ability to control his thoughts coherently. Instead, the memories rose up to taunt him with the same humiliating intensity he'd experienced so long ago. With a growl of fury, he stumbled to his feet and staggered toward the door.

He'd learned his lesson. One time was more than enough when it came to baring himself to a woman. Ruth's image fluttered into his head. Not even for her could he expose himself. He'd explain himself to her then walk out of her life forever. Once again, derisive laughter filled his head. Only this time the sound wasn't from the past. It was a mocking shout of amusement at the idea that he could part with Ruth so easily.

She persisted in her refusal to see him. What did he expect? That she'd be eager to see him after the way he'd humiliated her? And it had been nothing short of that. He'd had plenty of time over the last two weeks to think about those short moments after he'd pushed himself away from her. His words had haunted him since then.

His attempt to make her understand his reason for not making love to her could only be described as bumbling at best. The inept way he'd tried to explain his lack of sexual experience in the face of her seductive skills had only made things worse. In his efforts to account for his actions, he'd used words he was certain she'd misunderstood.

While he knew his inexperience in the bedroom wasn't the primary reason for rejecting her touch, it had been the best excuse he could come up with at the time. He was certain she'd interpreted his explanation as something completely different than his intent. There was no doubt in his mind that her sensitivity about her own age and the difference between them in years had been the cause she'd give his rejection. His words had been ill chosen. He clenched his jaw as he stared out the carriage window.

For the past two weeks, he'd done everything he could to see her. The flowers he'd sent every day with his note of apology were always returned. He'd known better than to insult her with jewelry, but desperation had taken hold of him three days ago. In hopes of at least securing the opportunity to explain himself, he'd commissioned white tulip earrings to match the brooch he'd given her.

They'd been promptly returned to the Crown Jeweler, who had immediately forwarded the earrings to him, along with the bill. All of it had made him even more disheartened. It was a state that made him irritable as hell, but had not stopped him from seeking her forgiveness.

He'd convinced himself that he was simply attempting to right a wrong, but he knew there was something much more troubling at the heart of his efforts. He'd deliberately refrained from examining the reasons for his crusade and focused all his attention on finding a way to reach out to her. Now he'd resorted to subterfuge. He was only grateful that Dolores had taken pity on him.

The carriage rocked to a halt in the mews behind Ruth's town house. The darkness of the narrow alley was broken by lanterns hanging outside the stables. He exited the coach and instructed Jasper that he'd find a hansom cab to bring him home. Without waiting for the driver's acknowledgment, he walked through the gate leading into Ruth's garden.

There was less light here, and he paused for a moment to allow his eyes to adjust. In front of him, he saw the light shining from the kitchen door Dolores had left open for him. His stride quick, he closed the distance between him and the house. When he stepped through the open doorway, Dolores jumped as he cleared his throat.

"Lord love me." Ruth's companion pressed her hand to her large bosom and shook her head at the sight of him. "You gave me a fright, my lord."

"My apologies."

"Well, come in, come in." She waved him into the warm room and closed the back door behind him before she took his overcoat from him.

"Thank you for taking pity on me, Dolores."

"I probably shouldn't, especially when her ladyship seems so distraught by whatever happened between the two of you."

"I hurt her, and I didn't mean to. I just need a chance to explain. Something I wouldn't be able to do if you'd not agreed to help me."

"Well, you *have* been persistent." The maid eyed him carefully. "And you're not like the other gents. You actually seem to care about her, which is the only reason I agreed to help you."

"I do care about her, Dolores. It's why I need to see her. I said something that hurt her, and I need to apologize."

"I only hope her ladyship doesn't throw me out for letting you in the house."

"You've been with her a long time, Dolores. I doubt she can do without you," he said with a smile. "But if the worst happens, come to me. I'll find you a position."

"I'm not too worried." The maid snorted softly with amused disdain and pointed toward a darkened doorway. "I think you'll charm your way back into her ladyship's good graces. You'd best hurry. I think she was planning on going out this evening."

With a quick nod, he headed up the back stairs and down the hall toward Ruth's bedroom. As he stopped in front of her door, panic swelled over him. What the hell was he going to say? He didn't have the foggiest notion as to how to plead his case with her. Would a man more intimate with women have any difficulty in coming up with a plan? The answer only emphasized his own lack of experience.

He'd been certain he could convince Ruth of his sincerity, but suddenly he wasn't sure of anything where she was concerned. The risk he was taking by exposing himself to her was enough to make him physically ill. She could easily view it as an amusing tale to share with her friends—Baron Stratfield's virginal status. Bile rose in his throat at the thought.

Christ Jesus, maybe he should just leave. Even if he managed to earn her forgiveness, in all likelihood he was only complicating matters between them. As he turned away from the door, an image of Ruth settled firmly in his head, followed by the memory of the pained humiliation in her voice. He clenched his jaw and wheeled about on his heel to knock on the door.

"Come in."

The closed door muffled Ruth's voice and opened quietly beneath his touch. The room seemed empty at first, until he saw her partially hidden behind the door of her wardrobe. He snapped the door closed then quietly turned the key in the lock and dropped it into his pocket. He didn't need her calling for Simmons. Hesitation swept through him again. *Now what?*

He didn't have to wait for an answer as she stepped away from the wardrobe. The sight of her made him suck in his breath. She wore a robe similar to the one she'd had on the other night, but to his disappointment the wrapper hid her lovely curves from him. For a moment she stared at him as if he were a ghost. She blinked, and her stunned expression disappeared as cold anger darkened her beautiful face.

"Get *out* of my house," she enunciated with a quiet hiss of fury.

"I realize you find me despicable, Ruth. But—"

"To find you despicable implies I bother to think of you at all, my lord." The icy contempt in her voice made him flinch before he narrowed his gaze at her.

"I have an explanation if you will just hear me out."

"I think you've said quite enough already, my lord. The thought of you baring your soul to me any further is not a welcome one."

Bare his soul to her. That was a good description of what he was trying to do. He bit down on the inside of his cheek as he walked toward her. Although she didn't move, there was an air about her that said she would take the first opportunity to flee. Her features revealed nothing as he closed the distance between them to mere inches, but he saw her tremble.

"I don't like hurting my friends, Ruth, but when I do I make amends."

"I am *quite* selective in my choice of friends, my lord." She displayed no emotion, but he heard the bitterness threading its way through her voice. "*You* are not one of them."

"Damn it, Ruth. If you'd just—"

"Therein lies the problem, my lord." The sudden smile curving her lips was cold and patronizing. "I have no interest in whatever it is you have to say. I simply want you to *leave*."

Despite his frustration with her stubborn refusal to show even a small amount of leniency, the scent of her overwhelmed his senses. Mere inches separated them, and she smelled of exotic flowers, enticing and mysterious. An unexpected tension gripped his body. It tightened every one of his muscles until he ached from the sheer intensity of the sensation as he found himself leaning into her.

Their gazes locked, and he swallowed hard at the sudden flash of emotion in her violet eyes. Sweet Jesus, what if she laughed at him—found him a pitiful excuse for a man? Desperately, he struggled with the fear continuing to rise inside him. The last time he'd felt this way had been the night Bertha and his uncle had humiliated him. He forced back the bile rising in his throat and shook his head.

"I'm not going anywhere until I've said my piece."

"Well, you can say it to Simmons as he escorts you to the front door," she snapped as she tried to push past him.

"No," he growled as he blocked her attempt, and her eyes widened in surprise. Without thinking, he grabbed her arms and jerked her toward him. "You might not be interested in what I have to say, but by God, you're going to listen. The other night, I came closer to making love to you than I have any other woman. Do you want to know what stopped me?"

"I *know* what stopped you," she said bitterly. "And I certainly don't wish to be educated on the subject a second time."

"Christ Jesus," he muttered as he breathed in. Her fragrance failed to subdue the fear churning in his gut. He was wavering between desire and panic, and he didn't know which was worse at the moment. "Do you have any idea how difficult it was—*is*—for me to keep my hands off of you?"

"Your passionate plea is worthy of the stage, my lord. Unfortunately for you, I've no interest in the performance."

With a vicious twist of her body, she broke free of his hold. The instant she was free, she took two quick steps until her back pressed into the mahogany wardrobe behind her. Despite her defiant stance, he saw a hint of fear in her eyes. He winced. Bloody hell, he didn't want her to be afraid of him. At no other time in his life could he remember ever feeling so helpless. Not even that night in his bedroom with Bertha and his uncle laughing at him had he felt this tormented.

A mix of terror and willpower kept him from closing the space between them. He'd come here to explain, not to complicate the situation by touching her. But damn if those beautiful eyes, wide with turbulent emotion, didn't make it hard not to do so. He took a deep breath and met her gaze with quiet determination.

"The other night—" His gut twisted painfully, and he almost bent over to retch. He had never imagined it would be this difficult to tell her even a small portion of the truth. He swallowed hard and turned away from her. "I told you I couldn't . . . that I couldn't make love to you because of the years of experience between us."

The sharp breath she sucked in at his statement emphasized how much he'd hurt her. Guilt swept over him as he rubbed the back of his neck. He'd hurt her worse than he realized. He knew Marston's leaving her for a younger woman had been devastating enough, and he'd only compounded that humiliation.

"You do *not* need to remind me of the age difference between us." Her voice had all the warmth of winter, and he spun around to face her.

"*Fuck*. Your age had nothing to do with it," he snarled. "I couldn't make love to you because I've never been with a woman before."

"*You bastard,*" she gasped as outrage darkened her face. "You must *truly* think me an old fool."

Stunned, he stared at her in disbelief. She didn't believe him. The fear rolled back over him again. He'd spilled his guts and for what? What could make her think he'd never made love to a woman before? He clenched his jaw at the look of contempt on her face. This was not going like he'd expected. What the hell had he *thought* was going to happen?

"It *is* the truth," he growled as he struggled with the fact that she didn't believe him.

"Is it? Then tell me why Lady Kent says you were the best lover she's ever had? Then there's Mrs. Campton who said your touch set her on fire," she scoffed with fury. "Not to mention the more than a dozen other women I've heard sigh over your sexual prowess. And what of the mistress you've kept for the last two years?"

He shook his head with incredulity at her words. As he slowly processed her fiery allegations, he remembered a few brief moments with Lady Kent in the Duke of Salisbury's garden a few years ago. The kisses they'd exchanged had been quite pleasurable, and it had been one of the more difficult situations to extract himself from. The same for Mrs. Campton.

What was it Ruth had said? *Sexual prowess.* The women of the Set considered him a skilled lover even though he'd never bedded any of them. They'd lied to protect their own reputations, and in return they'd helped craft the reputation he'd worked for. They'd done their work too well. The realization wound its way through him with a sluggish speed that left him speechless.

"You insulted me once before, my lord. Do not try to insult me again." Ruth neatly sidestepped him and headed toward the door.

"I am not in the habit of lying," he growled as he grabbed her arm and tugged her backward into his chest.

One arm wrapped around her waist, he subdued her struggles and prevented her from breaking free of his grasp. The sensual fragrance she wore flooded his senses and sent lust slamming into him.

Damnation, how was it he couldn't get near her without feeling this intense need to hold her and never let her go? This need to kiss every inch of her until she called out his name. But worst of all was the craving to bury himself inside her.

Fear lanced through him at the images filling his head. But this time his terror was born of the desire crashing through him. He closed his eyes against the delicious view her loosely tied robe offered him as he looked over her shoulder and saw the full curve of her breast. She was the most beautiful creature he'd ever seen. Even despite his lack of experience, he knew what to look for in a woman.

His friends had discussed the finer points of a woman's figure many times. Once or twice they'd even dragged him to a brothel despite his best efforts to extract himself from the visit. Although he'd managed to keep his secret under the pretense of being drunk, he'd received enough of an education so as to appreciate the lush curves of Ruth's body. She was beautiful.

"Please let me go." Her voice was a strained plea that made him flinch.

With a quick movement, he turned her to face him, his hands still holding her in place. Anger glittered in her eyes, but he could see the hurt and confusion reflected there as well. He drew in a deep breath and cleared his throat. He wanted her to believe him, but how could he make her understand without stripping himself bare—without giving in to the hunger tugging at him with vicious glee?

"I'm not lying to you Ruth. And telling you that I . . . my . . . about my lack of experience is damned difficult." He released his hold on her. "You're the first person I've ever shared this with. My family doesn't even know. And the *only* reason I'm telling you is because I know you thought I rejected you because of your age."

Her lovely mouth parted as if she was about to speak, and he pressed his fingertips against her lips. God, but her mouth was soft against the pads of his fingers. His insides knotted up with that familiar sensation she always aroused in him, and he clamped down on the desire building inside him.

"You're the most desirable woman I've ever met. Every time I'm near you, I have to fight to keep from touching you. God help me, but I can't get the image of you, emerging from your bathroom with water still clinging to every part of you, out of my head. You looked like a young Aphrodite, with your hair tumbling down onto your beautiful breasts."

He could hear how hoarse his voice had become as he met her gaze. The fact that she was dressed almost exactly as she'd been the other night was not helping matters. His cock had gone rigid in his trousers, and his tongue grew thick in his mouth as he remembered how badly he'd wanted her at that moment, almost as badly as he did now.

"The way your nipples became taut peaks the moment you realized I was looking at you made me come close to coming right then and there. Can you blame me for . . . I couldn't help taking you in my mouth when the opportunity presented itself. And Christ Jesus, I didn't know . . . never thought that a woman might think to shave . . ."

Bloody hell. He was stammering—acting just like he had all those years ago with Bertha. An inept schoolboy. He flinched at the memory and jerked away from her. This had been a mistake. A blunder of the worst proportions. Whether she believed him or not wasn't the real danger. It was whether she'd keep his secret.

Would she tell anyone? Why wouldn't she? The minute someone else knew about his lack of experience in the bedroom it would become fodder for the gossip mill. Christ Almighty, when Wycombe got wind of it, the man would be overjoyed. The earl had already come close to openly labeling him a sodomite; now the bastard would have even more ammunition.

Then there was his uncle. He was certain Beresford had already said way too much to Tremaine. It wouldn't be a short leap from his lack of experience in the bedroom to the fact that he was a freak of nature. The thought of the humiliation to come increased the gut-wrenching sensation that was threatening to make him violently ill.

"Christ Jesus, I'm a fool," he muttered fiercely. "I should have left well enough alone."

He turned away to leave but stopped as her hand caught his arm. The strange expression on her face made him feel even worse. The last thing he wanted or needed was her pity.

"Are you really telling me the truth?" she asked quietly. He hesitated, then gave her a short, sharp nod.

"Yes," he said between clenched teeth.

"Not even your mistress?"

"Mary needed protection from the man who'd ruined her," he ground out. "Having the world think I had a mistress helped keep my secret safe."

"But you parted with her." Suspicion clouded Ruth's face as she studied him carefully. It was evident she was struggling to believe him.

"She fell in love with the tutor I employed for her," he said with a pained grimace. "They were married several weeks ago and left for America."

"I see," she murmured with a sympathetic expression that made his jaw lock with tension. Her brow furrowed by doubt, she narrowed her eyes at him. "But I don't understand why you—"

"The why isn't important," he said harshly. "All that matters is that you believe me when I say that your age had *nothing* to do with my refusal to make love to you. You do yourself an injustice by thinking you're no longer young enough for a man to desire you."

The flush that crested in her cheeks emphasized the point he was trying to impress upon her. She looked half the age of her counterparts among the Set. Her face was smooth and youthful, and knowing a mere slip of fabric was all that hid her firm, supple body was enough to undo him. The thought of sliding into her made his cock stretch until he ached. What would it feel like to bury himself inside her? His hand was the only thing he'd ever known.

Christ, he'd probably spill his seed before he could even satisfy her. How *did* one satisfy a woman? He clenched his fists at the realization that no matter how much he wanted to know the answer to that question, it would go unanswered. The revelation he'd shared with her was all he dared to disclose about himself.

Coherent thought evaporated an instant later as she closed the distance between them. He breathed in her exotic fragrance, and suddenly, his entire body was raging with need. He stiffened as her hand touched his arm. Despite the light touch, the heat of her penetrated first his coat sleeve and then his shirt to warm his skin. He was going mad. Whenever the woman got close to him, he couldn't think straight.

"It must be difficult . . . the suspicions . . . the rumors people like Wycombe spread. Even if you—"

He didn't give her a chance to finish and tugged her toward him to capture her mouth in a hard kiss. The notion that she might be having second thoughts about his sexuality rammed through him like a wild boar. He probed her mouth with all the skill he possessed. A dark hunger ate away at him, pushing him to remove even the smallest doubt in her mind—to prove to her once and for all that Wycombe was wrong about him.

His hands slid beneath the thin robe to caress her breasts. They were warm and heavy in his palms. The moment his thumb brushed over a stiff nipple, she moaned softly and her tongue danced with his in an erotic fashion that heated his blood that much more. He wanted to suckle her again—wanted to hear her whimper with need like she had the other night. The thought pierced the haze of desire flooding his senses, and a shudder ran through him. He couldn't repeat his mistake with her.

Making love to her would openly expose him to more humiliation, and he wasn't willing to take that step, not even with her. Gently, he pulled her arms from around his neck and pushed her away from him. The sleepy, sultry look on her face slowly disappeared as she studied him in silence. He clenched his jaw against the banked fires threatening to take hold of him again.

"I am not a sodomite," he said stiffly as he turned away from her.

Damnation, the moment he'd even thought her about to suggest the possibility, he'd lost control in a way that alarmed him. He grimaced. When had he ever been in command of his senses where she was concerned? At least she'd shown him how the Marlborough Set would react to the truth. Bloody hell, if his inexperience became common knowledge . . . he ran his fingers through his hair as panic lashed through him. The silence hung between them like a heavy blanket. The heat of her hand pressed into his back and made him stiffen.

"I believe you, Garrick. Your inexperience. All of it. I believe you."

The quiet declaration released the tight vise wrapped around his chest and he sighed with relief. He hadn't realized how important it had been to him that he convince her of the truth. He cleared his throat as he turned toward her.

"I didn't mean to hurt you. If I were . . . if it . . . your age would *never* be a reason for me to reject you." His jaw tight with tension, he met her steady look for a brief moment before shifting his gaze away from her.

"I understand that now. So where do we go from here?" Her quiet question surprised him.

"Perhaps we could continue as before." He frowned. The one thing that had driven him to make amends had been their friendship. But if she suddenly decided she wanted more . . . he wasn't prepared for that.

"Is that what you really want?"

"What do you mean?" He narrowed his gaze at her.

"Are you sure friendship is the only reason you told me the truth? I'm a courtesan, Garrick. Although I do much more than fulfill a man's sexual needs, my skills in the bedroom *are* considered excellent."

"*Instruction?*" He choked out the word. Sweet Jesus, the woman was offering to tutor him in the art of lovemaking. How in the hell was he supposed to respond to that?

"If not that, then perhaps someone to confide in?" she said in a soothing voice. "There *must* be a reason why you've never been with a woman. I am a good listener, when I wish to be."

"That topic isn't up for discussion," he said through clenched teeth, not even smiling at her ironic comment about listening.

"As you wish."

The heat of her brushed against him as she walked past to sit down at her dressing table. Stunned by her ready acquiescence, he stared at her as she calmly reached for a jar of cream and proceeded to apply the emollient to her hands. Awkward. It was a sensation he'd never liked, and he was feeling extremely awkward right now. He clasped his hands behind his back then drew in a deep breath in an attempt to calm himself.

"You're going out this evening?" The question only reflected how ill at ease he was. She stopped rubbing her hands and met his gaze in the dressing table mirror.

"I was, but I've changed my mind," she said quietly.

"I see." A rush of pleasure surged through him. She hadn't said so, but he was certain he was the reason she'd changed her plans.

"And you? Do you have plans?" In a casual gesture, she shrugged one shoulder out of her robe to rub cream on her skin. He inhaled sharply as he saw the lush curve of her beautiful breast reflected in the mirror.

"No . . . I . . . I wasn't sure . . ." He swallowed hard as she finished rubbing cream on her shoulder and pulled her robe back up. His breathing eased for a mere fraction of an instant before she repeated the exercise with her other shoulder. A knot developed in his throat, making him cough.

"Are you all right, Garrick?"

She turned quickly to face him, her robe discreetly closed. The concerned look on her face would have eased his discomfort if he hadn't seen the flash of something far more dangerous in her eyes.

"I'm . . . fine."

With a shake of his head, he cleared his throat again. She tilted her head in contemplation. In the quiet glow of the gaslight, the movement emphasized the sweet curve of her shoulder and throat. A sense of impending doom swept over him, but he ignored it, unable to take his eyes off of her.

"Do you trust me, Garrick?" The softly spoken question took him by surprise, and he frowned.

"I would not have confided in you otherwise."

"There's nothing shameful about your innocence. In fact, I find it quite . . . arousing."

She turned to pull a long scarf from one of the dressing table's drawers. When she stood up to face him again, the gentle determination reflected on her face made him tense. In the next instant, the air in his lungs was dragged out of him in one large *whoosh* as he watched her slowly untie her robe. Bloody hell, why wasn't he racing toward the door?

"Desire is a pleasurable thing, Garrick."

Her voice was hypnotic, and he couldn't take his eyes off her as she trailed one hand across her throat and then downward. The languid movement parted her wrapper as she leisurely brushed her fingertips along the side of her breast. It was an erotic movement that sent heat blasting through him until his palms were damp.

"Let me show you what it's like to feel that pleasure." The thin robe hiding her from him slid to the floor with a whisper, and his mouth went dry at the sight. "Let me show you how wonderful it can be between us."

Why was he still standing here? He should have been at the door by now. He tried to move but couldn't. If he didn't do something fast there was no hope for him. His feet remained rooted to the floor as he watched her undo her hair so it fell down over her shoulders. God, she was beautiful. Her eyes closed, the scarf she still held in her hand drifted across the tips of her breast in a way that seemed natural, yet he knew it was deliberate.

"Do you like looking at me, Garrick?" The throaty whisper scraped across his senses.

"Yes," he rasped.

The scarf fluttered against her skin like a butterfly touching first one delicate curve and then another. Her hands cupped her breasts, and in a move that made it impossible for him to breathe, she circled her fingers around her rigid nipples. With great difficulty, he suppressed the raging need to stride forward and take her into his arms. Instead he forced himself to take a step back from her. It did little to assuage the hunger assaulting his rigid cock. Almost as if she could sense his need, her eyes flickered open, and she stretched out her hand to offer him the scarf.

"Tie me to the bed." It was a soft command that made him stare at her in astonishment. A sensual, yet gentle, smile curved her mouth. "I want *you* to be in control of your pleasure."

His brain struggled to process her words. This was a seduction of the highest order. She was giving him complete control. Deep inside his head a shout of alarm tried to keep him from moving forward. It failed. She was giving him the ability to make love to her on his terms.

With a guttural sound, he closed the distance between them and tugged her into his arms. She came willingly, her hands sliding up over his chest to cup the back of his head as her lips parted beneath his. A white-hot need thundered through him, and he swept her off her feet to carry her toward the bed. Despite the urgency tugging at his erection, he carefully laid her down, shrugged out of his coat, and knelt beside her. Hesitation hammered at him in a staccato rhythm. Christ Jesus, he must be insane to think this would work. He swallowed hard. She reached up to stroke his face in a tender gesture as their eyes met.

"I trust you, Garrick. I wouldn't have offered you complete control if I didn't."

Unable to speak, he nodded his head and took the scarf from her hands. He gently bound her wrists together then pulled them over her head to tie her to one of the brass spindles of the headboard. In the back of his mind he wondered how many other men had tied her like this. Jealousy streaked through him at the thought, but he pushed it away as he stared down at her. She was a feast for his eyes, every rosy flushed inch of her.

"Touch me." Her whisper was more plea than demand, and he

hesitated. Her eyelids were heavy with desire as she stared up at him. "I want you to touch me."

He nodded before he reached out to press his palm against her softly rounded stomach. The warm heat of her spread its way into him. He brushed his hand across her silky smooth skin to find the curve at her side. She was soft, pliant against his touch.

"You're beautiful," he rasped. A soft blush crested over her cheeks as she smiled up at him.

"Thank you. A woman never grows tired of hearing that." She bent her leg until her knee was almost touching his mouth. "We like to be kissed, too. Everywhere."

There was a veiled meaning to her words that he didn't completely understand. That awkward sensation he despised returned, but this time he crushed it beneath the weight of his desire to touch her. He'd come this far already, and the tantalizing vision in front of him was enough to make him overcome the minor resistance in the back of his head.

Instinct guided him to grasp her ankle and slowly slide his hand upward as he lightly kissed her kneecap. The quiet murmur of approval escaping her encouraged him to trail his mouth downward along her smooth leg to her ankle. She tasted of citrus and spice. Deliciously sweet.

He cradled the bottom of her dainty foot in the palm of his hand to nibble at the inside of her ankle. Another soft sound rolled out of her, and he looked back at her face. If possible, the heat in her gaze made his erection even harder. His heart slammed into his chest at the thought of sliding into her. Would he disappoint her? The old uncertainty embraced him again. He was only half a man; how could he possibly please this incredibly gorgeous creature?

"Don't think. Feel," she whispered as if she could read his thoughts.

"Where else do you like to be kissed?" he asked in a hoarse voice.

"Where would *you* like to kiss me?"

There was temptation in that question as his eyes drifted toward her breasts. He leaned forward to swirl his tongue around her aureole. Her soft gasp said he was proving an apt pupil. His teeth gently nipped at the hard tip, and she released a low cry of pleasure.

The sound pleased him. He liked knowing his touch had made her cry out. He wanted to hear it again. His tongue swirled around her nipple before he took as much of her as he could into his mouth and suckled her. Immediately, she arched up into him, the moan rolling from her throat exciting him even more.

He switched his attention to her other breast, and another mewl passed her lips. The sudden thought that she might be feigning her pleasure made him raise his head to look at her face. Deep inside, the old fears told him he'd find her laughing at him—mocking his inexperience. Instead, her expression of pleasure reassured him.

She didn't find his touch repulsive. Her eyelids fluttered open and he saw passion darkening her violet eyes. The look made his heart slam into his chest as his hand slid downward to caress her hip. She arched against the touch.

"I like what you're doing," she said in a low and throaty voice. "But I would like it even more if you would kiss me more intimately."

"More intimately?"

He frowned as he looked at her and followed her gaze downward. Sweet Jesus, she was asking him to kiss her cunny. He'd heard Charles talking about kissing a woman's sex, but he couldn't remember too much of the conversation as he'd been quite drunk at the time. Still, the thought of stroking her with his tongue excited him.

A new scent mixed with her sweet perfume as his hand lightly brushed over the baby soft skin at the apex of her thighs. The sharp breath she inhaled indicated her excitement as his fingers gently parted her soft folds.

"Stop," she gasped. He immediately froze and jerked his gaze up to meet her sultry look. "That nub of flesh you're touching. If you pay special attention to that—"

He didn't wait for her to finish speaking and rubbed the sensitive spot gently, yet firmly. The moment he fondled the small piece of flesh, she writhed against his hand. Another moan echoed out of her, and a sense of power sailed through him at the intensity of the sound. He wanted to hear it again.

Quickly shifting his position on the bed, he planted himself squarely between her legs. While still playing with her, he pressed a kiss to the inside of her thigh. He studied her face as he pressed his mouth against the inside of her leg, while stroking her with his thumb. A creamy substance coated his fingertips as he continued to play with her.

As he slowly kissed his way down her leg to the inner crease where her thigh met her hip, the look on her face made his blood pound its way through him. It engorged his cock, stretching him until he experienced a painfully acute pleasure. He recognized the precipice he was on, and he faltered. He was on the verge of exploding, and he didn't know how to keep from coming. How could he possibly please her if he spilled his seed now?

"Garrick, look at me." Her quiet command brought his head up to meet her understanding gaze. "You want me, now, don't you? You can't wait."

"Yes," he rasped.

"Then take your clothes off." He'd bent her leg at the knee and jerked as she ran her toe across his covered erection. "I want to feel your cock inside of me."

He recoiled from the touch, terrified she'd be able to tell he only had one ballock. The old memories returned as mocking laughter filled his head. He couldn't let her see him. If she realized what a freak he was . . . he shook his head at the fear rising up inside him.

"No." His voice was hoarse with panic.

"Please," she whispered. "I need you inside me now."

The words were a soft cry of passionate need, and he ached to obey her request. His entire body was shouting out for something he knew was within his reach, but he was afraid to take that last step. Frantic with a mixture of desire, need, and fear, he glanced around the room, for what he had no idea.

"It's all right if you don't want me to see you." Under the soft, reassuring words, he could hear the husky note of urgency in her voice. "There's another scarf in the drawer."

It was the crutch he needed. A way to keep his secret and yet possess her body. In a move that he recognized as being clumsy at best, he left her on the bed to retrieve the scarf. Seconds later, he was standing over her. Violet eyes looked up at him and a part of him cried out in protest as he blindfolded her. What he really wanted was to stare into her eyes as he plunged into her, but he knew better. He'd already taken more risks than he'd ever dared before with a woman.

Staring down at her, he drew in a sharp, deep breath. Tied and blindfolded, she was an erotic sight that tempted him in a way he'd never dreamed possible. His body was on fire as heat streaked through his veins. In seconds, he freed his cock from his trousers and knelt between her legs.

Hands braced on either side of her, he couldn't help kissing her sex. He wanted desperately to please her. His tongue slid between her damp folds, to taste her. She was white-hot against his lips, and she cried out as he savored her. Christ Jesus, he'd never thought a woman could be such a tempting morsel. He wanted to taste every inch of her. His mouth moved upward to caress her stomach then on to her breasts. The moment he captured a nipple in his mouth, she whimpered. It was a sound of pleasure, and he loved hearing it.

An instant later, his cock jumped as she bent her knee again, her foot glancing off the tip of him. Roughly, he forced her leg away from him, and with one hand guided his rod between her slick folds. A mewl of need poured out of her as he pressed into her. As he slid deeper, it felt as though her body was clutching at him, pulling him into her. It was an incredible sensation. His hand had never given him even one tenth of this kind of pleasure.

Blind need suddenly crashed through him and he withdrew before plunging back into her. Her tight grip was an exquisite friction against his cock, clenching around him like a hot vise. What little control he had slipped as he realized how close he was to exploding.

Unable to help himself, he began to drive in and out of her with fast, frantic strokes.

In seconds, a familiar rush made him stiffen and he exploded inside of her. The swiftness of his climax made him grimace with self-disgust. He'd not been able to hold his seed long enough to bring her to satisfaction, although he wasn't really sure what that entailed. Humiliated by his poor performance, he retreated from her and quickly pulled his trousers back on, hiding his diminishing erection.

When he'd concealed himself, he quickly undid her blindfold and freed her from the bed. Feeling like a schoolboy who'd failed to perform a simple task, he turned away from her and moved to stand at the fireplace. He stared into the flames with regret. He was a fool. He should never have allowed her to convince him to make love to her. His uncle had been right all along. He was half a man, and his performance just now proved it.

"Thank you." The scent of her wafted its way over his shoulder as she came up behind him. Shame prevented him from looking at her.

"For what?" he rasped. "It was a miserable performance by me at best."

"It was your first time. It takes practice to become a skilled lover." The gentleness in her voice didn't soothe his embarrassment.

"It was a mistake to think I could make love to you." He continued to watch the blue and yellow flames dancing across the logs in the hearth.

"But you *did* make love to me," she said quietly. "And I promise you, the next time will be even more pleasurable. For *both* of us."

"There won't be a next time," he ground out fiercely. The moment the words were out of his mouth, he flinched. The thought of not touching her again was a crushing blow.

10

Ruth stepped away from Garrick to pick up and shrug into her robe. A quick glance over her shoulder showed him still standing in front of the fireplace. The stark white of his shirt emphasized his dark features and black hair. His head bent, he stared into the flames as though contemplating some dark fate. It served to intensify the dangerous edge of his sinful good looks, but it was the bleakness to his posture that made her heart ache. Not a good sign. She needed to avoid growing attached to him.

She bit down on her lip at the thought. There had been other lovers in the past that she'd tutored in new techniques, but never a man who was completely inexperienced. There was something exciting about the idea of initiating him into the art of lovemaking. It was like starting with fresh clay and creating a work of art.

In Garrick's case, it meant teaching him how to please her. No, how to please another woman. She needed to remember that. In the end she'd be alone again. It had been that way since her mother died. That wouldn't change because there was no permanence to her life. Every man who'd entered her bedroom had always left. Garrick would be no different.

As long as she remembered this was a temporary arrangement, she could take pleasure in his company and his touch. And dear God, the man's touch was like a hot flame burning her skin. She couldn't recall ever feeling the kind of desire Garrick evoked in her. Perhaps it was because she'd sensed his lack of experience, and it aroused her.

She drew in a deep breath and turned to go to him. The moment she laid her hand on his arm, he jerked his head in her direction. She smiled at him and gently pulled him toward one of the chairs in front of the hearth. He hesitated.

"I should go," he bit out in a rough voice.

"Not yet," she said quietly. "It's considered rude to leave a woman's boudoir so soon after leaving her bed."

He nodded sharply and allowed her to guide him to one of the pale blue wingback chairs. His tall frame engulfed the chair, and her heart skipped a beat at how handsome he was. She studied him in silence as he stared at the crackling flames in the hearth. He seemed completely oblivious to her presence, his expression morose. Her heart went out to him.

The man seemed convinced that his lovemaking was worse than lamentable. He was clearly ashamed of his body as demonstrated by his refusal to let her see him naked. *Refusal* wasn't the right word. He'd seemed paralyzed by her request more than anything else. Helpless almost. The look on his face when she'd told him to undress had been nothing short of sheer terror.

At first she'd thought he was uncomfortable with his size, but the moment he'd slid into her, she'd found herself skidding along an edge of pleasure that had been a delicious torment. He'd been thick and hard between her thighs. And even though his climax had come quickly, she knew once he gained more experience, he'd drive her mad with want. The thought was both intoxicating and frightening at the same time.

With him settled in front of the fire, she went to a small sideboard in one corner of the room where she always kept cognac for her lovers. As she opened the doors, she saw a plate of cheese and hard bread. Dolores. It confirmed what she'd thought from the moment she'd first seen Garrick in her room.

Her maid had been instrumental in seeing to it that he had entrance to her bedroom. She knew she should be irritated that her friend had conspired with Garrick, but she wasn't. The plate of cheese and bread in one hand, and a tray holding the cognac and glasses in the other, she returned to the fireside. The moment he saw her full hands, Garrick quickly rose to take the tray of liquor from her, the glasses rattling slightly as he set it on the round table between the chairs.

With the small repast on the table, she poured him a glass of the French brandy and offered it to him. As his fingers brushed across hers a shock of electricity raced across her skin. The sensation was enough to make her tremble as she filled her own glass. It was unlike her to drink, but she suddenly had the need for something to steady her nerves. Although the expensive liquor burned as it sped down her throat it served to restore her composure.

She turned her head to study him. His profile was shadowed somewhat, but the firelight revealed his strong, angular jaw. The sensual line of his mouth was a tempting sight as she remembered how exquisite his lips had felt against her skin.

"I suppose I'm a creature of curiosity to you," he said bitterly without looking at her.

"Not at all." She tilted her head to one side. "Actually, I was thinking how lucky I am."

Startled, he turned his head to arch his eyebrow at her. "Lucky?"

"Yes. Of all the women you could have chosen to be your first lover, you chose me." She sent him a mischievous smile. "Besides, I have never cared for Mrs. Campton, and to know that you chose me over her is quite exuberating."

He laughed, and the sound pleased her. At least he wasn't looking quite so dour, and his laughter softened the harsh planes of his face. It was easy to understand why the women he'd never bedded had lied about being his lover. She knew what it was like to feel the sting of his rejection.

But of all the women in the Set, she was the privileged one. He'd chosen her as his tutor. There was more than a little sense of triumph at the thought, particularly where Louise Campton was concerned. The woman had insulted her on more than one occasion, and there was little love lost between them. Her gaze focused on Garrick, and she was happy to see his features had softened.

"There, that's better," she said softly. "You look much more relaxed."

"Do I?" The note of skepticism in his voice made her send him an admonishing glance.

"Yes. I want you to always feel comfortable here." She took another sip of brandy as he studied her for a minute before returning his gaze to the fire.

"I always feel that way when I'm in your company, Ruth." It was a simple statement that warmed her heart as she studied his profile.

"I'm glad." She smiled as she leaned forward to see his face in its entirety. There was still a grim twist to the corners of his mouth. "Tell me about your family."

The question made him look at her in surprise before a small smile curved his sensual mouth. It was a mouth designed for pleasuring a woman until she was begging for a release only he would be able to give. The images flooding her head made her swallow hard, and she set her glass down on the table in order to regain her composure. When she looked at him again, his expression had lightened somewhat from the morose one that had darkened his features a moment ago.

"You've already met Lily. Who, by the by, will be abjectly humble the next time she sees you. She's sincerely sorry for the pain she caused you."

The statement caught her off guard, and her eyes widened before she quickly looked away from him. The unpleasantness with his sister had been distinctly uncomfortable for many reasons.

"Her visit wasn't a new experience for me, and I'm certain her heart was in the right place where you're concerned. Just as it should be." Unwilling to discuss the matter further, she swiftly diverted his attention. "And the rest of your family?"

"Vincent is our bookworm. He has a habit of spending more time in our library than socializing with the Set. Although he's recently developed a fondness for certain soirees where a particular young lady is present. Something I intend to discuss with him when the opportunity presents itself." A dark scowl crossed his face.

"Isn't that a bit like the pot calling the kettle black?" she scolded gently as she smiled at him. "As I recall, you weren't all that happy with your sister's interference in your relationship with me."

"Lily's interest in my affairs was inappropriate. She's not the head of the family. I am. And it's my duty to ensure that my siblings marry people who will love and care for them properly." His mouth thinned to a firm line as an expression of unyielding determination hardened his handsome features.

"An admirable goal, but the heart cannot be dictated to," she said quietly.

"Perhaps not, but I've seen to it that Grace will be happy, and I am determined to do the same for Vincent."

His omission of Lily made her frown. Was Lady Lynmouth's marriage an unhappy one? Ruth knew little about the Earl of Lynmouth as the man rarely came to town, and Lily's appearance at St. Agnes's had been the first time she'd met Garrick's sister. Had his attempts to ensure the happiness of his siblings been far from successful?

"And Lily? You were able to ensure her happiness?"

The sudden expression of regret on his face told her Lily's marriage was anything but happy. He closed his eyes and rested his head on the back of the chair. The sorrow emanating off him made Ruth reach out to touch his arm in a silent show of support. He didn't open his eyes.

"Lily refuses to discuss Lynmouth with me or anyone. I would never have consented to the marriage if I'd thought she would get hurt." There was a touch of despair in his voice that emphasized how responsible he felt for his sister's happiness.

"You've always looked after them, haven't you?"

"Beresford, my uncle, wasn't a pleasant man. I once saw him whip a stableboy not quite as old as me until the boy's back was stripped of flesh." He emptied his brandy snifter, which Ruth quickly replenished. "I learned to draw the man's wrath down on my own head in order to keep the others safe from harm."

"Did he beat you?"

"Sometimes." His expression was unreadable as he nodded his head.

The brusque response said Garrick's uncle had done much more than beat him. Clearly, the man was a monster. She didn't know how, but she was certain Beresford was responsible for Garrick's emotional emasculation. Whatever his uncle had said or done to him, Garrick had come to believe that women would find his body repulsive in some way. And she was certain it was why he'd refused to bare himself in front of her.

A sudden sharp pain pierced her breast and made her draw in a quick breath. Sweet heaven, if Beresford had violated—no, please God no. Did she even dare ask the question? She swallowed the knot in her throat. Not only was it none of her business, but she'd said she wanted him to be comfortable here. Asking pointed questions would accomplish nothing, and would only make him feel ill at ease. He would tell her what he wanted . . . when he wanted.

His secrets were his to share or keep hidden. More importantly, she wanted to offer him sanctuary and peace, something she was sure he'd not had a great deal of in his life. Suddenly she wanted to cry, and she turned her head just a bit to swipe away a tear that had escaped. A strong hand grasped her forearm to tug on it gently. She jerked her gaze back to him.

"You're crying." He scowled at her as she shook her head.

"No. A piece of ash flew into my eye."

"Don't lie to me, Ruth," he said gruffly as he leaned closer to catch her chin in his fingers and forced her to look at him. "Are you crying for me?"

His amazement was easy to see, and she slowly nodded her head. An odd emotion flashed in his blue eyes, but it was impossible to read because it vanished so quickly. His thumb lightly rubbed across her bottom lip before he released her to recline in his chair again. Uncertain of what to say, she realized the tension between them had escalated again, and not in a good way.

"No one has ever cried for me before." The words were so soft, she wasn't sure she'd heard them at first. She stared at him in surprise.

"Not even your sisters?"

"Grace was too young to really understand what was happening in the house." His features could have been solid granite for all the emotion he displayed, and his voice was just as devoid of feeling. "Unlike you, Lily had no real knowledge of what life was like for me with Beresford in the house. I managed to keep most of it from her and Vincent."

"Just like you hide it from them now." Her soft statement made him jerk his head toward her. "If you let them, or anyone else, see your pain, you think it would make you less of a man in their eyes."

Although his expression didn't change, there was a dark emotion in his vivid blue eyes as he jerked his gaze in her direction. In that instant, she wanted to kill Beresford for the injuries he'd inflicted on Garrick. She understood the deep pain that others could inflict.

The pain of her father's rejection was always with her. It wasn't something she allowed herself to contemplate often, but the ache never eased. And she would never be able to forgive her father for what he'd done to her mother. Her father wasn't directly responsible for her death, but his actions had made her mother give up on living.

Like her, Garrick had endured pain at the hands of others and refused to give way to the hurt. Both of them had hid their feelings from the world to etch out their lives under their own terms. They'd survived despite the pain others had caused them, and they'd hidden the torture that survival had caused. The reflection made her remember what she was, and she flinched.

Their experiences had shaped them and made them hide their vulnerabilities. And she was terribly vulnerable where Garrick was concerned. He was completely oblivious to his ability to leave a woman breathless when he offered up that wicked smile of his.

Then there was the darkness buried deep beneath the surface that enticed her—mesmerized her. The force of his personality drew her to him with an intensity that excited more than frightened her. In truth, the man held far more sway over her than she cared to admit. She reached for Garrick's hand, determined to alleviate his emotional pain as much as she could.

"I think another subject matter would make both of us feel better. What if we plot the demise of those miscreants we find despicable and repulsive?" she asked mischievously as she smiled at him. "I know quite a few in the Set who the world would be better off without."

Her words lightened his features considerably as he offered her a half smile. "Again with this bloodthirsty mind-set. It's a side of you I've not seen before."

"It would be madness for me to display it often. I might lose all hope of enticing suitors into my company."

"I've told you before that you underestimate yourself," he said quietly. The emotion flickering in his blue eyes sent her heartbeat skidding out of control. In an effort to regain her equilibrium, she leaned toward him with a flirtatious smile.

"Well, I must confess I enjoy having a handsome man in my bedroom. Especially one who's such an apt pupil."

"Pupil?" He shook his head in silent refusal.

"Yes, and I won't take no for an answer," she said with a seductive smile.

She set her brandy aside and pulled a small piece of bread off the loaf Dolores had included with the cheese. Her hand outstretched, she offered the morsel to him. As he reached out to take it from her, she pulled her hand back.

"No, make it the sensual act of a lover," she said firmly.

Once more she extended her hand as she sent him an arch look. He eyed her carefully for a moment. She was certain he was about to turn away when she saw a flash of emotion cross his face. In that instant, she saw how quickly her liaison with him could become dangerous. She watched in fascination as he leaned forward to slowly nip at her fingertips with his teeth as he took the morsel from her.

His gaze didn't leave hers as he ate the bread. The air in her lungs disappeared as she struggled to breathe while watching him. The man was a born seducer. He just didn't realize it—or maybe he did. The one thing she was certain of was no woman would stand a chance with him if he made up his mind to have her.

"You do realize I can't agree."

"To what? Allowing me to instruct you in the finer points of lovemaking?" Her hand carried her glass to her mouth to take a small sip of brandy as a way of controlling the sudden trembling that threatened to shake her entire body. He looked away from her.

"Yes. What happened earlier cannot happen again."

"Why not?" Her question seemed to surprise him as he jerked his head back toward her. She frowned as she suddenly pondered the idea that her performance might have been a disappointment for him. The idea made her stomach lurch. He'd said her age wasn't an issue, but perhaps he'd changed his opinion. "Did I fail to meet your expectations?"

"What?" He choked out the one-word exclamation with obvious disbelief as he protested with a sharp shake of his head. "*No*, of course not. You were . . . you . . . it was incredible."

"Then make love to me again."

"I can't." There was a desperation in his voice that made her ache for him.

"Garrick," she said softly as she leaned forward to cover his hand with hers. He shuddered beneath her touch. "I know you don't want me to see you undressed. It's why I told you where the other scarf was."

"And it's why I can't make love to you again." The terse response made her nibble at her bottom lip. How could she make him understand he could trust her? In some ways he reminded her of a hurt little boy, unwilling to show his pain.

"Then you blindfold me again or we can make love in the dark. I meant every word when I said I want you to always be comfortable here."

She watched the conflicting emotions on his face as she met his gaze steadily. Beresford had much to atone for in making Garrick believe his body was ugly or that a woman wouldn't want him. In truth, she could see how easily she could develop feelings for him. He closed his eyes and turned away from her again. The resistance in him seemed to ebb slightly, and she left her chair to kneel in front of him.

"Garrick, I want you," she whispered. It wasn't a lie.

"It's not possible," he ground out between clenched teeth.

"You said you trusted me. Will you not trust me a little more?" She extended her hand to touch his chest. Beneath the crisp white linen of his shirt, she could feel his heart pounding frantically against her fingers. "Take your shirt off. Nothing more."

He stared at her for a long moment, and the now familiar glint of panic returned to his blue eyes. Something told her it wouldn't take much for him to recoil from her, and she remained silent even though she wanted to offer up words of encouragement. When he moved, she drew in a quick breath as he caught her hand and carried it to his mouth.

The tender way he brushed his lips across her fingertips made her heart skip a beat before it resumed its fast-paced rhythm. With a gentle firmness, he pushed her hand away to slowly unbutton his shirt. Fascinated, she watched as he shrugged out of it. The sight of him made her suck in a sharp breath. Sweet heaven, he was beautiful. Hard, powerful, and all male.

"You're magnificent," she whispered in awe as she reached out to trail her fingers across his chest. He jumped at the touch, and she immediately looked up at him.

Beneath her stare, he shifted uncomfortably and she saw a muscle twitch in his cheek as he locked his jaw. When he didn't say anything, she leaned forward to press her lips against his skin. Another shudder rippled through him, but he didn't move as she placed another kiss on his chest in a different spot.

Slowly, she brushed her mouth across his chest to his nipple. Her tongue flicked across it before she abraded him with her teeth. A dark growl rumbled out of him, and she glanced up at him to meet his gaze for a brief moment before she returned to the task of caressing his torso with her lips.

She couldn't remember the last time she'd ever taken such pleasure in worshiping a man's chest. Nor could she recall the last time she'd ever tasted a man so deliciously raw and spicy against her tongue. Hard muscles flexed slightly beneath her caresses as his breathing grew harsher with every passing second.

"Has any woman ever told you how beautiful you are?" she breathed against his skin.

"No," he rasped. The sound made her smile as she kissed his breastbone.

"Do you like what I'm doing to you?"

"Yes," he choked out as she abraded his nipple again with her teeth. He groaned. "Christ Jesus, yes."

"I'm glad, because I like pleasuring you."

With her hand pressed against his chest, the solid thud of his heartbeat pounded against her fingertips. The steady vibration accelerated dramatically as she slowly trailed her mouth down the center of his chest toward the fine line of hair diving downward into his trousers. A moment later, he grasped her shoulders and dragged her upward.

Startled, she didn't protest as his mouth parted hers with a skill that left her breathless. He might lack experience in bed, but his kisses were that of a talented seducer. It was a contrast that excited her even more. She responded eagerly, a tremor shaking through her as his tongue swept into her mouth to mate with hers. With each swirling caress, he tugged a response from her that made her tremble with need.

Heat rolled through her veins until she was on the verge of forgetting who was the pupil and who the teacher. As he lifted his head, she drew in a deep breath at the passion blazing in his eyes. Aware that he was still wavering whether to give in to her, she got to her feet and took his hand in hers to pull him out of his chair and toward the bed. The moment she sank down onto the mattress she smiled up at him.

"One of the most important things you need to remember when you make love to a woman is to treat her as if she's the only lover you've ever had that excites you to distraction." Her heart skipped a beat at the flash of emotion that flared in his eyes.

"That's not difficult where you're concerned, Ruth. You do drive me to distraction."

Dear God, if she didn't know better, she'd think the man well skilled in the art of seduction. The deep sound of his voice was nothing short of sinful. It contained an invitation to be wicked, and she shivered at the effect it had on her. Perhaps it was a mistake teaching him. The man was already devastating enough to her senses. The heated expression that swept across his face made her suck in a sharp breath as he reached out to run his thumb across her lower lip. Desire streaked through her and sent her heart skidding out of control until it slammed into her breast.

"Tell me how to please you." There it was again, that dark note of seduction that made her realize how easily he could master her. She swallowed hard as she slowly removed her robe.

"Touch me," she whispered.

A small gasp escaped her as he sat down next to her and his forefinger pressed gently against the base of her throat before sliding downward. He bent his head to follow the movement, his breath warming her skin with a heat that seared its way into every pore of her skin. With each slow inch his finger traversed across her skin, a stark need grew inside her until she wanted to cry out for a more intimate caress. As his finger circled the small indentation of her stomach she drew in a quick hiss of air.

"Does this please you?"

Behind the question she heard a slight note of hesitation in his voice. The fact that the man didn't realize the effect he was having on her made the moment even more intoxicating. She nodded.

"Yes, very much." Her gaze met his, and she slowly reclined back onto the bed, her hand brushing down the hard muscles of his arm. "Every woman has sensitive spots on her body, and every woman is unique as to where those spots are. You need to explore your lover's body to find them."

"I believe I've already found one of yours."

A smile quirked one corner of his mouth as his hand slid along her leg. He bent his head to kiss his way down to the inside of her ankle. Every nibble of his lips against her skin sent desire rushing through her until her breathing was wild and erratic.

Her eyes closed a moment later and she gasped as his mouth slowly made its way upward to her knee and along her thigh to the curve at her waist. She didn't know how much longer she could keep from demanding he make love to her immediately. She couldn't remember a time when she'd ever wanted a man as much as she wanted him, now, this instant.

The scent of him filled her nostrils as he shifted his body and hovered mere inches above her. For a moment, she simply breathed in the male essence of him until he enveloped her senses in all his raw maleness. When she opened her eyes his smoldering gaze made her feel as though he were devouring her. And dear Lord how she wanted him to do just that.

She saw him reach for one of the scarves still lying where he'd left it earlier. As much as she wanted him at that moment, she knew she had to put aside her own need if she was going to teach him how to be an extraordinary lover. Deep in the back of her mind, a warning screamed at her to stop the madness, but she refused to listen to it.

"Not yet," she breathed. She tried to clear the knot in her throat as he stared down at her. Oh God, when he looked at her like that it was almost impossible to think straight. Her voice husky, she lightly ran her fingertips over his shoulder. "A good lover knows how to please a woman, but an exceptional lover knows how to tease her until she's begging for a satisfaction only he can provide."

"Like this?" he murmured.

She gasped as his hand slid down across her stomach, and a moment later his fingers parted her slick folds to stroke the sensitive nub of flesh within. Her eyes closed as she arched upward to provide him greater access. A moment later the warmth of his breath brushed across her breasts as his mouth gently seized a nipple and sucked.

Raw, primitive sensations charged through her, pulling her closer and closer to the edge of an intense threshold of fulfillment before she spiraled downward into an erotic haze of pleasure. A sharp cry flew from her lips as the orgasm wrapped her in a white-hot heat that sent one shudder after another lancing through her. Pleasure flooded every inch of her until she was certain she was melting. As her trembling slowly subsided, he gently released his hold on her.

Sweet, merciful heaven. She'd never climaxed so easily at a man's touch. Trembling, she saw a look of satisfaction on his face. Her breath still coming in small pants, she tried to gather her wits about her. She'd known he'd be a quick study, but she'd not expected to find herself becoming addicted to his touch with each passing moment.

"I take it I've passed this particular examination in my studies?" It wasn't a question. The amusement in his voice said he knew full well he'd succeeded in pleasuring her.

"Most assuredly," she said and nodded in bemusement.

"I liked pleasing you." He lowered his head and nibbled at her bottom lip with his teeth. "But I especially liked watching you fall apart in my arms just now."

Heat flushed her cheeks at the provocative expression on his face, and she fought to control the emotions stirring deep inside her. What the devil was wrong with her? She wasn't some fresh-faced debutante staring up at an older lover. It was the other way around. *She* was the older, experienced lover instructing a younger man in the art of lovemaking. It was an important fact that would bear continuous repeating where Garrick was concerned. And she was determined to ensure he could bed whatever woman he desired with more finesse than any lover that woman had ever known.

"I'm certain any woman you bed will find your touch as pleasurable as I do." She gasped slightly as his hand stroked the inside of her thigh. The touch renewed the desire she thought her climax had quenched.

"I remain unconvinced, and I'm much more interested in delving deeper"—his voice was hypnotic as he dipped two fingers into her core—"into the sweet delights that I'm certain you've yet to teach me."

His touch tugged a low moan from her as she pushed against the heated stroke of his fingers. Instinctively her body clenched around him, and she trembled at the need growing inside her at an alarming rate. But she wanted more this time. Her heart racing wildly out of control, she raised her hand to caress his cheek as she fought to maintain control over her senses.

"Seduction—" She drew in a sharp breath as his touch sent her rushing toward the edge again. Desperately she struggled to continue a lesson that was quickly getting out of hand. "To seduce a woman . . . you must use . . . not only touch, but words . . ."

"If you wish to hear that you're lovely then I'm happy to oblige because I find you beautiful," he rasped.

"Yes, a woman loves compliments . . . like that . . ." She struggled to keep her voice steady. "But sometimes we like . . . it when your words are naughty."

"Naughty?" He frowned with puzzlement, and his pleasurable stroking slowed drastically. She wanted to beg him not to stop.

"Yes. Words that are risqué. Forbidden."

"Such as?"

He withdrew his touch, and she wanted to scream with frustration. Instead, she reached up to trail her fingers across the hard muscles of his chest. Then with deliberation, she dragged one finger down the middle of his chest toward the thin line of hair that dove toward his trousers.

"Words like *fuck*," she whispered, suddenly feeling terribly wicked for sharing such language.

"Women like to hear this?" His hand grabbed hers and pinned it to the bed, disbelief in his voice. Her desire eased somewhat, but she still craved his touch.

"Not always. But sometimes, when the moment is right, forbidden words can be exciting . . . shocking . . . erotic."

"And how do I use these words?" Excitement darkened his eyes until they were almost midnight blue.

"Sparingly, and at a moment when your lover is close to an orgasm." He lowered his head to kiss the base of her throat. It was a gentle touch, almost sweet in nature.

"So now would not be appropriate?" His mouth skimmed across her skin to nibble at the spot where her arm met her shoulder.

"No. But I like what you're doing."

"Good. I like it, too." The boyish satisfaction in his voice made her laugh.

He immediately jerked up his head. The shuttered expression on his face sent regret lancing through her. Whatever his uncle had done, laughter had clearly been part of the humiliation. She met his gaze with a steady look.

"Laughter in the bedroom is a joyful sound, Garrick. I laughed because I liked what you were doing, and I was happy you liked it, too." She didn't allow her gaze to waver from his until his expression relaxed. With a smile, she tipped her head toward her shoulder. "Now please resume."

Her firm command made him chuckle, and the sound sent a

shock wave through her. The man's laugh was rich as sin and equally devastating. His mouth caressed her shoulder again, and she closed her eyes at the pleasing touch. The heat of his breath gently stirred the hair against the nape of her neck and he swept it aside to nibble on her earlobe.

"Do you like this?" he murmured with a faint hint of vulnerability hiding deep behind the teasing note in his voice. It endeared him to her.

"I like it very much." She turned her head to kiss his bare arm braced next to her head. "I like it whenever and *wherever* you touch me."

He lifted his head to stare down at her with a pleased look on his dark features. He'd obviously heard how she'd stressed the word *wherever.* One hand cupped her breast as he circled the nipple with his thumb.

"And this?"

The question was rich and sinful in her ears as she trembled at his touch. Dear God, this tutoring session was wreaking havoc with her body. How easily he manipulated her senses with his voice and touch. He was devastating now, but when his last lesson was complete he would break hearts with just one look.

"Yes, but at the moment, all I can think about is how good it feels when you're inside me," she said softly. His hand stilled at her breast, and she saw passion sparking in his gaze as it warred with the fear inside him. For the first time, she pushed him. "Please, Garrick. I want to feel your hard cock driving into me, filling me until we're both satiated."

His throat bobbed as he swallowed hard, and she waited with bated breath for his answer. It came quickly. Desire engulfed his features at the same instant his head swept downward to capture her mouth in a hard kiss. She shuddered as he gently bit down on her bottom lip, forcing her to give him greater access.

The moment his tongue danced with hers a hot breeze brushed over her skin. Brandy and raw male heat flooded her senses with a force her mind registered as dangerous, but she ignored the warning. Instead she welcomed his heated touch as he teased and tormented her with each stroke of his tongue. When he lifted his head, she whimpered a protest. Her eyes fluttered open to see the dark desire on his face, and a flash of regret as he gently blindfolded her.

Garrick suppressed a groan of frustration as he covered Ruth's beautiful eyes. He wanted to see her full expression when he sank into her, but he didn't have the courage to bare himself to her completely. With a growl, he left her lying on the bed for a moment and turned his back on her to fumble with his trousers.

"Garrick?" The tentative note in her voice made him jerk his head toward her.

"I'm still here," he said gruffly. He shoved his pants off his legs and glanced downward with uncertainty. His cock was obviously ready—was he? She was a siren pulling him toward her, only he wasn't sure if he'd end up broken on the rocks.

"Are you . . . all right?" The concern in her voice did something unexpected to his heart, but he refused to define it. He turned around to face her, and the sight of her sucked the air out of his lungs. Exquisite. That's what she was. A feast for his eyes.

"I'm fine," he rasped. "I'm just enjoying looking at you."

"Wouldn't you rather be doing something else at the moment?"

The breathy sound of her voice slammed into him like a

sledgehammer. It sent lust pounding through every one of his muscles, and his erection expanded until he ached. Christ Jesus, what was this woman doing to him? Other women had tried to tempt him into their beds, but this one was accomplishing his seduction with little effort at all. He watched as her hand drifted down toward her sex in a languid move that made breathing difficult for him.

She arched her body slightly, her pink tongue flicking out to wet her lips. The instant her fingers slipped between the glistening folds of her sex, he forgot to breathe altogether. She was the most erotic sight he'd ever seen in his entire life. Part of him wanted to thrust into her hard and quick, while the other half of him wanted to go slow and prolong the pleasure of touching her. He leaned over her, and a smile curved her lovely mouth as if she could see him through the blindfold.

"There you are." She sighed as she blindly stretched out her hand to touch his face. "I love the way you smell. You should always wear bergamot so I can find you even in the dark."

"I shall remember that."

"I thought you'd changed your mind." Her quiet observation made him stiffen. How easily she could read him. Not until this moment did he realize he'd been contemplating doing just that.

"I almost did."

"I'm glad you didn't." Her hand slid around to the back of his neck to tug him downward.

He went willingly. The feel of her silky soft skin against his was a heady experience. His body covered every inch of her, and she warmed him until his blood was running hot and thick through his veins. Between her legs, his cock pressed against her sex, and he drew in a ragged breath as her hand reached for him.

"*No.*" The sharp command made her freeze against him. He grimaced and pulled her hand away from him. "Forgive me. I just don't—"

"It's all right. I understand."

Although the blindfold hid her violet eyes, he was certain that if he could look into her gaze, he would have seen that gentle understanding. He could hear it reflected in her voice, and see it in the sweet curve of her mouth. He shuddered. God help him, but he wanted to please her.

"Tell me what you want, Ruth. Tell me how to please you."

"You already know how," she said with a smile. It was the mischief in her voice that made him wish once more that he could see her eyes. He knew they'd be sparkling with an invitation he wasn't about to refuse. With a light kiss to her mouth, he brushed his lips along the edge of her jaw to where he could nibble on her ear.

She tasted of honey with just a trace of something deliciously seductive. The taste of it on his tongue was like an erotic aphrodisiac. It aroused him until desire sent hot tension charging through him. He drew in a deep breath of her scent, his body demanding he assuage his need for her.

"Is now the right time to say something wicked?" he asked as he pressed against the entrance of her sex. Her response to the small thrust was a sharp gasp. "Is that a yes?"

"Ye . . . yes." She trembled beneath him, and he sought the curve of her neck with his mouth. Gently nipping the skin just below her ear.

"Do you . . . I want to feel you tight around my cock." He choked back a groan at his awkward utterance and waited for her to laugh at him.

She didn't. Instead, she wrapped her legs around him, her heels digging into his buttocks. In a quick movement, she pushed herself onto his rod before he knew what was happening. Her body clenched around him tightly and dragged a moan out of him.

"Is it tight like you wanted?" she teased. The breathy laugh she released was a wonderful sound, but it wasn't the one he wanted to hear right now.

"Yes, you minx," he rasped as he thrust his hips forcefully against hers.

The small *oh* of surprise her mouth formed below her blindfold sent a rush of satisfaction through him. Swallowing the knot of desire rising in his throat, he gently rocked his body against hers. The slow precision with which he managed to thrust into her surprised him.

His body was demanding an immediate release, but unlike the last time, he wanted the pleasure to last.

He wanted to savor the way her soft, silky smooth body fit his. Breathing in her sweet, tangy scent, he sought her mouth in a hard kiss as he pushed deeper into the heat of her. God, she felt wonderful. He wanted to stay buried in her like this for a long time.

Suddenly, she moved her hips against his, and the friction it created made his cock jump with pleasure. She was slick and buttery around him. He groaned as the heat of her cunny tugged on him. It was like having a velvet vise wrapped around his rod. Her body squeezed then released the pressure against his erection with a mind-numbing pleasure his hand had never been able to give him. It fired his blood until he was sliding in and out of her in a natural, steady rhythm that surprised him. Her soft moan floated upward and filtered its way into his brain as he pressed his body deeper into hers. The sound excited him. It said he was pleasing her.

It encouraged him to increase the pace of his thrusts until she was matching him stroke for stroke beneath him. Suddenly, her fingers dug into his shoulders as she clung to him, and her hips jerked fiercely against his. Her body clenched tightly around him as spasm after spasm rippled over his cock until he groaned from the intense pleasure of it. Never in his wildest dreams had he ever imagined being with a woman would be like this.

She didn't stop shuddering around him as he continued to thrust into her. Each time he retreated, her body protested by clinging tightly to him. It increased the friction against his rod until every stroke of his body into hers was a delicious torment. A wild stirring in his blood sent a harsh demand for satisfaction streaking through him.

Lost in the hot, creamy feel of her, he drove into her at a frenzied pace. The harder his stroke the more intense the friction. It was an unbelievable sensation. He felt as though he were racing up a steep incline, his body demanding he reach the top before his lungs gave out.

The tension of the moment snagged its way through his back and arms until the pressure building inside him threatened to lock his body rigid. He slammed into her with one last thrust, and it pulled a shout from him as his cock jerked and throbbed inside her. His breathing labored, he hovered above her as wave after wave of intense pleasure assaulted his body. Ever so slowly the sensations abated until he found himself sinking down into her welcoming warmth with his forehead pressing into hers. God, he wanted to look into her eyes right now. His fingers reached for the blindfold, but a warning cry in his head made him caress her cheek instead.

"Another examination you've passed with flying colors," she said huskily.

"You made it effortless," he murmured as he kissed her. He wanted to go to sleep and wake up with her in his arms.

"And this?" She pointed to the blindfold, and his heart skipped a beat as the fear came rushing back.

He quickly rolled away from her and lunged for his pants on the floor. His trousers fastened, he turned around and stopped where he was to stare at her. They'd not bothered to undo the bed, and Ruth was nestled among the tousled bedspread and sheets. He'd never seen a more beautiful woman.

The gold bedding was the perfect foil for her luxuriant chestnut hair, and it emphasized the peach-colored hue of her flushed skin. The blindfold was still in place, and his throat bobbed as he marveled that he'd not even thought to tie her to the bed. It was a sign of how safe he felt when he was with her. Even more amazing was the fact that she was waiting on him to remove the blindfold. It was a simple gesture, but it indicated how sensitive she was to his needs. The realization shot a bolt of emotion through him, filling him with the sudden urge to tell her everything. But it wasn't a chance he was willing to take.

He tensed as he envisioned her looking at him. Would his deformity make her recoil from him? He grimaced as he removed her blindfold, and she blinked as her eyes adjusted to the soft light in the room. Her gaze met his and she smiled.

"Perhaps it's wicked of me to say so, but there's something erotically sinful about being blindfolded when you're pleasuring me." Her voice was sultry music in his ears, and another surge of desire barreled through him. The sensation was becoming all too familiar where she was concerned.

"So I pleased you?"

He winced. The words were nothing short of a cry for reassurance. Damn it to hell, he was far too transparent.

"More than any man I've ever been with," she whispered.

There was a catch in her voice that said she'd shared more than she meant to. Her words brightened the darkest corners of his heart. He instinctively knew it was a mistake to take pleasure in her comment, but he didn't care. A delicate yawn parted her lips, and he noted the way her eyelids drooped slightly. He lifted her hand to his lips and kissed the inside of her wrist.

"I'll leave you to sleep," he murmured.

"Don't go. Put out the lights and stay a little longer."

She shook her head and drew back the covers of her bed. The moment she slid beneath the sheets, he knew he wasn't going anywhere. The warmth in her violet eyes promised he'd find peace and comfort in her arms. He quickly doused the gaslights in the room so that the only light came from the small fire burning in the hearth.

As his eyes adjusted to the darkened room, he turned back to the bed and saw her lying on her side waiting for him. She stretched out her hand to him, and he crossed the room to accept her invitation. Lying down beside her, he wrapped his arm around her shoulder and tugged her into his chest. Without a word, she snuggled into him, her hand resting over his heart.

He liked the way she felt in his arms—the way he felt when he was with her. She aroused his protective instincts. He'd always watched over his sisters and Mary, but this was different. This was a territorial emotion at the most primitive level. He pushed the thought aside. It was simply a reaction to what had happened tonight.

Making love to Ruth had exceeded every erotic dream he'd ever had about her, or any woman for that matter. She'd not just instructed him on how to please her. She'd made him feel comfortable in her bed. It made her all the more beautiful to him. The gentle sound of her breathing brushed across his senses, and for the first time in memory something he could only describe as peace washed over him.

He closed his eyes to revel in the warmth of her curled up into his side. Contentment wasn't something he was acquainted with, but this came close. Deep inside, the fear and panic rose up to pound away at him, warning him not to let her get under his skin. He winced. That was water under the bridge. After tonight, it would be damned difficult to let her go. She uttered a soft murmur against his chest. He looked down at her and realized she was asleep. Had he worn her out with their lovemaking?

It was impossible not to feel a small sense of pride at the possibility. She'd said he'd pleased her, and he believed her. It filled him with a sense of satisfaction. The emotion vanished as old doubts pushed their way back into his head.

She was a courtesan. It was her job to please him, to tell him what he wanted to hear. He frowned as he looked down at her. Had she lied to him? Uncertainty held him hostage as he studied her lovely features. Instinct warred with doubt for a long time before he brushed a lock of hair off her cheek. *No.* He refused to believe she'd lied to him. There was no reason for her to do so. He yawned and breathed in her sweet smell.

The scent of her caressed his senses, and it was the last thing he remembered until his eyes fluttered open to see the dawn lighting the room. Groggy, he frowned as he pushed his way out of the depths of sleep. This didn't look like his rooms at Seymour Square or Chiddingstone House.

In a split second, the night before came rushing back to him as he recognized Ruth's lush curves cradled against him. Her back pressed against his chest, while her bottom spooned deliciously into his lower body. His arm was wrapped around her in a possessive fashion, and his cock stirred in his trousers at the soft curve of her breast just above his fingers.

As badly as he wanted to pull back the sheet covering her and make love to her again, he didn't. He needed to get the hell out of here and try to take in everything that had happened since last night. Everything in his world was upside down, and he wasn't sure what it meant going forward. Last night had been incredible, but if he continued down this path there would eventually be a reckoning.

He needed time to think about the consequences of what had happened. As quietly as he could, he pulled away from her and slipped out of the bed. She protested with a soft murmur before burrowing into her pillow. He hated leaving her without saying good-bye, but he was afraid of what would happen if he stayed.

The risks he'd taken last night would double in the bright morning light. He glanced down at his rumpled trousers. Damnation, he couldn't go home to Chiddingstone House looking like he'd slept in his clothes. He'd have to go to Seymour Square. Later today he could send several extra pair of trousers to Ruth's house.

The progression of his thoughts dismayed him. Automatically assuming his relationship with Ruth would continue without considering the risks was a dangerous thing to do. With a quiet grunt, he quickly gathered the remainder of his clothes scattered between the bed and the fireside. When he was dressed, he looked back at Ruth.

While she slept, the sheet had slipped downward to reveal a lovely breast, and his mouth went dry as he remembered suckling her the night before. The memory instantly made him hard as a rock, and he ached to take her again and again until she was out of his system. He ignored the mocking laughter in the back of his head at the possibility of succeeding. He moved to the secretary near the window to retrieve pen and paper.

Staring down at the paper, he tried to think of something to say that wouldn't make him sound like a smitten schoolboy. In the end, he settled for a brief message that he'd escort her to supper and then the Westerham affair this evening. He deliberately omitted the fact that supper would be in the company of Grace and her fiancé. Somehow he knew she would balk at the idea of meeting his youngest sister. And he wanted Grace to meet her. She would like Ruth as much as he did. He ignored the question of why it was so important to him that the two women meet. He left the note on the bedside table then quietly left the room.

Downstairs, he met Simmons coming out of the back hall. Aware of his disheveled state, he expected the butler's eyebrows to rise. When the man simply bowed his head in a polite greeting, Garrick awkwardly acknowledged the man.

"Shall I hail a hansom cab for you, my lord?" The man's offer sent relief rushing through him. The possibility of someone seeing him so untidy had just decreased immensely.

"Thank you, Simmons."

With a nod, the man disappeared through the front door as Garrick paced the hall floor. He wasn't sure whether his nervousness was due to the possibility of Ruth coming after him or the fact that it was a struggle not to race back up the stairs to her. Moments later, Simmons reentered the house to announce he'd secured a cab. He nodded his thanks at the butler and headed out the door.

As he hurried down the front steps, he saw a carriage roll to a stop several doors up the street. At the same moment, he saw young Worthington emerge from the town house. Startled, he paused for a brief second on the sidewalk just as the younger man jogged down the steps toward his carriage.

Almost as if aware he wasn't alone in his early morning departure, Worthington turned his head toward Ruth's house. Embarrassment darkened the younger man's cheeks as he offered a sharp nod in Garrick's direction then bolted into his carriage. Following the other man's lead, he climbed into the cab and ordered the driver to proceed to Seymour Place.

Several minutes later, he emerged from the vehicle and strode quickly up the steps to unlock the front door of the town house. As he crossed the hall toward the stairs, he called for Carstairs. The butler quickly appeared in the foyer.

"Have Willie bring up hot water for my bath."

"Yes, my lord."

"And send the boy . . ." He frowned as he tried to remember the lad's name.

"Samuel, my lord?"

"Yes. Have him fetch Blackstone." He continued up the stairs. "I want the man here in an hour."

When he entered his bedroom, he slammed the door shut behind him in a fit of frustration. Christ Jesus, what had he been thinking last night? He hadn't. His cock had done all his thinking for him. In less than twenty-four hours, he'd broken every rule he'd ever made when it came to his involvement with women.

But Ruth had been impossible to resist. How the hell Marston or any other man had been willing to part with her was beyond his comprehension. The problem facing him now was how to avoid repeating his mistake of last night. And God help him, it was a mistake he wanted to make over and over again with her, even though he recognized the folly of it.

The fact was, she'd made it so easy for him to break his vow never to bed a woman. She was a courtesan, trained in the art of pleasing a man, but last night she'd shown him the other attributes of her trade. She'd emphasized that her skills weren't just about offering up her body to a man for their mutual pleasure.

Her talents also meant seeing to her lover's comfort. Something she'd done with remarkable skill. In allowing him to tie her to the bed the first time, she'd displayed a trust in him that he found amazing. Even more astounding had been her ability to read him so well that she'd offered him another scarf to blindfold her.

The trust she'd placed in him had enabled him to experience the delights of a woman's body, something he'd never thought to enjoy in his lifetime. He winced as he recalled his first effort with her. It had been a disastrous event. One she'd excused with a gentleness that had eased his acute embarrassment.

A knock on the bedroom door pulled him out of his thoughts as Willie entered the room with hot water. The young footman quickly filled the bath then darted out the door to retrieve more. It took the servant another fifteen minutes to fill the tub with steaming water, and all the while, Garrick paced the floor reflecting on the previous night's events. When the door closed behind the footman for the last time, he strode across the room and turned the key as was his usual habit.

Quickly shrugging out of his jacket and then his shirt, he stopped to stare at his reflection in the mirror. Just thinking about Ruth, and the way she'd caressed his chest with her sweet lips, aroused him still. Not only had she made him believe he was the most important man in the world, she'd desired him. He had no doubts about that.

The fiery passion in her gaze had been bold and uninhibited. Other women had looked at him just as boldly, but they'd never succeeded in stirring his senses the way Ruth did. She'd seduced him with ease, and his ability to subdue his own desire had been nonexistent.

He grunted as he moved to stand in front of the oak washstand. Hot water splashed out of the blue-speckled porcelain pitcher into the matching basin, a few drops stinging his hand. Instead of letting the water sit for a moment, he splashed it onto his face in a form of penitence. If he'd known what would happen last night he would never have attempted to see her again.

As he viciously mixed his shaving cream into a stiff lather, he grimaced with disgust. He'd told Ruth he couldn't abide someone lying to him, and he was doing just that to himself. Nothing would have stopped him from seeing her last night. He just hadn't expected things to proceed in the direction they had. Nor had he anticipated talking so openly with her.

Last night he'd shared things with Ruth he'd never told anyone. Things he'd never thought possible to share as easily as he'd done with her. She'd listened quietly and without judgment. Would she have been equally sympathetic if he'd told her the complete truth? The thought made him quickly lather his face then slam the shaving mug down on the washstand. Only a fool would think such a thing.

He reached for his razor and brushed it rapidly back and forth across the leather strap hanging off the side of the oak furniture. When the blade was ready for use, he scraped it across his skin with quick, sure strokes. As he shaved, he recalled his reaction when he'd realized Ruth was crying for him. It had twisted his heart with an emotion he hadn't wanted to label then nor did he wish to now.

Even though she didn't know the true cause of his suffering, she'd spilled tears he'd never been able to shed himself. It was as if she understood everything he'd been through. He could only believe her own life experiences had been the reason for her empathy. She'd shared enough of her past for him to know that her life might have been vastly different if her father had been less of a bastard. The last bit of shaving cream removed from his face, he quickly finished undressing and slid into the bath.

The water was still hot, but it wasn't as hot as Ruth had been in his arms. Closing his eyes, he leaned back against the cool porcelain. She'd seduced him. There wasn't any other way to describe it. She'd quietly broken through every one of his defenses and enticed him to make love to her. It had been erotic and incredible.

The problem facing him now was where to go from here. Last night had been an unbelievable introduction into the pleasures she had to offer, and like a powerful drug, he wasn't sure he could give her up easily, despite the risk involved. Even if he could avoid the temptation of her bed, it wasn't possible for him to just walk away from her.

The pleasure of her company was something he enjoyed too much. When he was with her, things were simple and comfortable. He just wasn't sure which way to turn where she was concerned.

If there was one thing he couldn't stand, it was not having a plan of attack. Having a blueprint to follow meant he was prepared if something went wrong. Being unprepared meant being exposed to unknown possibilities, things that could make him vulnerable. He grabbed the bar of soap off the dish and savagely rubbed it over his body.

He'd find a way to address his problem with Ruth later. He needed to clear his head for a while, think of something else for the time being. Answers always came to him if he forgot about the problem for a short time. At the moment he needed to find out what Blackstone had discovered. The man had been watching his uncle for several years now, and had taken to observing the Viscount Tremaine as well. Blackstone would know how often the two men had met over the last several weeks.

It didn't take him long to finish bathing, and less than a half hour later he stepped into the study to find Blackstone sitting in one of the chairs situated in front of the large mahogany desk. The minute the man saw Garrick, he sprang to his feet.

"Good morning, my lord."

Bowler hat in hand, the husky man bowed slightly. Watching his uncle for the past several years wasn't the only thing John Blackstone had done for him. The man had taken on numerous roles whenever it came to fulfilling Garrick's directives. Garrick circled the desk to sit in the large leather office chair. With a gesture toward the chair Blackstone had been occupying, he silently told the man to retake his seat.

"Well? What do you have to report?"

"Beresford owes Lord Tremaine money, my lord. A great deal of money."

"How much?"

"Ten thousand pounds, maybe more."

Garrick drew in a sharp breath. With that kind of a hold on his uncle, Tremaine might easily know the truth. That night at the Marlborough Club, the bastard had been far too smug for his comfort then or now.

"How often do they meet?"

"Two or three times a week. They spend a great deal of time in gaming establishments or brothels. Lord Tremaine generally backs

Beresford at the card table, paying off his debts when your uncle loses." Blackstone scowled darkly. "Their brothel visits have seen them banned from the more respectable whorehouses. Your uncle whipped one girl who objected to being buggered. She was barely conscious when he sodomized her anyway."

The obvious disgust in Blackstone's voice matched his own abhorrence for his uncle's actions. The son of a bitch deserved a taste of his own medicine.

"How stable are Tremaine's finances?"

"The man's suffered several deep losses in the last year that have clearly affected his desire to invest in risky ventures. His situation isn't dire, but it could be if he were to suffer another substantial loss." Blackstone frowned in puzzlement. "In fact, I'm surprised he's willing to continue covering your uncle's extensive gambling losses."

"And my uncle's situation?" He pushed back the fear stirring inside him at the other man's words.

"You have the controlling interest in all but a few of his smaller investments. If you were to call in those interests, he would have no way of meeting his financial obligations."

What would his uncle do if Tremaine called in his gambling debts? Garrick rose to his feet and strode to the window that looked over the small garden at the back of the house. Now that the time had come to ruin his uncle, the taste of revenge was slightly sour in his mouth.

The sound of Bertha's and his uncle's vicious laughter suddenly reverberated in the back of his head. Just as quickly came the images of his uncle trying to enter Lily's bedroom, the whippings he'd endured, and the torment the bastard had inflicted on all of them. The dark memories taunted him until tension held him rigid, and the bitter taste on his tongue vanished.

"As I recall, I hold the liens on several cotton mills Tremaine financed last year." Hands clasped behind his back, he turned around to face Blackstone. At the man's silent acknowledgment, he smiled tightly. "Have the bank call in the loan on the smallest one. Then in another week call in the loan on the mill he has in Haltwhistle."

"Do you have a time frame for when you want the monies paid?"

"The man has three weeks from the recall of each loan."

"*Three* weeks, my lord?" Blackstone sent him a startled look.

"Correct." He drew in a deep breath. "If Tremaine appears to be having trouble meeting the deadline, I want you to immediately call in the liens I hold on my uncle's properties."

"And if Tremaine manages to make payment?"

"Then you're to call in the next largest debt until the man's back is against the wall." At his command, Blackstone nodded.

"Is there anything else you wish me to do, my lord?"

"No. Simply provide me with a daily report as to any changes in their activities."

Blackstone nodded his understanding as he stood up and bowed in his direction before leaving the small office. As the door closed quietly behind the stockily built man, Garrick turned back to the window overlooking the garden. With his plans for his uncle and Tremaine moving forward, the only other matter of importance was Ruth.

The question of what to do about their relationship hadn't changed in the past hour. He refused to give her up, and it was impossible to go back to the way things had been before last night. For all intents and purposes, she was his mistress now, and he'd provide for her accordingly. He would simply have to limit his time in her bedchamber. With a grunt of disgust, he realized he was living in a fool's paradise if he thought that would happen. Staying out of Ruth's bedroom was the last thing he was capable of doing. He would simply have to secure her agreement that their lovemaking continue under the same conditions as last night. It was reasonable to assume she'd agree to his request. But for how long?

Hopefully long enough for him to formulate an alternative plan, although God only knew what it would be. The one thing he was certain of was that he wanted to make her happy. He wanted to shower her with presents, something she would no doubt protest, but he wasn't going to let her refuse any more of his gifts. Today's small token would be the first of many he intended to give her.

He crossed the office to open the small safe tucked next to a large file cabinet in the corner of the room. The tumblers rattled quietly as he spun the dial back and forth until he heard the click that said the safe was unlocked. He opened the strongbox and pulled out a box covered in blue brushed velvet. The safe snapped closed, and he spun the tumblers before opening the box in his hand.

The white tulip-shaped earrings winked up at him. When the Crown Jeweler had forwarded the jewelry to him, they'd noted that Ruth had returned the package unopened. At the time, he'd been deeply frustrated, but the fact she'd never opened the jewelry meant he would have the pleasure of seeing her expression when he gave them to her this evening.

He made a mental note to stop by Garrard's later this afternoon to arrange for a matching necklace. Pulling his watch out of his pocket, he flipped the timepiece open. Today was his regular midday visit to Caring Hearts. It had become a habit of his to read to the younger children after lunch before Lily and one of the maids put them to bed for their early afternoon nap. As a child, his governess had read to him every night. It had instilled a love of reading in him, and he hoped to foster a similar love in the children who lived at the home.

A quiet knock on the office door interrupted his thoughts as Carstairs entered the room with a breakfast tray. The butler placed the tray on the desk then retreated as quietly as he'd entered. Garrick shoved his watch back into his vest pocket and poured himself a cup of coffee. He reached for the folded paper tucked under the plate of toast and fresh fruit and frowned.

Carstairs had arranged the paper so that the Society page was blatantly front and center. With a scowl, he quickly skimmed the gossip column then stiffened as the initials L.S. and L.R. caught his eye.

Known for his discreet, secretive liaisons, L.S. has surprised many among the Set with his recent display of infatuation with the L.R. However, it would appear that L.S. and his new amour the L.R. have had a falling-out since their last appearance together at the performance of Così fan tutte *several weeks ago. We can only hope that both parties have come to their senses in recognizing that love is for the young and not those of advancing years.*

He drew in a sharp breath at the last sentence. Christ almighty. As sensitive as Ruth was about her age, the minute she read this malicious gossip she'd be devastated. And this anecdote was particularly vicious in reference to the differences in their ages. Without a second thought, he leaped to his feet and jammed the jeweler's box into the inside pocket of his coat.

If he was lucky, she might not be awake yet. He uttered a dark expletive and bolted toward the door. That was wishful thinking on his part. The best he could hope for was that she'd not yet seen this morning's London *Times*. If she read that piece before he arrived, all bets were off as to whether or not she'd allow Simmons to let him through her front door.

Ruth awoke to a raw male scent embedded in her pillows. It was Garrick's, and it brought a smile to her lips. Her eyes still closed, she reached out for him, but the space where he should have been was empty. Disappointment crested through her as she raised herself up to rest on her elbows and looked around the bedroom. The first thing she noticed was that his coat was no longer draped over the back of the fireside chair. The rest of his clothes that had been scattered on the floor were gone as well. He'd left without saying good-bye. She didn't know why she'd expected to wake up in his arms, but she had. Her gaze fell on the folded parchment standing up on the table beside her bed. The strong handwriting on the note made her slide quickly across the mattress to snatch the missive off the nightstand. It was a brief note, and she smiled at his shy, almost awkward message.

Thank you for last night. I shall call for you at seven for a small dinner party Lord and Lady Ashford are hosting prior to the Westerham affair.

She fell backward into her pillows with the note clutched to her breast. Slowly she rolled over to bury her face in the pillow Garrick had used last night. The rich spicy smell of him permeated the bed, and her mind flitted back to the pleasure she'd found in his arms. Despite his inexperience, he'd been an amazingly quick study.

The second time he'd made love to her, he'd already learned how to control his own release until he secured her climax. Sweet heaven, but the man had been incredibly thick and hard inside her. When she'd shattered in his arms that first time, she couldn't have imagined a more exquisite moment. But she'd been wrong.

With the innate skill of a born seducer, he'd pulled her toward another precipice. In a joint release of pleasure, they'd climaxed together. The memory of how he'd throbbed inside her flooded back to make her body ache with a need to feel him inside her again. It had been a wonderful experience, and the only thing she could have wished for was to see his face at the moment of his release.

She sighed. Although Garrick had trusted her with one of his secrets, there were deeper layers to be explored. It would take time for her to gain his trust until he was willing to reveal himself further. Whatever Beresford had done to him, it was obvious Garrick didn't want her to see or touch him below his waist.

When she'd reached for his cock, his rejection of her touch had been so swift it had startled her, and the fear in his voice had touched her deeply. She had wanted to kill Beresford at that precise moment. Kill the bastard for the torment he'd caused Garrick. But in a blink of an eye, Garrick's touch had pulled her back to him and the delicious way her body responded to his.

With every touch, he'd made her feel desirable, wanton, and young again. She couldn't remember the last time she'd felt this alive, euphoric almost. It was as if she were fifteen years younger. It was a glorious feeling, and she loved it. Loved the way he made her feel both physically and emotionally. It was a heady experience.

A quiet knock sounded on the door before it opened and Dolores entered with a breakfast tray. The maid eyed her warily, but she was too happy to berate her friend. Thanks to Dolores, she'd experienced a night unlike any she'd had in a very long time.

"So are you going to fire me?" There was just a trace of smug contentment in the maid's voice, but Ruth didn't care.

"No."

"Good. I knew it was the right thing to do to let his lordship into the house. After the bleak mood you've been in for the past three weeks, I'm happy to see you smiling."

"I've not been that bad," she protested.

Dolores arched her eyebrow at her in disbelief before she set the breakfast tray on the table in front of the hearth. In a limber move for a woman her size, the maid retrieved Ruth's robe from the floor where it had fallen the night before.

Ruth scooted out of bed and accepted the silk garment the maid handed her. The robe brushed softly against her skin, reminding her of the warmth of Garrick's breath on her cheek as she'd fallen asleep last night. The robe's belt tied around her waist, she reached for the glass of juice on the tray.

"Do you know what time Lord Stratfield left this morning?"

"Simmons said he hailed a cabbie for his lordship around seven this morning," Dolores said as she bustled her way into the bathroom to run Ruth's bath.

Her heart skipped erratically at her friend's comment. So Garrick hadn't left immediately after she'd fallen asleep. The realization sent happiness spiraling through her. Inside, a small voice of warning tried to obliterate the blissful feeling, but it failed. She knew it was a mistake to take pleasure in the notion that he'd been unwilling to leave her, but she couldn't help herself.

Ruth glanced at the mantel clock. Nine thirty. There would barely be time to enjoy her breakfast and dress before she needed to leave. Yesterday she'd arranged to visit the Caring Hearts orphanage to speak with Lady Lynmouth about making their current partnership a permanent one. Deep inside she knew her motives for the visit had not been completely selfless.

She knew she'd been hoping to catch a glimpse of Garrick or at least have word of him from his sister. No matter how much she wanted to deny it, his continuous attempts to see her over the past three weeks had begun to wear her down. It was why she'd been unable to resist listening to his heartfelt explanation last night. She took a small bite of toast and frowned as she stared down at the tray.

"Dolores, where is the morning paper?" The question was met with an indistinguishable reply. "What?"

"I said you don't have time to read the paper." The older woman avoided her gaze as she emerged from the bathroom.

"I'm not that short on time." Ruth frowned at the stubborn look crossing the maid's face. "You're hiding something from me. What is it?"

"It's nothing." Dolores sniffed with annoyance. "Come along now. You need to be getting your bath or you'll be late for your appointment."

"The paper, if you please, Dolores." She stretched out her hand in a silent demand. With great reluctance, the maid pulled the paper from a deep pocket in her skirt.

"Don't you pay them no mind, my lady."

Her friend's words sent tension skimming along every one of her nerve endings as she accepted the London *Times*. With trepidation she opened the paper to the Society column. Her gaze scanned the article until she saw Garrick's initials combined with hers.

A shudder raced through her as she read the last sentence of the paragraph. Oh God, *advancing years*; she reached for the back of the nearby chair as she swayed on her feet. Behind her, Dolores clucked with concern and touched Ruth's arm. Her stomach lurched unpleasantly as she shrugged off her friend's touch.

"Leave me, Dolores." It was a quiet order her friend disobeyed.

"Don't let it upset you, my lady. It's all—"

"Go, Dolores," she bit out coldly. "Now."

She closed her eyes in an effort to control the nausea rolling over her with increasing strength. Why hadn't she listened to the warning bells in her head when Garrick had first suggested they be friends?

And last night . . . dear lord . . . last night had been a mistake of the worst kind. She shuddered.

Just moments ago she'd felt so young, but she'd been pulled back down to earth by a harsh reality. She was far too old to be involved with Garrick even if the age difference was only a few years. The newspaper crumpled and crackled beneath her tight grasp. *Advancing years.* Even with her eyes closed she could still see the words.

Last night couldn't happen again—no matter how much pleasure Garrick brought her in bed. She refused to play the role of a woman desperately clinging to her youth by being paramour to a man several years younger than her. And that was exactly how she appeared.

Desperate and old. The gossip column had bluntly made that point all too clear. The clock chimed the quarter hour, the sound piercing its way into her thoughts. She remembered her appointment with Lady Lynmouth. She couldn't cancel at the last minute.

As humiliating as this piece of gossip was, she refused to let anyone see how much it cost her emotionally. She would break with Garrick as soon as possible. He might protest, but she would have to be firm in her resolve and not let him persuade her to his way of thinking. She bit her lip as her head filled with images of Garrick attempting to overrule her decision.

Sweet heaven, would she be able to resist him? Her walk unsteady, she headed toward her waiting bath. She had no other options where Garrick was concerned. Their current relationship would eventually end, and the degradation of another man leaving her for a younger woman was far too painful a thought.

When a reasonable amount of time had passed, she would retire to Crawley Hall. The moment the next scandal took center stage in the Society column this humiliating experience would end. Chilled by the thought of how long that might take, she made her way into the bathroom to bathe. She would have to continue as though untroubled by the gossip.

God, if only she were younger. It would be hard to part with him. Last night he'd been such a willing pupil, and she'd never enjoyed herself so much in bed before, despite his lack of experience. But even if they were the same age, it would still be a mistake to continue seeing him. She was quickly growing infatuated with the man.

When she was with him, she didn't feel old at all. He made her feel vibrant, beautiful, and it was as if there was no question of age between them. Her eyes suddenly blurred with tears, and she blinked them away quickly. She was being ridiculous. It would be too short a jump from the passion they shared to something deeper where her feelings for Garrick were concerned.

Heaven knew she was already far too close to the edge as it was. And that was something she could afford even less than her current humiliation. Heartsick, she proceeded to bathe and dress for her appointment with Lady Lynmouth. The thought of Garrick's sister made her flinch. There was little doubt that the woman would be quite pleased to see an end to her association with her brother.

Her thoughts continued to center around Garrick, and by the time her carriage drew up in front of the Caring Hearts orphanage, her spirits had not improved. The young maid that greeted her at the door seemed a bit rattled, and Ruth frowned at the girl's distressed expression.

"I've an appointment with Lady Lynmouth. Would you please tell her I've arrived."

"I don't know that I should, my lady. Lord Tremaine arrived a quarter of an hour ago, and told us not to interrupt them."

Ruth stiffened at the maid's words. Was it possible Lady Lynmouth was involved with the bastard? It seemed unlikely, and she was certain Garrick would have put an end to such a relationship the moment he discovered Tremaine anywhere near his sister. But then perhaps Lady Lynmouth had kept it a secret from her brother.

Uncertainty filled her as she considered that possibility. Garrick's sister had not struck her as a woman who would dally with a man such as Tremaine. Drawing in a deep breath, Ruth's hand brushed across her drawstring reticule. Ever since the day she'd freed Jenny from the tyranny of the pickpocket who'd bought the child, she'd learned to carry a small revolver whenever she came to the East End.

She'd never used the weapon before, but Garrick's description of Tremaine told her the man was no different than his father. Somehow she doubted it would take much for her to at least wound the man. Without a second thought, she moved quickly down the hall to the office and its closed door. She raised her hand to knock when she heard the sound of a chair scraping across the floor.

"Let me go." Lady Lynmouth's voice was sharp, but there was a note of panic behind her command.

Ruth immediately tested the doorknob. It turned easily and she experienced a rush of relief that Tremaine had not had the forethought to lock the door. She quickly pulled her revolver from her drawstring bag and entered the office. The sight of Garrick's sister struggling to escape Tremaine's grasp sent a chill through her. Had her father witnessed a similar scene between the viscount's father and her mother? Pinned between Tremaine and the wall, Lady Lynmouth was trying hard to free herself from the man's hold.

"Let her go, my lord, or I shall be forced to shoot you." The moment she spoke, Tremaine jerked his head in her direction.

Garrick's sister didn't hesitate to take advantage of the man's distraction and jerked free of his hold to put several feet between them. A feral smile on his face, the viscount offered Ruth an arrogant bow of condescension.

"My dear Lady Ruth, this is a surprise."

"One you should be grateful for, my lord," Ruth said quietly. "I feel certain that had I been Lord Stratfield, it is unlikely you would still be alive."

"Ah, but you are not Stratfield, my dear lady." The man arched an eyebrow at her, clearly not intimidated by her weapon. He took two steps toward her, and Ruth cocked the small handgun. He immediately froze in his tracks.

"I have no wish to shoot you, Tremaine, but I will if necessary." She saw him weighing his options before he bowed again.

"It appears I've outstayed my welcome." He glanced at Garrick's sister. "I look forward to our next meeting, Lady Lynmouth."

Out of the corner of her eye, she saw the other woman pale. Angered at the way the viscount was threatening the woman, Ruth eyed the man coldly.

"I would advise you not to come anywhere near Lady Lynmouth in the future. I doubt her brother will be as generous with your well-being as I have been."

"Stratfield?" The viscount raised his eyebrow in contemptuous amusement. "I am quite certain the man's secrets will ensure his dealings with me are quite generous."

"Then you're a fool," she snapped. "The man won't hesitate to kill you if provoked."

The viscount's beady eyes narrowed as he assessed her. After a long pause he shrugged. "Stratfield doesn't strike me as a man capable of murder and mayhem."

"Stratfield might not be, but when it comes to my wife, I am more than capable of violence." The deep voice behind her startled Ruth, and she jerked her head to look over her shoulder at the tall man standing in the doorway. The room suddenly seemed much smaller as he entered the room, and as she glanced back at Tremaine, she saw the man's face had gone gray.

"Ethan," Lady Lynmouth gasped.

Her husband didn't look at her, keeping his eyes fixed steadily on Tremaine. The scowl he sent the other man made the viscount clear his throat nervously. Edging his way forward toward the door, Tremaine watched Lord Lynmouth warily.

"My apologies, Lynmouth. I had assumed you were done with the lady."

"What's mine, I keep." There was something dark in the earl's voice, and it said the words weren't intended for Tremaine alone.

The tension in the room took a sudden, accelerated leap forward, and it was evident she wasn't the only one to feel it. The viscount jerked his head in a placating gesture and abruptly headed toward the door. As the man disappeared from the room, Ruth sagged with relief. A large hand gently took the revolver from her and released the firing pin before returning the weapon to her.

"Are the two of you unharmed?" Although his question seemed calm and nonchalant, the tension vibrating off the man said he was far from either of those things.

"I am fine, my lord." Ruth nodded her head as she returned her revolver to her drawstring bag. "Although I am grateful for your arrival."

She glanced at the woman across the room and drew in a sharp breath. Garrick's sister seemed on the verge of collapse. Without hesitating she hurried to the woman's side and guided her to the office chair.

"Come, sit down. You've had a horrible fright."

"Thank you, Lady Ruth." The countess's whisper barely reached Ruth's ears, and she noticed the woman's gaze had yet to stray from her husband.

"I, too, owe you a debt of gratitude, my lady. If you hadn't intervened, I might have arrived too late." The man's deep voice resonated with gratitude, and beneath her hand, Lady Lynmouth's body grew rigid.

"Why are you here, Ethan?"

There was a harshness to the question that made Ruth immediately cast a glance in the earl's direction. She almost didn't catch the flash of emotion that flitted across the tall man's face, but the brief glimpse told her the earl was in deep torment. When he didn't answer his wife's question, Ruth glanced first at the countess then at the earl. The sign of a battle brewing was visible on both their faces, and the last thing she wanted was to be caught in the middle.

She straightened in preparation to leave the couple alone.

"I think we should reschedule our appointment for another time, Lady Lynmouth."

"Oh no, I am—"

"I believe you're correct, Lady Ruth. I'll take my wife home and see to it that she rests."

"Then if you'll excuse me, my lord. Lady Lynmouth," she said as she quickly headed toward the door. She'd almost reached it when she heard the sound of running feet. Tension drew her muscles taut as Garrick shouted for his sister from the corridor.

"Lily. Lily, are you all right?" The moment he barreled through the doorway, Garrick slid to a halt in amazement and stared around the room in angry confusion. "They told me Tremaine was in here."

"He was, but Lady Ruth prevented the man . . . then Ethan . . . arrived." The countess's stammering explanation made Garrick frown darkly as he looked at Lily's husband.

"Stratfield." The earl nodded in his brother-in-law's direction.

"What the devil are you doing here, Lynmouth?"

"I've come for my wife." The earl's stoic reply prompted a stubborn look to harden Garrick's face, and he shook his head.

"Lily has made it quite clear she wants nothing to do with you."

"Nonetheless, as my wife she will come home. Now I'd like a word with her. In private."

Lord Lynmouth turned to his wife, his expression harsh and unrelenting as he silently demanded she acquiesce. He was an intimidating man, and it surprised her that Garrick's sister didn't flinch in the face of her husband's obvious determination. Still not looking away from her husband's face, she gave her brother a slight wave of her hand.

"It's all right, Garrick. I'll listen to what he has to say."

Eager to escape the volatile emotions flooding the room, Ruth didn't wait to hear him argue with his sister. As quickly as she could, she slipped past Garrick and hurried down the hallway. At the front entrance to the orphanage, she released a quick breath of relief that Simmons was exactly where she'd left him. She took a step forward only to have a strong male hand prevent her from leaving the orphanage.

"Is there a reason you didn't wait for me?"

"You were occupied with family matters, and I had no wish to pry," she murmured.

Before she could protest, he pulled her back into the orphanage and into a small storage room off the main entryway. He closed the door behind him and leaned against it with his arms folded across his chest. She shuddered at the memory of her hands caressing his bare chest. She quickly glanced away from his penetrating gaze in an effort to quiet the desire curling in her belly until it sped downward and made her ache to feel him between her legs again. Her entire body pulsed a primitive rhythm at his nearness, and she tried to quiet the rapid beat of her heart.

"Have you seen the morning paper?" he asked.

"Yes." There wasn't much else she could say, even if she wanted to.

"It won't work, Ruth." The emphatic note in his voice sliced into her like a carving knife. The fact that he'd come to his senses made her stomach churn. She had hoped she'd be the one to walk away this time, but like others before him, he was finished with her. She winced.

"I understand." Even to her the words were stilted.

"Do you?" Garrick's voice was firm. "When I say it won't work, I mean I will not give you up simply because people choose to gossip."

Startled, she jerked her gaze toward him. The determined expression on his handsome features tightened her throat. He was serious. A knot swelled in her throat, and she shook her head.

"You make it sound so simple when it's not."

"Damn it, it *is* simple." He sent her a fierce glare. "I'll not let a few narrow-minded half-wits dictate who I should or shouldn't see."

"It's not the gossip."

She winced at how her awkward response made him slowly push away from the door to stand tall and rigid in front of her. Her gaze flitted down to where his hands had fisted at the side of his legs before she looked back at his stone-cold features.

"So I was little more than one evening's entertainment to you. An amusing tale to share with others." His icy statement appalled her.

"*No.*" She quickly stepped forward to wrap her hand around his hard fist. "Last night was wonderful."

And it had been, more wonderful than she'd ever thought possible, and that was part of the problem. She was frightened that if she were to continue seeing him, her age would only ensure heartbreak. The tension making him hard against her slowly abated as his fingers unfurled to grasp her hand, and he bent his head to kiss the inside of her wrist.

"Then why deny yourself—or me for that matter—the pleasure of experiencing it again?"

The heat of his caress sank its way through her skin until it warmed her blood and sent a tingling sensation spiraling through her body. Sweet heaven, the mere touch of the man's mouth against her skin was more arousing than any kiss she'd ever exchanged with any of her lovers. She gently pulled her hand free of his grasp.

"There is more than pleasure to consider." Her heart beat erratically in her breast at the passion she saw burning in his gaze. "My lifestyle has never been viewed as . . . respectable . . . in some circles, but I have always been discreet."

"So the gossip does bother you."

She shook her head in denial. It was difficult to put into words that it wasn't the actual comments that bothered her. It was how they reinforced her own feelings about her age. She'd never been one to really care what the Set thought with regard to most situations, but this was different. She was struggling with the fact that she was no longer young.

There wasn't a sign of gray in her hair, and her skin was still wrinkle free, but it was coming. She'd seen it happen to others—almost overnight, and the Set had mercilessly shoved them aside for younger women. Without patrons, their incomes had dwindled to nothing, consigning them to a life without home or family.

For the first time, she realized she'd been hoping that she wouldn't be one of those women. Deep inside she'd actually believed in the possibility that her life would be different than that of others she'd seen disappear into obscurity. The realization that it wouldn't left her feeling alone and frightened.

"What are you really afraid of, Ruth?" His astute question made her mouth go dry.

"I'm afraid that when you leave—" She raised her hand as she saw him frown. "It's inevitable. You will leave. And when you do, the price I'll pay is going to be dear."

"Do you think I'll break your heart, Ruth?" The intensity behind the question alarmed her. It was unexpected, and the answer that fluttered in the back of her head scared her.

"No." She shook her head vehemently, despite knowing it was a lie. "I learned a long time ago to protect myself from unrequited affection. But it's the way you make me feel that I like far too much."

He leaned toward her, and the spicy scent of his cologne filled her senses. It reminded her of last night and falling asleep in his arms. The memory was exactly what she meant when it came to liking how she felt with him.

"Tell me how I make you feel, Ruth." The smooth velvet command drew a frisson across her skin and she fought to suppress a shudder.

"You make me feel alive . . . and young."

"Young?" He caught her chin in his hand and forced her to meet his gaze. "You're obsessed with this idea that age is a number. It's not."

"For a woman in my position it is," she said firmly. "Age and beauty are what my livelihood is based on. Without them, the only option left to me is retirement. Something I intend to do shortly."

"There is another option." His blue eyes studied her intently as his thumb rubbed its way across her lower lip. "You can let me provide for you."

The statement made her stiffen with a mixture of shock and resignation and she jerked her head back from his touch. She'd been right. Last night had dramatically changed their relationship. Deep inside, she'd known this might happen where he was concerned, but she'd chosen to ignore the possibility rather than consider what she would do if he offered to be her patron.

"I won't take no for an answer, Ruth." His beautiful mouth

thinned to a hard, stubborn line as his gaze challenged her to try and defy him.

"And you have the audacity to call me stubborn," she snapped with frustration.

"When it comes to you, yes I am." There was a gleam of something dangerous in his eyes that made her heart slam violently into her chest as he put several feet between them again. "I've wanted you from the first time I saw you. I think I've always known you were meant to grace my bed. I simply didn't know how to accomplish the task given my—my inexperience."

Despite the strength and resolve in his voice, she was certain he'd almost revealed his dark secret. Whatever his shame, she knew it tormented him, and her irritation vanished as her heart made her want to reach out to him. Afraid that her ability to read him might prove embarrassing for him, she moved to the small window that looked out on the dingy home fronts across from the orphanage.

Living here in the East End could have just as easily been her fate, but providence had made life much easier for her. She should be grateful for what she had, and not long for the dream she'd always kept buried deep inside her. She'd be a fool to reject Garrick's patronage. But would she be an even greater fool for accepting? Her feelings for him were already far stronger than she liked.

"I have something for you," he said quietly.

She looked over her shoulder to see him pull a jeweler's box out of his coat pocket. It reminded her of the one she'd returned to the jewelers several days ago unopened. He popped the lid of the box open and waited as she closed the distance between them. The design of the white tulip earrings nestled in the satin interior of the box matched the brooch he'd given her. A second apology.

The white diamonds sparkled in the subdued lighting of the storage room, and she would have been a liar if she'd said she was unmoved by the beauty of the earrings. The custom-made jewelry showed what a thoughtful lover Garrick was. Not even Westleah had ever given her jewelry custom designed for the purpose of an apology.

She closed her eyes for a moment. She'd made up her mind about him several minutes ago, but she'd not realized it until just now. It was probably the worst decision she'd ever made, but her feet were already on the path to hell, and there was no turning back. The heat of him washed over her body as he leaned into her. His lips brushed across her mouth then her cheek as he nibbled his way to her ear. A shudder streaked through her as he gently abraded her earlobe with his teeth.

"Give me your answer, Ruth."

"Yes," she whispered as she turned her head and sought his mouth.

Heat exploded and spiraled its way through her body the minute their lips met. He pulled her into his embrace, his hands cupping her face as he teased her mouth apart and his tongue danced with hers. With a skill that belied his inexperience in the bedroom, he kissed her slowly and deeply. The caress was maddening in its restraint, and she murmured a protest as he pulled away from her. He stepped away from her with a shake of his head, and her mouth went dry at the desire burning in his gaze.

"As much as I want you right now, sweetheart, I have a commitment I need to keep."

Disappointment seeped its way through her, and she nodded with an understanding she didn't feel. The fact that she didn't want him to leave signaled her need to keep her head where he was concerned. She'd never clung to a lover in the past, and she refused to do so now, even if it was exactly what she wanted to do at the moment.

"I shall see you later this evening," she murmured as she started to move past him. His hand grasped her arm as she came abreast of him, and he turned her to face him.

"No. Stay with me." He smiled at her. "I always read to the children every week at this time."

The explanation made her stare at him in surprise. Garrick's commitment was far from the frivolous engagement she'd immediately assumed he'd scheduled. She didn't know why it surprised her so much, except that it was unlike anything her other lovers had done.

They'd all donated their funds, but never their time, to a charity. That Garrick was donating not only his money but his time to the children in the home revealed a great deal about his character.

It was one more aspect that made him so very different from any other man she'd ever been with. It endeared him to her. Unable to resist the charm of his smile, she placed her hand in his and nodded her acquiescence. The moment his smile widened to a grin, her heart skidded out of control. It was a vivid reminder that she traveled a perilous road and would have to guard her heart well.

Her hand clasped in his, she allowed him to lead her through the orphanage to a bright, cheery schoolroom where a young woman was drawing letters on a blackboard. The minute the children saw Garrick, the room erupted with squeals of delight. He released her hand and the children immediately surrounded him.

It was clear they adored him, and in the back of her head, a small voice whispered all the reasons why. Oh how easily she could lose her heart and soul to this man. Garrick accepted the book the young teacher offered him and smiled his thanks. The moment he turned back to the children, Ruth caught the look of adoration on the young woman's face. The teacher's reaction to Garrick wasn't surprising, but the strength of her own territorial reaction alarmed her. She quickly brushed the emotion aside and focused her attention on Garrick as he sat on a stool and opened up the book.

"Now then, what shall I read today?"

He glanced around at the children who had gathered at his feet and arched his eyebrows as a chorus of suggestions resounded loudly in the room. Garrick looked down at the boy who was tugging roughly on his trouser leg.

"Yes, Arthur?"

"'The Ugly Duckling,' please, my lord. It's Hannah's favorite."

"All right then, 'The Ugly Duckling,' because Hannah likes it."

Garrick smiled at the little girl sitting next to the boy, an odd expression flickering across his face as he opened the book. It was the sign of a man remembering his past, and his own efforts to look out for his siblings. Quietly finding a chair in the far corner of the room, she sat and watched Garrick enthrall the children for the next half hour with his reading of Hans Christian Andersen's popular fairy tale.

When he'd finished, the children immediately beseeched him to read another story. He laughingly refused to give way to their demands, his hand tousling several of the children's heads. It was an affectionate gesture, and Ruth suddenly imagined him with several dark-haired children of his own clinging to his legs. He would make an excellent father.

The thought made her chest constrict with a sharp pang. The fact that she had no children was her deepest regret. It made her envy the woman who would eventually bear Garrick's. His wife would be an extremely fortunate woman. Her throat tightened as his gaze met hers across the room.

There was an intimacy in the brief glance that took her breath away and made her feel as though she were the only woman Garrick would ever desire. She stiffened at her sudden wish that something more than desire existed between them. It was a reckless thought. One that would cause her terrible heartache in the future. She needed to keep reminding herself that their liaison would endure only as long as his desire for her lasted.

That fact would have been easy for her to accept when it came to any other lover. But when it came to Garrick she was certain that her heart would not go unscathed. Her body warmed as he drew closer to her, and she didn't hesitate to link her arm with his when he offered to escort her out of the room. The future be damned. She would allow herself this one last pleasurable affair before she retired to Crawley Hall. For once in her long life, she would consider her own needs just as much as she would her lover's.

A wild frenzy pitched its way through his blood as Garrick thrust into Ruth one last time then convulsed violently inside her. With equal intensity, her body clutched at him, extending the pleasure of his release. He opened his eyes and stared down at the blindfold across her eyes in frustration. How could he know he'd pleased her when he couldn't read the emotion in her gaze?

With a grunt of self-disgust, he withdrew from her and left the bed. He quickly cleaned himself, and as he pulled his trousers on, he glanced over his shoulder at Ruth. For more than a week now, she'd willingly allowed him to blindfold her every time they made love. He was now beginning to realize how unfulfilling it was not to be able to look into her eyes as he brought her to a climax.

And he had no doubt of his ability to do that. He'd experienced her over and over again in the last few days since she agreed to be his mistress. He'd memorized every inch of her. She was etched into his senses in a way he never dreamed possible. He returned to the bed to remove the scarf from her eyes, while he gently cleaned the remains of their lovemaking from between her thighs.

The soft sigh she released pulled his gaze to her face. She was smiling at him, and the bolt of emotion blasting its way through him made him tense. It was a sensation he couldn't afford to feel. Lust was the only thing he could allow himself to feel where she was concerned. It was bad enough he hid his body from her. The last thing he needed was to learn how to hide his heart from her as well.

"Have I told you before what an apt pupil you are?" There was more than a hint of satisfaction in her voice, and he could feel a smile tugging at his mouth.

"On more than one occasion," he said with amusement, his black mood lightening considerably. "But then I've been tutored by an exceptional woman."

She laughed, and he loved the sound of it as it filled his ears. His gaze swept over her exquisite curves, relishing the sight of her. She looked far younger than her forty-one years, and he wished she could see herself the way he saw her. How any man could be so easily parted from her was beyond his comprehension.

It would be a long time before he was willing to part with her. *If ever.* He quickly crushed the small voice threatening revolt in the back of his head. He lay down next to her and propped himself up on his elbow while he stroked her softly rounded belly with his forefinger.

"I think I shall enjoy having you as my mistress very much. Always at my beck and call whenever I have need of a new lesson in the art of seduction." He paused to smile wickedly at her. "And I am certain I shall require a great many lessons."

"Then you do not regret my offer of instruction." She sent him a teasing smile, but there was a hesitancy layered beneath her question that made him eye her carefully. He shook his head.

"Do you regret accepting my offer to provide for you?"

"No, I want to be with you. I would not have agreed otherwise." She smiled at him, but a hint of sadness darkened her violet eyes.

She turned over onto her stomach to cradle her head in the crook of one arm, and he lightly stroked her back. Her response hadn't been quite convincing enough for him. Something was troubling her. Lowering his head, he playfully nipped at the small of her back, while exploring her shoulder with his fingers. She murmured a soft noise of pleasure at the caress.

"This pleases you?"

"Anytime you touch me, I find it pleasurable." Her breathy words ended in a quiet gasp as his hand slid along the line of her back to slip beneath her and cup her breast.

He loved the warm, lush feel of her in his hand. Every part of her seemed made for him. Her breasts fit nicely in the palms of his hands, while she fit his cock perfectly. Even her head nestled against his shoulder felt right. He gently tweaked her nipple.

"Good. Because I like touching you very much." He kissed his way up her spine expecting her to say something else, but she remained silent. Raising his head, he studied her profile. "Tell me what's troubling you."

The moment she hesitated, he knew he could make a good guess as to what was wrong. She didn't have to say it. Not once had she protested when he'd covered her eyes. Each time she'd smiled up at him with not only desire, but an open expression of trust on her face that twisted at his gut. He knew leaving the blindfold off when they were making love would signal his reciprocating trust, but he'd not had the courage to bare his soul completely. He couldn't, not even with her.

"Tell me," he commanded.

"It's nothing."

"My inexperience did not—"

"You are no longer *inexperienced*," she said with mischievous amusement. He playfully smacked her bottom.

"I might not be fully indoctrinated into the arts of the bedroom, but having sisters has taught me how to tell when a woman is worried about something." He rolled her over onto her back. "Is it the blindfold?"

"I don't mind it, but it would . . . it would be nice to see your face when you're making love to me." The gentle understanding in her voice made him wince.

"You ask a great deal of me."

"Garrick, have I betrayed your trust yet?" When he responded with a sharp shake of his head, she touched his face. "Then could you not trust me further?"

"It is not a matter of trust," he rasped.

"Then what is it? You have a beautiful body." She pressed her hand into his chest as he grimaced. "You *do*. Even blindfolded, I can *feel* how splendidly male you are."

The blindfold had done its work well. He was far from the magnificent specimen of manhood she thought him to be. She had no inkling he was a freak of nature. And he was too much of a coward to risk telling her the truth about his deformity. If she were to react the same way Bertha had, it would destroy him.

Images from the past flooded his head, and he clenched his jaw at the pain the memories brought. The clock on the mantel chimed the two o'clock hour. He'd promised to meet Charles at the Club for breakfast and then he had an appointment with Smythe to view a piece of property on the outskirts of town. He pushed himself up off the mattress and headed toward the chair where he'd laid his clothes.

"I have an early morning appointment, and I have no wish to wake you, so I'll leave now."

With his back to her, he didn't see her climb out of bed, and he jumped as she took his coat from his hand to help him slide into it. There was a tenderness to her gesture that gripped his heart and he turned around to pull her into his arms. Even through his clothing and the silk of her robe, he could feel her warmth boring its way into him—his soul. He swallowed hard at the emotion pounding through his veins. Lowering his head, he kissed her gently, wishing he didn't have to leave her. When he raised his head, he smiled.

"You make it difficult for me to leave you, sweetheart."

"Do I?" Happiness lit up her face as she smiled at him. "I'm glad."

"I'll call for you this evening around eight. I believe a new opera is playing at the Lyceum." He gave her a gentle push toward the bed. "Go get some sleep. I intend to keep you up even later tomorrow night."

He grinned at the slight blush that crested over her cheeks, and with one last quick kiss, he left the room. The moment he was in the hallway, he experienced the need to go back and hold her close. It was as if he'd left a part of himself behind with her. Grunting at the sentimental thought, he strode down the hallway and made his way downstairs.

Unlike his usual habit, Simmons didn't materialize from the back of the town house. Quietly letting himself out, he locked the door behind him with the key Ruth had given him several days ago. It didn't surprise him that the street was deserted. He should have asked Jasper to wait for him, but the man deserved a decent night's sleep. With a shrug of resignation, he headed toward Chiddingstone House.

He found himself wishing he'd not made his early breakfast appointment with Charles. It would have meant he could have stayed with Ruth a few more hours. His thoughts returned to his current dilemma. What the hell was he going to do? There were only two options open to him, and he wasn't willing to accept either one.

As long as Ruth was willing to accept him as he was, then they would continue as they had from the beginning. He walked through the beam of the gaslight illuminating the sidewalk into the softer shadows. A cat screeched nearby and set his senses on alert. He glanced behind him and saw nothing. While this part of town was generally safe at all hours, it still paid to be careful.

He grimaced. He'd been cautious all his life, always on guard, whether it was preparing himself for his uncle's next lesson in cruelty, protecting his siblings, or doing whatever it took to keep his secret safe. But in the last few weeks he'd learned what it felt like to not be continuously vigilant with his thoughts or his words. Ruth was easy to talk to, and he'd shared more of himself with her than he ever thought possible to share with any woman.

A clatter of noise echoed out of the alley he was passing, and he drew up short as a man stumbled out of the darkness toward him. Staggering to first one side and then another, the drunk saluted him with a mumbled greeting before passing. A smile pulled at the corners of his mouth at the man's inebriated state.

The last time he'd seen someone that drunk had been the night of Charles's birthday celebration last year. Everyone had imbibed a bit more than usual, but Harrington had been the worst. The earl had reeked of alcohol, unlike the man who'd just stumbled—a blow to the back of his head sent him sagging toward the ground. One knee pressed into the pavement, he tried to shake off the pain making his gut churn.

Before he could come upright, two pairs of hands dragged him backward into the alley. Still reeling from the attack, it took him several seconds to regain his senses enough to struggle. His feet scrabbling for a foothold on the alley's slick cobblestones, he turned his head and bit down on the hand gripping his bicep until he tasted blood. The man released Garrick with a sharp cry.

"You bloody bastard. I'll show you who's in charge 'ere," his first attacker snarled. "Hold 'em."

With a vicious twist of his arm, Garrick jerked free of his second assailant and landed flat on his face. A heavy foot barreled into his side, and with a grunt of pain he quickly rolled away. His hand pressed into his side in a futile effort to ease the screaming protest of his insides, and he scrambled to his feet. Standing upright, he swayed like a drunk and could have sworn someone was using a sledgehammer on the back of his head. In front of him, he saw two dark figures eyeing him with caution. He was apparently proving to be more trouble than they'd expected.

The taller of the two men was built like a wrestler, and he was nursing his hand where Garrick had bit him. The other man was far from skinny, but he didn't appear to have the strength of his friend. Furious that the bastards had targeted him for robbery, Garrick stepped to one side so he could keep an eye on his assailants while looking back toward the street.

His jaw clenched with tension at the distance between him and the street. Running wasn't a good idea given the fact that he was barely able to stand upright as it was. His gaze switched back to his assailants. The smaller attacker would be easier to shake off. Not so the larger man. The sooner he took the brawny one out of the equation, the less likely he was to lose his wallet or his life.

He darted forward in a light move and landed a hard right to the jaw of the bigger man. The man's head snapped sideways from the force of Garrick's blow, and the result was a low roar of anger. It wasn't exactly the sound he'd been hoping to hear.

Pain shot through his side as he leaped backward. His retreat wasn't far enough. With surprising speed, his opponent jumped forward to tackle him around the waist and drive him backward into the alleyway wall. Once again the air left his lungs as the man's beefy hands grabbed him by the throat and squeezed.

Garrick clawed at his attacker's fat hands to no avail. The lack of air and the pain gripping his body made it hard to focus as he fought to stay alive. An image of Ruth filled his head. God, he might never see her again. The thought sent adrenaline surging through him, and he drove his forefinger into the man's eye.

The bastard instantly released him to stagger backward, his hand covering his injured eye. Air rushed into his lungs again as he dragged in several deep breaths. A noise off to his side made Garrick lurch away, but not fast enough. The second assailant had decided to enter the fray, and the man's left hook ricocheted off his jaw, snapping his head to one side with a loud crack.

Shock clouded his vision as blood filled his mouth, and he had no time to recover as the man rammed his fist into his side again. His breathing ragged from the pain assaulting every inch of his body, he stumbled away from the man in the direction of the street. He'd been a fool not to try running. He staggered two steps before he fell forward, breaking his fall with his hands. Now it was too late.

Another foot landed in the one side of him that didn't hurt, and it drove air out of his lungs with a loud *whoosh*. Once more Ruth's face pushed its way through his pain. He wasn't willing to give up yet. His breathing labored and his body screaming a protest, he straightened as quickly as he could to face his attackers. In the dim light, he saw his burly assailant glaring at him with malicious fury.

"You're a stubborn one, ain't ye, guv."

Garrick tried a retort, but his jaw was too sore. Instead, he spit blood in the man's direction. The act of defiance cost him dearly as his jaw protested with a vicious stab of pain. The man lunged forward and in the darkness, Garrick failed to see the club swinging in his direction until it was too late.

The minute the stick hit his leg with a sickening crack, Garrick sank to the ground. The excruciating pain shooting up his leg sent bile rising in his throat. As he choked on it, he slumped onto the slimy, damp cobblestones. Somewhere in the back of his head a voice shouted for him to get up. He couldn't.

His entire body was in agony, and a black morass was winding its way around his conscious thought. Not even the foot ramming into his side produced enough pain to pierce the fog clouding his brain. A low moan echoed in his ears. It struck him as odd that the man who kept kicking him would be moaning until in the depths of his brain he realized the sound was coming from him.

"Damn it, Billings, what the fuck are you doing? We're not supposed to kill the bastard."

"What difference does it make?"

"I'll not get hung for murder, you stupid lout," Billings's partner snapped. "We was just to rough him up a bit, and I'd say you done more than that. Get his wallet, and that ring there."

Barely aware of his surroundings, Garrick heard his attackers' conversation as if they were far away. Someone leaned over him and tugged at his jacket. The rough movement sent more pain lashing through his body. Unable to move, he didn't fight the fog sweeping over him, and Ruth's smile filled his head as he hovered on the edge unable to move or speak.

The sounds of his attackers had vanished, and he vaguely realized he'd been out for God knew how long. He tried to move, but when he did a raging fire assaulted his body. Sleep. All he needed was a little sleep. He drifted off again and when he came to it was to a fiery pain that covered his entire body.

Christ Jesus, it hadn't been a dream. He rolled over with a groan, and lay still for a moment. Lifting his head, he saw the street in front of him. It looked as though it were a hundred miles away. With a sharp breath that breathed fire through his sore throat, he got up on his hands and knees to crawl toward the street.

Vaguely, he noted the first light of dawn was brightening the sky, before he collapsed again to the slimy stones beneath his hands. He wasn't sure how long it took to gather his strength again, because he kept drifting in and out of consciousness. The next time he came to, he managed to gather his strength and get to his feet.

By some small miracle, he was able to stagger into the wall of the side street, where he stood braced against the stone for a moment. Slowly gathering his strength, he slid his body along the wall toward the end of the alleyway. Every step was agony, but he refused to collapse and give way to the pain. Step after step, he forced his body forward.

He wasn't sure how long it took him to get to the street, but as he reached the sidewalk, he stumbled out into the open. Without the alleyway wall to brace himself against, he lurched to first one side of the sidewalk and then the other. Unable to think clearly, he swayed on his feet as he stared around him. Where was he? Ruth. He'd been at Ruth's house. Which direction was that?

A door slammed nearby, and with an awkward stagger, he turned around to see a small phaeton waiting for the man striding down the steps of a town house. The man seemed familiar. Garrick took a step forward only to fall to his knees. Defeat pounded against him as he tried to crawl forward. His throat swollen and aching, he tried to cry out for help but failed.

"I say there, are you all right?"

The man's voice was one he'd heard before, but he couldn't remember where. He shook his head at the question, the movement dragging a groan of pain from him. Although he could barely lift his head, he managed to look up at the man bending over him. Worthington.

"*Good God.* Stratfield. What the devil . . . Johnson, get down here *now.*" With a gentle hand, the younger man touched his shoulder. "Where are you hurt?"

The question made him laugh, but the sound he made was anything but. His mouth swollen on one side, all that came out was a grunt. When the driver reached them, Worthington gave the older man directions and together they lifted Garrick to his feet. Another groan rolled up into his burning throat, and Worthington muttered an expletive.

"Sorry, old man. You've a new bird, haven't you? The Lady Ruth?"

"Yes." It was a mangled response.

"Johnson, it's just a few houses down. We'll take him there." Worthington bowed his head toward him. "This is not likely to be pleasant, Stratfield, given your condition."

He could only groan as the two men half lifted, half carried him toward Ruth's town house. In the back of his head, he heard a voice calling a warning to him, but he couldn't figure out what it was saying. Instead, he felt himself sagging between the two men as he slipped back into the darkness again.

When he next rose up into consciousness, it was to the sounds of exclamations and the sweet music of Ruth's voice. He tried to lift his head, but found it difficult to do so. There was the sudden sensation of being weightless as several hands carried him up the steps to Ruth's bedroom. Another groan escaped his lips as he was placed on a soft mattress. A cool hand caressed his head, and he opened his eyes to see Ruth bending over him. Fear darkened her eyes, and as terrible as he felt, his spirits lifted slightly. She was afraid for him. He tried to smile at her reassuringly. All he managed was a grimace before he lost consciousness.

Uncertain how much time had passed, he awoke to the sound of quiet voices nearby. He licked his dry lips and tried to clear his throat to ask for water. In seconds, Ruth was at his side. Despite the pain he was in, the first thing he noted was how beautiful she looked. He'd thought he'd never see her again. Her arm gently slid under his shoulders so she could cradle him against her as she offered him a sip of water. After three sips, she pulled the cup from him. In protest, he stretched out his hand for the cup, but she moved it out of his reach.

"Just a little now, my darling. Too much might make you sick." The soothing sound of her voice stroked his senses and he tried to nod as he closed his eyes again. A feathery kiss brushed against his brow just before he drifted back into an unconscious state.

He was cold. The sheets shifted around him as he rolled over. The action turned the dull throbbing in his body into a sharp stabbing pain that jerked him fully awake. Christ Jesus, what the hell was wrong with him? He opened his eyes and frowned at the drapes covering his windows. Who the devil had changed the curtains? Slowly the room came into clearer focus, and he realized he wasn't at home. He was in Ruth's bedroom. In her bed.

Naked.

He shot upright, and the minute he did so, a sharp pain made his stomach lurch as it tugged a low cry past his lips. Why the devil did he hurt so—the alleyway. Anger blasted through him as he remembered the two men who'd attacked him. The minute he was able, he'd send for Blackstone and have him find the sons of bitches who'd done this to him.

Damnation, his throat hurt as though he'd been sick, but he was certain it was from the beefy fingers of the attacker who'd throttled him. Gingerly, he bent his head and lifted his arm as high as possible to examine the bruises on his side. Bloody hell, almost every inch of him hurt, some places more than others. Moving quickly would be difficult at best.

His jaw was sore, and he brushed his fingers lightly over the side of his face that was the most painful. The touch wasn't pleasant, but it wasn't quite as tender as he'd expected given the battering he remembered. Probably the worst pain of all was his leg. It ached down to the bone itself. Something told him a cane might be necessary for a while.

The sound of the door opening made him jerk his head up to see Ruth walk into the room. Dressed in a blue day dress, she looked tempting enough to eat. God, and to think he might never have seen her again. The sight of her stirred his cock for a few seconds before he went flaccid and a slow, nauseating horror rolled over him.

He was naked. Someone other than his uncle now knew he was half a man. Was it her? Did she know the truth? Bile rose in his throat at the thought, and his body grew rigid with tension, which only intensified the pain gripping every part of him.

"You're awake."

Delight enhanced the excitement in her voice, but all he could think about was the need to know who knew his secret. He watched her move quickly to set down the tray she carried before she hurried toward the bed. He winced as she sank down onto the mattress beside him to reach for his hand. Tenderly, she carried his hand to her mouth to kiss his scraped knuckles then turned it over to kiss the inside of his palm.

"Do you feel up to eating some broth?"

"No," he said hoarsely.

He shook his head sluggishly as he glanced down to study her hand holding his. Despite the fear holding him hostage, a small part of him welcomed the warmth of her touch. It indicated an affection for him that almost eased his fears, but his terror was stronger. He tugged his hand out of hers with a grimace as the movement affected the rest of his body.

"Who . . ." he rasped and looked away from her. Christ Jesus, he couldn't even ask the question.

"I did." Her quiet response made him jerk his head toward her.

"You what?" He knew what she was referring to, but he didn't want to believe it.

"I undressed you," she said gently. "There was little choice, we needed to see the extent of your injuries. I knew you wouldn't want anyone to see you, so I'm the *only* one who . . . who knows."

Her words battered their way through him with the same ruthless power as the beating he'd taken last night. Worse, she'd stumbled over her explanation. A strong indicator of her revulsion.

Fuck. Fuck. Fuck.

The violent oaths built slowly in his mind until the last instance of the word was a roar of fury resounding in his head. She'd seen him. She knew his secret. Humiliation swept its way through him. Christ Jesus, what was he supposed to do now? If she told someone, he'd be the laughingstock of the Set.

Worse, he'd be an object of pity for others. The sudden urge to run latched onto his limbs, and he glanced around the room for his clothing. Out. He needed to get out of here. He needed to find a quiet place to think.

"Where are my clothes?" The rough edge of his voice made her flinch, but he didn't care. He had to leave. He couldn't stay here knowing she knew the truth.

"They're in the wardrobe, but you're not well enough to get out of bed, let alone dress."

"*My clothes*, Lady Ruth," he ground out. The flash of pain that flitted across her face was easy to ignore when the panic inside him refused to subside.

"Don't be ridiculous," she snapped. "You're far too weak to go gallivanting about town."

"I'll be the judge of how strong I am. *Bring* me my clothes."

"Get them yourself."

The words were sharp with exasperation, and the noisy rustle of her skirts emphasized her outrage as she stood up. Her mouth tight with anger, she took several steps back from the bed and waited for him to move. He glared at her then started to scoot his way to the edge of the bed, taking care to keep the sheet close to his waist. Even though she knew about his defect, the idea of exposing himself to her was unthinkable.

His efforts to reach the side of the bed pulled a hiss of pain from him, and he stopped to take in a breath. *Bloody hell.* What part of him didn't hurt? He inched forward again, and the grunt he made pulled a small noise of dismay from Ruth. Damn it, the last thing he wanted was her pity. But he didn't have much choice about getting out of bed. She was right. He didn't have the strength to leave.

The realization made him sag back into the feather bedding. He wasn't used to being so helpless, and he'd never had need of a physician's care before. He stiffened. *We.* She'd said "we had no choice." Christ almighty, she had to have sent for a doctor. She *wasn't* the only one who knew the truth. Horrified, he clenched his jaw only to have it shoot pain up into his head, but it didn't stop him from pushing himself up into a sitting position once more.

"You said *we*," he rasped.

"I had Simmons examine you. He served in the army as a medical corpsman." Her tone was calm and serene, but her irritation remained just below the surface. "He's quite skilled, and I trusted his judgment that you were in no serious danger."

A servant. She'd allowed a servant to examine him. His gut twisted violently at this newest revelation. Servants were notorious for gossip. It was like spoon-feeding the Marlborough Set. One servant whispered a juicy piece of information into the ear of a servant from another household and suddenly something private was public fodder.

"You allowed a servant—"

"I was with Simmons the entire time. And even though I trust him implicitly, I know for a fact that his examination did not uncover your secret." She returned to the bed to straighten the pillows behind him. God help her if she was lying to him.

"Leave me be, Ruth." His throat hurt, and their conversation only exacerbated his pain.

Each new revelation she offered up added to his misery. And the last thing he wanted to do at the moment was think about how his life would change—had changed, and not for the better. Exhausted, he closed his eyes.

"Oh, so it's not *Lady Ruth* anymore," she muttered. He grimaced as she jabbed a pillow behind him. "I ought to crown you for being so stubborn and trying to get out of bed."

"Christ Jesus, leave me *alone*."

His vicious growl sounded as sharp as his throat felt, and he opened his eyes to see her jerk back from him as if bitten. He half expected her to flee the room, but she didn't. Instead, she stood there looking down at him for a long moment before she shook her head.

"I'll do no such thing." Her firm manner reflected the remnants of her irritation. "You need me, and I understand some of what you must be feeling."

"How in the hell could you possibly understand?" he snarled, and as her gaze met his, she sighed softly.

"You're not the first man I've seen with only one ballock, Garrick."

The quiet confession caught him off guard, and he stared at her in stupefaction. He shook his head in denial. She had to be lying. To what end, he had no idea, but she couldn't be telling him the truth. Violet eyes flashing with anger, she stiffened.

"I am not in the habit of lying, and while I *never* reveal the secrets of any man I've been with, I can assure you that your physical condition is one I've seen before."

At a loss for words, he looked away from her. Was it really possible one of her other lovers had the same physical flaw as him? Was she telling the truth? He could think of no reason not to believe her. And he wanted to believe—trust her to keep his secret as she'd kept the secrets of other men. She sank down on the mattress beside him, and he breathed in the scent of her. It soothed him, despite the horror still holding him rigid. Her fingers lightly touched the back of his hand, but he refused to look at her.

"Whatever your uncle told you about your condition, he was wrong." She wrapped her fingers around his and squeezed his hand.

"I believe you are an exception in this particular matter," he muttered with a grimace.

"I highly doubt that," she said with conviction. "I cannot believe that any woman would find you repulsive."

"Then you would be wrong." He turned his head and eyed her coldly. "I was seventeen when I learned just how revolting I was to women."

"All women or just one?" The soothing quiet of her voice made him close his eyes. The woman was far too skilled at convincing a man to open up his soul.

"It wasn't necessary to expose myself more than once." He shook his head. "The event persuaded me that every woman would have the same reaction Bertha did."

"Please do *not* put me in the category of 'every woman.'" She was clearly annoyed, and a small smile tugged at his lips as he studied her peeved expression.

"You're an exceptional woman, Ruth. I would be hard-pressed to categorize you."

"Then I forgive you," she said with a smile. Her hand reached out to stroke his brow. "What role did your uncle play in this woman's rejection?"

The memory of Beresford slamming into his bedroom that terrible night made his mouth tighten with humiliation and anger. He clenched his jaw, and the pain that followed the action made him draw in a sharp hiss of air between his lips.

"My uncle knew I was enamored with Bertha. When she invited me to her rooms one night, she did so with my uncle's knowledge. It was obvious they staged the entire event merely to have sport with me." His fingers curled inward until his nails dug into the palms of his hands.

"It was a cruel thing to do."

"My uncle is a cruel man. Poking fun of my infatuation with Bertha as well as my inexperience is something that would appeal to his sadistic nature."

"Then your uncle knew nothing of your condition."

"No," he rasped as the humiliation of that specific moment rolled over him again. "If Beresford had known about my . . . my condition, I have no doubt he would have tormented me with the fact long before that night. I'm certain he didn't know until he charged into my room at the sound of Bertha's laughter."

The moment the bastard had discovered Garrick only had one ballock the man had zealously made use of the knowledge to torture him. Beresford had taken great pleasure in tormenting him with the threat of revealing his secrets. Even worse, he had relentlessly taken every opportunity to remind Garrick he wasn't really a man.

Over and over again, his uncle had reiterated how Garrick's physical flaw guaranteed that no woman would want him. He supposed he should be grateful the man hadn't shared his secret with anyone, at least not until recently. Even now he couldn't be sure his uncle had kept his end of the bargain they'd struck when he'd tossed the bastard out of Chiddingstone Manor.

"It explains a great deal."

"What does?" He stiffened. He would have none of her pity.

"The fact that you never wanted me to see you—touch you." Her quiet response held no pity, only sadness, and relief inched its way through him.

"That's not entirely true. I *did* want you to touch me."

It was a bare statement that left him more vulnerable than he'd ever been since the night his uncle and Bertha had played their vicious game. He met her gaze for a fleeting moment before he looked away. The woman had the ability to turn him inside out. Even when he'd been fighting so hard to survive, his only thought had been to return to her. He released a sigh as a sudden weariness gripped him hard.

"Sweet heavens, what was I thinking? You're fatigued. And you've not eaten anything."

She sprang to her feet and hurried toward the fireside table where she retrieved a large bowl off the tray. Steam still drifted off the contents, and he shook his head as she approached. Attempting to eat when his jaw and throat hurt so badly was the last thing he wanted to do.

"No," he rasped.

"Surely you can eat a spoonful or two. Dolores made it especially for you, and she'll be disappointed if you don't try and eat even a little bit." She sat down on the bed close to his shoulder and gently stirred the soup. He tried to smile at her wheedling tone.

"Guilt?"

"Absolutely, if it means you'll eat something. Just a few spoonfuls, then you can sleep some more."

The smile she offered him would have been more than enough to secure his obedience. With a slight nod, he opened his mouth and sipped from the spoon she held up. The broth smelled wonderful, and to his surprise it tasted even better. He managed to eat almost half the bowl before he gingerly held up his hand to silently signal he was done.

She set the bowl aside then wet a small towel in the basin resting on the nightstand. When she'd wrung it dry, she tenderly cleaned his face with the moist cloth. With that task complete, she quickly checked his bandages then helped ease him down lower in the bed. Bent over him, she cupped the uninjured side of his face.

"There," she said softly. "Try to get some rest. I'll be here if you need me."

A deep weariness settled into his bones as she made him comfortable. It made his limbs heavy as lead and barely able to move as she covered him with the sheet and light blanket. The sweet smell of her filled his senses and it was the last thing he remembered as he drifted off to sleep.

Sunlight warmed Garrick's face as he reclined in Ruth's conservatory with his eyes closed. The indoor garden was sunny and warm, despite the slight nip in the air outside. It had been four days since the attack, and he was already feeling like himself again.

Incapacitation wasn't something he was accustomed to, and he certainly hadn't enjoyed it. Particularly when he hadn't been able to move quickly enough to box his brother's ears. Ruth had sent word to his siblings the morning after the attack, and Vincent had come to see him as soon as the message arrived at Chiddingstone House.

His brother's comments about the impropriety of his confinement in Ruth's house had infuriated him. He knew his brother meant well, but Vincent's observations about the age difference between him and Ruth enraged him. He'd liked even less his brother's concern about chatter amongst the Set because it had reminded him of the last piece of gossip concerning Ruth and him.

Fortunately, thanks to Worthington, the Set was convinced he was at death's door, and at the moment, it was the only thing the Society pages were fixated upon. Soon though, the gossips would begin questioning his recovery time. It was one thing to be seen in public together, but to openly reside in Ruth's home would simply make her a target for the gossips and their vicious tongues. That was something he wished to avoid at all costs, and was the reason he'd decided to return home tomorrow.

He frowned. No, that wasn't the real reason, and he knew it. When she'd agreed to be his mistress at the orphanage, he'd thought their relationship would remain essentially as it had been with a few minor adjustments. He should have known better. Planned better. He might even have avoided being attacked if he'd been thinking more clearly. He should have known he was inviting trouble by walking home the other night. He snorted with anger.

That hadn't been the problem. He could have easily defended himself if he'd been paying attention. By the time he'd realized his attacker wasn't just another bumbling drunk, it had been too late. It was one thing to box with an opponent in the ring under the Marquess of Queensbury rules. A street fight was completely different.

If one wasn't prepared for an encounter like he'd had . . . the truth was, he was damned lucky to be alive. He looked down and glared at his bare hand. The bastards had beaten and robbed him, even taking the ring that bore the Stratfield family crest. It was the one thing of his father's that Beresford hadn't touched.

The crest would make it impossible for the thieves to sell the jewelry in one piece, but they would have no trouble prying the stones out of the ring. The minute he got home, he'd send for Blackstone for a report on what the man had found out about his two attackers and his missing ring.

Another grimace tugged at his mouth. Thanks to his assailants, Ruth had discovered his secret. Now everything had changed between them, and he had no idea which way to turn. Especially when the idea of parting with Ruth was unthinkable. Even when he'd barely been conscious he'd known when she was near.

Between the laudanum and the pain, it had taken him almost a day to realize Ruth had been sleeping in one of the fireside chairs.

He'd immediately insisted she share the bed with him. Although she'd protested, he'd finally gotten his way, and for the past two mornings, he'd woken up to the sweet sensation of Ruth curled up into his chest. It was a physical sensation that hovered between pleasure and torment.

Even the occasional twinge of sore muscles when her body bumped his in the middle of the night had been bearable just to have her in his arms. Unlike the past few days, when he'd awoken to find her gone from the bed, he'd been the first to awaken this morning. His physical reaction to her had been immediate. That hadn't been a surprise, but the revelation that followed had stunned him.

He loved her.

It was a simple, straightforward insight that had taken him by surprise. And it complicated matters between them that much more. Despite her words of understanding, he was still uncomfortable with the idea of exposing himself to her. Now it would be even more difficult. He was certain she was very fond of him, but love?

The idea of her rejecting him was far more painful than he cared to consider. He had no desire to experience the humiliation he'd experienced at the hand of Bertha. Not that he believed Ruth could ever be that cruel, but losing her would be unbearable. The question he really wanted an answer to was whether she had feelings for him.

But how to broach the subject? She was already sensitive about the age difference between them. When she discovered it was an even greater gap than she believed, the likelihood of her casting him aside was far greater than he wanted to think about. He needed to come up with a plan that would allow him to break the news to her gently before someone in the Set did it for him. He just wasn't sure how to do that without jeopardizing their relationship.

All of these thoughts had pounded their way into him when he'd awakened with her sweet body curled up against his. It was why he'd left her sleeping and rose to dress. His thoughts were too chaotic to keep her from thinking something was wrong, and the last thing he wanted to do was confess his feelings for her until he knew exactly how to address the situation to ensure a favorable outcome.

His jaw was still sore, but the swelling had almost disappeared, yet the bruising looked like he'd forgotten his morning shave. His sides were still bruised, but the only part of him that really hurt was his leg.

Simmons had stated Garrick had been lucky the leg wasn't broken considering the size of the bruise he bore. Walking was still painful, but he didn't let it keep him from making his way downstairs. The minute Dolores had seen him in the foyer she'd fussed over him like a mother hen, ordering him into the conservatory where she'd brought him breakfast and the London *Times*.

The paper had failed to hold his interest as thoughts of Ruth had relentlessly pushed their way into his head. She'd not been shocked by his condition and had discounted the thought that other women would find him repulsive because of his birth defect. It made him love her all the more, but it didn't ease his fears.

Despite her reassurances, to his recollection, she'd not expressed whether or not she would want to lie with him again. Perhaps she'd simply been waiting for him to recover before she welcomed him back into her bed. And he wanted that very much. Even with his injuries, his body was more than ready to experience her again.

He wanted to feel her creamy center wrapped around his cock, while his mouth worshiped her beautiful breasts, her delicious mouth, and every silky inch of her. Still, it wasn't just the thought of making love to her that tugged at his heart. He loved everything about her. There was the sweetness of her smile, the way her brow wrinkled slightly when she was concentrating on a problem.

But it was the sound of her laugh that gave him the greatest joy. Especially when he was the one to have made her laugh. She'd never said it outright, but he knew her life had not been the fulfilling one she wanted. Her father's betrayal had cut deep, and there were moments when she'd stopped herself from expressing the sadness she felt at the life she could have had. He wanted to protect her from anything that threatened to harm her.

If there were one thing he could do for her, it would be to convince the Marquess of Halethorpe that the man had wronged his wife and his daughter. He just needed to find a way to prove it. Considering Tremaine's character, it was impossible not to think that his father had been any less of a cad. If he could find a way to reconcile the two, it would give her one more reason to consider spending the rest of her life with him.

He knew the thought shouldn't have surprised him, but it did. He'd always believed Vincent would produce an heir for the family line. The idea of him marrying had been as remote a thought as fathering a child. But he knew he wanted more from Ruth than what they had now. He wanted her for his wife. The thought of losing her to another man made his gut clench. He dragged in a deep breath, and his nostrils filled with an exotic fragrance he knew well. Her lips were soft and warm against his as she bent over to kiss him.

"Good morning," she said as she sat down next to him on the chaise lounge. "I'm surprised to see you up and about so early. How are you feeling?"

"Much better, thank you." He forced a smile to his lips.

"I'm glad."

Her hand grasped his, and the touch launched a flood of tension through his body. The speed with which it blasted through him showed him how close to the edge he was where she was concerned. The wrong word or move would reveal parts of him that he'd kept hidden away for years. Parts he wanted to share with her, but not knowing how deep her affections went made it impossible for him to open up to her.

It only reinforced the fact that he needed a plan. Although he didn't have the slightest idea what that plan would entail. How did one court a courtesan and convince her to marry oneself, particularly if she were older and sensitive about her age? He swallowed the knot swelling his throat closed.

"You've been such an excellent nurse I feel strong enough to return home today."

"But you're still not well!" she exclaimed with dismay.

"I'm well enough. I have business affairs that need attention, and my presence here . . . I've been enough of a burden."

"Why would you think yourself a burden?" Her violet gaze narrowed at him with an astute look he recognized.

"Do you deny that your routine has been disrupted over the last few days due to caring for me?" He met her gaze unflinchingly, but it was clear she was able to read him better than he realized. God help him if she were to guess his feelings.

"I see." She paused for a second then shook her head. "This has to do with my knowing the truth about you, doesn't it?"

"I don't know what you're talking about," he said quietly, grateful that she hadn't stumbled upon the real reason he needed to put some distance between them.

"You know exactly what I'm saying," she said with exasperation. "I'm disappointed you could even *think* I would reject you simply because nature made you different from other men."

"I don't recall saying anything to that regard. However, we both know it's an issue that bears consideration." He scowled at her. It was true. There were two hurdles to overcome when it came to their happiness. His defect and her unwillingness to see that age was a state of mind, not a number.

"Does it? I see it differently." The moment her hand came to rest on his stomach he went rigid. Sweet Jesus. Whenever she touched him, she lit a fire inside him that threatened to consume him. "Shall I tell you what I saw the other night when I undressed you?"

"It would change nothing," he replied stoically as he acknowledged he wanted to be whole, if only for her sake.

"I disagree. It changes everything between us, and I think it's a conversation that is long overdue."

Her fingers reached for the buttons beneath the flap of his trousers, forcing him to grab her hand. The steady look she gave him made him pull in a sharp breath, which in turn immediately filled his senses with her sensual fragrance. The scent combined with the determined look in her expression made his throat tighten painfully. God, how he loved her when she looked at him like that.

"If you feel the need to prove something to me," he rasped, "don't."

"The only thing I wish to *prove* to you is that your uncle was wrong. Your body is a work of art."

She gently unlocked his fingers holding her wrist prisoner then undid the first and second buttons of his trousers. His traitorous body reacted with astonishing speed. He shook his head in protest, and her fingers pressed against his lips.

"No. Don't say anything. Just listen to me," she said as her fingers continued to undo his trousers. "When I removed your clothing the other night, I was appalled by all the bruises marring your incredible body. But not even the ugliness of your injuries could hide what I'd always known. You are beautiful."

He grunted with disbelief before his heart slammed into his chest. She looked at him for a moment before she exposed him completely. It was like a sledgehammer hitting his chest as her fingers splayed open his trousers to reveal his erection. Christ Jesus, he wanted to believe her.

"I love looking at you—touching you," she whispered, her forefinger circling the edge of his cock's mushroom cap before applying an exquisite pressure to the thick vein directly beneath its rim. "When I look at you, I want to please you. Do you know how I want to please you, Garrick?"

"How?" he asked roughly. His question made her lips curve upward in that mysterious smile of hers. It sent fire churning its way through his veins until he wanted to jerk her skirts up and settle her honeyed core over his cock.

"Like this."

Somehow he'd known what she intended to do, and the minute she bent her head toward his rod the air disappeared from his lungs. The heat of her tongue trailed a fiery path from the base of him upward to swirl around the tip of him. The touch made him draw in a sharp hiss of air.

He'd heard his friends talking about a woman tending to one's cock, but he'd never imagined it would be like this. It was a touch unlike anything he'd ever dreamed of. One moment the fiery stroke of her tongue caressed his rod then in almost the same instant she cooled his skin with a puff of air. It was an amazing sensation that hardened him until he ached with pleasure.

"Am I pleasing you, Garrick?"

"Yes." His response was little more than a guttural sound in his ears.

"And this?" The heat of her tongue blazed its way down to his ballock before her mouth engulfed it. *Bloody hell.* She had to ask? Of course it pleased him.

"Yes," he rasped, and he groaned as she sucked on his ballock.

An instant later his hips jerked upward as she made a low humming sound that vibrated his sac. Christ Jesus. Just when he thought the woman had taught him everything he needed to know about pleasure, she managed to do something else that told him how little he really knew. An incredible sensation stretched through him until his cock expanded and hardened more than he ever thought possible.

As she hummed, her hand wrapped around him like a gentle vise. The stroke of her hand combined with the vibrations on his ballock had him gripping the sides of the chair as if that would control the pleasure. God help him, but the woman's skill was taking him to places he'd never imagined. A groan rolled out of him as her hand tightened on him. The friction her stroke created almost made him spew his seed.

"Sweet . . . heart," he choked out. "Sweetheart, if you . . . ahh . . . don't . . . stop . . . I won't . . ."

She immediately lifted her head, but her hand continued to slide up and down his erection at a slow, yet steady pace. His senses clouding his head, he tried to focus his gaze on her features. There was a smile of gentle triumph on her face.

"Do you believe me when I say you're beautiful?"

The question made him tremble. Could he believe that? After

Bertha's rejection, after all the times his uncle had reminded him that he was only half a man and even Wycombe's insinuations—all of it—was it possible they'd been wrong? He desperately wanted to believe her. Conflicted with emotion, he shook his head. She was trained to please a man, and she'd made it her goal to teach him how to make love to a woman. Her gaze narrowed slightly at him.

"I told you I'm not in the habit of lying," she said in a firm, yet soft voice. "Your body is a work of art only God could have made."

"He made a mistake," he rasped as the memory of Bertha's disgust lashed through him.

"No, see how hard and thick you are." Her hand slid up and down in a swift stroke that tugged a groan up out of his chest. "You're beautiful. Don't believe what your uncle has told you over the years."

"It's not—"

"You've believed your uncle's lies for so long, you can't see yourself the way I do. The way any woman in her right mind would." Her thumb rubbed against the pulsing vein that rested just beneath the cap of his erection. It pulled another sharp breath from him. "Your body is a wonderful specimen of male beauty. And your cock is one of your most beautiful attributes. Just looking at it makes me ache for you."

She bent her head again and stroked him with her tongue from the base of his rod to the tip. The seductive caress pulled a wild shudder from him. God, he wasn't sure how much more of this he could take. He reached for her, but she threaded her fingers through his hands and held them away from her.

"Your uncle was wrong."

As she lowered her head again, he expected to feel her tongue laving the length of him, but when she took his cock into her mouth, he barely managed to bite back a shout of surprise and pleasure. God help him, she was determined to undo him completely. Her mouth on him was hotter than anything he'd ever experienced in his life.

The exotic scent of her wafted up into his nose, heightening the intensity of the pleasure she was giving him. His hands reached for her, his fingers threading through her beautiful, silky hair. Damnation, the woman was hell-bent on driving him insane with these slow, maddening strokes of his rod.

He wanted her to move faster, but when he applied a gentle pressure to her head, she resisted his silent plea. Hot and moist, her lips clutched the tip of him as her tongue swirled around the rim before her mouth suddenly engulfed him in one swift move. It sent a rush of pleasure shooting through him, and he released a guttural sound at the intensity of it.

Just as quickly as she'd taken him into her mouth, she began to suck on him with increased speed. Watching her caress his cock was the most erotic sight he'd ever seen. God, her mouth was a wicked hot vise around him. There were no words to describe the sensations rolling through him. The startling touch of her fingers on his ballock made him draw in a sharp breath. Gently, her thumb massaged his sac as her mouth tightened around his erection. A familiar pressure built inside him, and he groaned.

"Stop sweetheart . . . I can't hold . . ."

His words only made her suck harder, and the moist friction gripping his rod was one of the most amazing things he'd ever felt. Another guttural sound passed his lips, and with a shout he exploded in the white heat of her mouth.

"*Christ Jesus*," he cried out as she swallowed his seed and sucked on him as he throbbed between her lips. He was swimming in an ocean of blind pleasure as wave after wave of incredible sensations crested over him. It was impossible to think. His body was in complete control as it sent one blistering message of delight after another to his brain. And still she continued to caress him with her mouth. Wild shudders rippled through him at her slowing strokes, and he shuddered again as she slowly let him slip out of her mouth. She sat upright and stared at him with a small smile of satisfaction.

"Do you believe me now when I say I think you're beautiful? Especially your cock," she whispered.

"Yes," he rasped. Arguing with her was something he didn't have the strength for. Not when it was taking every bit of willpower he possessed not to say he loved her. "Thank you for . . . for . . ."

"You're welcome."

There wasn't one iota of amusement in her voice or expression, but he still felt like a schoolboy with his first woman. He grimaced at the thought. Damnation, in many ways he still was, and it would take a great many more lessons to achieve the skill he needed to seduce her—please her. And pleasing her was what he intended to do.

Somehow he'd find a way to make her love him. As a courtesan she would know better than to grow emotionally attached to a lover. But if there was one thing he knew about himself it was his determination. When he set his mind to do something, he did it. His fingers curled into his palms. He'd make her fall in love with him. If it were the last thing he did, he'd make her see they belonged together. He didn't have a choice. It was a simple acceptance of his fate.

His gaze met hers, and she tilted her head slightly as she studied him with a puzzled frown. She'd admired his body, but he was the beast to her beauty. He reached out to cup her face. When she looked at him like that, he wanted to carry her off to some remote spot in the country. Far away from the gossips and wagging tongues who tried to hurt her.

A place where he could indulge himself listening for her laughter or the sweet music of her voice. Somewhere quiet, like Chiddingstone Manor, where he could savor every smile, scent, and touch for years to come. And the last thing he wanted to do was leave her.

"It will be hard to leave you." The moment he spoke, an odd emotion flew across her features and vanished almost as quickly as it appeared. His heart jumped. Had that been fear? Was she afraid that he meant to leave her for good?

"I cannot imagine why," she said with a soft laugh that rang hollow in his ears. "I'm certain you've been bored these past two days with nothing more to do but lay in bed."

"I won't deny that I've missed my morning routine and workout at the Club, but I will miss waking up with you in my arms."

"And I shall miss you, too."

Although Ruth's tone was light, her words seemed forced. He studied her carefully. She'd said she'd miss him, but something about her tone bothered him. Her gaze darted away from his as she busied herself with buttoning his trousers and restoring his appearance to a more circumspect one. Despite her matter-of-fact manner, there was a nervousness about her that made him frown.

"What's wrong, sweetheart?" He caught her chin in his hand and forced her to look at him. For the briefest of moments, he saw fear darkening her eyes.

"Nothing at all," she replied with a bright smile that he was certain was forced. She sprang to her feet and offered him her hand. "Come, I'll have Simmons ready the carriage while you pack your things."

He accepted her hand and got to his feet. She started to walk away, but he immediately tugged her back to him and pulled her into his arms. Her eyes were wide with surprise as she stared up at him. But there was something else. An emotion he couldn't decipher, and it struck a note of fear inside him. He'd believed her when she'd said his physical flaws were inconsequential.

And the way she'd ministered to his cock with such great fanfare had helped shore up that belief. But she was hiding something from him, and suddenly he wasn't sure of her anymore. Courtesans were skilled lovers *and* actresses. Had she been playing him for a fool? Had she simply told him what she thought he wanted to hear? They were questions he didn't want to learn the answers to. He struggled to keep his voice empty of the fear twisting its way through him.

"I know you, Ruth. Something's troubling you, and I want to know what it is."

"I told you. There's—"

"Goddamn it. Tell me," he growled with frustration and a growing fear that he might have met the one thing in his life that he couldn't control. The one objective he couldn't obtain. Her heart. "Are you so eager to see the back of me—now that you've proven you can suck my cock without flinching?"

"*No*," she snapped fiercely. "I told you I think you're beautiful, and I meant it."

"Then why the bloody hell are you so eager to get rid of me?"

"I am *not* trying to get rid of you." Her angry glare made him frown with confusion, and she turned her head away from him. "I was . . . I was thinking . . . how hard it will be when you leave me for good."

Leave her? Christ Jesus, if the woman only knew how difficult he was finding it simply to leave her today, let alone in the future. Hope soared in him once more. He quickly tempered the emotion. Instinct told him now wasn't the time to test her emotions where he was concerned. Deliberately, he forced himself to lighten her mood.

"Given the ink on our arrangement is barely dry, isn't it a bit soon to think about saying good-bye?" he teased, hoping to bring a smile to her face.

"I am a realist. When your lessons are finished . . ." Her violet eyes were dark with vulnerability as she looked up at him and shook her head. "You need an heir, and I would prefer you find your young bride after we've parted."

He grimaced. There it was again, the fact that he was younger than her. God help him when she learned he was twelve years younger. She'd composed her features now into a serene mask. It was the same look she'd worn the night they'd set tongues wagging at the opera. The thought that she might be thinking of ending their liaison made him tense. He cupped her chin firmly and gently forced her to look at him.

"I have no intention of parting with you for a long time, Ruth." *Never.*

"I do not regret agreeing to our liaison. I am simply being practical. Our relationship will end when one of us has no need of the other."

Her stilted response made him grimace. What she really meant was when he had no further need of her instruction. God, if only he could tell her the truth. But the truth was even more dangerous than when he'd been unable to explain about his physical flaw. As long as she was his mistress he had the chance to woo her. Convince her that they could be happy together despite the difference in their ages. If she pushed him away, she would make it difficult, if not impossible, for him to court her.

"Although I enjoy your lessons in seduction very much, Ruth, that's not why I asked to be your patron," he said quietly as he stared down into her eyes. "You told me that you wanted me to feel comfortable with you. I do. *That's* the reason I proposed our arrangement. I like being with you. I *want* to be with you. I want to take care of you."

Because I love you.

Slowly, her features softened as her gaze met his. The vulnerability was still there in her violet eyes, but something else gentled her expression. Did she have feelings for him that she was afraid to share? A fear of the obstacles only she thought stood between them?

They'd found pleasure in bed together, but it didn't mean her emotions were involved beyond the desire she felt for him. Still, she was no longer holding herself rigid in his arms.

"I like being with you, too." A small smile curved her lips. Her body was suddenly pliable again, and he immediately pulled her tight against him.

"I should hope so, as I am in need of a great many more lessons in seduction."

"Be careful what you wish for. Some lessons are not to be learned in the bedroom," she said with a smile as she relaxed slightly in his embrace.

"As long as I'm in your company, I will find my time occupied quite pleasantly."

"See, you've already mastered the art of complimenting a woman." This time a small laugh parted her lips. "Soon you'll master the art of pleasing a woman."

He saw through the lighthearted statement and bent his head to kiss her. The softness of her skin was like silk against his lips as he caressed the line of her jaw to her pink earlobe. When he nipped at the small piece of flesh, he heard her inhale a quick breath.

"Since you are convinced I am an exemplary student, there is only one thing for me to do."

He lifted his head so he could stare down at her. A frown of confusion furrowed her brow, while her white teeth bit down on the plump fullness of her bottom lip. She looked like an innocent young girl trying to think through a difficult problem. She eyed him carefully.

"And what would that be?"

"I shall find it necessary to abandon my studies and focus solely on pleasing you."

Satisfaction rolled through him as a rosy blush crested in her cheeks. An expression of genuine delight lit up her face. She had no idea how young and adorable she looked. But he'd find a way to make her see herself as he saw her. Somehow he'd convince her that age didn't matter. Not when two people loved each other.

Ruth descended the stairs knowing Garrick would be waiting for her in the salon. Whenever they had plans for the evening, it had become his habit to enjoy a glass of cognac while he waited for her to finish dressing. It had been more than two weeks since Garrick's assault, and he'd recovered completely from the attack.

Although the police had taken Garrick's statement, they had no leads as to who had attacked him. Even Garrick's man, Blackstone, had failed to learn anything as to the identity of the two men who'd robbed him and left him for dead. She'd had Simmons query his sources as well, but like Garrick's man, her longtime servant had turned up nothing. When she reached the bottom of the steps, she stopped to check her appearance once more in the mirror.

The evening gown she wore was a muted gold satin accented with small bits of black lace. She'd ordered it almost two weeks ago, and it was the first time she'd worn it. The vain part of her was convinced she looked elegant without looking too mature, and she hoped Garrick would find her pleasing to the eye.

She wanted to please him in every way, and not just in the

bedroom. Her thoughts flitted back to the night before. In recent days, his lovemaking had contained a deep-seated passion that had intensified each moment he'd brought her to climax, but last night had been different.

The emotional intensity of that moment had struck something deep inside her that thrilled her almost as much as it frightened her. It had ignited a tiny flame of hope. A small fire she'd not been able to extinguish. The grandmother clock struck the hour of seven.

Tonight they were dining at the Rothschilds'. She knew it would be a relatively small affair, but more importantly, the insults would be minimal as those in attendance would mostly be friends. The thought of more gossip was enough to send a shiver down her spine.

The *Town Talk* had been particularly vicious of late, and Garrick had demanded she stop reading the scandal sheet. She'd tried, but like someone with an obsessive fascination for the morbid she still scanned the Society column every few days. She heard the soft clink of crystal and crossed the foyer floor to the salon doorway.

Garrick was standing at the sideboard, pouring himself a cognac. When she'd learned the French brandy was his favorite drink, she'd instructed Dolores to see that they always had some of the liquor on hand. She paused in the doorway to look at him. He was the handsomest man she'd ever seen. There was a dangerously wicked air about him that held her under his spell like a mesmerist, and it was at moments like these that she was certain he'd bewitched her.

Every time he came near her, it was easy to forget the future—forget how he would eventually disappear from her life. Through his eyes, she'd come to view herself as desirable again. Even despite all the vicious gossip, she was able to ignore it because Garrick was always there to remind her that the malicious talk meant nothing.

He was convinced the gossip indicated how envious others were of their obvious happiness. And she *was* happy. For the first time in her life she was living with little thought of the future. Being impractical was a dangerous thing to do, but she didn't care. She was without a doubt the happiest she'd ever been in her life, and she was willing to trade the joy of the present for the pain of the future. She watched him as he raised his glass then froze as he realized she was in the room. A frisson raced across her skin at the knowledge he could sense her as easily as she could him. Slowly, he turned to look at her.

"My God, you look exquisite," he rasped. The naked desire on his face accelerated her heartbeat until the sound of it thundered in her ears.

"One might call you prejudiced, but I appreciate the compliment," she said with a small laugh as she moved deeper into the room.

With the measured movements of a predator, he set his glass down on the sideboard without looking away from her. Although it took only seconds for him to reach her, it felt like an eternity. Beneath his penetrating gaze, her body vibrated with a pleasurable tension that sent a shudder through her.

Even though they had known each other not quite two months, every part of her responded to him with the same intensity as the night they'd first met. He stopped in front of her, his hand reaching out to glide his fingers across her bare shoulder. The touch warmed her skin until the heat of it spread its way throughout her body and she ached for more.

"Prejudiced or not, I've half a mind not to take you tonight. Any man worth his salt will take one look at you in this dress and want you for himself. And I have no intention of sharing you with any man."

The possessive growl made her heart skip a beat. It was impossible not to take pleasure in the fact that she'd aroused his territorial instincts. It made her feel even more desirable than usual. The fact that it strengthened the small flame of hope in her breast alarmed her, but she ignored it.

Instead, she chose to revel in the way he made her feel. Young, vibrant, and alive. With every touch, the age difference between them vanished. When his fingers reached the curve of her shoulder, they slowly traced the line of her bodice down to the vee between her breasts.

The entire time his fingers blazed their way across her skin, his gaze remained locked with hers. Gone was the inexperienced man who'd come to her bed an innocent. In his place was a man who was devastating to her senses. In the past few days, he'd begun to exhibit more and more skill in the art of seduction, but tonight his touch was sinfully erotic and tempting.

It made her feel hot and feverish. Like him, she found herself wishing they didn't have to go out. Her breathing ragged, she inhaled the delicious male scent of him. His cologne had hints of sandalwood that tingled her nose with a raw, woodsy aroma. She found herself leaning into him with the overwhelming need to be kissed. A slow, wicked smile curved his lips and he took a step back from her.

"We'll be late if we don't leave now."

"You did that deliberately," she said with a gasp of surprise.

"Did what?" The innocent note in his voice didn't fool her as she sent him a look of amused exasperation.

"You were trying to seduce me."

"Did I succeed?" Laughter filled Garrick's voice telling her that he knew exactly what he was doing.

"You know perfectly well you did." She wrinkled her nose at him.

"Good." He quickly reached for her and pulled her into his arms. "I would not want your tutorials to go to waste."

She pulled in a sharp breath as his mouth seared hers. The blood in her veins flowed hot and wild as he gently forced her lips apart and his tongue explored the inside of her mouth. His skill at kissing was the one thing that had always been at odds with his inexperience in the bedroom. The way his tongue danced with hers was an invitation to join him in sin, and her heart raced at the image of his naked body melding with hers. She moaned softly as his mouth brushed across her cheek before reaching her ear. The warmth of his breath teased her ear.

"Tell me what tempting lesson you have planned for me tonight, Lady Ruth?"

The dark, playfully seductive note in his voice made her stomach flutter with wild excitement. Sweet heavens but the man had learned his lessons well. A slight shudder sped through her as she drew back from him to meet the wicked gleam in his eyes.

"Perhaps a game," she whispered in an unsteady voice.

"A game?" Puzzlement furrowed his brow.

"Yes," she said with a secretive smile as the intriguing idea took root in her head. "At supper tonight, let us pretend we've just met and formed an immediate attraction to each other."

Excitement flared in his eyes as he rubbed his thumb against her lip. She immediately pulled it into her mouth and swirled her tongue around the tip. He drew in a sharp breath as she sucked on him for a long moment. The rumble in his chest indicated his growing arousal, and she slowly released his thumb from her mouth.

"As you said, we'll be late if we don't leave now," she said as she slipped out of his arms.

She headed toward the foyer, sending him an inviting look over her shoulder. The stunned expression on his face made her suppress a laugh. He hadn't expected her to turn the tables on him. When she reached the coatrack, she picked up his top hat and cane then turned to offer them to him. The annoyance on his face made her laugh, which only served to increase his exasperation.

"That will cost you, my sweet," he murmured as he settled his hat on his head with a resolute gesture.

"And I look forward to hearing what price you demand, my lord." She almost laughed at his scowl as he helped cover her shoulders with the wrap she'd retrieved.

"I can assure you, it will come when you least expect it, my lady."

Out of the corner of her eye, she caught the sudden flash of amusement on Garrick's face, and it shot a shiver of anticipation down her spine. As they moved out into the night she peeked another quick look at him, and he arched his eyebrow at her.

He was planning something. She could see it in his expression as if he were enjoying a private joke. She narrowed her gaze at him as he joined her in the vehicle, and the mischievous smile he directed at her as he seated himself opposite simply confirmed her suspicions.

The devil. He meant to keep her on edge, wondering when he might extract punishment from her.

Suddenly, the game she'd proposed only a few moments ago had taken on a completely different meaning. Garrick truly was an exemplary student. If she didn't take care her heart would belong to him completely. Her mouth went dry at the thought. No, she wouldn't let that happen. She couldn't afford to. This time the small flame inside her breast was easy to extinguish.

They spoke little during the short ride to the Rothschild residence in Mayfair. It seemed Garrick had apparently decided to begin their game ahead of schedule. He seemed to take enormous pleasure just watching her, which made her nerves tingle with a mixture of pleasant apprehension and excitement.

There was something thrilling about the way he'd taken control of the situation. Her tutoring had simply intensified the masterful side of him that she'd seen in his day-to-day activities. The carriage rocked to a halt, and Garrick assisted her out of the vehicle with his hand supporting her elbow.

As she reached the sidewalk, his fingers brushed across the side of her breast in a seemingly innocent graze. Her gaze flew to his, and the heated look he sent her said his touch had been anything but an accident. As the carriage door snapped closed behind them, he bent his head toward her.

"Let the game begin."

The velvety note of seduction in his voice was disturbing enough, but the warmth of his breath against her ear heightened the sensation. Excitement spiraled down into her belly then moved lower until she ached to feel him inside her. It was the same type of feeling she'd experienced the night they'd first met.

The frisson skimming its way across her skin set her heartbeat racing as he escorted her up the wide, marble front steps of the Rothschild mansion. Tonight her pupil clearly intended to apply his tutoring toward a goal she was certain would bring her enormous pleasure.

Once inside, Lady Rothschild greeted them warmly. They were quickly separated as Baron Rothschild pulled Garrick away to join a discussion of finance in another part of the room. As her hostess turned to greet a new arrival, Ruth saw Allegra across the room. With a warm smile she moved toward the Countess of Pembroke. Her friend was in the middle of a conversation with another guest, but the minute she saw Ruth, she excused herself and hurried forward. Allegra beamed at her as she released Ruth from her embrace.

"Look at you! Lord Stratfield is obviously good for you. You look stunning." The delight in her friend's voice made her smile.

"Well, I won't deny I'm happy."

"You're *radiant*, Ruth. There's no other word for it." Allegra's words were adamant. "And you deserve happiness."

"I shall accept it for the time I have it," she said quietly. Her friend shot her a look of admonishment as she looked over Ruth's shoulder then frowned with annoyance.

"Blast, I was hoping she hadn't been invited this evening."

Allegra's irritable exclamation made Ruth look over her shoulder. She stiffened as she saw the latest arrival entering the Rothschilds' salon. Louise Campton. Ever since the Viscount Bexhill had left Louise to pursue Ruth, the woman had gone out of her way to be as vicious as she could toward her.

Generally, the woman's verbal snipes were of little consequence, except when Louise took pleasure in commenting that Ruth's mother was a whore. The woman deserved to be slapped, but Ruth knew her mother would have expected her to simply walk away. Beside her, Allegra sniffed her disapproval.

"I don't know what Emma sees in that woman. Louise Campton is interested in one thing and one thing only, any man she can coax into her bed."

"Lady Rothschild is kind and thoughtful. I think she sees the good in everyone."

"No doubt," Allegra said with a sharp nod. "But one must look long and hard to see the good in Louise Campton."

Ruth didn't reply as she watched the woman make a beeline toward Garrick. Her heart sank at the radiant smile her nemesis flashed at him. Jealousy snagged its way through her as he returned the woman's smile. Dear God, would he apply his newfound talents on the younger woman?

She saw Garrick glance her way, and the astute look he sent her caused her heart to sink. *He knew.* He knew she was jealous of Louise. Heat stung her cheeks as she abruptly turned away from him. If this was the type of game he intended to play, she wanted no part in it. Suddenly, she found herself wishing the evening was over, and it was with a sense of relief she heard the butler announce supper.

To her dismay, Lady Rothschild asked Garrick to escort Louise Campton into the dining room, while Ruth was paired with an older gentleman who was a business acquaintance of the baron's. Throughout the meal, she struggled to keep her eyes off Garrick, but it was impossible to avoid doing so completely.

Once or twice when she glanced his way, their eyes would meet, but it was impossible to tell what he was thinking. Worse, the moment Louise saw Garrick looking in her direction, the woman would immediately distract him. Over the years, Ruth had worked hard never to be jealous of a patron's interest in another woman, and she didn't like knowing she'd failed where Garrick was concerned.

Jealousy was a foreign concept to her, and the intensity of the pain it could cause startled her. It was extremely unpleasant. The grating sound of Louise's laughter at the opposite end of the table pulled her gaze back to the woman and Garrick. He seemed enthralled by Louise, and it sent a fiery anger streaking through her veins. The woman laughed again, and Ruth had a sudden urge to push her head into the crème brûlée they'd just been served.

Unable to bear watching the woman flirt with Garrick any longer, she turned her attention back to the gentleman who'd escorted her into dinner. The man's conversation had been tediously boring throughout the meal, but it was a far better pain to bear than watching Louise Campton attempting to seduce Garrick. Especially when it seemed as though she was succeeding.

Shortly after the last course of the meal, Lady Rothschild invited the ladies to join her in the parlor while the gentlemen enjoyed an after dinner drink. Ruth didn't bother looking in Garrick's direction as she left the room, but she could feel his eyes on her.

As she followed the women back toward the parlor, she had the sudden urge to plead a headache and leave before the men rejoined them. But Louise Campton would notice, and she wasn't about to let her know she was upset by Garrick's interest in the woman.

A footman politely stopped her.

"My lady." The young man offered her a note and stepped back to wait patiently as she opened it up.

I wish to see you. Now. While the note was unsigned, she was reasonably certain it was from Garrick. It looked like his handwriting, although his previous notes had never been so authoritative, but this—this missive was an order. She could read it in the hard, bold strokes of the ink. When had she become his to command? Especially when he'd been so attentive to Louise Campton. She raised her head, and the footman immediately stepped forward, clearly expecting her to do as the note bid.

"If you'll follow me, my lady. His lordship is waiting."

"Tell his lordship he can continue to wait," she snapped and returned the note to the footman with a sharp thrust of her hand. She turned on her heel, only to have the footman touch her arm.

"Forgive me, my lady, but Lord Seymour was most insistent. He said he has information regarding Lord Stratfield."

"Lord Seymour?" For the first time, she wondered if she'd mistaken Garrick's handwriting for someone else's. She stretched out her hand. "Let me see the note again."

The footman handed her the note in silence, and she frowned as she tried to determine whether she'd been wrong. She didn't know a Lord Seymour, nor did she remember being introduced to him. But if she was wrong and it wasn't Garrick summoning her, it might be someone who wanted to hurt him. And no matter how angry she was that he'd been so engrossed with Louise Campton, she wouldn't let anyone hurt him if she could help it.

As the last of the women disappeared through the doorway she silently gestured for the servant to lead the way. The footman guided her deeper into the Rothschild mansion, stopping in front of a nondescript door and opening it for her. She walked into a small office dimly lit by a tiny gaslight on the far wall. Centered in the middle of the room was a large desk, while several tall cabinets lined the walls.

It was difficult to see much of anything in the near darkness as she moved toward the center of the room. She'd almost reached the desk when she heard the door close behind her and the key turn in the lock. Startled, she whirled around and raced toward the door. Grasping the doorknob, she shook it in a futile attempt to open the door. Fear nipped at her as she slapped her palm against wood.

"Come back and open this door," she called out. "Do you hear me? Let me out of here this instant."

She pounded at the door in anger. Whoever had arranged for her entrapment might find it amusing, but she didn't. Not one bit. Lord Seymour indeed. A sudden tingle on the back of her neck made her stiffen as she suddenly realized she wasn't alone. Before she could turn and face them, a warm body pressed into her back and gently crushed her against the beveled panels of the walnut door.

The woodsy scent of sandalwood filled her nostrils as resentment spiraled its way into her muscles and she stiffened. Garrick. He'd tricked her. She tried to turn and face him, but he held her fast. His hands forced hers to lie flat against the walnut door, while he braced his body against hers in a manner that stirred her arousal despite her irritation with him. She tried to slide out from underneath him once again, incensed by her body's reaction.

"Don't fight me, my lady. We both know Stratfield is likely to be jealous if he knows you've been with another man."

One cheek resting against the door, she could barely see him out of the corner of her eye, but the husky sound of his voice caressed her like an invisible piece of velvet. Furious at her inability to feel nothing at his touch, she angrily latched onto his ludicrous statement in an effort not to succumb to the desire threatening to take over her body.

To even suggest that he'd be jealous at the thought of her with another man was ridiculous. He'd been so busy flirting with Louise Campton, he'd paid no notice to her at all. The memory of his attention to the other woman fired her anger again.

"*Another man—*"

"I've been watching you all evening."

"I find that highly unlikely." She sniffed with umbrage. The bastard had been too preoccupied with someone else. Her teeth clenched at the thought.

"Unlikely?" A quiet laugh breezed across the back of her neck. "You barely ate your meal, you toyed with your necklace throughout the evening, and you had no idea that you are the most beautiful woman here tonight."

She stiffened against the door. Had he truly been watching her after all? Impossible. She would have known. Perhaps the one thing the man hadn't noticed was how she couldn't keep her eyes off of him and his flirtation with Louise Campton. But she *had* eaten very little and *had* nervously played with her necklace. She drew in a breath as she realized she was giving way to him.

"Forgive me, Lord Str—" A warm hand covered her mouth to silence her effectively. The touch had a dangerous edge to it and a small shiver of excitement skated down her spine. She immediately berated herself for letting his touch make her feel anything.

"No names, my lady." His voice was a rough whisper breathing fire across her back as his mouth grazed her shoulder. "Remember the rules. We've never met before."

The game. Her heart skipped a beat. Sweet heavens, she'd been so angry with him, it had never occurred to her that this might be the game she'd suggested before they'd left the town house. And she'd expected a mild flirtation, not an intimate seduction in the house of their host, especially with the danger of someone noticing their absence. His hand left her mouth to caress the side of her neck. It was a slow, sensual touch that burned its way through her until her body grew warm with anticipation.

"You are presumptuous in your attentions, my lord." She forced the words past her lips as his hand moved downward to cup her breast. The touch pulled a gasp from her, and his teeth lightly abraded the side of her neck.

"And I think your protest is a façade," he whispered in a low, velvety tone that made her legs weaken beneath her.

"Even if what you say was true, this is hardly the place . . ." Her words died in her throat as his hands left hers to slowly draw her skirts up and bunch them at her waist, while his hard body held her in place against the door. She gasped the moment his hands gripped her thighs, the heat of his touch spreading its way into every part of her body.

"Don't try to deny you're enjoying yourself, my lady."

His mouth seared the back of her neck, and she breathed in the rough male scent of him. Oh God, he smelled wonderful. He was right. She *was* enjoying this—far too much. His fingers kneaded her flesh as he pressed his legs into the back of her thighs.

Through his trousers and the thin material of the short drawers beneath her corset, she could feel him growing hard against her. Surely he wasn't planning to seduce her completely. Someone might come looking for them. Her breathing grew erratic at the dangerous thought. She knew it was reckless to feel excitement, but she did. Still, she forced herself to try and make sanity prevail.

"I don't think—"

"I once had someone tell me not to think, but to feel."

Sinful. It was the only word she could think of to describe his voice. The sound of it was a dark caress that hinted at something decadent as he quoted her own words back to her. Her mouth went dry as she suddenly realized he was no longer a student. The way he'd planned this small tryst and the masterful way he was seducing her said he'd paid close attention to everything she'd taught him over the past month.

She inhaled sharply as his hand slid across her leg to reach the spot just above the apex of her thighs. A familiar liquid warmth dampened the fragile silk drawers. Merciful heaven was he planning to make her have an orgasm right here and now? Her heart slammed into her chest at the deliciously wicked idea. She shuddered. They couldn't. There was enough scandalous talk about them as it was.

"Please . . ."

"Please what, my lady?"

The confidence in his voice was something she'd never heard before. It reinforced the fact that he'd graduated from inexperienced pupil to devastating seducer. A man capable of enticing her to submit to his bidding. His hand moved again to press into her stomach at a spot just below her corset.

A moment later, his hand tugged forcefully at her drawers, and she gasped out loud with shock. Seconds later, desire spiraled through her belly only to explode in her nether regions as his fingers brushed across the top of her mound. Dear God, she'd never experienced an erotic seduction like this before.

Her entire body tingled with desire, and every touch of his hand intensified the sensation until her breathing was coming in short pants. Suddenly, his fingers parted her folds to lightly stroke the nub between them. The hedonistic caress pulled a low moan out of her.

"You like that, don't you." His satisfaction was clearly evident in his words as he moved his hand back to her thigh. She whimpered at his withdrawal.

"Yes," she gasped.

"A teacher of mine once told me that some women like to hear a man whisper naughty words into their ears." His teeth nibbled at her earlobe. Her knees gave way, and only his body kept her from sliding to the floor. "Are you one of those women, my lady?"

"Oh God," she whispered hoarsely. She couldn't remember any man ever arousing her to such a fevered pitch before.

"Answer me, my lady." The low growl rumbled in her ear like a distant thunderstorm. A tempest that would most likely strip her of every sense or sensibility she possessed.

"Yes," she whispered with a ragged breath.

His hips shifted against the back of her thighs, and she could feel the hard length of him leaving its imprint on her buttocks. His fingers threaded with hers against the door as his mouth left a trail of fire across her shoulder. She wanted to kiss him. Needed to feel his mouth on hers, on every inch of her body. She tried to turn toward him, but he easily held her in place.

"Do you know how beautiful you are?" The words were harsh against her ear as his hand brought hers downward to touch his stiff erection. "From the first moment I saw you, I've wanted nothing more than to bury my cock inside you."

She gasped at the images his words produced. Only two or three times had he spoken to her in such a manner. In both instances, he'd been uncomfortable, almost shy, using the words. Now, his voice was strong and demanding. He was in complete command of his words and his desire, and that was more shocking than his language.

It sent a frisson dancing down her back as she stroked him through his trousers. Touching him like this only intensified the need inside her. Her body ached for a completion she knew only he could give her. God, she wanted him now. At this moment in time, she didn't care if someone discovered them here. She didn't care what people might think. All that mattered was her need to have him inside her bringing her to a climax only he could give her.

"Please, I want—"

"*Want*?" he rasped tightly and with a fervency that thrilled her. "You have *yet* to understand the meaning of the word, my lady. When I'm done with you tonight, your sweet cunny will be weeping for my cock."

The raw, coarse words sucked the air from her lungs, leaving her breathless. Never in her life had she ever wanted a man so badly. A soft sob ripped from her throat at the realization that for the first time in her life she was no longer in command of her own senses. She was the one out of control and desperate for fulfillment. The abrupt departure of his warmth stunned her.

Still pressed against the door, she waited for some other delicious torment to assault her senses. When that didn't happen, puzzlement and an intense frustration caused her to stiffen. Slowly, she turned around, her back against the door as her only support because she was certain her legs were still too weak to bear her weight.

In the dim light of the office, she saw Garrick standing a few feet away. A small smile of satisfaction curved his sensual mouth, but it was the blazing desire in his gaze that made her tremble once more. Her hand went to her throat as she stared at him with uncertainty. Why had he stopped? She'd been more than willing to do whatever he'd asked of her.

"I like this game of yours, my lady," he said in a husky voice filled with amusement. "The anticipation is quite . . . exhilarating."

"Anticipation?" She stared at him in bewilderment.

"Yes. The expectation of the pleasure to come."

"To come?" she choked out. He'd teased her into a frenzied state, knowing full well he didn't intend to satisfy her until later. And the fact that he seemed completely unaffected by his seduction of her was just as frustrating. She wanted to strangle him, while a small part of her took pride in her creation.

"The night is far from over, my lady. I have it from Stratfield himself that I may deliver you home at the earliest possible moment."

So the game wasn't over. The confidence in his expression made her want to remind him that he wasn't the only one who was skilled at seduction. She pushed herself away from the door, determined to show him that he didn't hold all the cards in this contest. She halted when she was just out of arm's reach and flicked her tongue out to wet her lips. His reaction was to inhale a sharp breath, and she smiled at him.

"And what is it you think will happen when you take me home, my lord?"

The slow wicked smile curling his lips made her heart skip a beat before it went skidding out of control. The man had become more devastating than she could have dreamed possible the first night she'd initiated him into the art of pleasure.

"I'm going to undress you. Not quickly, but ever so slowly. I intend to worship every inch of your beautiful body with my mouth." He reached out and trailed one finger along the edge of her jaw. "And I confess the prospect of seeing you naked beneath me excites me immensely. It excites me to know that you will be mine and mine alone."

It was nothing less than a declaration of possession. He was stating emphatically that she was his, and no other man could have her as long as he wanted her. The flame she'd tried to quench earlier sprang from the embers as hope flared to life inside her.

"Then perhaps we should return to the party for a reasonably discreet time until you can escort me home, my lord," she whispered in a sultry tone. "The thought of us pleasuring each other is exciting to me, too. Particularly when I know how delicious you will taste when my mouth is sucking on you."

He took a quick step toward her and kissed her hard before he released her just as hastily. Withdrawing a key from his pocket, he unlocked the door and opened it.

"*Go. Now.* Before I forget we're playing a game and take you right here on the desk."

The strangled sentence indicated he'd reached his breaking point, and the sound relieved her. The nonchalance he'd displayed after his seduction of her and even when she'd tried to seduce him illustrated nothing more than an iron will on his part. It was a relief to know she'd affected him far more than he'd allowed her to believe.

Without a word, she hurried past him, her body tingling as she heard the door close behind her. Weak-kneed, she moved down the hallway as quickly as she could. She had no idea how long she'd been gone from the gathering, and she was certain her disheveled appearance was bound to raise eyebrows.

Ahead of her, she could hear the sound of voices, and the sight of a mirror on the wall made her draw in a breath of relief. She paused to examine her image and stared with something akin to shock. There was a glow to her face she'd never seen before. Even her eyes sparkled, and she tried to dismiss the cause.

Lust was the reason she looked like a woman in her late twenties or early thirties, nothing more. Quickly, she pinned several strands of hair that had fallen down to brush the side of her face. Satisfied that she'd repaired her appearance sufficiently to not arouse too much suspicion, she forced herself to enter the Rothschilds' main salon.

An empty chair just inside the parlor's doorway seemed the perfect place to sit quietly in hopes that no one had noticed her missing. Relief spread through her as no one turned to study her with suspicion, and after a minute or two, she was able to breathe much more easily.

Allegra met her gaze from across the room and sent a conspiratorial smile in her direction as Garrick appeared in the doorway. Heat flooded her cheeks at her friend's amused expression. She didn't look at him as he came to her side and bent his head.

"Plead a headache in a few minutes," he rasped. "If you wait any longer, I'll drag you out of here in spite of the scandal it will cause."

He didn't give her a chance to respond as he walked away, his stride rigid. As she watched him join their hostess, Ruth marveled at the fact that he wanted to be alone with her so badly that he was willing to cause a scene. A rustle of silk caught her attention, and she glanced at the woman who'd sat down next to her. She immediately went rigid in her seat as she met Louise Campton's malicious gaze of amusement.

"My dear Lady Ruth, might I say you look lovely this evening. It's obvious the young baron's attentions have done wonders for your spirits."

"You're too kind, Mrs. Campton," Ruth murmured as she turned her gaze back toward the small gathering in front of her.

"I only wish I had half your daring."

"Daring?" She straightened in her chair as she saw Garrick turn his head to look in her direction.

"Of course." Louise sounded like a cat toying with a bird caught in its claws. The woman's purring voice set Ruth on edge. "After all, there are few women in the Set who have such adventuresome natures that they take a younger man for a lover."

There it was. Louise's reason for sitting next to her. She thought to make her feel uncomfortable for being with Garrick. She refused to listen to the woman's prattle. Louise was no better than the *Town Talk* or other scandal sheets. She turned her head and sent the woman a disdainful look.

"My relationship with Lord Stratfield is no one's concern, even if there are a few years' difference in our ages."

She arched her eyebrow in disdain, hoping the woman would go away and leave her be. The headache Garrick had told her to plead was quickly becoming a reality.

"A *few* years?" Louise laughed unpleasantly. "Oh you poor dear. I thought you knew. Lord Stratfield is much more your junior than a few years. He's a good twelve years younger than you."

Ruth couldn't remember ever being so cold. It was as if someone had dropped her in an icy lake. Her gaze shifted downward, expecting to find her clothes drenched with water. Frozen in place, she struggled to absorb Louise Campton's words. *Twelve years.*

The woman was wrong. She had to be. Garrick couldn't possibly be any more than three to five years younger than her. He was far too mature to be a man of . . . she quickly calculated the number in her head. Dear God, he was only twenty-nine.

Her stomach started to churn. Twenty-nine. No wonder the scandal sheets had been so vicious. She was in love with a man young enough almost to be her son. She gripped the seat cushion beneath her as she fought not to faint.

Love. How could she possibly be in love? The nausea made her clutch at her stomach as she looked up and saw Allegra heading toward her with a look of concern on her face. Beside her, Louise Campton leaned toward her with contrived worry.

"Are you all right, Lady Ruth?"

"Yes," she said hoarsely and shook off the woman's artificial gesture of concern. "I think I ate something this evening that doesn't agree with me."

"Let me call for someone to assist you. Lord Stratfield, perhaps?"

"Mrs. Campton, there you are. Lady Rothschild was just looking for you. I believe she wants to introduce you to someone." Allegra's tone was clipped as she gave the woman seated beside Ruth a cold look of dislike. With a haughty smile, Louise Campton rose to her feet and glanced down at Ruth.

"I do hope you'll forgive me any pain I might have caused you, Lady Ruth. I can assure you it was unintentional."

Again, the woman reminded her of a cat. Only this time she'd finished toying with her prey and swallowed it whole. Ruth choked back the bile rising in her throat and forced herself to meet the woman's malevolent gaze.

"You give yourself far too much credit, Mrs. Campton. But I thank you for the service you so willingly provided me. Generosity is so contrary to your nature."

It amazed her that she even had the wherewithal to insult the woman, but she could tell her words struck home as Louise's head snapped back. With a vicious glare at her and then Allegra, the woman stalked off as though she was the one who'd been injured during the exchange. Sitting down in the chair Louise had vacated, Allegra took Ruth's hand and uttered an appalled gasp.

"Dear God, your hands are like ice. What did that woman say to you?"

Ruth didn't answer as she tried to organize the chaotic thoughts flying through her head. How could she have not realized he was twelve years younger than her? She fought back tears of humiliation. Why hadn't she read about his age in the scandal sheets? How could she have missed that? She turned to Allegra.

"Did you know?" she rasped.

"Did I know what, dearest?"

"Did you know that Garrick is twelve years younger than me?" She watched her friend shake her head.

"*Twelve years*. Is that what Louise told you?" Allegra exclaimed. "I don't believe it."

"The woman took far too much pleasure in relating the news for her to be lying." Ruth shook her head as she blinked tears out of her eyes.

"I knew he was younger, but I never thought . . . does it really matter?" Allegra squeezed her hand. "He's good for you, Ruth."

"He's too young," she said hoarsely. "God, I was a fool. I knew it was a mistake to agree to a liaison with him. But he made me feel . . . and I . . ."

"Oh Ruth," her friend murmured. "You're in love with him, aren't you?"

"Yes." The knowledge weighed heavily on her chest, making it difficult to breathe. "I need to go. I can't . . . I don't want her . . . *anyone* to see me like this. I want to go home."

A familiar frisson rolled over her skin, and she flinched. *Oh God.* She couldn't face him now. One hand pressed to her stomach, she fought to control the panic flooding her limbs. His hand touched her shoulder as he bent over her.

"Christ Jesus. You look like you're about to faint." The concern in his voice made her tremble. Struggling to remain composed, she shook her head.

"It's nothing. It will pass," she said sharply.

If only that were true. Her gaze flitted around the room. Several guests were beginning to look in her direction with curiosity, and it heightened the mortification making her so ill. But it wasn't true. It would take a very long time before she was no longer the laughingstock of the Set. She could see it in their eyes. They thought her desperate for being with a man so much younger than herself.

"I'll take you home."

"No." She shook her head vehemently. "Allegra and the earl were about to leave. I will go home with them. You stay and enjoy the rest of the evening."

"*I'll* take you home," he growled. "Come."

She looked at the hand he offered her and stood up without his help. Allegra rose to her feet as well and gently pressed her hand into Ruth's back to steady her.

"My lord, if you'll call for the carriage, I'll see to Ruth." Her friend's pragmatic tone made Garrick nod in agreement, but his dark frown didn't disappear.

His hand briefly touched her arm in a gesture of concern, and she stiffened. For a moment, he hesitated as if he were going to question her, but Allegra waved him away. As he left the salon, Lady Rothschild appeared in front of her, followed by the baron.

"My dear Lady Ruth. Are you feeling unwell?"

"Yes, my lady. Please forgive me, but I think it's best if I go home." It took a great deal of effort, but she was able to keep her voice steady as she responded to her hostess.

"But of course," Lady Rothschild exclaimed softly. "I'm so sorry you're feeling ill. Is there something the baron or I can do for you?"

"No thank you, my lady. I'm certain I'll recover soon enough."

The words were bitter on her tongue. She might recover from the humiliation, but she would never find a way to mend her heart. With a slight nod to the Rothschilds, she moved toward the salon's open doorway, all too aware of the prying eyes following her departure.

As she reached the hall, she saw Garrick waiting for her. He was at her side in several quick strides, but she shrugged off his assistance. The footman draped her wrap over her shoulders, but the garment didn't alleviate the chill that had seeped into her muscles and down into her bones.

Her entire body felt stiff and awkward, and the numbness washing over her made her feel as though she were drowning in a slow-moving river. Something she was almost grateful for as it made it easier to bear Garrick's touch when he helped her into the carriage. Huddled in the corner of the vehicle, she stared out the window with a sense of helpless despair.

She loved him. From the beginning, she'd told herself to guard against losing her heart to him. How could she have allowed it to happen? Her relationships had always been fleeting. She knew better than to fall in love. And yet she had.

Worse, she'd fallen in love with a man who was barely out of the schoolroom. Her stomach lurched at the thought. Oh God, what was she going to do? Eyes closed, she found herself praying for the night to be over. Praying for the sanctuary of a faraway place where she could curl up and wait for all the pain to recede.

But she couldn't go anywhere until she'd resolved things with Garrick. There was no doubt in her mind that he would fight her on the matter, but as far as she was concerned, their liaison was at an end. The carriage rocked forward, and she tensed as Garrick leaned toward her.

"Are you with child?"

The question shocked her, and she jerked her head around to look at him. He was serious. The realization almost made her laugh and cry at the same time. The idea that she might be carrying his child would have been heart-wrenching under any circumstance. But the knowledge that she would never be able to give him a son or daughter was far more devastating.

"I'm too old to have a child," she snapped.

"Don't be ridiculous. Of course you can still have children. The question is whether I can father a child." There was a morose note in his voice that made her heart weep for him in spite of her humiliation and pain.

"I'm sure that when you find a bride younger than me you'll sire many children."

The thought of him with another woman was abhorrent to her, and she heard the resentment in her voice. Garrick caught her hand in his and she stiffened, expecting a familiar hot sensation to skim up her arm. It didn't. The numbness was still there. She couldn't help but breathe a soft sigh of relief. It was her only protection from the fire she knew his touch always ignited in her.

"Goddamn it. *Stop* emphasizing your age. It has nothing to do with us," he snarled in a manner that said he knew something was deeply wrong between them.

"It has everything to do with us. You deceived me."

"Deceived you? How?" His grip on her hand tightened.

"You let me believe you were only a few years younger than me. However, Mrs. Campton kindly opened my eyes to the truth this evening. She told me . . . she said you were *twelve years* younger than me." There it was again. That sickening churning sensation in her stomach. She bit back a sob as she tugged her hand free of his.

"*Christ almighty*," he rasped. "Louise Campton is a poisonous bitch, and the difference in our ages means nothing."

"*Now* who's being ridiculous? We both know what everyone thinks about a woman of *my* age consorting with a man *your* age." Mortified by the words, she shivered with cold and clutched her wrap tightly around her in a futile effort to warm herself. "God knows, the papers have taken me to task regularly on the subject. Although I am amazed they haven't mentioned the exact difference in our ages before this."

"They didn't until this week," he bit out through clenched teeth. She stared at him in openmouthed horror, and he released a fierce noise of self-disgust. "When Dolores showed me the article, I instructed her to dispose of it."

"The *Town Talk* has been on my breakfast tray every morning this week."

"Except one."

She frowned then drew in a quick breath as she remembered the morning he was talking about. He'd surprised her by joining her in the bathtub. It was a pleasurable memory that the fear of this moment crushed. He hadn't just deceived her, he'd manipulated her. Appalled, she stared at him in shock as the carriage jerked to a halt. Tonight need not have happened if he'd simply been honest with her.

No, it wouldn't have happened because she would have ended their relationship the moment she'd learned the truth. She would not have waited for someone like Louise to make her a figure of fun. But that was precisely what had happened, and it was why she intended to be done with him tonight. Her heart splintered in her chest at the thought.

It would be even more arduous than when she'd asked her father to visit her mother in the days before she died. Her stomach churning again, she flung the Berline's door open. All she wanted to do was escape this nightmare. She half tumbled, half threw herself out of the vehicle in her determination to flee.

Behind her, Garrick uttered a violent oath, but she didn't pause in her haste to put distance between them. She had no choice but to have it out with him, but not in the close confines of the carriage. It was too intimate, and she was terrified the numbness controlling her limbs would evaporate any minute. It would make her vulnerable to him—to his touch.

She gathered her skirts up to keep from tripping then hurried up the steps to the front door of the town house, which was slowly opening in front of her. Inside the softly lit foyer, she handed off her wrap to Simmons and glanced at the stairs. She wanted to retreat to the comfort of her bedroom, but she knew that would be a terrible mistake. The intimacy of her bedroom would eventually work in his favor. Garrick was excellent at persuasion, and she'd need her wits about her when she told him they were through.

Without another thought, she bolted into the salon. She rarely drank anything other than wine, but at the moment, the fire of a stiff brandy would give her the confidence she needed for the fight to come. Her nerve endings were already dancing on a thin wire, and as the salon door crashed shut, the violent sound made her jump, but she didn't turn around. Instead, she poured a glass of brandy with trembling hands and threw it down her throat. The result was a coughing spasm that left her clutching her breast until it passed. Strong hands grasped her arms and jerked her into a warm chest.

"Damn it, Ruth. You can't drink brandy like that," he chided her with exasperation.

The warmth of him sank its way into her body, thawing her more quickly than the cognac. The numbness slowly rolled back as she breathed in his scent. *Sandalwood.* Dear God, he always smelled so deliciously of the outdoors. Her nostrils drank in the essence of him, strong and incredibly male. Whenever he held her like this, she felt safe from anything that might harm her.

She gasped with dismay when she realized what she was doing. With a hard shove, she broke free of his embrace and darted away from him. Part of her expected him to pursue her, but when she turned to face him, he hadn't moved. Blue eyes glittering with assessment, he studied her in silence. She was already so on edge that if he'd taken a single step in her direction, she most likely would have fled the room. The residue of brandy still burned her throat, and she coughed again.

"I'm not letting you go, Ruth." The harsh determination behind his words made her stiffen.

"And I refuse to continue a liaison with a man who's twelve years my junior." Her voice was just as inflexible as his.

"*Bloody hell*, it's a number, Ruth." He shoved his fingers through his dark hair in a gesture that illustrated his frustration as he began to pace the floor. "It's just a number."

"Even if I could accept that, which I cannot, you manipulated me. You deliberately hid the truth from me."

"Of course I hid the truth from you," he growled as he stopped his prowling to face her. "You're so damned convinced you have nothing left to offer a man, and I wasn't about to let the papers destroy what little progress I'd made in convincing you otherwise. I knew how you'd react—"

"And did you know how I'd react when someone else told me that you were twelve years younger than me?" The question sent mortification crawling across her skin again. It was like an insidious piece of ivy threatening to choke her. "Do you have *any* idea how I felt when Louise Campton so kindly informed me of the difference in our ages?"

She clutched at her throat as she remembered Louise gleefully pointing out the twelve years' difference between her and Garrick. Only minutes before that terrible revelation, his masterful, seductive caresses had made her forget she was older than him. Then in one ugly sentence, Louise Campton had reminded her what old really felt like.

The humiliation would have been painful enough, but to realize she was in love with him at the same moment in time had been a crushing blow. Louise had known it, too. The woman had enjoyed seeing Ruth struggle with the knowledge that she'd fallen in love with Garrick. If she'd felt old before, it was nothing compared to what she'd felt at that moment and now.

"I made a mistake, Ruth," he rasped. "I should have told you the truth." Regret darkened his handsome features, but she refused to absolve him of his sin.

"But you didn't tell me the truth. Louise Campton did. And she enjoyed every damn minute of it," she said bitterly. "I have no doubt the woman will be certain to take credit for our falling-out in the days to come."

"What the hell is that supposed to mean?" he growled.

"It means your lessons are at an end, my lord. I wish to break our liaison."

She steeled herself to maintain a detached manner as he narrowed his eyes at her with a calculating look she'd seen before. It was a look that said he was determined to have his own way, and it alarmed her. The silence stretched between them and grew heavier with each passing second. She averted her gaze from his penetrating look.

Why didn't he say something? He'd been so persistent throughout their affair at getting his own way, yet now he chose to remain silent. Perhaps he didn't think her serious about ending their liaison. No, she was certain he knew she was earnest in her intent to end things between them; he was simply strategizing how to persuade her otherwise.

Did she have the willpower not to give in to him? A lump rose in her throat, and she immediately reproached herself for even thinking she was willing to accept more heartache where he was concerned. The decision to end their affair was the only thing that would save her further humiliation. Not just at the hands of the Set, but from him as well if he were ever to discover the way she felt about him.

"I think not." For a simple statement, it had a harshness to it that made her jerk her gaze back to him. An impassive expression hardened his features making it impossible to read his thoughts.

"*What*?" she exclaimed. She'd expected an attempt to persuade her, not an autocratic refusal.

"I will not have others dictate who I choose to be with, nor should you."

"It is not a question of anyone governing my actions. It's a question of propriety," she said with apathy. "I'm too old for you."

"And yet you agreed to be my mistress knowing full well that I was younger than you. You just didn't know by how much," he said with a savage intensity as he closed the space between them.

"Don't you *dare* lay the blame for this evening at my feet," she bit out, holding her ground despite the sudden urge to run.

There was far more truth in his statement than she cared to admit, and it made it harder for her to ignore her body's reaction to his close proximity. Every part of her was suddenly on fire, making it difficult to ignore his delicious male scent, or worse, the tug of desire she felt winding its way through her. Resignation and regret twisted his lips into a thin line.

"No. I take full blame for tonight. If I could take it back, spare you the humiliation, I would. But I can't."

"Then spare me any further humiliation and find a new mistress," she whispered as the full impact of him on her senses threatened to make her give way to the apology in his voice.

"I don't want another mistress," he growled. "I want you."

Despite her desire not to feel anything, the possessive note in his voice sent a shiver of arousal down her back. She shook her head in silent protest, and this time she did retreat. He didn't give her the chance to widen the distance between them. With lightning speed, his hand grasped her arm, and he pulled her into his arms. The moment his mouth covered hers, the fire of his kiss made her body melt into his without any resistance whatsoever.

Heat pulsed its way wildly through her veins with a speed that startled her. Her heart rejoiced at his touch, rejecting the warnings in the back of her mind as she yielded to the passion spinning a web of delight across her skin. His lips teased and cajoled a fiery response from her, and she moaned softly as his mouth skimmed its way along her jawline to her ear.

"Do you have any idea how exquisite you are?" His breath was a sinful heat against her ear, while his honeyed voice made her legs weaken. "No matter how old you become, your beauty will never fade. You're timeless in a way other women can only dream of."

The intense desire threading through his words made her sex tighten in a tactile response that was so strong it was as if he'd physically stroked her. She drew in a sharp breath hoping to hide her reaction to him, but something in his gaze warned her that he knew exactly what she was feeling. Desperately she reminded herself that he'd deceived her—that twelve years was too great a divide between them.

But it was almost impossible to remember anything but the pleasure of his touch when she was still reeling from his kiss. It was even more difficult when he was looking at her as if he wanted to devour her. A voice deep inside her fought to reject logic and urged her to take even the smallest bit of happiness she could find with him. It would be a foolish thing to do.

If she thought her heart was breaking now, it wouldn't survive when he left her in the future. The knot in her throat threatened to choke her as she met his smoldering look. His gaze suddenly narrowed as if he realized she was struggling not to give way to him.

She tried to calm her racing heartbeat as she forced herself to go rigid in his embrace. She was on the verge of succumbing to him, and if she allowed him to see it, he would press her until she surrendered.

"*Timeless* is such a pretty word. Unfortunately it's wasted on me."

"Is it?" he rasped. "Your lips say one thing, Ruth, but your body says something completely different."

The intensity in his voice made her mouth go dry with fear as she stared up into his astute gaze. Dear God, had he surmised the truth? No. He couldn't have. He would have used the knowledge to his advantage if he suspected she cared for him. Perhaps he fancied himself in love with her. The thought made her heart squeeze painfully in her chest.

It made sense he might be infatuated with her. She was the first woman he'd ever been with. But that wasn't the same thing as the type of love she felt for him. Even if he did feel a deep affection for her, she would never be able to reconcile herself to the difference in their ages.

She met his gaze and saw the resolute gleam in his blue eyes. He truly thought she would give in to him. If she didn't break with him now, he would have his way. She had little choice but to drive him away by any means possible, no matter how cruel.

"And you forget that I am trained to respond when a man caresses me. *Any* man," she said coldly as she pushed her way out of his suddenly lifeless arms. "You were special because you afforded me the opportunity to teach, rather than perform the usual tricks of my trade."

The heartless words made his head snap back as if she'd hit him. He looked stunned, and her muscles tightened as she fought not to rush forward and beg his forgiveness for her cruel words. In the blink of an eye, his facial expression became cold and empty.

Even the angular planes of his face were drawn tight until the muscles in his jaw were hard and inflexible. The withering look he directed at her drove an icy shard into her heart. With what little self-control she had left, she struggled not to cry out in pain at the contempt in his blue eyes. He took a rigid step back from her and bowed.

"Then I shall not stand in the way of you performing your trade, my lady."

The scorn in his voice made the insult all the more agonizing.

Without another word, he turned and walked out of the salon, the door closing quietly behind him. Rooted in place, she stared after him as the numbness returned. Slowly, she sank to the floor, her arms wrapped around her waist as a cold weariness settled into her limbs. Only one other time in her life had she ever felt so lost as to which way to turn. A tear rolled down her cheek. In the back of her mind, a voice screamed at her to go after him. She ignored it. Another tear landed on her arm as the ache in her chest spread its way into every part of her. The only other man to break her heart was her father, but the pain of losing Garrick was far greater. Unlike her father's abandonment, Garrick's departure bit down into her soul in a way that said she would never be whole again. The tears flowed hot and heavy down her cheeks. It was as if she'd awakened to find it was nighttime, only to realize dawn would never come again. Garrick had been right. Her age was little more than a number. She wasn't afraid of growing old. Her biggest fear was realizing she would never know what it was to be loved.

Ruth stared down at the paperwork in front of her. She'd been sitting inside St. Agnes's small office for the better part of the day. She'd yet to balance the orphanage's books, despite her usually meticulous bookkeeping. She frowned at the numbers for another long moment, before she relented to the pressure in her head.

Her pencil falling onto the ledger in front of her, she closed her eyes and gently rubbed her throbbing temples. It had been more than a week since she'd broken off her liaison with Garrick, and every day had been a painful exercise in living. Invitations continued to be delivered, but she'd not accepted any for fear of seeing Garrick.

She was certain some people in the Set would find it amusing to ensure that the two of them were together in the same room, simply to see what might happen. Not even Allegra had been able to console her, although her friend was insistent that Ruth visit Pembroke Hall for an extended visit. She refused despite Allegra's pleas.

She'd decided to close her town house, until a tenant could be found, and move to Crawley Hall. There was little reason for her to remain in town. The only thing to do now was finish up a few last-minute business matters related to St. Agnes's. Lord Pembroke had provided her with the names of several strong candidates to attend to the orphanage's daily operations when she was no longer in town.

The young man she'd finally settled on, James Turcot, was an affable fellow. It was clear he enjoyed children, which meant he would do his best to see to their well-being, not just managing the books. She would still come to town for the quarterly meetings of the orphanage's board, but the day-to-day task of running the business she would leave to James. He was due to start next week, and she'd already set Dolores to work in preparation for her move to Crawley Hall.

The pain in her head unabated, she retrieved her pencil to study the column of figures she'd yet to calculate properly. The sound of the office door opening made her raise her head, and she stiffened at the sight of the Viscount Tremaine. She immediately opened the desk drawer, her fingers sliding the small pistol out of her drawstring bag for ease of access.

Cunning filled the man's smile, and she rose to her feet so she would not be at a disadvantage.

"Lord Tremaine," she said coldly.

"My dear Lady Ruth. I'm delighted to see you again."

"What do you want, my lord?" She didn't care that she sounded rude. She neither liked nor trusted the man.

"Straight to the point. I like that in a woman." His smile sent an icy finger skimming down her spine. "I have a proposition for you."

"A proposition?" She arched her eyebrow at him in her haughtiest manner.

"Yes. I've learned that Stratfield is no longer your sponsor, and I thought we might get along nicely."

She could not have been more stunned than if her father had walked into the orphanage to beg her forgiveness. The viscount was clearly amused as he sent her a mocking smile. He was a handsome man, but it was his mannerisms that made him unattractive. Collecting her wits, Ruth shook her head.

"While I am . . . flattered by your offer, I must decline."

"I urge you not be too hasty in your decision, my dear lady. I think you should consider the far-reaching consequences of your decision."

The man was gloating. There was no other word for it. She frowned in puzzlement. What sort of consequences could he be referring to? To her knowledge, he had never had anything to do with the orphanage. But what else could he be referring to?

"Consequences, my lord?"

"I'm referring to Stratfield."

"I'm afraid I don't understand. Lord Stratfield and I are no longer, as you said, involved."

The viscount strolled forward, causing her fingers to slip into the desk drawer in search of the comforting ivory grip of her gun. The man's gaze drifted down to where her hand was, and he smiled as he pointed to the chair facing the desk.

"Perhaps I should explain. May I?" He gestured toward the chair and she nodded then sat down as well. "Lord Stratfield and I are—how shall I put this—not the best of friends. Recently it's come to light that the man has been attempting to bankrupt me, which I find most distressing."

"Of course," she murmured as he eyed her expectantly. The feral smile on his lips made her uncomfortable. The man looked like a wolf hunting its prey.

"However, I've acquired a unique piece of information that I believe will make Stratfield reconsider his efforts to meddle in my finances." Something in the viscount's manner chilled her, and she immediately feared for Garrick.

"How does any of this involve me?"

"While I'm certain the information I have is enough to persuade Stratfield not to tamper with my finances or that of my informant's, I prefer to make the stakes a bit more painful for the baron."

"Again, I fail to see how this affects me." She folded her hands tightly in front of her and worked hard to keep her expression serene.

"I have it on excellent authority that you're in love with the young baron." At the man's amused smile of confidence, her composure slipped.

"I . . . I don't know what you're talking about." She could feel a knot swelling in her throat until it was difficult to breathe.

"It's quite all right, my lady. Your secret is safe with me as long as you agree to help me."

"If you think to blackmail me with the threat of announcing to the world that I have a tendré for Lord Stratfield then feel free to do so. It will do you no good," she snapped. Infuriated that the man thought to use her in his attempt to injure Garrick, she sprang to her feet. "I've heard quite enough, my lord. I think it's time you left."

"You have a fiery spirit, my lady. I see we shall get along famously."

"I think you're delusional, Lord Tremaine, and I have no intention of accepting your patronage." Furious, she wanted to shoot the man for even daring to blackmail her. Palms flat on the desk, she glared at him fiercely. "Now get out."

"As you wish," he said smoothly without moving from his chair. "Of course, I'm confident the papers will be delighted to receive word from the Lady R. regarding her recent liaison with Lord S. and how his lordship is minus a ballock. It will be the most sensational news they've printed in years."

Ruth gasped in horror at the viscount's words. How in God's name did the man know about Garrick's disfigurement? Garrick had paid his uncle to stay away from his family. For the first time, she wondered if what he'd really been doing was paying for the man's silence. But how had Tremaine learned the truth? Did the man know Garrick's uncle?

She sent up a fervent prayer that the bastard hadn't found the woman who'd humiliated Garrick and learned the truth from her. Something told her the viscount would take pleasure in tormenting

Garrick with such knowledge. But it was the thought of what Garrick would think when he read the papers that sickened her.

The public humiliation would be devastating for him. And if she didn't do as Tremaine demanded she'd be responsible for his pain. She met Tremaine's smug look in a state of shock as her knees threatened to give out beneath her. She loved Garrick, and she refused to let anyone humiliate him in such a fashion. She knew all too well what that type of mortification was like.

Slowly, she sank down into her chair. Think. She needed time to think. Time to figure out a way to beat this bastard at his own game. She wet her dry lips and lust swept across Tremaine's features. She immediately regretted the action. Somehow she'd find a way out of this quagmire, she just wasn't sure how. She sent her blackmailer a look of intense loathing.

"What makes you think I'll agree to your blackmail scheme?" she bit out between clenched teeth.

"Because I understand people, Lady Ruth," he said with a venomous smile. "You're in love with Stratfield, and you'll not betray his secret."

"Even if what you say were true," she said, refusing to confirm the man's suspicions, "I fail to see how my participation in this scheme of yours serves any purpose where his lordship is concerned. Lord Stratfield holds me in contempt and has no interest in me at all."

"Have you not read the papers of late, my dear?" Tremaine arched his eyebrows at her. "The young man has taken to drinking heavily and boxing with commoners. He bears all the signs of a man infatuated with a woman."

Young man. The silent insult behind the words didn't escape her. Despite his determination to make her his mistress, even Tremaine thought Garrick too young for her. The sudden image of Garrick drinking and fighting to excess made her heart skip a beat.

She'd not had the courage to read the papers for the past week, and she'd spent the majority of her time at the orphanage. The behavior the viscount described was clearly unlike Garrick. Was it possible he cared about her more than she'd given him credit for? No. If Garrick were in love with her, he would have found a way to try and change her mind. He was far too persistent not to do so.

"You have still not explained your reason to include me in your scheme."

"There is a personal score to settle between you and me." The viscount leaned forward, his gaze narrowing at her in a way that frightened her. "No one interferes in my personal business without consequences."

"If you're referring to Lady Lynmouth, it was clear to me the lady didn't want your attentions."

"I would have persuaded her otherwise, except you interfered." There was a vicious note of anger in the viscount's voice as he got to his feet. "I've decided to teach you a lesson, while ensuring my financial stability. Stratfield has been a thorn in my side for some time. I shall enjoy pointing out to him that only a real man, such as myself, could ever satisfy his one-time mistress."

Dear Lord, what was she going to do? She had to find a way to let Garrick know what Tremaine was up to. The bastard strolled around the desk toward her. The smile on his lips didn't reach his flat gaze as he pulled her to her feet.

"I think we have an understanding, don't we, Lady Ruth?" His hand cupped her chin and forced her to look at him. "Stratfield will pay for my silence, and because you are my mistress, I shall maintain your secrets. Shall we seal our bargain with a kiss?"

She couldn't remember ever being frightened of a man before, but she was of this one. His arm snaked around her waist and he tugged her against him. His lips met hers, and a shudder wracked her frame at the way her skin crawled from his touch. He wasn't unskilled, but as his tongue probed her mouth, her stomach roiled. Dear God, how was she going to stand welcoming this man into her bed?

Garrick. She needed to remember this was all for Garrick. In the back of her head, she could hear the wonderful sound of his voice, and the viscount stiffened against her. As he stepped back from her, Tremaine turned his head and smiled. It was a terrible smile, and dread trailed a stream of icy water down her back and spread its way all over her body.

Her gaze followed the viscount's, and the sight of Garrick standing in the center of the room made her heart shatter. His face was white with anger and something else she didn't want to label for fear it would make her sob with misery.

Rage. It consumed him with a white-hot heat that threatened to obliterate his sense of reason. He'd wanted Tremaine dead for some time now, and perhaps today was the day to take care of the bastard. The man's sneering smile only intensified the fury inside him. Fists clenched, he remained rooted where he stood, despite the urgent need to charge across the room and savagely rip the man apart.

And Ruth.

He couldn't believe she was in Tremaine's arms willingly, even if she wasn't making any effort to free herself from the son of a bitch's embrace. If anything she seemed shocked, almost frightened, by his appearance in the orphanage's small office.

"Ah, the illustrious Baron Stratfield. How convenient. You've saved me the trouble of calling on you."

"Let her go, Tremaine." Despite the softness of his voice, the words possessed a lethal quality that made the other man flinch. The viscount recovered quickly.

"Perhaps the lady doesn't wish to be free."

Tremaine smiled with far too much confidence as he turned his attention to Ruth. When the man didn't release her from his arms, Garrick swung his gaze to her. The minute his eyes met hers, she quickly looked away. She was afraid. He looked back at Tremaine. The man was far too pleased with himself—he was holding something over her head. But what?

"I find it difficult to believe that Ruth is remotely interested in you, Tremaine. After all, your father was responsible for the destruction of her parents' marriage, and she knows what you did to Mary," he said as he looked at the man with disgust.

"Your recently departed Mary was not the sweet miss you think she is." Tremaine snorted. "Be that as it may, I've explained myself to Ruth, and she's agreed to my patronage."

The viscount glanced at Ruth with a smile of satisfaction before he turned back to Garrick. The man was lying. How in the hell could Ruth possibly consider a liaison with this bastard? She knew what the man was.

Unless—he dismissed the possibility in the blink of an eye. She might be a courtesan, but her reaction to him had never been that of a woman merely servicing her lover. There had been something more between them. She'd ended her affair with him for one reason and one reason only—he was younger than her. He'd been so certain of it, he'd come here today to convince her the gossips were wrong. His ability to satisfy her hadn't played any role in her decision. He refused to believe otherwise.

"I don't believe you," he snarled.

"I can assure you it's quite true, Stratfield," the viscount said with a condescending smile. "At least Lady Ruth will be able to welcome a real man into her bed."

Garrick froze. His gaze shifted back to Ruth. Still in Tremaine's arms, she kept her face averted, but there was something in her demeanor that troubled him. Despite the warning in the back of his head, he dismissed it. He didn't think for one minute that she'd betrayed him. Still, it troubled him that she wouldn't look at him. Not taking his eyes off her, he cleared his throat.

"Tell me why you'd be willing to let this bastard into your bed, Ruth." He watched as she freed herself from Tremaine's arms and turned toward him. It was impossible to tell what she was thinking.

"I am free to see who I wish, my lord." Her voice was devoid of any emotion. His jaw locked tight with frustration. She'd not answered him.

"You see, Stratfield. The lady has come to her senses." Tremaine's smile was malicious.

"Has she?" he replied in a sardonic tone. "I sincerely doubt Ruth would even consider getting into bed with a bounder like you under any circumstances. Something tells me there's more to her agreement than either of you are saying."

"True. But then I have it on good authority that the lady wasn't satisfied with a man who has only one ballock."

The viscount's words ripped into him like a gunshot. Desperately fighting to collect his wits, he forced a strained smile as he met the man's snide look. His uncle. That son of a bitch had told Tremaine about his defect. His fears had become a reality. The question was, what did the viscount want? He arched his eyebrow at the other man.

"You have an active imagination, Tremaine." The amusement in his voice was sufficient for the man to eye him with a calculating frown. An instant later, the viscount smiled with contentment.

"You surprise me, Stratfield. Personally, I'm amazed at your ability to perform at all despite having only one ballock. But did you really think Lady Ruth would keep your secret?"

The man's words sucked the air from his lungs. Rigid with disbelief, he focused his gaze on Ruth. Although she was pale, her expression revealed nothing. When she didn't contradict Tremaine, his heart twisted so violently in his chest he wanted to shout from the pain of it.

She'd betrayed him.

In the next breath he rejected the notion. He didn't believe it. It had to have been his uncle who'd revealed his secret. It couldn't have been Ruth. She wouldn't have betrayed him in that way. A mocking voice in the back of his head sneered at his pathetic protests—of course she'd betrayed him. If it had been his uncle, Tremaine would have no reason to involve Ruth.

Although she was no longer in Tremaine's arms, she'd made no effort to put any significant distance between herself and the bastard. She'd agreed to become the man's mistress. What further proof did he need that she'd told Tremaine his secret? Perhaps hearing the fact straight from her lips. Again a voice deep inside taunted him with his desire not to believe what was so plainly visible.

"You seem at a loss for words, Stratfield." The viscount's smug tone made him narrow his gaze at the man.

"Not at all." He feigned nonchalance with a shrug. "I'm simply puzzled as to why my physical traits are of such great interest to you. Between you and Wycombe, it would seem buggery is becoming one of your favorite pastimes. A diversion that holds no interest for me."

Fury darkened the other man's face, and Garrick smiled bitterly. The balance of power had shifted in his direction.

"I doubt you'll be quite this complacent when the Set discovers you're a freak of nature."

"You say that as if I care what people think." Garrick shook his head in a fatalistic manner before glancing at Ruth. Despite her pale color, her features remained composed and unreadable. Guilty, simply by virtue of the fact that she didn't deny Tremaine's allegations.

"I think you care a great deal," Tremaine said with a calculated look. "In fact, I think you'll pay me to keep silent."

"Pay you?" He laughed at the man.

The fact that he'd managed to do so amazed him. Tremaine was threatening to expose him to the world, something he fought long and hard to prevent. He didn't know whether to choke the son of a bitch or to simply walk out and take his chances that no one would believe the man. But then there was Ruth. People *would* believe her.

The bitter taste of bile rose in his throat at the thought of her betrayal. If there was anyone's throat he wanted to wrap his hands around, it was hers. How long had it taken her to run to Tremaine with his secret? He glared in her direction, and what little color she had left in her face drained away.

For a brief moment, he found himself thinking she was merely a pawn in Tremaine's hands. The bastard could be holding something over her head. He swallowed hard as her betrayal pushed itself back into the forefront of his mind. He was making excuses for her again. She'd told this bastard his secret, and now he was supposed to pay for Tremaine's silence.

He'd paid his uncle to keep quiet. Paying Tremaine would be no different. That wasn't true. Despite providing his uncle with a living, *he'd* made the terms of agreement, not his uncle. He'd been the one to stipulate what Beresford could or couldn't do. He'd clearly outlined the consequences if his uncle failed to abide by the agreement, and it appeared the man had kept to their bargain.

Instead, the least likely of sources had been his undoing. A woman. It was as if Bertha was taunting him all over again. The memories of the past welled up over him, and his body hardened with tension. He'd never thought it would be a woman who would betray him. Especially not Ruth.

A savage desire to hit something snaked its way through his body. She'd destroyed him. She'd told Tremaine the truth. Even if he paid the man, what would stop the bastard from revealing his secret to someone else? The blackmail would never end. The viscount uttered a grunt of frustration as he glared at Garrick.

"You seem to have lost your tongue, Stratfield." The man's amusement was edged with anger.

"On the contrary. I'm simply trying to understand if I heard you correctly."

"You did. I'm not asking for much." Tremaine sent him a glare of intense dislike. It was obvious their conversation was not going the way the man expected. "I simply want you to revoke your demand for payment on all my investment loans."

"I still fail to see why I would do such a thing. Your claims would be unsubstantiated."

"Ah, but I have Lady Ruth," Tremaine said smoothly as he took a step toward Ruth and caressed her cheek.

A bolt of anger lanced through him at the man's gesture. The thought of Tremaine touching her at all, let alone bedding her, enraged him. He immediately condemned himself as a fool. The woman wasn't worth the emotional effort. In the back of his head, a sharp voice protested the thought vehemently.

"You seem quite confident of your ability to bring me to heel like some dog, Tremaine." He eyed the man with scorn.

"I don't see that you have much choice."

"There is always a choice," he said as his gaze darted toward Ruth. She'd turned away from both of them, and there was a forlorn look about her that he recognized. He snorted softly. Why was he so damned determined to find an excuse for her betrayal?

"Then perhaps you should consider the *best* choice to make in this matter."

"And I suppose that in exchange for my coin you'll remain silent." He narrowed his gaze at Tremaine.

"Precisely. And because your uncle's investments directly affect mine, I shall expect the payment demands on his investments to cease as well."

"Naturally," Garrick said as he narrowed his gaze at the man.

The request to cease and desist in his attempt to ruin his uncle wasn't all that unexpected. But it made him consider once more the possibility that Ruth really was a pawn in some twisted game Tremaine was playing.

He looked in her direction and studied her profile for a moment. Almost as if she could feel his gaze on her, she turned her head.

Was that sorrow in her beautiful violet eyes? No, she wasn't any different than Bertha. She didn't have a heart. She'd betrayed him in a span of days. No doubt, it had amused her to tell Tremaine his secret. He crushed the protest echoing in the back of his head.

"Well, are we in agreement then?" The viscount eyed him with confidence.

"I don't think so." As he met the man's gaze, he knew he wasn't going to agree. The fact amazed him.

"*What?*" Tremaine's angry roar wasn't surprising. "I'll expose you, Stratfield. Don't think I won't."

"Oh, I've no doubt you'll *try* to do your worst"—he smiled coldly at the man—"but I'm wondering who's going to take the word of a whore or a bounder who hovers on the fringes of fashionable Society."

Without waiting for the man's reply he turned and headed toward the office door. Behind him, Tremaine was sputtering with fury, and it filled Garrick with a small nugget of satisfaction. His life in the Set was over, but telling this bastard to go fuck himself had felt good. He turned the knob on the door and opened it as Tremaine shouted out after him.

"You'll regret this, Stratfield. I'll see to it that this ruins your family, too. That young brother of yours won't be marrying up in Society with everyone knowing your secret."

An icy rage engulfed him at the threat. Slowly, and with great control, he turned around to face the man. The contented look on the viscount's face dissolved into a look of fear as Garrick studied him with a deadly calm.

"If you do anything, *anything*, to hurt my family, Tremaine, I'll kill you."

The menacing sound of his voice echoed loudly in the room, and the viscount swallowed hard. The man's expression suddenly changed back to one of malicious satisfaction, and Garrick saw Ruth's eyes widen in horror as she stared at something over his shoulder. In the deepest recesses of his mind, he wondered why she would be horrified for him. He turned his head and met the wide-eyed look of a stockily built gentleman he didn't recognize.

"Mr. Millstadt, what a surprise."

From her breathless greeting, Ruth knew the man. But then she knew a great many men, he thought bitterly. With a sharp grunt of fury, he pushed his way past, and strode down the hall without a backward glance. In less than a minute he was out on the street, where he ordered Jasper to drive him to the Club.

Throwing himself into the leather-cushioned seat of the Berline, he seethed with a fury unlike anything he'd ever known. Not even the night he'd caught his uncle trying to enter Lily's room or the day he'd caught Tremaine in Seymour Place had he been this angry. If he'd given way to his impulses moments ago, he would have pulverized Tremaine until the man couldn't walk and then repeated the exercise.

Ruth.

The image of his hands wrapping around that beautiful neck of hers wasn't satisfying at all. He wanted to hear her pleading for mercy. Bertha had made a fool of him all those years ago, and he'd allowed Ruth to do the same thing. How could he have been such a simpleton?

Once more a woman had humiliated him, but this time he wasn't infatuated. He was in love, and the pain of her betrayal was a knife carving into the heart of him. His jaw clenched, he drew in a sharp breath between his teeth. Arms folded across his chest, he dug his fingers deep into his biceps.

She'd betrayed him.

The knowledge still left him stunned. It was almost impossible to believe given everything they'd shared. The image of her in Tremaine's arms filled his head again, and it made his blood flow hot with anger once more. The thought of her with that son of a bitch sickened him. Christ Jesus, how could he still love her in spite of what she'd done?

Her betrayal cut deep. So deep he knew there was little Tremaine or anyone else could do to him that would come close to the excruciating pain of her treachery. Ever since that terrible night in Bertha's room, he'd lived in fear of his uncle revealing his secret. Lived constantly on edge at the thought of someone exposing him for the freak of nature he was.

The irony of it was that it was a woman who'd revealed his secret. Something that never would have happened if he'd simply stayed away from Ruth. His fist hit the buttoned leather seat as the vehicle rocked to a halt in front of his club. To hell with Tremaine. He refused to let the bastard dictate to him. Not waiting on Jasper, he stepped out of the small carriage and climbed the steps of the Club, two at a time.

Lord Tremaine was going to find himself ruined by the end of the month. The bastard could do his worst, but Garrick refused to be blackmailed. Ruth might have betrayed and lied to him, but there was one thing he'd learned from his experience with her. His physical defect didn't define him. He'd been a fool to care what others thought.

He charged through the Club toward the gymnasium. He needed to hit something, and if he couldn't hit Tremaine, then a punching bag would have to suffice. Tremaine might find it pleasurable to humiliate him, but it didn't matter anymore. Nothing would be as painful as knowing the one woman he wanted above all others had deceived him.

Ruth stared at herself in her dressing table mirror. The dark circles under her eyes only emphasized her age. Her elbow resting on the well-polished maple tabletop, she cradled her forehead in her hand. She couldn't remember the last time she'd been this exhausted.

She'd barely slept last night as the entire scene with Garrick at the orphanage yesterday afternoon had played in her head over and over again. Although Tremaine had said he would visit her last night, he'd never showed. For that she was grateful. It had given her time to think about how the bastard had coerced her into doing as he wanted.

At the time, she'd been terrified of Garrick discovering she was in love with him. But seeing him struggle with Tremaine's threats yesterday had nearly done her in. The thought of his being blackmailed was abhorrent, particularly when Tremaine had made her a part of Garrick's pain. A teardrop rolled down her cheek, and she brushed it away. With shaky hands, she swept her hair up and used hairpins to hold the shape she'd created on the top of her head.

She'd invited Allegra to come for breakfast several days ago, and she needed to put on the best front possible where her friend was concerned. She'd not even managed to formulate an explanation as to Tremaine's sudden presence in her life. Something Allegra was not going to let go so easily. With one last glance in the mirror, Ruth stood up and headed downstairs. When she reached the foyer, Simmons emerged from the back of the house. She forced a smile to her lips.

"Good morning, Simmons. I expect Lady Pembroke to arrive shortly. Please let Dolores know that I'd like breakfast to be served as soon as her ladyship arrives."

Simmons always had a serious expression on his face, but today he appeared grimmer than usual. She frowned as he bowed his silent acknowledgment of her command before handing her the morning paper. As she took it from him, she noticed him hesitate for a fraction of an instant.

"Is everything all right, Simmons?" A shiver streaked down her back as his hesitation became even more pronounced.

"I believe the *Town Talk* is particularly ugly this morning, my lady. Perhaps the *Times* would be a better choice of reading material."

His words made Ruth's heart skip a beat, and her fingers curled around the paper Simmons had given her until she heard it crackle softly. *Tremaine.* The bastard had changed his mind. It had taken more than an hour for her to convince him that it was in his best interest to try one more time to persuade Garrick to accept his terms. But something told her the bastard hadn't waited. What had he told the papers?

"Thank you for the suggestion, Simmons, but gossip is rarely kind. I'll be in the salon. You may show Lady Pembroke there when she arrives."

Without waiting for a reply, she turned and walked toward the drawing room with the paper at her side as if it contained nothing of concern to her. The moment the door closed behind her, she tore the paper open in a frantic effort to reach the Society section. The moment her gaze fell on the gossip column, she quickly skimmed the words downward.

A moment later, her stomach lurched, and she swayed on her feet for a second before stumbling to the nearest chair. She sank into the lush cushions with the paper clutched to her stomach as if doing so would help ease her nausea. Although she knew she'd not misread the column, she slowly opened it again to ensure she'd not dreamed the words.

It appears the Lady R. has revealed a most interesting fact about a certain Lord S. The gentleman in question seems to have a round, exceedingly prominent piece of his anatomy missing. However, Lord S. is apparently quite capable of performing his manly duties, despite being only half a man.

Bile rose in Ruth's mouth. The paper fell from her hands, and she leapt to her feet to rush to the sideboard and pour a glass of brandy. She tossed the liquor down her throat then proceeded to cough violently from the burning sensation. The memory of Garrick chastising her the night of the Rothschilds' party flooded her mind, and she squeezed her eyes shut hoping that he would come charging in to do so again. It was a futile wish.

One hand pressed into her stomach in an attempt to ease the churning, she offered up a prayer that this was all a nightmare and she'd wake up soon. A voice in the back of her mind scoffed at her. The sound of the doorbell ringing made her stiffen. Allegra had arrived. Behind her the door opened and she turned to see her friend sweep through the doorway followed by Lord Pembroke. She'd only expected her friend for breakfast, not the earl.

"Oh my dear, we're too late." Her friend hurried forward as she glanced over her shoulder. "Shaheen, my darling. She looks ready to faint."

Lord Pembroke quickly followed his wife's forward movement, and in seconds she was in between the couple as they escorted her to the sofa. She shook her head as Allegra sank into the cushions next to her.

"I'm quite all right," she whispered. "It's of little consequence."

"*All right? Little consequence?*" Allegra's green eyes widened as she gasped in obvious horror. "What the devil is wrong with you? It's terrible."

"I know that. But I had nothing to do with it. I can't change what he did."

"What *he* did?" Lord Pembroke said sharply. "How do you know he's guilty?"

Confused, she stared up at the earl with a frown of puzzlement then turned to look at Allegra. Their expressions of horror and dismay made her heart sink. Had something else happened? Dear God, she didn't think she could take any more. She pressed her fingers to her forehead as she suddenly realized her head was throbbing.

"Because I was there. I heard Tremaine threaten Garrick with exposure, and now he's done just that." She gestured to the paper on the floor with a sharp wave of her hand. "And the bastard blamed me for it. He had the paper say *I* betrayed Garrick. But I didn't. I would never . . ."

She swallowed hard, unable to finish the sentence. Her eyes went to Allegra, who blanched slightly as she looked up at her husband. The earl's expression was grim, and she heard Allegra draw in a sharp hiss of air before she caught Ruth's hands in hers.

"Then you haven't heard." The note of alarm in Allegra's voice made Ruth uneasy as she met her friend's troubled gaze.

"Heard what?" she whispered as a wave of dread washed over her. Something was terribly wrong. She gripped Allegra's hands. "Garrick. Is he all right?"

"Oh my dear . . ." Allegra shook her head slightly, the auburn color catching the morning sunlight streaming in from the salon window. "Shaheen, I . . . please, I can't."

"Oh God," she whispered. "He's dead, isn't he?"

Lord Pembroke shook his head. "No, he's not dead, but Tremaine is, and Stratfield has been arrested for his murder."

Suddenly feeling light-headed, a shudder ripped through her as Ruth struggled to comprehend the earl's words. Tremaine was dead, and she was glad. But Garrick—he couldn't have killed the man. In the background, she heard the doorbell ring, but she ignored it as she met the earl's forbidding look and Allegra's sympathetic gaze.

With a shake of her head, she silently rejected their fears. Garrick had been furious yesterday. She understood that. He'd believed she'd betrayed him. Something she'd promised she'd never do, and yet Tremaine had deliberately blamed her, and in an effort to protect Garrick, she'd remained silent.

She had gladly borne that burden, in exchange holding Tremaine to his bargain with her and keeping him from announcing Garrick's secret to the world. But she was certain Garrick hadn't killed Tremaine. He wouldn't have done such a thing. It wasn't in his nature.

"No. He couldn't have. I know—" She didn't get to finish as Simmons entered the room.

"My lady, an Inspector Cooper is here to see you." The butler stepped to one side to allow a tall, gangly man in a brown tweed coat to enter the room. The inspector bowed in their direction.

"Lady Ruth?" His gaze flitted back and forth between her and Allegra. Struggling to maintain her composure, she stood up to face the man.

"Inspector." She nodded in his direction. "How may I help you?"

"I'm here about Lord Tremaine's murder." The words made her hands cold and clammy as she clasped them in front of her.

"My friends were just telling me the terrible news." She gestured toward Allegra and the earl. "May I present the Earl and Countess of Pembroke."

The inspector offered her friends a bow before his cool gaze shifted back to her. "Forgive me, my lady, but may we talk in private?"

"I have nothing to hide from my friends, so ask whatever questions you like."

"As you wish, my lady." The inspector sent her a calculating look.

"As I said, I'm investigating the murder of Lord Tremaine. I suppose your friends have informed you that Lord Stratfield has been arrested in connection with the case."

"Yes." A voice in the back of her mind whispered for her to remain calm and in control. "Although I'm sure you've made a mistake in doing so."

"I spoke with Mr. Millstadt about the matter first thing this morning. One of the orphans at St. Agnes's indicated that the gentleman visited the orphanage yesterday afternoon. About the same time Lord Tremaine and Lord Stratfield were there." The man eyed her carefully.

"Yes, he did. Lord Tremaine called first. Lord Stratfield arrived a short time later. Mr. Millstadt arrived just as Lord Stratfield was leaving."

"Yes, that's Millstadt's story as well, although he says that Stratfield threatened Lord Tremaine." The inspector's stoic manner unnerved her slightly, but she managed to maintain her composure.

"I can assure you that it was an empty threat. Mr. Millstadt arrived at the end of the conversation. He didn't hear the threats Lord Tremaine made."

"Ah yes, the gossip column in *Town Talk* this morning." The policeman nodded with understanding. "An excellent motive for murder, wouldn't you say, my lady?"

"If the column is true," she said coldly at the man's snide tone. "But Lord Stratfield didn't kill Lord Tremaine."

"Do you have proof of that, my lady? Because as of right now his lordship doesn't have an alibi." The words made her heart race, and her mouth went dry as her fingers ached from the way she was clasping them so tightly.

"Is that what he told you?"

Her heart raced as she realized what she was about to do. In the past, every fashionable home of the Set had welcomed her. But that was about to end. Talk of her liaisons had been just that—talk. It was one thing for gossip to occur, but to openly admit to an affair was unacceptable. It was social ruin. She no longer cared. It would most likely make a difference in her ability to ensure donations to St. Agnes's didn't subside, but Garrick's life was at stake. She'd find a new way to encourage people to donate to the orphanage. All that mattered was Garrick's safety. She was willing to do whatever it took to ensure his freedom.

"Actually, my lady, he said he spent the night walking the streets."

"A logical answer if he was protecting someone."

"Protecting someone, my lady?" For the first time, the inspector displayed puzzlement.

"Yes. He was protecting me," she said as she heard the sounds of surprise and shock behind her. In seconds, Allegra was at her side, grasping her hand.

"Ruth, we know Garrick is innocent. We'll find some other way to prove it. He wouldn't want you to sacrifice yourself like this for his sake." Her friend squeezed Ruth's hand, but she shook off Allegra's grasp and kept her gaze firmly locked with the inspector's look of assessment.

"Lord Stratfield was with me from approximately eight o'clock last night until the morning's first light," she lied with a quiet firmness that amazed her. "Naturally, you understand this is not something I would willingly admit in polite society, but I sincerely doubt Lord Stratfield had time to kill anyone because he was busy pleasuring me."

"And you have others who can corroborate this, my lady?" Cooper's eyes narrowed at her as he tried to determine whether she was lying. The silence in the room pushed its way into her as she realized she might not have managed to save Garrick at all.

"I can, Inspector." Simmons's voice was like thunder in the stillness of the room. As the inspector jerked his head toward the butler, Ruth sagged slightly until Allegra's fingers pressed into the back of her arm. She straightened her shoulders and calmly met the policeman's gaze as he turned back to study her with a narrowed gaze.

"You do realize the penalty for providing misleading information to Scotland Yard is quite severe, my lady?"

"Not nearly as severe as the penalty the Set is going to extract from me the moment it's learned that I openly confessed to Lord Stratfield sharing my bed, Inspector."

"This presents somewhat of a problem for me," the investigator grumbled.

"I see no problem." Ruth nodded toward Simmons. "You have my word and that of my butler that Lord Stratfield was here all last night. It's obvious his lordship couldn't have killed Tremaine."

"Perhaps, but there's the question of his ring."

"His ring?" Ruth's heart skipped a frantic beat.

"Yes, my lady." The policeman frowned, clearly baffled. "Lord Stratfield's signet ring was found in Lord Tremaine's hand at the crime scene. It's a clear link to his lordship."

Ruth stiffened her body as she fought not to collapse under the strain of lying to the authorities. Think—there had to be an explanation for the ring. She just couldn't think straight.

"If I may, Inspector. Lord Stratfield was attacked several weeks ago and his personal effects stolen." Simmons's quiet explanation made Ruth briefly close her eyes in relief.

"My butler is correct," she said in a firm voice. "His lordship was beaten severely and remained incapacitated for almost a week."

"So there's a police record of this?"

"Yes, and you may ask Lord Worthington about the incident as he's the one who found Lord Stratfield and brought him here that night."

"Is there a doctor who can testify to his lordship's injuries?" The inspector sounded suspicious still, and she shook her head.

"Simmons served in the army as a medic, and was more than qualified to take care of Lord Stratfield."

"I see." The inspector scowled his displeasure as he saw his open-and-shut murder case evaporating into thin air. "This does put a different light on things. However, it still doesn't address what Mr. Millstadt heard yesterday when he arrived at the orphanage. Why did Lord Stratfield threaten Lord Tremaine?"

The question made Ruth hesitate as she met the inspector's narrowed gaze. God, would the man never stop asking these questions? She shrugged.

"Lord Tremaine was threatening to blackmail Lord Stratfield. He'd already blackmailed me to assist him in his extortion of the baron."

"And what was Lord Tremaine threatening the baron with?"

An icy chill skated over her skin as she turned toward the chair where the morning's paper had dropped to the floor. Lord Pembroke quickly reached for it then handed it to the inspector. Ruth sent him a silent look of gratitude then pointed toward the horrible paragraph she'd read earlier.

"Lord Tremaine had discovered that Lord Stratfield has a . . . a birth defect of a sensitive nature."

"It says here that the Lady R. provided this information to the paper." The investigator eyed her suspiciously. "Is that a reference to you?"

"Yes. When Lord Stratfield refused to agree to Tremaine's demands, the viscount threatened his family. Lord Stratfield warned Lord Tremaine against doing anything of the kind, and it was at that moment that Mr. Millstadt entered the office."

"I see." The officer rubbed his jaw in contemplation. "It appears that there is more to this than I realized. I trust you'll make yourself available for more questioning, my lady."

"Of course."

"Very well," the inspector said with a nod of his head as he turned toward the door. He'd reached the threshold when he suddenly turned around. "You said Tremaine was blackmailing you, my lady. Might I inquire what he was holding over you?"

The question sent a bolt of panic slicing through her. If she told the man the truth, he might see through her lie about Garrick being with her last night. No, Simmons had attested to Garrick's presence here as well. She swallowed hard as she met the calculating look in the man's eyes.

"Lord Tremaine knew I was privy to Lord Stratfield's private physical condition, and the man threatened to make the matter public record, if I didn't help him in his attempt to blackmail the baron." She took in a deep breath as the investigator arched an eyebrow. "Lord Tremaine knew I was in love with Lord Stratfield. He was certain I'd agree to do his bidding to protect the baron and his secret. He was right. I gave in to his coercion."

Cooper eyed her in silence for a long moment, before he nodded his head. "Thank you, my lady, for your cooperation. I'll be in touch."

With that, the man was gone from the room, and Simmons followed him, the salon door closing behind him. For a long moment, Ruth stood looking after him. He was gone. Garrick would be safe. With Simmons and her giving him an alibi, he'd be safe. Free. From a distance, she heard Allegra say her name then say something sharp to Lord Pembroke. A moment later, she fell into a strong embrace.

"Garrick," she whispered as she fainted.

"When was the last time you ate something?"

The quiet question made Garrick straighten upright as Lily entered his office. With a surreptitious movement of his hand, he pushed aside the copy of *Town Talk* he'd been studying.

"Cook sent in some cold cuts earlier."

His sister went to the table where the covered lunch tray sat. When she lifted the silver cover it revealed the untouched meal. Lily turned her head and glared at him. He offered her a shrug. He'd not been hungry, despite the fact that he'd eaten little in the past two weeks.

The cover made a sharp sound as Lily placed it back on the tray in an obvious display of frustration. A moment later, she was reaching over the desk for the newspaper. Obviously his effort to hide what he'd been doing had been for nothing. He caught her wrist to stop her.

"Leave it," he rasped.

"You need to let it go."

"She betrayed me."

The quiet words emphasized the icy contempt he felt as he released his sister and pressed his fingertips into the top of his desk. Lily didn't flinch under his cold stare.

"I don't believe that, Garrick. You know good and well the *Town Talk* will print anything from any source they have. Anyone could have told the paper about your . . . condition."

Garrick didn't even flinch at his sister's slight hesitation or the light pink that crested in her face. He'd neither confirmed nor refuted the paper's claims, and Lily's reaction was the one he expected everyone in the Marlborough Set to have if he ever ventured out into public again. All of which he owed to Ruth. He grimaced.

It didn't matter now. Murder accusations had a way of making one prioritize what was important. But deep inside he knew it did matter. Worse, it hurt like hell. He clenched his jaw at Lily's continued persistence in pleading Ruth's case. His sister had always taken up lost causes, but Ruth was not one he was willing to let Lily browbeat him with.

"You don't even like the woman, and yet you defend her."

"I've misjudged her. She's done a great deal for Caring Hearts, all without my asking. And it's obvious the children of St. Agnes's mean the world to her." Lily shook her head as he snorted his disgust. "That is not the description of a woman cruel enough to submit such venomous tripe to *Town Talk*."

"Then she's fooled you, like she fooled me. If she weren't guilty, she would have said something while that bastard tried to blackmail me. She betrayed me. It's as simple as that."

"The viscount could have easily delivered a note to the newspaper *before* he was murdered. Have you sent Blackstone to see if the paper will say who *did* leave the note?"

"It doesn't matter who delivered the note. She told Tremaine."

"Why are you so determined to believe the worst of her? You sound as though she's broken your—good Lord. You're in love with her."

"This conversation is over, Lily. Don't say another word."

"Why?" His sister gave an unladylike snort of irritation. "Because you say so?"

"Yes, goddamn it." He slammed his fist onto the desk. The resounding crash filled the office. At least Lily had the good sense to jump with surprise before she sniffed in a dismissive manner.

"If you're in love with her, you should at least try to hear her side."

"I heard her side," he growled. "She said nothing."

"Even if she told Tremaine truth or fiction, it doesn't mean she gave the information to *Town Talk*. You should worry about who tried to frame you for Tremaine's murder!" his sister exclaimed with frustration. "And I certainly don't think the Lady Ruth fits that mold."

As much as he hated to admit it, his sister was right. Ruth might have betrayed him to Tremaine, but she had no reason that he could think of to frame him for murder. He winced at the memory of his arrest. He'd been exhausted *and* hungover the morning after discovering Ruth with Tremaine.

After boxing himself to the point of exhaustion, he'd left his club and spent the remainder of the night walking the streets of the city, searching for what he wasn't sure. Perhaps another fight? A way to end the pain holding him prisoner? Whatever the reason, he'd not arrived at Seymour Square until shortly after dawn. He'd been eating breakfast when Scotland Yard arrived to arrest him for Tremaine's murder.

He turned away from Lily to stare out the window of his office that overlooked the garden. When his jailer had opened his cell door later that day, the man had simply told him he was free to leave. He'd assumed that Vincent had posted a bond for his release, but there had been no one to greet him as he'd left the jail. He'd come straight to Chiddingstone House. For once, he'd wanted—no, needed—to hear the noise that came with a houseful of siblings.

Of course, the mood had been subdued since his brief incarceration, but in recent days, a sense of normalcy had returned to the house. With each passing day, he grew less uneasy about the possibility of Inspector Cooper coming to say they'd made a mistake.

Halfheartedly, he noted the flower beds were riotous with color. They were a stark contrast to the chilly, damp prison cell he'd inhabited for an entire day. A shudder rippled through him at the memory. The door to his office opened, and Martin stepped into the room.

"Inspector Cooper has arrived, my lord. He wishes to speak with you."

Garrick stiffened at the butler's announcement and ignored Lily's gasp of fear as he nodded toward the servant. "Show him in, Martin."

A short moment later, Inspector Cooper's tall, lanky form crossed the threshold of Garrick's office. A fisted hand clasped behind his back, Garrick nodded to the man, certain the officer was bringing bad news.

"Forgive the intrusion, my lord. I'm sure I'm the last person you wish to see at the moment." There was a note of apology in the man's voice that puzzled him. He frowned, unwilling to exchange pleasantries.

"Are you here to arrest me again, Inspector?" The bitterness in his voice was evident, and Cooper grimaced.

"No, my lord. In fact, I have some good news to report, and Scotland Yard wishes to offer its apologies."

"Apologies?" His body taut with tension, Garrick wasn't sure what to make of the inspector's statement.

"Yes, my lord. I can't say much at the moment, but a new suspect has come to light in the Tremaine murder." The man's words sent relief crashing through him. Vindication. The relief only lasted a moment as the memory of Ruth and her treachery returned to haunt him.

"This is wonderful news!" Lily exclaimed as she moved to stand at his side, her hand squeezing his arm.

"Are you saying I'm no longer a suspect?" Garrick swallowed the knot in his throat.

"Correct, my lord. In fact, that's why Scotland Yard owes you an apology. I've only just learned that the jailer who released you two weeks ago didn't relay certain information to you."

"What information?" Garrick's muscles locked into a rigid

position as he sent the inspector a hard look. Outside the office he heard a shout, but was willing to ignore it to hear what the man had to say. Inspector Cooper had heard the noise as well and turned his head in the direction of the sound. "*What* information, Inspector?"

Cooper turned back to face him, his attention still obviously on the noise outside the office. Shouting that was growing louder by the minute. "Yes, my lord, it's about your alibi—"

"Alibi? What alibi?" Garrick snapped as he heard Martin yelling at someone.

The inspector's head turned toward the cries outside the office. Clearly he would have to wait for the man's explanation. With an oath of disgust, Garrick started toward the office door. He'd only gone a few steps when the door flew open with a violent bang. Garrick narrowed his eyes as he watched his uncle stagger into the room. The man reeked of alcohol and something that smelled like the sewer. Obviously, his uncle had visited one of the seedier establishments in the city before coming to Chiddingstone House. He struggled not to gag from the man's stench.

"What do you want, Beresford?" His mouth tightened into a hard line.

"I want my life back, you little prick," the man said viciously. "You've ruined me. You've taken everything from me."

"You ruined yourself," Garrick said coldly.

"No. You did this to me, and I'm going to make you pay." Beresford snarled like a wounded animal as he gave a drunken lunge in Garrick's direction.

"Exactly how might you do that, my lord?" Inspector Cooper's quiet voice made Garrick's uncle start with surprise as he turned to see the officer studying him with great interest. Swaying slightly, Beresford eyed the investigator with a look of panic on his face.

"*You*. What the hell are you doing here?"

"Solving a murder case," the officer said calmly.

"I didn't kill Tremaine." Beresford's voice was a piteous sound as he shook his head vehemently.

"I don't recall mentioning Lord Tremaine's name." The inspector's words sent another look of panic across Garrick's uncle's face. "Take a seat, Beresford."

The inspector gestured for the man to sit in one of the chairs in front of the desk. When Beresford was seated, the inspector went to the office door. As it opened, Garrick could see Martin standing there with an expression of stark dismay on his face.

"My lord, I'm so sorry." The unflappable butler looked as though he were ready to come undone. "I tried to stop him, my lord."

"It's all right, Martin. Everyone is safe." His reassurance seemed to help the butler regain some of his composure.

"Yes, but I have two incompetent officers who have some explaining to do as to why they didn't stop Beresford from entering the house," Cooper said in a grim voice.

"I am not quite as stupid as you might think, Inspector. I came in the back way," Garrick's uncle said with a sneer, clearly having regained some of his bravado. Cooper sent Beresford a look of disgust before he turned to Martin, who was still hovering in the doorway.

"If you would please, ask Officer Brown to bring his prisoner in here. And would you have one of the policemen outside the *front* of the house join us in here." The inspector glared at Beresford over his shoulder, obviously irritated that he'd been unprepared for the man's arrival.

Martin hurried away without any further prompting as Inspector Cooper turned back to face Garrick and Lily. A sympathetic look crossed his face as he studied Lily's pale features.

"Perhaps you might like to lay down, my lady." The man's words made his sister stiffen and push away from Garrick's side.

"I'm quite well, Inspector. Thank you just the same."

A scuffling sound came from the hallway outside the office, and a moment later, a blue-suited policeman dragged a reluctant prisoner into the room. A second officer followed them into the room. Garrick frowned at the size of the prisoner. He had the look of a dockworker. The moment the prisoner saw Beresford, he released an ugly sound.

"What the fuck is he doing here?" The man's distinct voice made Garrick stiffen. He knew that voice. The inspector glanced in his direction.

"My lord, this is Billy Turner. Do you recognize him?" Inspector Cooper waited quietly for Garrick to answer.

"I recognize his voice. I believe he's one of the men who attacked me more than a month ago," Garrick replied quietly.

"That's a lie. I ain't never seen this gent before, guv." The husky prisoner glared at him, and Garrick arched his eyebrow.

"During the attack, I bit the hand of one of my assailants hard enough to draw blood." Garrick studied the prisoner's face, and wasn't surprised to see the man flinch. "Might I ask that this man show his hands?"

"Let's see his hands." The inspector nodded toward the officer standing beside Turner. The prisoner struggled to keep his hands hidden, but the officers forced the man to show them. On Turner's pudgy left hand, the almost healed scars of a deep bite were still visible.

"He made me do it," Turner exploded as he nodded in Beresford's direction. "Him and the other gent. He told me he wanted to see something personal of the guv's to prove we'd done the job."

"You and who else," Inspector Cooper bit out in a cold voice.

"Me friend, Harry. We done the odd job for his lordship before, and Beresford here pointed out the guv to us." Turner jerked his head in Garrick's direction, suddenly a fount of information as he realized he might be blamed for something worse than assault and thievery. "We just roughed his lordship up a bit. We did the same thing with the other gent. But like the guv here, we left him alive, Inspector. I swear it."

"I find that hard to believe, Turner." Cooper's tone was ice-cold.

"I swear it. His lordship told us not to kill him."

"His lordship?" the inspector snapped. The prisoner hesitated and Cooper frowned angrily. "A name, Turner. I want a name."

"Marston. Lord Marston." The dockworker's fear was so bad he almost wept the name. Garrick jerked in surprise. What the devil had he ever done to Marston? He tried to think back over the last several months, but could come up with nothing that would warrant the man trying to frame him for murder. His attention quickly returned to the interrogation at hand.

"And the ring you took from his lordship, here?" The inspector nodded toward Garrick as he narrowed his gaze at the burly man.

"Harry and I gave the ring to him." Turner bobbed his head in Beresford's direction. Clearly unsurprised by the man's response, Inspector Cooper nodded and turned back to Beresford.

"Do you have anything to add before I arrest you, Beresford?" Cooper asked in a harsh tone.

"For what? I didn't do anything," Garrick's uncle snarled.

"Perhaps you're forgetting the ring." The inspector's voice was quietly menacing. "The ring you put into Tremaine's hand to blame your nephew for the murder you committed."

"*No.* That's not true! It was Marston!" Beresford shouted as he jumped to his feet. "Yes, I put Garrick's ring in Tremaine's hand, but I didn't kill the man. It was Marston."

"And I'm sure Lord Marston is saying the same thing about you right now to my colleague, Inspector Watson," the policeman said in a critical tone.

"I'm telling the truth." Beresford's face had the look of a madman as he pointed wildly at the burly Turner. "This one and his partner beat Tremaine senseless then Marston finished the bastard off with a brick."

"Why would Marston do that? You were the one who owed Tremaine money," the inspector snapped.

"Marston owed Tremaine money, too. When my nephew called in Tremaine's loans, he called in our markers. Marston and I didn't have enough funds to cover what we owed him. Tremaine was about to take what little we did have." Beresford turned sharply to face Garrick. Although his face was beet red with anger, the man looked more terrified than anything else. "This is your fault. You set out to ruin me and Tremaine and now I'm the one being framed for murder."

"Just like you tried to frame me, uncle?" Garrick was surprised by the evenness of his voice as he sent Beresford a cold look. "Look in the mirror if you want to see a guilty party."

"You sorry little prick." Beresford was almost foaming at the mouth as he lunged forward, but the inspector threw himself in front of the half-drunk man whose eyes were dark with hate. "Just like your father. Only one ballock and a taste for traitorous whores because no other woman will have you."

Raw fury streaked through Garrick's veins at the reference to Ruth, and he took a quick step forward. The moment he moved, his uncle threw back his head and cackled with glee. Garrick froze. He recognized that laugh. It was the same sound he'd heard all those years ago in Bertha's bedroom. His uncle's laughter filled his ears, and he grew stiff as he waited for the familiar humiliation to painfully wash over him.

It didn't.

He stared at Beresford with a sense of amazement. He was truly free. Walking away from Tremaine and the man's effort to blackmail him that day in the orphanage hadn't been an illusion. He really had accepted himself for who he was, not what his uncle had made him believe for so long. Lily gripped his arm, and he glanced down at her.

The look of sisterly concern on her face made him shake his head as he gently patted her hand. Almost as though Beresford realized his words no longer had any effect on Garrick, the man's laughter died abruptly. Inspector Cooper gestured to the second officer, who stepped forward to lead Beresford out of the office. The inspector turned back to Garrick.

"If you'll excuse me, my lord, I'll take Beresford and Turner here back to Scotland Yard so I can finish sorting this case out," Cooper said quietly. "As I said earlier, we owe you an apology. I am certain your involvement with this sad affair is at an end, except for the possibility of being called to testify as to today's events."

The inspector started toward the door, and Garrick felt a wave of relief wash over him. He could go back to living his life again without fear of the police pounding on his door, demanding his arrest. An image of Ruth fluttered through his head, and his gut clenched. His life would be completely empty without her. Cooper stopped at the office door and turned back to Garrick.

"I almost forgot, my lord. Your man Blackstone was of immense help with the investigation. I appreciate your agreement to let him work with us."

"You're welcome," Garrick replied quietly.

"It might interest you to know that he was able to get the *Town Talk* to reveal that it was a man who provided them with the . . . offensive gossip they printed. From the description it would appear it was Tremaine. I'm sure we'll know for sure once we finish questioning all concerned." The inspector frowned as if trying to remember something else before his expression became one of revelation. "Ah yes, and I didn't get to finish what I was saying earlier. About your alibi."

"My alibi?" Garrick frowned. Didn't the man remember he didn't have one? "Under the circumstances is that irrelevant?"

"It is now, but as I said we owe you an apology." Inspector Cooper grimaced. "The officer on duty should have told you that the Lady Ruth claimed you were with her from approximately eight o'clock the night of Tremaine's murder until the next morning."

"What?" he exclaimed with stunned disbelief. Beside him, Lily clutched at his arm.

"Dear Lord," she gasped with horror. "There won't be a respectable house in London open to her."

"Her butler confirmed her claim as well," Cooper said quietly as he looked in Garrick's direction. "It says a great deal about the lady's character when she's willing to sacrifice her reputation to save an innocent man."

Garrick stared at the inspector in stunned silence. What the hell had possessed Ruth to lie to the police? Why the devil would she do such a thing? Guilt. That had to be the answer. In the back of his head, a small voice whispered a different explanation. He crushed the thought. He knew better than to even think she might be innocent. She'd been in Tremaine's arms. There was no explanation for that. Inspector Cooper bowed slightly.

"I'll leave you then."

With that the policeman left Garrick and Lily standing in the office. He stood there staring after the man, still trying to grasp the reality of everything that had transpired in the last few minutes. When Lily touched his arm, he shrugged her hand off and returned to his desk. He sat down and reached for some bills that he'd not paid yet. It represented a normalcy about his world that was very unsettled at the moment. As he pulled out a ledger from the desk drawer, his gaze fell on the two-week-old copy of *Town Talk*.

"What are you going to do?" Lily asked quietly.

"Do? There's nothing to do." He met his sister's gaze for a brief moment then returned his attention to the ledger.

"Don't be a fool. You heard the inspector. The Lady Ruth didn't tell the *Town Talk* about your condition. For heaven's sake, she even saved you by providing you with an alibi, knowing she'd pay a high price for doing so. Is that the sign of a woman who would betray a man?"

"Let it go, Lily," he muttered. "It's over."

"It's not and you know it. But I'll tell you what that behavior does signify. It says she loves you." Startled, he jerked his head up to stare at his sister in amazement. She glared at him. "That's right you muttonhead. She loves you. No woman in her right mind would have made a sacrifice like she did unless she was in love. And if you don't go to her and beg her forgiveness for doubting her, well I . . . well, you're not the man I think you are."

With an angry flounce, Lily whirled around and stalked out of the office, leaving him staring after her. Was his sister right? Was it possible Ruth loved him? How could she when she'd betrayed him by running to Tremaine? He leaned back in his chair and closed his eyes as he recalled those dark moments in St. Agnes's office.

Ruth had been so pale when he'd entered the office, and she'd looked horrified to see him. And then there had been that look of anguish in her eyes when he'd refused to pay Tremaine his coin. If she loved him, what would have possessed her to help Tremaine? He frowned. There was only one way to find out. He would have to ask her.

Ruth laughed as she splashed bathwater up over one of her youngest charges at Crawley Hall. At two years of age, Thad was already a charmer, and his cheeky grin had captured her heart the moment he'd toddled through St. Agnes's front door with his hand locked in that of his big sister, Clara. The pair had been living off scraps of food for weeks since their mother had died, and she'd known she would bring them to Crawley Hall with her from the moment she'd first seen them. She rubbed soap on the washcloth she held, and smiled at Thad.

"No more arguing, Thaddeus Nelson," she said in a voice she'd meant to be no-nonsense, which was anything but. "I'm going to wash behind those ears whether you like it or not."

Thad shook his head and giggled, making it impossible for her not to laugh with him. Leaning forward, she glared at him fiercely. His eyes widened and she laughed as he folded his ears down so she could clean the dirt off him. Gently she washed his skin, and in another moment, she had the back of his dirty neck covered with soap bubbles.

"How in heaven's name did you get so dirty, little man? You look like you've been rolling around in the stable yard again."

She arched her eyebrow at him, and Thad just giggled before his small hands hit the water to send it flying all over the front of Ruth's blouse. Laughing, she rinsed him off then lifted him from the tub and rubbed him dry with a large towel. The back of her neck tingled, and she absently reached up to rub her nape.

The moment she did so, she saw Thad's gaze shift to a spot past her shoulder. She turned her head, and the sight of Garrick sent her reeling. At a loss for words, she just stared at him. With one shoulder pressing into the door frame, his nonchalance was that of a man accustomed to getting his way. He was devastating, and her heart pounded wildly in her chest as his vivid blue eyes met hers.

He looked just as handsome as the first time she'd seen him. Only today he looked leaner. Older. She swallowed the derisive laughter bubbling up in her throat. She was the older one. It was impossible to tell what he was thinking, and she wasn't sure she wanted to know. What was he doing here? Beside her, Thad stuck one hand out of his towel and tugged at her arm.

"Mama. Play." The child's demand interrupted Ruth's preoccupation with Garrick's presence, and she immediately turned back to Thad.

"No my darling. It's time for supper." She shook her head. "Let's go get dressed, shall we?"

Her hand gripped the edge of the bathtub for leverage in standing when fire seared her middle as Garrick lifted her to her feet. His familiar scent wafted over her, and she closed her eyes for a brief moment, remembering other times his hands had been wrapped around her waist. Moments when she'd been unbelievably happy. Reality set in, and she shuddered. This wasn't the past.

"Thank you, my lord."

She didn't even send him a glance over her shoulder, but his fingers tightened at her waist for a brief instant before he released her. He had never liked it when she was so formal with him. With Thad's hand in hers, she led the small boy from the bathroom, all too aware that Garrick was following.

What did he want? She knew Marston and Garrick's uncle had been charged with Tremaine's murder. She'd been relieved to read that in the paper, but beyond that, she'd refused to read the gossip columns or anything else that might have mention of Garrick. The thought of it had been too painful.

As they moved along the corridor toward the room Thad shared with several of the other younger children, she saw Dolores hurrying toward her. The older woman glared over her shoulder at Garrick.

"Simmons told me his lordship was here," her friend said fiercely. "I thought you might need help with Thaddeus."

So it hadn't been Dolores who'd let Garrick have the run of the house. Never in a hundred years would she have guessed Simmons would let Garrick into the house. She frowned and nodded toward her old friend.

"Thad, go with Dolores." She bent over to kiss the boy's cheek. "I'll tuck you in at bedtime."

The boy smiled at her and nodded his head before he turned toward Dolores. As the child toddled away pulling her maid with him, her heart expanded with love. He was such a sweet boy. A familiar sensation tickled the back of her neck, and she darted a glance over her shoulder at Garrick.

"I'm not sure why you've come, my lord, but whatever you have to say would be best said in the library."

She didn't wait for him to answer her, but hurried forward and down the stairs into the front hall. As she reached the foyer, she heard the sound of voices coming from the main salon. The sound grew muted as Simmons closed the doors to the room. She paused a few feet into the vestibule to send the man a hard look. Her longtime butler had the grace to look uncomfortable as she glared at him.

"Do we have visitors, Simmons?" She prayed he would answer yes. It would give her time to gather her wits.

"Yes, my lady. They're friends of Lord Stratfield's."

The man's response made her look over her shoulder at Garrick, who was standing at the foot of the stairs watching her with interest. Why would the man bring friends with him? Perhaps donors for St. Agnes's. No, he and his sister had Caring Hearts to support. Damn him. Frustration and fear coursed their way through her veins as she gave Simmons a brief nod and turned away to walk down the hall to the library.

She'd had Crawley Hall's large library converted into a schoolroom. The large number of volumes that had come with the house served as a resource for the older children in their lessons and a source of solace for her in the middle of sleepless nights. The room was empty, and she hastily crossed the floor to stand behind the large desk the local tutor used when he came two days a week to provide lessons to the children. As she faced Garrick, her heart skipped a beat at the dark look on his handsome features.

"You have a son." There was a demand for an explanation in his statement that annoyed her.

"All the children here are mine to care for and love."

"The boy called you mama," he bit out. Something akin to jealousy swept over his features. It alarmed her. Why had he come here?

"Thad is an orphan, like his sister, Clara," she snapped. "But they're as much mine as if I'd given birth to them. Not that it's any of *your* concern."

"I see." The short statement was filled with an emotion she refused to define.

"Perhaps you should tell me why you're here, my lord," she said coldly.

"I told you the last time we were together here at Crawley Hall that I wanted you to call me Garrick," he growled as he crossed the room to brace himself on the desk as he leaned across the furniture that separated them. "That hasn't changed."

"As you wish, *Garrick*," she said in a detached voice that gave her a small measure of satisfaction. "Why are you here?"

"I imagine you've heard that Marston and my uncle are being charged with Tremaine's murder."

"Yes." She didn't dare say anything else. The less said the better, particularly when she was so relieved that he'd been vindicated. She also didn't want him asking her about the alibi she'd given him.

"Before I came here, I visited my uncle. I asked him if he'd told Tremaine about my condition." He eyed her carefully as if waiting for a reaction from her. When she didn't respond, he grimaced. "Beresford said he'd told Tremaine about my birth defect almost four months ago over one too many glasses of brandy."

"I'm sorry," she said quietly. She was. When she'd read that terrible accusation in the *Town Talk*, she'd been horrified and humiliated for him.

"I'm not." His quiet statement startled her, and she stared at him in surprise. He cleared his throat. "I'm glad it was Beresford and not you that betrayed me to Tremaine."

A knot developed in her throat as she watched him straighten upright. His vivid blue eyes locked with hers as he studied her for a long, quiet moment. The intentness of his gaze set her on edge.

"I want to know why Tremaine was with you that day in the orphanage." The demand caught her by surprise.

She stiffened, and her heart skipped a beat before it slammed into her chest. The air vanished from her lungs as she fought to gather her wits. As she struggled to breathe, she noted the arrogance in his demeanor. His posture said he intended to have an answer. With as much aplomb as she could muster, she shrugged.

"He offered to be my patron, and I accepted."

"Don't lie to me, Ruth." His voice was quiet.

"I am *not* lying." She glared at him. It *was* the truth. Tremaine had made an offer and she'd accepted. She'd simply omitted the fact that the bastard had been blackmailing her into accepting his proposal. Garrick studied her carefully, and the look in his eyes made her tremble. He was up to something.

"There's more to it than you're admitting," he said as he narrowed his gaze on her. "In fact, I have a strong suspicion Tremaine was blackmailing you, just like he was me."

"Even if that were true, the man is dead. He can no longer blackmail anyone." She fought to maintain her composure so her features revealed nothing.

"Then you admit he was blackmailing you." The look of triumph on Garrick's face made her nervous.

"I didn't say that," she protested with a shake of her head. "What could the man possibly blackmail me with?"

Garrick quickly circled the desk and caught her by surprise as he towered over her. Although he didn't touch her, he might as well have done so, the way her body was responding to his. Every part of her was on fire, humming in a way that only happened when he was near. It was a sensation no other man could arouse in her. She swallowed hard and took a step back. He followed. One hand going to her throat, she stared up at him, her eyes fixating on his sensual mouth. The memory of his lips caressing her in the most intimate of places made the knot in her throat swell even larger threatening to cut off her breathing completely.

"Tell me what he was blackmailing you with, Ruth."

"I didn't say he was blackmailing me," she said in an effort to come up with something that would divert him from the truth. She couldn't bear for him to discover that she'd been protecting her own secret.

"I think I know what he was holding over you, Ruth, but I want you to tell me." He leaned into her, his mouth so tantalizingly close.

Dear Lord, surely he didn't know how she felt about him. She forced herself to forget everything but the need to hide the truth from him. He'd already broken her heart when he'd hidden his true age from her. She couldn't bear it if he learned that she'd been hiding her own secret. Her heart would break all over again if he learned she was in love with him.

"What is it you want from me, Garrick?" she asked with a quiet serenity she didn't feel. Her composure seemed to startle him, and he narrowed his eyes.

"I want to know why you let me believe you'd betrayed me to Tremaine."

"As I recall, the only thing I said to you was that I was free to see whom I wished," she said.

"And yet you knew I believed the worst when Tremaine told me he knew that I have only one ballock." There was a grimness about the statement that said the memory of that moment hadn't left him.

"Would you have believed me if I'd said otherwise?" She shook her head. "You chose to believe what you wanted."

It was the truth. She'd seen his condemnation in his eyes the moment he'd found her in Tremaine's arms. Even if she could have told him the truth that day at the orphanage, Garrick wouldn't have believed her. His expression lightened as if she'd said something that pleased him. She frowned. Why did she suddenly feel as though she'd revealed something she shouldn't have?

"And my alibi. What made you willing to openly declare that you were my mistress when it meant you'd be ostracized?"

"You were innocent." She shrugged slightly. "I'd already made plans to move to Crawley Hall. I had nothing to lose."

"Nothing except donations to St. Agnes's." His husky response made her flinch. A mistake.

His lips brushed against hers like a gentle breeze. The faint touch held a delicious hint of seduction in it. She shuddered, suddenly feeling light-headed. Dear Lord, she'd taught him well. That hadn't been a kiss. It had been a declaration of war on her senses.

The raw, male scent of him washed over her, and she struggled not to let her body melt into his. God, he smelled so wonderful, and the low sinful sound of his voice was wreaking havoc on her sensibilities. He was on a mission, and she knew it was her surrender. She'd known it from the moment she'd seen him standing in the bathroom doorway upstairs. She closed her eyes to relish this last moment with him. It would have to last her a very long time.

"I want to know why you did it, Ruth. I want to know why you publicly admitted you were my mistress." It was a command, and his expression warned her that capitulation was the only thing that would satisfy him. He cupped her face in his hands, and his touch sent a wild tremor racing through her. "Would it be easier for you to answer me, if I said I love you?"

His words made her sway on her feet. It wasn't possible. He couldn't be in love with her. He was infatuated—convinced they could overcome the twelve years between them. But she knew better. When he was in his prime, she would be a doddering old fool. In a few years, he'd regret being with her. He'd leave her, and she refused to bear the heartache of his leaving.

The pain she'd lived with over the past two weeks had been far greater than anything she could have imagined. To experience something worse wasn't a risk she was willing to take. Panic welled up inside her as she met his blue eyes. Whenever he looked at her like that it always took her breath away. Now wasn't any different. Brushing his hands aside, she took a quick step backward.

"I don't know why you came here, my lord, but—"

"I came here to ask you to marry me, Ruth."

His words stunned her. A confession of infatuation was one thing, but this? The thought of marriage shot a bolt of horror through her. A long-term liaison would be scandalous enough, but marriage? Impossible. How could she possibly agree to marry him? She was almost old enough to be his mother.

"Don't be ridiculous. I'm far too old for you," she snapped. "Even if I were foolish enough to agree to such a mad proposal, you'd be neglecting your duty."

"My *duty*," he growled.

"As head of your family you're required to produce an heir. I'm too old to bear you a son. You need a younger wife."

Defiantly, she glared at him. Courtesans never married, any more than younger men married women who were too old for them. They glared at each other for a long moment, the silence between them thick with tension. Garrick's eyes had turned dark blue with anger, but she didn't care. He was acting like a spoiled schoolboy who'd been denied something he wanted. She turned to walk away from him, but his hand flew out to grasp her arm and force her to look at him. Eyes narrowed, he gave her a slight shake.

"This isn't about age at all, is it, Ruth?" His mouth thinned with anger. She gasped at the ferocity of his statement. "It's about fear."

"*What*?" she exclaimed as she tried to twist free of his grasp.

"*Fear.*" He emphasized the word with a force that sent a shiver down her spine. "Every man you've ever known has left you, just like your father abandoned you."

"My father has *nothing* to do with this." Her mouth went dry as a tiny voice in the back of her head called her a liar.

"He has everything to do with it. Your age isn't the real problem. It's your fear that I'll abandon you, just like your father did you and your mother." The harsh words held a ring of truth in them and it terrified her.

"My lifestyle makes it inevitable that my lovers and I are destined to quit each other. You're no different." Her voice sounded hollow in her ears.

"I won't leave you, Ruth," he said firmly. "I'm not your father or any of your other lovers. I want to spend the rest of my life with you."

She stared up at him, unable to respond. Garrick's assessment of her was frightening. What he'd said about her father was so close to the truth that words failed her. He knew her far better than she knew herself. Her father's refusal to visit her mother on her deathbed had always troubled her deeply, but looking back, she realized it had been more painful than she'd ever allowed herself to admit. She'd felt abandoned and all alone after her mother died. There had been no one to turn to, and she'd done what was necessary to survive. She wet her lips with her tongue, and Garrick growled softly.

"I know you love me, Ruth. You wouldn't have sacrificed yourself by giving me an alibi otherwise."

"I don't," she said hoarsely. Even she could hear the words for what they were. A lie.

"I don't believe you. Say it. Tell me that you love me."

He pulled her into his arms, staring down at her. Oh God, what was she supposed to do? He'd said he wouldn't leave her. Could she believe him? She squeezed her eyes shut as she took a leap of faith.

"I love you, Garrick," she whispered.

In the next instant, his mouth devoured hers as he crushed her against him. The kiss demanded her complete surrender, and she willingly succumbed. Every inch of her was on fire as she melted into him. She was certain she was making a mistake, but at this precise moment she didn't care. All that mattered was his touch and how it made her feel. Young. Alive. Desirable.

Loved.

Even now it was hard to comprehend that he really loved her. Her lips parted to give him access to her mouth, and a soft whimper escaped her as his tongue teased hers in a familiar dance of seduction. She'd missed him so much. Never in her wildest dreams would she have thought it possible that she could give her heart to a man. But she had with Garrick. His kiss deepened until she was deaf and blind to everything around her.

Garrick's skill at kissing had never been in question, but there was a new level of confidence in him that said he would never be her pupil again. Instead, he would be the master, and she welcomed his possessive touch. His lips left hers and hungrily skimmed across her cheek to her ear. A low groan rolled out of him.

"Christ Jesus, you go to my head. I want nothing more than to carry you upstairs to bed this instant." His breathing ragged, he rested his forehead against hers. "But there are some people I want you to meet."

"Your friends?" she rasped as she tried to calm her racing heart at the thought of making love to him.

"Yes. They're here to help my cause."

"Your cause?"

"I intend to marry you, Ruth. I won't take no for an answer." His emphatic tone made her stiffen in his arms.

"You'll have to," she bit out fiercely. "It's just not done. You cannot marry your mistress, let alone a woman so much—" His fingers pressed against her mouth.

"Don't," he warned with a harsh look.

She closed her eyes for a brief second, her heart aching at the thought of not being able to bear him a son. God, if only she were a few years younger. She brushed the thought aside. It wasn't possible. She loved him, and nothing mattered except him. When it came time for him to produce an heir then she would bear the pain of that moment for his sake. If she couldn't give him a son, she would set him free when the time came for him to do his family duty.

"You need an heir, and you know I can't give you that."

"Vincent will carry on the family line," he bit out through clenched teeth. He clearly expected her to fall in step with his demands, but she refused to let him make a mistake he would no doubt regret in the future.

"We shall continue in the same manner as before or not at all."

"That's not good enough for me. But we shall see. Come."

He didn't wait for her to answer. Instead, he simply grabbed her hand and led her out of the library toward the salon. When they reached the closed doors of the parlor, he opened them and pulled her into the room behind him. An older couple sat on the room's love seat waiting patiently. The moment the door opened the gentleman quickly stood up. The couple smiled as Ruth and Garrick came to a halt in front of them.

"Ruth, I'd like you to meet Squire Cranston and his wife, Mrs. Cranston." Garrick swept his hand toward the older couple. "Their property abuts Chiddingstone Manor. Squire, Mrs. Cranston, may I present the Lady Ruth. My fiancée."

Garrick's announcement made her gasp as the Cranstons immediately offered them best wishes. She was so outraged with Garrick that she barely found the wherewithal to greet the squire and his wife with any modicum of politeness. Furious, she sent Garrick a glare, but he simply smiled with the satisfaction of a man who'd just gotten his way. Somehow she managed to keep her wits about her enough to invite the couple to stay for supper. Mrs. Cranston's voice helped to suppress her anger, and she focused her attention on the woman.

"The baron tells me the Hall is actually an orphanage."

"Yes, but it's not a typical one. I've taken a page from Lord Stratfield and his sister's administration of their home." She sent Garrick a quick look, but he'd already pulled the squire aside to discuss local politics. "Crawley Hall offers children a safe haven as well as the opportunity to learn a skill or trade."

"How wonderful," Mrs. Cranston said with great enthusiasm. "I grew up in an orphanage, and it was nothing like this lovely home."

It was impossible not to be drawn to the woman. There was something warm and pleasant about her demeanor. And she'd mentioned her past without rancor or the slightest amount of self-pity. Ruth smiled at her.

"Whatever your circumstances once were, you are clearly happy now."

"Very. Albert makes me very happy." Mrs. Cranston beamed. "And what wonderful news about you and Lord Stratfield. I hope you will be very happy."

"The baron was a bit premature in his announcement," she said quietly as she glanced at Garrick, who was deep in conversation with the squire. "I've not yet given his lordship an answer."

"Ahh, so he intends to coerce, if not embarrass, you into accepting his offer." Mrs. Cranston chuckled.

"Yes. And his tactics do not sit well with me." Ruth turned her head toward Garrick again, and as if he knew she was watching him, he looked in her direction. Passion blazed in his eyes, but his love for her was easy to see in the fiery look.

"Well, it's evident the man is deeply in love with you. Perhaps he's worried you might say no." The quiet observation made Ruth jerk her gaze back to the older woman to find Mrs. Cranston watching her with great interest.

"You say that as if the baron had expressed his concerns to you." Ruth scrutinized the woman in a fashion that made Mrs. Cranston blush.

"I am convinced the baron came to us out of desperation," the squire's wife murmured. "He knew that . . . well, that Albert and I have something in common with you and Lord Stratfield."

"I'm afraid I don't understand." Confused, Ruth shook her head. Mrs. Cranston frowned slightly before a lovely smile brightened her features.

"How old do I look to you, Lady Ruth?" The woman's question made Ruth gape at her in astonishment, and Mrs. Cranston laughed softly. "Forgive me, but I have a good reason for asking. You see, I'm older than Albert. His lordship knew that, and he asked us to come help him plead his case with you."

"I see."

Ruth sighed with resignation. Garrick was bound and determined to see to it that she had no arguments to use against his proposal. No doubt he assumed that a couple where the wife was older than her husband by a few years would serve to aid his case.

"I'm not sure you do, my dear. It's why I asked you how old I look. You see, I'm nine years older than Albert."

"Nine years," she breathed with amazement.

"Yes, and like you, I was resistant to my lover's marriage proposal. I refused him three different times, and he finally threatened to compromise me if I didn't say yes." Mrs. Cranston reached out to pat her hand. "Lord Stratfield explained he had reason to believe you would be reluctant to accept his suit for one of the same reasons I was hesitant to accept Albert's proposal."

"You hesitated because of the age difference."

"Yes, I was thirty-six when I met Albert. My age and not knowing who my parents were made me *more* than hesitant. But Albert didn't care about either of those things. All he cared about was me. I've not looked back since the moment I agreed to be his wife." Mrs. Cranston glanced at her husband, and happiness lit up her face. Instinctively, Ruth knew the squire had sent his wife a look of affection. It was the only explanation for the woman's glow.

"It's obvious you're exceedingly happy."

"We are," Mrs. Cranston said with a nod of contentment. "We've been married more than twenty-five years now, and we have four wonderful children to add to our happiness. Three sons and a daughter. Our youngest just turned twenty last month, and she's as hardheaded as her father." Mrs. Cranston's comment made Ruth's eyes widen in surprise. Even if Mrs. Cranston had had four children in four years, it would still have made her at least forty when her daughter had been born. Trying to hide her amazement, Ruth was relieved when Simmons entered the parlor to announce supper.

The meal was a lively one, as the Cranstons regaled them with several amusing stories of their children. Despite knowing the reason for the couple's visit, she found herself enjoying their company immensely. Garrick seemed especially pleased with himself, and whenever his gaze met hers, the determination she saw in his blue eyes said he intended to get his way. Reluctantly, she had to admit the Cranstons had easily dismantled her reasons for rejecting him. With each passing minute, her ability to refuse his proposal grew weaker. The knowledge filled her with a happiness she wasn't sure was real. The hour was late when the Cranstons indicated they should return to the inn where they were staying the night until their return trip home in the morning. As she and Garrick saw the couple to their carriage, Mrs. Cranston stopped at the front door and grasped Ruth's hands.

"I understand the fears you have, Lady Ruth," the older woman said with a gentle smile. "But do not let happiness slip away from you, no matter what the reason. Even a half-wit could see Lord Stratfield adores you."

With that parting remark, she moved out the door and down the steps to the waiting carriage. Squire Cranston said his good-byes as well, and as the older couple departed, Garrick slowly closed the door behind them. He stood there with his back to her for a long moment before he turned to face her. Emotion flashed across his face as he studied her, and she was certain it was fear. Despite his confidence and determination, he was afraid of losing her. It was at that moment, she knew he would never lose her. She was his forever and always. As if he'd suddenly made up his mind about something, he stepped forward, and with his hand at her elbow, he guided her back into the parlor. The sound of the key turning in the lock made her send him a questioning look. He shrugged.

"I don't wish to be interrupted until I have the answer I want," he said as he walked toward her with a slow, purposeful stride.

Despite the concern she'd seen on his face moments ago, he now exuded confidence and determination. Her heart began to pound wildly in her chest as he stopped less than a foot away from her. Sheer, raw male. It was the only way to describe him. It wasn't just the spicy hot scent of him, but the harsh sound of his rapid breathing and the way his body was rigid with tension. Eyes closed, she leaned into him to breathe in his scent, and she heard the sound of his breathing change to a dark rasp that signaled his rising desire.

"An answer requires a question," she murmured. She took a small step forward until there were mere inches between them. A low growl rumbled in his chest.

"Then hold out your hands." The harsh command caught her by surprise, and she looked up at him in puzzlement. The unrelenting expression on his face made her step back slightly to offer her hand to him. "Both of them, palms up."

Growing more puzzled by the minute, she did as he asked and watched as he pulled a small sack from his pocket. He turned the bag upside down and more than twenty diamonds spilled out into her hand. She gasped at the number and her gaze flew upward to meet his.

"I intend to have these made into a necklace for you to wear on our wedding day," he said quietly as he picked up the largest jewel in her palms. He held it up to the light. "Look at it, Ruth. Have you ever seen anything more beautiful?"

"No," she said quietly as she studied the sparkling gem in the room's soft light.

"I have." The emphatic note in his voice made her jerk her gaze back to him. "I think you're the most beautiful thing I've ever seen in my life, Ruth."

There was a look in his eyes that filled her heart with an emotion that spilled its way throughout her body until she was warm. This was what it felt like to be loved unconditionally. She was certain of it. The largest diamond still in his hand, Garrick held the sack in front of her so she could pour the smaller ones back into the velvet bag. He studied the diamond he held for a long moment, before dropping it into the sack and pulling the drawstring closed. The small bag disappeared into his pocket before he cupped her face in his and kissed her gently. Raising his head, he stared down at her.

"It takes thousands of years for a diamond to be made, Ruth. And no matter how old a diamond is, its beauty is incomparable," he whispered. "You're my diamond, sweetheart. You banished the darkness from my life, and I can't live without you. Marry me."

Tears welled up in Ruth's eyes at the deep love and passion echoing in Garrick's voice. As her vision grew blurry, he bent his head to kiss away her tears. He pulled her into his tight embrace, waiting patiently until she composed herself.

"Well?" he asked in a masterful manner.

"Yes, I'll marry you," she whispered. "But only if you promise to pleasure me whenever I ask."

"Spoken like a demanding tutor, my love," he said as relief flashed in his eyes and a smile curved his mouth upward. Her heart skipped a beat as his blue eyes suddenly darkened with fiery passion. "Shall we start pleasuring each other now?"

Garrick didn't give her a chance to respond as his mouth captured hers.

Epilogue

Ruth sat in a chaise lounge on the rear lawn of Chiddingstone Manor. With the large, lush green lawn stretching out before her, she leaned forward as she saw Thad chasing his sister with a stick.

"Thaddeus Stratfield, put that stick down, *now*," she called out sharply. The five-year-old immediately halted in his tracks and turned to look at her with a scowl on his face.

"But Clara called me a baby."

"Your sister didn't mean it, did you, Clara?" There was an unspoken demand for her adopted daughter to apologize, which the girl did with reluctance.

With the minor altercation resolved, Ruth leaned back and closed her eyes to enjoy the heat of the sun as it warmed her face. A sudden spasm in her belly made her grunt with discomfort as her hand rubbed over her rounded stomach. This child was far more active than Jack had ever been at this stage of her pregnancy. The thought of her firstborn made her smile. He was such a happy child. Another kick made her gasp. Perhaps a walk would soothe the babe. She was about to sit up when a shadow fell over her. Startled, she looked up to see Garrick's face looming over her. A second later, he was kissing her warmly. When he lifted his head, he glanced down at her belly.

"Let me guess. The child has been kicking harder than usual."

"Yes," she sighed. "Jack was *never* this active."

"What you need is a walk." Garrick tugged her to her feet then wrapped his arms around her.

"I thought you were going to take me for a walk," she said with a soft laugh.

"Is it a crime to hold my wife in my arms for a moment?" There was a mischievous glint in his eyes that she'd seen in their son's as well.

"Not at all," she murmured as she pulled his head down so she could brush her mouth over his. "In fact, I wish I wasn't such an elephant at the moment. Although this *is* your fault you know."

She stepped back and touched her belly as she sent him a playful scowl. He offered her his arm with a cheeky grin. "I seem to recall my wife pleading with me to pleasure her, and I willingly obliged."

"You're incorrigible," she said as she wrapped her arm in his and they began to stroll toward the fountain at the edge of the lawn.

"But deeply in love." The quiet confession made her smile as she rested her head on his shoulder.

"So you're happy then?" Although she knew the answer, she wanted to hear him say it.

"Happier than a man deserves to be. And you, Lady Stratfield?"

"Well, despite my current size and level of discomfort, I am happy as well."

They walked for several minutes in silence before Garrick cleared his throat. Ruth came to a halt and stared up into his handsome features. Concerned by the troubled expression on his face, she touched his arm.

"What is it, my love? Has something happened?"

"I'm afraid I've done something you won't like."

"Oh Garrick, did you bring home another stray dog?" She glowered at him. "I know it teaches the children responsibility by caring for them, but there are fifteen in the stables now. Even with the children's help, the groomsmen are having trouble keeping up with them."

"Not exactly." Garrick's voice betrayed a hint of uncertainty that astonished her. The man was always confident.

"What do you mean, not exactly?"

"Do you remember me telling you that Tremaine's estate was sold off a year ago since he had no heirs?" His words made her shudder as the memory of the man darkened the sunny day. She nodded and Garrick frowned slightly. "The new owners have a child who is an avid reader, and the boy came across some papers in the estate's library recently."

"What sort of papers?" Ruth asked as she tried to understand how Tremaine's papers might be of interest to them. Garrick frowned.

"The boy found a private journal Tremaine's father kept."

"I still don't see what this has to do with us," she snapped.

In the three years they'd been married, Garrick rarely did anything to upset her, but this particular topic was far too sensitive for her. The old viscount had ruined her mother's life *and* hers because of his lies. Falsehoods that her father believed as truths, even to this day.

"The new owners turned the diary over to your father." Garrick caught her hands as she tried to turn away from him. "The old viscount wrote it all down."

"Wrote what down?" Ruth's heart skipped a beat as Garrick's hands tightened on her suddenly cold fingers.

"The old man's journal detailed the truth about your mother, and how she refused him. Apparently the man gloated about having created the illusion of ruining her when she refused him." The disgust in Garrick's voice equaled the revulsion she was experiencing as well. She pressed her hand against her stomach to calm the churning. "The old viscount apparently took great pleasure in the way your father cast her aside. It's no wonder his son was such a bastard."

Garrick's voice faded to a soft murmur as she realized the importance of what he was saying. Her father finally knew the truth. Knew that Viscount Tremaine had lied about her mother. An icy chill swept over Ruth, and she was suddenly trembling so bad she could barely stand. Garrick immediately pulled her into his arms and held her tight, his hand rubbing her back as he whispered soothing words in her ears. It took several moments for her to stop trembling, but when she'd grown still in his arms, Garrick grasped her shoulders and gently put her at arm's length.

"Better?"

"Yes. I'm simply shocked, that's all. I suppose the *Town Talk* is rife with gossip on the matter." She nodded her head, and didn't try to keep the bitterness out of her voice as she mentioned the newspaper. She remembered how vicious the Society paper could be when it came to private matters. "Is that how you learned of it or did Vincent inform you of it?"

"No, your father notified me of the situation."

"Why on earth would my father feel the need to—" She sent Garrick an appalled look and tried to pull free of his touch, but failed.

"He's asked to see you," Garrick said in a quiet voice.

"No." She shook her head vehemently. "I don't want to see him. The day my mother took me to see him was the last day she was truly alive. She gave up living after that."

"Ruth, don't you think the two of you have suffered enough? Don't you think your mother would want you to forgive him?"

"Forgive." She jerked free of Garrick's arms and sent him an appalled look. "I'm to forgive what he reduced me to? A woman who had to sell herself to survive. I'm to forgive him for abandoning my mother? Me."

"Yes," he said in a firm tone. The look on his face was a familiar one. It meant he intended to get his way. Well, this was one time she refused to give in.

"Well, I won't," she snapped. "This is none of your affair, Garrick. The Marquess of Halethorpe made his bed years ago, and I hope he rots in it."

"Anything that affects my wife *is* my affair." The sharp words made Ruth wince, and she quickly reached up to touch his cheek.

"I'm sorry, my love." She sighed. "But I can't. I can't forgive him for what he did."

"The man wants to make amends, Ruth."

"Amends? How does one make amends for abandoning one's wife and child?" She narrowed her gaze on him. "Would you be so eager to welcome your mother back if she suddenly reappeared in your life?"

"Eager?" He grimaced, and his expression made her realize it wasn't the first time he'd considered the possibility of his mother's return. "No, but I would not reject her outright. You gave me the world the day you married me, sweetheart. With so much happiness in my life, I could afford to be charitable if she returned."

"I'm not sure I can be that charitable."

"*We* have so much, Ruth, and your father has so little." Garrick bent toward her and cupped her face with his hands. "We have what your father lost long ago. Happiness. With all that we have, can you not find it in your heart to at least give him the chance to speak with you?"

At his question, she wrapped her arms around his waist and pressed herself into his warm, solid frame. Did she really want to see the man who was responsible for so much misery in her life? She closed her eyes as the memories washed over her. Images of her parents arguing so horribly that one last time.

The memory of her father ordering her mother and her out of his house. Then the day she'd steeled herself to go plead with the man to come visit her mother on the woman's deathbed. The way he'd cruelly rejected her mother's request. Could she forgive the man all that? It was a lot for Garrick to ask of her.

"Mama! Mama!"

Jack's excited cry pierced her thoughts, and she turned toward the sound of her three-year-old son's voice. The sight of him bounding out of the house and running toward them made Ruth's heart expand with joy. He was the image of his father and had a mischievous streak in him that mimicked Garrick's.

As Jack raced toward her, it was impossible not to wonder what it would have been like for her to race toward her parents on a warm sunny day such as this. The image created a bittersweet sensation inside her as she contemplated what it would have been like to grow up in a home where her parents had been together.

She would most likely have grown up like any other young woman. Married someone her parents had deemed suitable. She might never have met Garrick, or worse, they might have fallen in love and been unable to be together. She drew in a sharp breath. The thought of being married to someone else other than Garrick made her tremble with dismay. Beside her, Garrick brushed his fingertips across her cheek.

"Are you all right, sweetheart?"

The sound of his voice made her catch his hand in hers so she could kiss his palm. The what-ifs of the past would never be answered, and it was pointless to dwell on the possibilities of what might have been.

"I'm wonderful," she whispered. "You're right, I have everything I could ever want right here. I can afford to be charitable."

An instant later, Jack was wrapping his small arms around her legs as Garrick entwined his fingers with hers. Just as quickly as he'd arrived, Jack was dashing off to where Clara and Thad were playing near the fountain. Slowly, she and Garrick followed him, and as the sound of laughter reached her ears, Ruth released a sigh of happiness. The future was bright with possibilities and all the love she'd ever longed for in her life. All of it was more than enough to forgive the past.